FOREVER AFTER ALL

A CHRISTIAN COWBOY ROMANCE

WOLF CREEK RANCH
BOOK SIX

MANDI BLAKE

Forever After All
Wolf Creek Ranch Book 6
By Mandi Blake

Copyright © 2023 Mandi Blake
All Rights Reserved

Holy Bible, New International Version®, NIV® Copyright ©1973, 1978, 1984, 2011 by Biblica, Inc.® Used by permission. All rights reserved worldwide.

Published in the United States of America
Cover Designer: Amanda Walker PA & Design Services
Cover photographer: Macie Shubert
Cover models: Madie Tidwell and Landon Nix
Editor: Editing Done Write

Above all, love each other deeply,
because love covers over a multitude of sins.
1 Peter 4:8 NIV

CONTENTS

CHAPTER 1
JESS

Jess swirled the wedding mint in her orange punch with a spoon. "It's not melting."

"You have to stir it a lot," Ben said, sloshing his own punch over the side of the cup.

"Come on. Remi will gripe at both of us if you get that orange punch on your church shirt."

Ben shrugged, clearly unbothered by his mom's wrath. "She gets all of my stains out."

"That doesn't mean it's okay to mess up your clothes."

Ben's shoulders sank an inch. "I know. She's tired a lot now."

Jess looked for her friend over her shoulder. Remi was pregnant and was looking a little sluggish earlier, but there wasn't any sign of her now.

Dozens of people filled the reception hall. Jess hadn't attended a single wedding before the ranch opened their event venue. Now, she couldn't go a month without getting an invitation to dress up and look classy.

Well, as classy as she could. You could dress up a pig, but it was still a pig.

Not that Jess cared. She preferred to spend her time in the stables, and she didn't need to apologize for it.

"Where is your mom?" Jess asked Ben as she continued to scan the room.

Ben slurped loudly as he licked the punch-and-mint mixture off his spoon. "She went to get the present she left at home."

"I could have gotten it for her." Jess had been looking for an excuse to bow out of the event since she arrived. Sure, she was excited for her brother and Thea, but wedding parties weren't her thing.

Her gaze drifted over Lincoln North and stilled. He wore a white dress shirt that contrasted with his darker skin, navy slacks, and his church boots. No sign of the cowboy hat she saw him wearing most days. He stood with his hands in his pockets while their friend, Colt, rattled on about something.

Nope. Not hanging around that tree. If she stared too much, everyone at the ranch would have them hitched. They were all coupled up, except for the older ones. Though she had a feeling Paul and Vera were heading toward the altar together, she couldn't be sure. Those two were about as quiet as Jess and Linc.

That she could get behind. Everyone else thought marriage was the best thing since sliced bread. Jess was so far from marriage that the wedding bells hadn't even been made yet, much less ringing.

"What are you waiting for?"

"What?" Jess asked, jerking her attention back to Ben.

He pointed at her punch cup. "Your drink is ready."

Jess raised the concoction to her lips and drank. The foamy punch was thicker with the mint mixed in.

She licked her lips a few times, savoring the last of the flavor. "It's not bad. I've had better."

Ben's eyes widened. "I love it."

"I can tell. Did anyone give you a limit on those wedding mints?"

Jess wasn't sold on the whole idea of kids. They probably weren't in her future, considering she didn't have a man in her life. Well, besides the wranglers at the ranch. Those men were definitely in her life, and thankfully, they all respected her.

That was all she wanted and all she could ask for. Respect.

"Dad just told me not to jump off of anything. I promised I wouldn't."

Jess took another sip of the punch. "Fair enough."

She made the mistake of glancing out into the crowd again. Everyone was dancing with someone.

Here she was, hanging out at the kids' table with Ben–the only man who had asked her to dance. The eight-year-old had tried to swing her around a little too much for her liking before she convinced him to have some punch with her.

Punch and wedding mints. It was actually pretty good. Who knew?

"You want to dance, Miss Jess? I bet Jacob would dance with you."

Jess caught sight of the pre-teen from church and quickly shook her head. "No, thanks. I don't like dancing."

"You sure? I could ask Mr. Linc to dance with you."

Now that was funny. Linc wouldn't be caught dead dancing at a wedding reception. She glanced over at Linc as he snuck out the door.

Did that mean she could sneak out too? There was probably some rule of etiquette about how long to stay and hobnob at a party, but Jess didn't know the first thing about fancy parties.

"I'm good. Really. Thanks for hanging out with me."

"I don't mind." Ben squirmed in his chair and tapped his fingertips on the table.

"Why are you being so jittery?" Jess asked.

Ben looked around the room. "Can I go play with Jacob?"

Jess quirked a brow at him. "I'm not your babysitter. Go do whatever you want."

Funny, the kid assumed she was the responsible party here. His mistake.

"But won't you be lonely?"

Jess threw up her hands. "Okay. I'll go hang out with other people too. Happy?"

"Yes." Ben jumped up from his seat and ran off toward his friend.

Jess stood and brushed her hands down the front and sides of her dress. She loved the olive-green color, but it was a little too snug in a few places. Why had Remi insisted the tight-fitting dress was "the one?"

Never again. Jess would be shopping for comfort from now on.

She scanned the room, looking for anyone who didn't seem to be coupled up or already involved in a private conversation.

Too bad Linc had already skipped out. He was the one she could always count on to be available, mostly because he was one of the only single wranglers left on the ranch.

It hadn't bothered her before to be single. Now that she and Linc stuck out like sore thumbs, it was a little hard to ignore the implication that they should just do as others do.

They weren't the "relationship" types. She and Linc did well as loners and didn't need anyone. She liked knowing they were alike in that way. They could even be alone together most days and enjoy it.

Now, she was alone in a room full of people, and why did it suddenly seem like everyone was looking at her?

Mrs. Scott was making her way over, waving one hand in the air. The other was dragging a man in a suit behind her.

Oh no. Not another setup. Good grief, the woman was persistent.

"Jess!" Mrs. Scott pointed at the man trying to keep his feet beneath him as she pulled him along. "Meet Hanson."

Hanson. Was that his first name? It would have helped if Jess had paid a little more attention the first four times Mrs. Scott had tried to set her up with him.

Hanson straightened his shoulders and fixed his surprised expression into a friendly smile. "Hi. It's nice to finally meet you."

Jess stuck out her hand before he got the bright idea to go in for a hug. "Hi."

She wasn't about to tell him it was nice to meet him too. The jury was still out on that.

Lying for the sake of being polite was overrated.

Hanson took her hand in his and gently shook it. "My aunt tells me you've lived here a long time."

"Yep." Not knowing what to say, she swirled her drink in the plastic cup. If he already knew she was a local, why did he want her to confirm it?

Mrs. Scott patted a hand on Hanson's chest. "I'll let you two get to know each other." She gave Jess a wink before walking off like she was proud of a job well done.

Jess looked up at Hanson. He was at least six inches taller than her. His tawny hair was longer on the top and swept to one side. He had straight, white teeth.

He looked like a decent guy, but she'd always had trouble judging a person by looks alone. A handsome smile could hide an evil heart.

Great. Now he was looking at her like she was supposed to say something. Or respond?

"So, I'm new in town," Hanson said. "My mom is getting older and needs more help now. Thankfully, I can work from anywhere. I'm an IT tech."

"Oh, cool."

So cool that she had no idea what he meant. If her computer issues involved anything more than turning it off and on again, she was out of her element.

"Can I get you a drink?" Hanson asked.

Jess lifted her minty punch. "Thanks, but I already have one."

He held up his cup and studied it. "That looks different from mine."

"It has a mint melted in it. Ben told me it was good. He was right."

"Ben?"

Jess pointed to the kid doing the hokey-pokey with his little sister, Abby, on the dance floor.

"Ah. Sounds good."

Hanson turned his attention back to her, and his friendly smile hadn't faltered. Maybe he was a nice guy. They'd been talking for two whole minutes, and he hadn't looked at her like she was horse manure on the bottom of his boot.

This guy wasn't even wearing boots. Could she see herself with a man who wore shiny shoes?

She studied him one more time. His smile was even warmer now.

Okay. He probably deserved a chance.

"That's nice of you to take care of your mom," Jess said. "My mom is a narcissist, and I haven't talked to her since I moved out five years ago."

Hanson's smile faltered then. "That's terrible."

Jess shrugged. "It is what it is."

She'd stopped trying to win her mother's love when she was still a kid. The woman was as mean as a snake, and the only way to escape her bite was to stay out of her sight.

And Jess intended to do just that for the rest of her life.

"What about your dad?" Hanson asked as his brows pinched together.

"He died. Murdered."

Hanson jerked back, and his eyes widened. "Murdered?"

This was why she didn't date. Her past was riddled with bullet holes and sad songs. It wasn't exactly dinner talk.

All of her dating opportunities went just like this. Guy shows interest, Jess tells the truth and puts all the cards on the table, and guy runs away.

Lather, rinse, repeat.

And that was how Jess had remained very, very single her entire life.

Hanson scratched the back of his neck. "I'm sure you don't want to talk about that right now. Would you like to dance instead?"

Well, surprise, surprise. This one wasn't a scaredy cat. "Sure."

Hanson offered her a hand, and she took it, following him to the open dance floor just as a slower love song started playing.

When his hand touched her waist, she tensed. Her instinct was to recoil from touch, but knowing they were dancing and preparing her mind for the contact lessened her reaction. Once she relaxed, the dance was actually kind of nice.

Hanson definitely liked cologne. With his chest at face level, she got a good whiff of the spicy scent.

"Listen, I know we just met, but would you be interested in going on a date with me?"

Jess shrugged. "Sure."

She'd finally been asked out on a date by a seemingly-normal guy. Was this how dating was supposed to feel?

Hanson grinned. "How does Monday night sound?"

"Sounds great. I should warn you that my schedule will be extremely limited once the tourist season starts. I work six days a week. Sometimes on Sundays if necessary."

"I understand. My job is kind of intrusive too."

Intrusive? Did she say her job was intrusive? Because it wasn't. She loved her job. She might have a house, but she basically lived in the barn.

The song ended, and Hanson looked over his shoulder. "Aunt Betty wants me to meet some of the ladies from her church group. Can I get your number?"

"Sure." She rattled off the number, and he keyed it into his phone.

"I sent you a text so you could have my number too."

"Thanks. My phone is at home. No pockets on this dress." She slid her hands down the sides.

Hanson glanced at her dress. "I see that."

Normally, she'd feel uncomfortable if a man

looked at her, but Hanson's gaze didn't linger. That was refreshing.

He looked up with a smile. "It was nice meeting you. See you Monday."

Jess waved. "Nice meeting you too." She could finally speak the truth about that now.

Maybe dating wouldn't be so bad after all, but it was better to be realistic. What were the chances her first real date would end up being "the one?"

Yes. *First* real date. She was twenty-two years old and completely new to the dating game.

It didn't have to be scary, right?

CHAPTER 2

JESS

She went back to the kids' table to grab her shawl. It was really just a piece of cloth she was supposed to hang over her shoulders, but Remi said it looked better with the dress than the jean jacket she usually wore.

The reception had been going on for a few hours. Surely, it was okay to leave now.

Jess groaned. She'd ridden here with Remi, who was nowhere to be found. And she'd left her phone at home.

Everyone else seemed to be deep in conversation. No one looked ready to leave.

Linc had to be around somewhere. He'd give her a ride. She looked down at her feet. The heels were going to be a pain, but she'd survive.

Jess found Brett and Thea and said her goodbyes. Her brother wrapped her in a big hug, then Thea did the same.

She'd never been much of a hugger, but Brett was. Now that Thea was part of the family, they'd been getting along much better.

That had not been the case a month ago. Jess had been ready to ship Thea back to Alabama, where she came from. With good reason, too.

Jess didn't have many people she could count on, but her friends and brother were special to her. She'd always be in their corner. She hadn't known whether Thea was on their side or not, and Jess had been slow to trust.

Now, Thea had proven herself to be a good partner to Brett. Their conflict wasn't a problem between them anymore, and as much as Jess disliked it, she'd apologized. Thankfully, Thea had been quick to forgive.

The April wind was mild for once, and the little bit of snow left on the ground only lingered in the shades of the trees. The shawl was useless, and Jess was going to give Remi a piece of her mind the next time they spoke.

Jess shielded her eyes from the sun as she looked up the gravel drive leading from the reception hall to the heart of the ranch. There was no way the pointy-heeled shoes would work on the gravel, so she shuffled over to the grass that crunched beneath her steps.

She'd check Linc's cabin first. It was closest anyway. If he wasn't there, she'd try the garage, then the main stables.

Her knees were frozen, knocking against each other as she rounded the path leading to his cabin. When she saw his truck wasn't parked outside, she turned and headed for the garage.

Trudging up the path to the garage, she silently prayed Linc would be there. She could walk all the way to the stables, but she'd probably sacrifice a toe to frostbite along the way.

Jess topped the rise and spotted Linc's truck at the garage. She had a feeling he would be itching to get back to work after the reception. She wished for a change of clothes herself.

The maintenance garage was part of the private side of the ranch, and while it wasn't messy, everything was covered in a thin layer of dirt or grease. It didn't get a regular cleaning like the main areas.

This was where Linc got his signature smell. The metallic scent she associated with him didn't come out of a bottle. It came from underneath a pickup truck.

She made her way over to the garage, where she spotted him hanging out from under one of the trucks.

Yep, she'd know those legs anywhere. The stained loose-fitting jeans and boots that had been resoled a few times too many were a dead giveaway.

"Can I help?" she asked, careful not to lean against anything.

"Probably don't want to mess up that outfit," he said as he cranked the wrench.

Jess crossed her ankles, wondering if she could return the dress after wearing it. She should have just borrowed something from one of the other women at the ranch.

"Can you give me a ride home when you get finished?"

"Sure."

"Thanks."

It was a good thing she could always count on Linc. There were others she could call if she needed a hand, but Linc was first on her list when she had to phone a friend.

"I hate standing around. Are you sure I can't do something to help?"

Linc shuffled a little, planting the heel of one boot beside the creeper to adjust. "Let me get this oil draining, and we'll go. In the meantime, you can just stand there and look pretty."

"Ha! That's rich."

Jess didn't care one cent about being pretty. Beauty was confusing if it didn't match what was on the inside.

She'd heard plenty of whispers about her looks. Most people thought she was pretty. They also thought she was too bold, and she simply couldn't understand why honesty wasn't a virtue in a woman.

Linc's wrench clanked against something underneath the truck. "Think of it as helping with minimal effort or expense."

"That's the definition of not helping at all," Jess said.

Words had meanings, and she preferred when people used them accordingly. Say what you mean and mean what you say.

Hanson's date proposal crept into her thoughts. She didn't like the tightness that seeped into her shoulders. It was just a silly date. What was there to be nervous about?

More importantly, how was she supposed to handle nervousness?

She'd seen a few counselors in her teen years, mostly before her dad died. After that, she hadn't wanted to talk to anyone. But one thing the counselors agreed on was that Jess hadn't learned how to handle emotions and filter her reactions.

She still battled with it every day, but at least she was aware of it.

Linc bumped against a few things under the truck. She liked the fact that she could trust him to tell her the truth, even when it wasn't what she wanted to hear. He'd be upfront with her. And he wouldn't laugh about her lack of dating experience.

Guys didn't like a woman like her. She was too blunt and didn't stroke their ego enough. It also didn't help that she could change her own flat tire and cut her own grass. She could do almost anything on her own. What she didn't know how to do, Linc could teach her.

That's why he was a good one to come to with this particular problem.

Jess readjusted her feet and cleared her throat. "What do guys like on a date?"

"Wha–?"

A bang came from beneath the truck, and she had a hunch it was Linc's thick skull hitting the frame.

"You okay under there?" She couldn't afford to lose her co-worker. Not right before the tourist season.

Linc moved around on the creeper for a few seconds before answering, "Fine."

He slid out from under the truck, and her body warmed. There was something about seeing Linc that made her feel better. Every time.

Like, right now, she didn't care that her nose was frozen.

She reached out a hand to help him up, and that peaceful warmth seeped into her hand.

Then he pulled, and instead of helping him up, she was falling toward him.

She landed on his chest with a loud grunt from both of them. Linc was flat on his back, and Jess was…

She was on top of him. Somehow, she hadn't ever pictured herself in this position with Linc. Or any man, come to think of it.

When she lifted her head and looked at him, his nose was about an inch from hers.

So close. Closer than she'd ever been.

And he wasn't looking at her like he was annoyed or any of the other usual looks she got from men once they realized she wasn't as sophisticated as her blonde hair and feminine frame would suggest.

Linc's eyes were wide, his mouth was open, and he looked like she'd just waved a snake in front of his face.

He hated snakes, but she promised him she'd never tell a soul.

To this day, she hadn't. And she would keep her word.

Jess shrugged a shoulder. "Oops."

It seemed funny, until Linc continued staring. She had a hard time reading social cues on a good day. What was she supposed to make of his frozen silence?

And his arm was around her, keeping her from falling the remaining three inches to the dirt beside him.

There was a good chance she was supposed to be doing something, but all she could think about was why Linc was looking at her like that.

Instead of hanging around for the awkward party, Jess got her bearings and stood to her feet.

The stupid shoes were to blame. And the dress. Never, ever again.

She focused on brushing off her knees and swiping down the front and sides of her dress.

Huh. Linc still wasn't moving.

Jess offered him her hand again. Maybe she should just brace herself better this time.

Linc finally grinned and waved her hand away. "I got it."

Jess assessed the damage. He didn't seem to be bleeding. "Are you okay?"

"You might weigh a hundred pounds. I think I'll live."

Now that warmth that usually brought her peace was rising to her ears. That wasn't a good sign. "Sorry."

Linc gave a quick huff that was probably meant to be a chuckle. "If you wanted to throw yourself at me, you could have waited about thirty more seconds, and I would have caught you."

And just like that, the heat in her face and ears began to subside. She hadn't scared him off or offended him. He might be the only person left who hadn't been ruffled by something she did, and she needed to hang onto this one remaining person she hadn't damaged with her "personality."

"For the record, I think you did catch me."

Linc wiped the wrench on his pants. "Happy to do it, ma'am."

Jess rolled her eyes and crossed her arms in front of her chest. At least he wasn't laughing at her. "Like I was saying, can you help me? I have a date tomorrow, and I'm lost as a goose."

"Do geese get lost? That seems unlikely."

She huffed and brushed a hand down the side of her dress. "Focus, Linc. I need to know what guys expect on a date."

Linc put the wrench away and took his time doing it.

"Please? I don't know what I'm doing," Jess said, almost pleading. He was her best chance of doing this whole dating thing the right way.

He closed the drawer on the toolbox and wiped his hands on a rag. "I think you should talk to someone else."

"I can't go to any of the girls here. They'll get all mushy and talk about how it's time to settle down and do the whole ring, babies, and minivan thing."

Truly, she was tired of being told she needed those things. Sure, she wanted a husband. She'd settle for a boyfriend at this point, but the idea of having just any man as her partner didn't appeal to her one bit.

Spending her life with someone she clicked with? That's what she wanted. She wouldn't settle for anything less.

"What about your brother?" Linc asked.

Jess's shoulders sank. There was no way on earth she'd take dating advice from her brother. "I don't want anyone to know about it. I'm not even sure I want to date, so I don't want there to be expectations when this falls apart before it even gets started."

Linc rested a boot on the creeper and rubbed his jaw. At least he wasn't telling her a flat-out no. And if he wanted to, he would.

When his silence continued to drag, she asked, "What if he wants to kiss me?"

Linc jerked his chin up, and his wide eyes settled on hers. His foot propped on the creeper went flying, and he was on his back before she could get her head on straight.

"Ow," Linc murmured. His brows knitted together, and his eyes closed tight.

Could they get through this humiliating conversation without Linc taking another hit? Maybe she should just try again later.

"Are you okay?"

He groaned and rested his head back on the dirt. "Yep."

Jess leaned over him, unsure what to do to help when she couldn't see any obvious injury. "Good. If you could compose yourself long enough to stay on your feet, I'll be waiting in the truck."

CHAPTER 3
LINC

L inc took a deep breath and stared at the ceiling of the garage. Jess was going on a date, and she wanted his help.

He'd rather be trapped in a small room full of snakes than talk about Jess dating another man.

In the guy's defense, he had guts. Linc had seen Jess intimidate many men. Not just scrawny wimps. She'd stood her ground with some of the biggest men in Blackwater.

Linc liked that about her. She didn't cut any slack.

So, whoever this guy was, he'd made it past Jess's first line of defense–her abruptness.

Linc had thought about asking her out himself a few times. Then, he reminded himself of all the reasons why he shouldn't.

They were co-workers–ones who worked together very closely.

Jess hadn't shown the slightest bit of romantic interest in him.

And the biggest reason? He was a criminal. With a felony under his belt and a decent list of misdemeanors, he wasn't any woman's first pick.

But Jess didn't know that. At least, he didn't think she knew.

Mr. Chambers knew, only because his boss had been the only person in Wyoming to give him a chance with that felony on his record.

It was bad enough explaining that employment gap during job interviews, but it was a huge red flag on a date.

Hence the reason he hadn't dated since his release. It was a pretty good reason not to act on his feelings for Jess.

Jess was the definition of literal. She took everything at face value because that's what she gave. If you told her the rules, she followed them to the letter. If you asked her to do something, she did it. Right then.

Linc had a ten-year crime spree under his belt. There weren't many rules out there he hadn't broken.

He sat up with a groan. It had been a while since he'd hit the ground like that, but nothing felt broken. He got to his feet and propped his hands on his hips. Now or never. It was time to face Jess.

He tossed his grease rag onto the toolbox and grabbed his hat from the hook.

Just as she'd promised, Jess waited in the passenger seat of his truck. She'd occupied that spot hundreds of times, and having her beside him always felt right.

Couldn't they just skip this part? Fast forward through the dating and kissing conversation and get back to their easy, casual existence?

Linc climbed into the driver's seat and started the truck. He glanced over at Jess and instantly regretted it.

If her shiny blonde hair and sleek green dress weren't enough to kick him in the gut, her faded red lipstick did him in.

She'd asked about kissing, and now he couldn't stop thinking about kissing. Specifically, kissing Jess.

"So, what should I do? Mrs. Scott introduced me to her nephew, and he wants to take me out on Monday."

Jess rubbed a thumb over her knuckle. Hmm. He'd never seen her fidget with her fingers before. Usually, her hands were busy. She always knew what she needed to be doing.

The unwelcome thought that she might actually

be interested in this guy really struck a chord. "What's his name?"

"Hanson. He's new in town."

Linc raised a brow. "Hanson? Like, the old teenie-bopper band?"

"I think so. Anyway, he was nice. His shoes were a little too shiny, but he didn't run scared when I told him my dad was dead and my mom is probably one of Satan's minions."

Linc focused on the path leading out of the ranch. Thankfully, Jess didn't live far. "Listen, I'm not the person to talk to about this."

Jess leaned back against the seat and sighed.

Letting Jess down wasn't on his list of things to do. It was in his makeup to be there for her, but he couldn't help her with this.

"Why are you even asking me? I don't date, and I don't have any advice for you."

In fact, it had been years since he'd kissed a woman, and there didn't seem to be any Xs or Os in his future.

Unless Jess had a great awakening and decided she wanted him. Kissing Jess would be great for him and bad for her.

No, it would be *glorious* for him. He'd imagined it plenty of times. Jess was the only woman who had captured his interest in years, and boy, did she have it all.

"What do I do?" Jess whispered.

Was she even talking to him now? Or was she just asking herself?

"Be yourself."

She huffed. "I can't do that."

"Why not? If he doesn't like it, then forget about him."

"No one likes me," Jess said.

Linc's chest tightened. This must be what a broken heart felt like because it caused him actual pain when she was upset.

Not only that, she was wrong. Linc liked her plenty.

Jess covered her face with her hands. "Ugh. What do I do if he tries to kiss me?"

Linc's foot slipped off the gas, jerking the truck to a much slower speed.

Jess grabbed for the door handle but didn't seem bothered by his distracted driving.

Okay, this whole conversation was stirring up some frustration he really didn't want to deal with. He jerked the truck to a stop and shifted into park.

Linc turned toward her and propped his arm on the steering wheel. "Jess, calm down. I finally have some advice for you. If he tries to kiss you on the first date, deck him."

Jess laughed. "I'm serious."

"So am I. You can tell him it's from me."

She was actually smiling now. Hopefully, she'd interpret his words as literally as he'd meant them.

"Maybe I should just call it off. I'm only twenty-two."

Linc pressed his lips together. It was always nice to be reminded that there was a six-year age gap between them. Not that six years was a lot as a general rule. It just translated to lightyears between him and Jess.

"Maybe I'm not meant to be in a relationship," she whispered.

There she went again, breaking his heart into a million pieces.

"Do you want to be in a relationship?" Linc asked. Did he really want the answer?

"I don't know. That's the thing. I usually don't do something unless I want to do it. Dating feels like something other people want me to do because they don't want me to feel left out."

"Well, there's your answer. Don't let anyone push you into something you don't want to do."

Jess sat up straighter. "You're right." There was a second of hesitation before she went on. "Well, maybe I do feel a little left out. But here's the thing, I don't know what it feels like to be left out because I've never cared before."

"Do you care now?" Linc asked.

Jess slowly looked at him. He caught the movement in his peripheral vision and turned to find her staring at him with a look of sadness he'd never seen before.

"No. Not really. I'm happy right now."

"Right now?"

"Yeah, like anytime I'm at the ranch or church or just hanging out with you."

Linc finally took a breath. He hadn't lost her yet.

But was it fair to hope she didn't find someone when he still didn't know if he should make his own move? He wanted her to be happy, and she was happy when she was with him.

She meant during the day-to-day work they did. She didn't mean sharing a life with him. She didn't mean dealing with his checkered past.

While he was making a lot of progress in moving away from his old life, he hadn't actually made the move with the Big Man.

Jess was happy when she was at church. So was he. But as much as he believed in God, it was hard to reconcile his massive sins with such an easily accessible forgiveness.

So, yeah. He believed in God, but he hadn't taken the leap yet. It was like he could see the green grass on the other side but couldn't figure out how to get over the fence.

"He was really nice," Jess said as she stared out the window.

"Then maybe he deserves a chance."

As much as it killed him to say it, if Jess thought he was a good guy, Linc trusted that judgment. Who was he to stop her if she was confident in her discernment?

"Okay. I'll go. It's not like it's a lifetime commitment, you know?"

"Right."

At least, he hoped she was right.

CHAPTER 4
JESS

Jess parked in front of Marshall's, the nicest steakhouse in town. She was three minutes early.

Was Hanson usually on time, or would he be late? Was that a fireable offense if he was?

The girls at the ranch had told her a few horror stories over the years, and she'd kept a log of the red flags they mentioned. Ava had been stood up before, but no one had mentioned a late date.

Her gut said being late was bad. He wasn't taking things seriously. He didn't respect her. He didn't care.

But she'd been accused of being too strict before in many areas of her life. It was possible she was being that way now.

There was a knock on her window, and she jumped.

Hanson stood beside her truck, waving and wearing a smile like he was genuinely happy to see her.

Was he, or was that goofy grin just his normal happy expression?

This was never going to work. She wasn't the smiling kind. If Hanson turned out to be all bubbles and rainbows, they were already on the fast track to destruction.

She made sure her truck key was in one pocket of her coat and her money in the other before opening the door. "Hey. You made it."

"I've been waiting on you," Hanson said as he hooked a thumb over his shoulder at a sleek silver car.

"Is that yours?" Jess asked.

"Yep. Bought it myself." His smile got even wider. "Sorry, it's kind of exciting for me. I have a mound of student loans, but it's pretty exciting to say I don't have a car payment."

Jess studied the little car. It was way too tiny for her liking, but she could appreciate a big, responsible purchase.

"That's cool. I was excited when I bought my own place."

Hanson offered her his arm, but she just stared at it. She'd never been a big toucher. If the job warranted it, then yeah. Just holding onto the arm of a stranger? Not so much.

He must have picked up on her hesitation because he lowered his arm. His smile, however, didn't falter. "You have your own place?"

"Yeah. It's not much, but it's mine."

There was something about having a place she could call home. It was almost like her safety blanket. After growing up in a house that felt more like a prison with regular corporal punishment, it was an immense relief to go home alone in the evenings.

No one would slap her to the floor.

No one would tell her she was a waste of space.

No one would remind her that she was too stupid to live.

Just the blessing of silence. Her little house was worth every penny she paid for it.

Hanson opened the door to the restaurant and stepped to the side for her to enter first. "That's so cool. I've been living with my college roommate. Well, I was before I came here. Now I'm living with my mom."

"How long will you be here?"

Hanson shrugged. "I guess until she doesn't need me anymore."

So, had he agreed to be his mom's caretaker until she died, or just until she recovered from an injury? That was a big commitment either way. Yet, he didn't seem bothered or inconvenienced.

The dark-haired hostess greeted them with a warm smile. "Hello. Welcome to Marshall's."

Hanson stepped up beside her and rested a hand on the small of her back. "Table for two."

Jess stiffened. Why was he touching her? Maybe he was expected to touch her. What did she know? She should have bucked up and asked one of the girls about dating. Linc hadn't mentioned touching, but he'd seemed pretty convinced a kiss shouldn't happen on the first date.

At least there was that. If she was this wound up by a touch, she might take Linc's advice and deck him if he came in for a kiss.

When Hanson's hand pressed firmer against her back, she followed the hostess at a quick enough pace that he couldn't keep up.

When his hand fell from her back, she took a much-needed breath.

The hostess led them to a table, and Hanson took his seat across from Jess.

Hanson picked up the menu. "So, what—"

"I don't like being touched."

There was probably a better way to get the point across, but she didn't know how to soften it.

Hanson nodded. "Okay. I'm sorry. You're absolutely right. I shouldn't touch you without permission."

He didn't seem mad. In fact, he seemed to truly agree with her. He sounded sincerely sorry.

"Thanks. I just... I know lots of people hold

hands and hug and stuff, but it's always made me uncomfortable."

Should she skip the part about how her mom had jerked her to the floor by her hair? Or the way she'd twist the skin of her arms in opposite directions until they burned?

Yeah, touch had never been fun for her. This guy probably wouldn't understand.

"I get it. I was actually really sick when I was little, and I had to take this medicine that pretty much killed my immune system. I couldn't hug my family for almost a year."

Jess stared at Hanson. "Wow. That sounds bad."

Hanson looked down at his menu, but he didn't seem to be reading it. "Yeah. It was. It took a while to get back to..." He waved his hand in the air. "I don't know. It took a while to understand what touch even meant."

Jess looked at her menu. What *did* touch mean?

The waiter stepped up to their table and introduced himself. "What can I get you to drink?"

They both ordered water, and the waiter explained the specials.

"Are you ready to order?" Hanson asked. "I'm starving."

Jess picked up her menu. It was a good thing Hanson was so open. It was nice knowing what he was thinking so she didn't have to guess.

"Sure."

Hanson nodded, indicating she should go first.

That was one of the signs Ava had talked about. She'd noticed which of her dates had allowed her to order first and which ones put themselves first.

Apparently, there was a difference.

"I'll have the pork chop," she said as she handed the menu to the waiter.

"Are you sure you don't want a steak?" Hanson asked. "They're fantastic here."

"Of course I want a steak, but they're pretty expensive."

If they were splitting the bill, she'd rather not blow a week's paycheck on one meal. If he was paying, she didn't want to order the most expensive thing on the menu.

But he'd asked if she *wanted* a steak, and she did want it. She just had reasons not to order it.

"Go ahead. It's my treat tonight," Hanson said.

Jess waited two full seconds before reaching for the menu she'd just given the waiter. "I'd like to change my order to the ribeye."

"Twelve ounce or fifteen ounce?" the waiter asked.

"Twelve."

"How would you like it cooked?"

"Medium."

Hanson handed over his menu. "I'd like the New York strip. Medium."

The waiter took down the last of their orders. "I'll get this right out to you."

Hanson linked his fingers together on the table and returned his attention to her. "So, you have any siblings?"

"It's complicated."

Hanson laughed. "What an answer. Now I can't wait to hear more."

"I have a brother. He's just a little more than a year older than me. We've always been close, even though he drives me crazy half the time. We're different."

"You're saying he isn't blond?"

Jess chuckled. "I'm saying he likes to goof off. Don't get me wrong, we work together, and he's a good worker. He just likes to have fun."

"And you don't?"

Wow. She actually had to think about that answer. She wasn't the kind to seek fun things or even make her own fun. Brett made everything into a game or made people laugh when the work was hard. She liked that about him, but it wasn't in her nature.

"I like fun. I like working. I like the horses."

Was that all she did? Pretty much. She hung out in the stables, and she liked it.

"You just used working and fun in the same breath," Hanson pointed out.

"I like them both."

"That's a good thing. I like my work too."

Oh yeah. He fixed computer problems or something. Sounded like the opposite of fun to her, but it was good that he enjoyed it.

"So, it's just you and your brother?"

"Well, it was just me and Brett until recently."

Hanson leaned over the table. "The plot thickens."

"It did. We found out we have a half-sister."

"When?"

"A month ago. I still don't know what I think about her."

It didn't bother Jess that she had a sister. The part she got hung up on was *who* the sister was.

The waiter arrived and filled their glasses with water. As soon as he walked away, Hanson dove back into the conversation.

"You like her?"

"I haven't decided."

Hanson laughed. "I like your honesty."

"Good. Some people don't. What about you? Any siblings?" Jess asked.

"Loads. I have two sisters and two brothers."

"That seems like a lot of kids," Jess said.

"Yep, but my mom and dad are great. I couldn't imagine growing up without a houseful of siblings. It was fun."

Okay, Hanson definitely had a different childhood than the one she'd experienced. It was hard not to be jealous.

She'd only had Brett, and while he'd been enough, maybe things would have been easier if they'd had someone else on their side. They'd watched each other's backs without a break for their entire lives.

Did Linc have any siblings? She'd never asked. The topic hadn't come up, but she suddenly wanted to know the answer.

Jess was beginning to understand the upside of dating. Getting to know someone was much easier when you had nothing to do except talk.

Maybe she should have more casual conversations with Linc. But she also enjoyed the peaceful silence when he was around.

"You have any friends around here?" Hanson asked.

"A few. Aside from my brother, I guess I'm friends with the people at work. I definitely see them the most. And there's Linc."

She stopped talking and replayed the last sentence. Why did she want to list Linc separately?

"Who's Linc?"

Swallowing hard, she tried to push Linc out of her thoughts. Why was she thinking about him when she was on a date?

How did Linc feel about touch? Was he stunned when she fell on top of him a few days ago? Why hadn't it bothered her to touch Linc when she was laid out on top of him?

"Jess?"

"Yeah?"

"Who is Linc? You just mentioned him."

"He's my friend at work."

Was he her friend? They'd never actually defined the relationship, but she liked him enough. She'd just listed him separately from the others she worked with, and she didn't know what that meant.

Her mouth was dry all of a sudden, and she reached for her glass of water and took a few gulps.

What would it be like to kiss Linc?

She flattened her palms against the hard wood of the table. They were starting to sweat. Kissing Linc? That was way outside of the safe zone. Was it getting hotter?

Why was she thinking about her kissing conversation with Linc when her actual date was sitting in front of her? She wasn't thinking about kissing this guy at all.

"He works with the horses too?" Hanson asked.

She could focus on horses and get her wayward thoughts back on track.

Horses were safe. Linc was not.

"Yeah. He leads the pack rides, so I get the horses ready, and he packs the supplies."

"Sounds like teamwork makes the dream work,"

Hanson said, tilting his head from side to side. "I'm not a big fan of horses."

Jess jerked like someone had just pulled her out of a daydream. "What?"

"They're huge. And they have big eyes," Hanson explained.

"Their eyes are proportionate to their size. And they're big, but they're not all scary."

"Tell that to my overthinking brain. There are dozens of ways a horse could hurt me. It's intimidating, looking up into those big, mysterious eyes."

Jess couldn't fight the urge to grin. "I can't believe you're scared of horses."

"I'm not scared. I just don't want to make friends with them," Hanson said.

"Well, I won't tell anyone you don't like horses if you don't tell anyone I don't like frogs."

Hanson mouthed, "Frogs?"

Jess nodded. "I know they won't hurt me. I just think they're creepy." She snapped her fingers when the reason occurred to her. "They have big eyes."

Hanson slapped a hand on the table. "Big eyes are scary!"

"Shh," Jess whispered. "Keep it down or the whole town will know we're weirdos."

"I just got in town a few days ago. Please don't ruin my chances here," Hanson pretended to whine. "I want to fit in."

"You will."

The waiter placed a basket of bread on the table, and Jess felt her tension disappear as he left.

Hanson was a nice guy, but things would never work with him. Unfortunately, not liking horses *was* a fireable offense in her world. Horses were her life. They were the only things she was passionate about.

She woke up before the sun, spent her days at the ranch until after sundown, slept, then did it all again on repeat. There wasn't any room in there for a relationship.

Especially not with a man who didn't understand the one thing she loved most.

A smile grew on her lips. "I think—"

"Don't say it," Hanson interrupted with his hand in the air. "Let's just have this one nice date, and then you can kiss me goodbye."

Jess's eyes widened. "I don't think—"

"You're going to tell me we're not right for each other, or that you think I'd make a good friend, or something about it's not you, it's me."

She paused to give each of those reasons a thought. "No, I was going to say I don't think I could see myself in a serious relationship with someone who doesn't like horses."

Hanson grinned. "Well, I was taking the cliche route. Of course, you settled on the straight truth."

"So, you're not mad?"

Hanson picked up his glass. "Why would I be mad?"

"Something tells me you should be at least a little upset."

Hanson took a drink, put his glass down, and rested his arms on the table. "I like your honesty. So many people prefer to dance around on their tiptoes, and it's exhausting. Hanging out with you tonight has been a breeze."

Jess's shoulders sank as she relaxed. "Really?"

No one had ever told her she was easy to hang out with. In fact, most people avoided being around her.

"Really. I won't ask you out on another date, but I hope we can still be friends."

Jess reached a hand across the table. "It's a deal."

Hanson took her hand and gave it a strong shake. "Why are we shaking?"

"It's like a new start. New expectations and all."

"Got it. Does this mean you'll help me make more friends?"

"Of course." She looked around. "I think I'm going to go to the restroom before our food gets here."

She could count the times she'd been to Marshall's on one hand, and she was second-guessing whether the restroom was at the front or the back. Starting with the front, she made her way through the lobby area and found what she was looking for on the other side of the restaurant.

She took her time washing her hands and

avoiding her reflection in the mirror. Why was she relieved that the "date" with Hanson was over? Maybe she wasn't ready to date after all. The anxiety didn't seem worth the prize.

Pulling her phone out of her pocket on the way back to the table, she fired off a text to Linc.

Jess: How is Star?

She held the phone as she walked, waiting for a response. Star had cut her hind leg open, and Jess hadn't wanted to miss the visit from the vet.

"She's fine."

Jess jerked her head up at Linc's response. Instead of a text, his words were real. He leaned against the wall in the lobby, looking like he'd just popped out of her thoughts.

"What are you doing here? Why aren't you with the vet?"

"Brett's there. The vet just left. Star is fine."

Jess looked around. Was God trying to be funny? She'd thought about Linc, and he appeared. "And my other question. What are you doing here?"

"Picking up takeout."

Jess narrowed her eyes. "From a steakhouse?"

"Brett wanted steak," Linc said, not missing a beat.

Her attention cut to the table where Hanson sat waiting for her. "Did Brett send you to check on me?"

"Nope. Just to get food."

She accepted the answer. Linc would always be honest with her.

"Want to get out of here?" he asked.

Jerking her attention back to Linc, she furrowed her brow. "What?"

"Is that your date?" Linc asked, pointing directly at Hanson, who tapped furiously on his phone.

"Yes. His name is Hanson."

"You told me." Linc took a step toward her and whispered in a deep voice, "You want to get out of here?"

Jess furrowed her brow. "I can't do that."

"He's pretty interested in his phone. He probably wouldn't notice."

Jess rolled her eyes. Spending too much time on his phone was one of those red flags she'd heard about. She didn't understand the appeal, since she only used hers when she needed it, but Hanson said he could work from anywhere, and that probably included using his phone.

Linc also didn't know he'd hit the nail on the head. Hanson probably was more interested in his phone than he was in her. Romantically, at least.

"You've been gone for a while. How long do you think it'll take before he notices?" Linc asked.

Jess groaned. "Did you tell Brett about my date? I don't want anyone to know."

"I didn't. You told me not to."

She had, and she hadn't expected him to tell.

Confirmation of his loyalty was pretty unnecessary, but it was a good thing he hadn't mentioned it to anyone because there wouldn't be a second date.

Linc crossed his arms over his chest and tapped one finger against his bicep with every second, drawing her attention to the spot. Hanson was a nice-looking guy, made even more attractive by their new friendship agreement.

Even so, the guy didn't hold a candle to Linc. She'd always thought he was handsome. Almost too handsome. She didn't need him to draw attention to his bicep to know it was big. Linc had the kind of muscular build forged by hard work, and it showed.

When she attached his quiet kindness, hard work ethic, and fierce protectiveness to it, his looks were beyond compare.

At least, they didn't compare to any man she'd ever met, and the pickin's were slim in Blackwater.

"He still hasn't looked up. You think he's been brainwashed?" Linc asked.

"Hanson is a nice guy. Cut him some slack."

"Don't settle for a guy you have to give slack. He doesn't seem bothered that you're over here talking to another man."

Jess glanced at the table, and sure enough, Hanson was watching them. He gave them a little wave and a friendly smile.

Fair enough, but Hanson's new position as her friend meant she didn't have to care if he was giving her all of his attention or if he cared that she was talking to another man.

Linc waved and gave Hanson a daring grin.

"Stop that. Once again, what are you doing here?"

"Like I said, waiting for my food."

"Well, if you'll excuse me, I need to get back to my table."

She started to walk off, but Linc straightened.

"Wait."

"Yeah?"

"Will you meet me at the barn later?"

"Is something wrong with one of the other horses?"

"No, they're fine. I just wanted to talk to you about something."

There weren't many things Linc would need to tell her. Her first, second, and third guesses all had to do with the horses.

"Sure. I'll be there."

Linc relaxed back against the wall and jerked his chin in farewell.

She turned and headed back to the table where Hanson waited. She'd started the evening nervous about her date. Now, she couldn't stop wondering what Linc wanted and why she was still completely flustered.

Not because of her date but because of Linc.

CHAPTER 5

LINC

Linc paced next to Kiwi's stall. He hadn't considered how long he'd have to wait for Jess's "date" to be over when he asked her to meet him after.

If things were going well, sparks were flying, chemistry was happening, he could be left waiting for hours.

He checked his watch. Shouldn't it be over by now? Wasn't two hours enough time to figure out if you liked someone or not?

Linc huffed and paced, and Kiwi did the same.

"I feel you, girl. You think she needs help? Don't women usually have a signal they send their friends when they want to get out of a date?"

He lifted his hat, pushed his hand through his hair, and propped an arm on the wall beside the stall. "She'll come back to us, right?"

Kiwi blew out a thick breath and nodded, seeming to agree with Linc.

"Right. She likes us. She won't leave us for a pretty boy." Linc rubbed a hand over his jaw. "Unless she likes that. I'm not pretty, and, well... you're not a boy."

Kiwi hung her head. Linc had taken up with the roan for casual conversation because she seemed to be the most responsive. His own horse, Thunder, still had a wild heart and didn't care for chitchat.

"Don't worry, girl. She'll be here."

The rumble of a diesel engine outside had both Linc and Kiwi straightening.

Linc turned to Kiwi and put a hand on either side of her jaw. "Act cool."

The barn door opened, and Paul's wolf-dog, Thane, darted in. The older cowboy followed and gave Linc a small chin jerk in greeting.

Not the face Linc had been expecting, but at least it wasn't Jess's brother, Brett. He'd have too many things to shoot the breeze about, and Linc only had one thing on his mind right now.

Thane ran up beside Linc and brushed up against his legs. The massive, intimidating beast had been stoic like his owner, until the women on the ranch basically turned him into an attention hog.

Apparently, men had soft hearts for women in every species.

Paul stopped and narrowed his eyes at Linc. "You okay?"

"Yeah."

Linc wasn't acting cool enough, if Paul broke his silence to check on him.

"Mkay then." Paul disappeared into the tack room, and Linc bumped his forehead against the wall.

"Stupid, stupid, stupid."

Thane whined at Linc's feet.

"I'm fine. My stomach is just tied up in knots."

Paul emerged from the tack room with a saddle blanket and whistled for Thane to come. A minute later, Linc was alone with the horses and his thoughts.

His heart pounded, and his hands were sweating. "She's not coming."

Kiwi turned, giving Linc her massive behind.

"Some friend you are."

The barn door opened again, and Jess strolled in. She must have pulled up as Paul was leaving because he hadn't heard her truck.

She'd dressed up for the date, which only served to fuel the riot in his stomach. The guy probably hadn't even noticed. She wore a flannel shirt and jeans like she always did, but Linc knew the pattern wasn't one she wore to work, and the jeans were a darker wash than usual.

Her long blonde hair was down, resting over one

shoulder like a waterfall. He never complained that she wore it up most days. He liked seeing every bit of her face.

But when she wore her hair down, he had problems. He spent way too much time fighting the itching in his palms. What would it feel like to run his hands through it?

"Everything okay?" she asked.

"Yeah. Everything's fine. How was your date?"

So much for acting cool and being subtle.

Jess shrugged. "He's a good guy, but it didn't work out."

"What do you mean? What did he do?"

"Nothing." Jess gave her attention to Kiwi who had turned back around.

So, she was going to leave him hanging. Her date was a nice guy, but it was a bust. Did that mean she had high standards? Good. She should.

That also meant Linc was completely out of the running. He might live by the straight and narrow now, but he had a lifetime of bad blood behind him.

"Too bad," Linc said.

Too bad for Henderson or whatever his name was.

Linc tapped the heel of his boot against the toe of the other. He shouldn't wish her dates to crash and burn, but his jealous heart had a mind of its own.

He cleared his throat. "Can I ask you something?"

"Yeah," she drawled.

This was his moment, but the words were mixing with the rocks tumbling in his stomach. The question stuck in his chest like concrete.

Jess propped her hand on her hip. "Spit it out while I'm young."

Right. Jess didn't like beating around the bush, but she had no idea about his sweaty palms and the bubbling in his gut.

"I was thinking...wondering if you would go with me to Ridge and Cheyenne's wedding."

Jess tilted her head to the side. "Like a date?"

Great. This was a define the relationship moment, and Linc was fighting back vomit.

"Um, I was thinking I could pick you up, and we could ride together."

Jess quirked one brow up. He was butchering the whole thing.

"And maybe we could dance a little. I'll take you home after."

Lord, save him. He'd just brought up dancing, and neither of them were the dancing type. He was really selling the farm on this one.

Desperate times called for desperate measures.

"So, is it a date?" she asked again.

Leave it to Jess to expect nothing but the straight

truth from him. He knew better than to be vague with her.

He pulled his hat off and scratched his head. "Well, let's see how it goes. No pressure."

She could call it courting or the preliminary round for all he cared. He just wanted her with him, and he didn't want to give her a chance to ask anyone else first.

Jess's piercing stare relaxed. "I'll have to think about it."

What? Think about it? Was she trying to give him a heart attack?

"When? How long?"

He'd given plenty of thought to the many ways she could turn him down. He hadn't considered a dangling response.

Torture. Jess was a master of torture, and Linc was caught in her trap.

"I'll let you know in the morning."

A whole night of torture? Jess would be the death of him.

But really, he'd asked for it.

"Okay." The word came out surprisingly casual, despite the panic drumming in his head. "Well, I'm just going to refill the feed bins before I head out."

"Thanks for that."

Jess had her hand over everything in the stables, and she held her own like no one he'd ever met before. But the feed bags were heavy, and he made a point to take that weight off her shoulders when-ever he could. It wasn't that she couldn't do it, it was that he didn't want her to have to do everything.

She rubbed Kiwi's mane. "I'm going to stick around for a while."

Linc tipped his hat at her. "See you in the morning."

Hopefully, she'd put him out of his misery before breakfast.

CHAPTER 6
JESS

J ess tacked the feeding schedule to the bulletin board and picked up the chalk. She rolled it between her fingertips as she tried to quiet the unrest in her head.

She picked a verse or some kind of motivational quote to write on the chalkboard next to the bulletin board every day. The stables were her place.

Well, Brett had just as much sway in the stables, but he'd never said a cross word about her verses and sayings.

Thankfully, he hadn't asked. She didn't want to talk about how she'd started the habit when one of her counselors suggested it. She also didn't want to talk about how much it helped target her focus every morning.

Sometimes, she left the sayings for a few days or a week. Sometimes, they changed daily.

Today, she wasn't feeling the William Langewi-esche quote she'd written yesterday.

So much of who we are is where we have been.

It was true, and sometimes, she wanted to embrace the hardships that had led her to the place she was today.

Other days, she wanted to scream until her throat was sore and beg God for a redo.

She grabbed the eraser and wiped away the chalk before making up her mind and writing the words on her heart.

Above all else, guard your heart, for everything you do flows from it. Proverbs 4:23

The storm inside her was doing a good job of firing up her indecision.

She turned over Linc's words from the night before until they stopped making sense. Had he been asking her to be his date to the wedding, or was he just saying he could pick her up?

When she'd asked him to clarify, he hadn't, and that was unlike him. She appreciated Linc's directness, and she'd always thought he knew the reason why she preferred the straight-edged approach.

Jess stared at the verse on the board. It was one she'd written and read many times. She'd memo-rized hundreds of verses, and this one spoke to her on a deep level.

Guard your heart. She'd been doing that her

whole life, and if God's word said it, then it was truth.

Thankfully, this one was something she'd learned well, and there were few people she trusted wholeheartedly.

Linc was one of those people. Why was she over-thinking his invitation to be his date to the wedding?

Because he hadn't actually said "date."

He'd given her a non-answer, and she hadn't known what to do without a definite understanding of the expectations.

Expectation was the root of all heartache. Or so she'd heard. She knew expectations, but she'd learned to shut off heartache. She was probably immune to it, along with ninety-five percent of the other human emotions she either didn't possess the capacity for or didn't understand.

Jess tossed the chalk back into the tray and wiped off her hands. She headed for her office and checked her watch. She'd skipped breakfast at the dining hall on purpose.

Every time she skipped a meal with the whole ranch clan, Linc brought her a plate to the barn. She'd never asked him to do it, and she'd never told him not to.

She liked that he noticed when she didn't eat, and she liked sharing a quiet meal with him in the barn much more than a loud meal in the dining hall.

Jess had always sought out routine, and she knew Linc would walk through the door with their breakfast in the next fifteen minutes.

She hadn't made it to the office when Linc appeared. Wearing a brown cowboy hat, a brown flannel shirt, worn jeans, and his work boots, he could blend into the dirt at his feet if necessary.

Linc lived a quiet existence. He never asked for attention and did everything that was asked of him, sometimes more. He loved the land and the horses just as much as she did, and he always took the lead and prayed before every meal they shared.

If the only thing the man said to her all day was a prayer, she'd take that as a good sign.

Jess stopped and waited as he walked toward her. Whatever her mind and heart decided about Linc, her body dove in headfirst. A swirl of heat rose up her spine, and her fingers tingled. Despite her best efforts, her breaths grew shallow, and the air was thicker.

As he stepped up to her and jerked his head toward her office, every muscle in her body relaxed. There was a peace that followed Lincoln North, and it wrapped around her when she was with him.

She hadn't deciphered what that meant, but she trusted her instincts. Whether he wanted to go to the wedding as her date or her friend, everything would work out for the best.

He pulled boxes of food out of a bag and opened

them on her desk. They ate and talked about work at least once a week, and every casual meal she spent with him was a reprieve from the noise outside the barn.

She sat in her usual chair and moved things around on the desk to make room for the food.

Linc didn't speak, which was typical. He didn't ask about her answer, and he didn't act like she'd imagined the whole thing either.

When he sat and pulled off his hat, she bowed her head as he prayed.

Yes, there was something to be said about a man praying. Linc was a man of few words, but his prayers were always honest and straightforward.

Just like hers.

He hung his hat on the back of his chair and dug into his food.

Jess watched him for a few seconds before the words came out. "I want to go to the wedding with you."

Linc had a mouthful of hamburger steak, but the edges of his lips tilted up into a slight grin as he chewed. When he finally looked up at her, he winked and turned his attention back to his food.

This was Linc. Her Linc.

Everything would work out. One way or the other.

Hadley pulled a light-pink dress off a rack and held it up in front of her. "What do you think about this one? Does it make me look washed out?"

"No, that's actually a really good color for you," Thea said. "Try it on."

Hadley, Thea, and Everly each had an armful of dresses, and Jess had empty hands.

It would help if she knew what she was looking for. At least the others knew what colors and styles they liked. Jess just knew she needed something fancier than her jeans and boots to wear to the wedding.

When they'd invited her to go dress shopping with them, Jess had gone into things knowing she was out of her element.

She was out of her element anywhere that wasn't at the ranch or her house, so she'd grown used to being the one who stuck out like a sore thumb.

It didn't bother her much, but she actually did want to look nice for Ridge and Cheyenne's wedding. It was going to be the fanciest wedding of her life. Ridge was loaded with a capital L, and they'd gone all out for the celebration.

Too bad Jess's fashion sense didn't know what that meant.

"What style are you looking for, Jess?" Everly asked.

Jess shrugged and moved a pink fluff of fabric across the rack. "I don't know."

"Linc really liked that green dress you wore to the reception last weekend," Thea said quietly.

Jess gave her new sister-in-law a pointed stare. "What do you mean?"

"She means Linc liked that green dress," Hadley said.

A weight pressed on Jess's chest. "Why does it matter what Linc liked?"

"It doesn't. Unless you want it to matter," Everly said.

Jess looked back and forth between the other women. "Did Linc say anything about the wedding?"

"No," Hadley drawled in her sweet, Southern accent. "If he did, what would he have said?"

Jess shook her head. "Nothing. He's picking me up for the wedding."

Everly grabbed the rack beside her, but her wide-eyed stare stayed fixed on Jess. "Really?"

"He's picking you up for a date?" Hadley asked, slowly and carefully.

Jess sighed and continued looking at the dresses. "He didn't say it was a date."

"But he didn't say it wasn't either, did he?" Hadley asked.

"Double negatives confuse me," Jess admitted.

"What did he say?" Everly asked.

"He said he could pick me up, we could ride to the wedding together, maybe dance, and then he would take me home."

Thea's eyes widened as she looked at Hadley, then Everly.

"What?" Jess asked.

Everly pretended to be interested in the dresses again. "He didn't say it was a date, but did you ask him if it was?"

"Yes. I did. And he said just what I told you. He didn't say it was a date."

He hadn't. That fact hadn't escaped her. It wasn't a date, or Linc would have said it was.

That was the only thing keeping her from pulling her hair out over it. When she was confused, she asked for clarification. She usually got it.

Not this time.

But it was safe to err on the side of caution. If it wasn't a date, that meant they'd be at the wedding together, but there weren't any expectations.

"Like I said. Linc liked you in the green dress," Thea continued. "Maybe look for something dark. Navy would be a nice contrast to your light hair."

"Liked it? He couldn't take his eyes off of her," Everly added with a chuckle.

Jess fought the panic rising in her throat. "You're seeing things. Linc is my friend. He's my co-worker. That's it."

He was not her love interest.

But... lately, she'd been wondering if things could work out between them.

Then again, it probably wouldn't.

"You two are just alike," Everly said. "You don't say anything unless something needs to be said, you don't beat around the bush, you're both hard-working and responsible, you're both honest to a fault."

"Yep, the same person," Hadley agreed.

"And yet, Linc has never said anything about feelings," Jess said. "Your assumption is debunked."

"Well, have you ever said anything about *your* feelings?" Hadley asked.

"No. I don't understand feelings." Jess hated having to point that out all the time.

Feelings and emotions were hard to decipher because they weren't absolutes. She understood rules. She understood schedules. She understood yes and no.

Anything in between wasn't just gray. It was invisible.

Everly hummed. "Well, maybe you're right. If either of you had feelings, one of you would have spilled the beans by now."

"I don't know. Linc is so sweet when it comes to Jess. Is silence a love language?" Thea asked.

Jess found a long, navy dress and held it up in front of her. It hit about mid-calf and had a slit up one side.

"That one!" Everly exclaimed.

Jess hung the dress over her arm and started toward the back of the store. "I'll be trying this one on."

"We're coming too," Thea said.

Sighing, Jess found an empty dressing room. She'd hoped to escape the Linc talk, but it seemed the conversation would be following her.

Jess slipped into the dress, and the silky fabric was cool against her skin. After zipping it under her arm, she ran her hands over the softness at her hips.

She actually liked it. Without a doubt in her mind, this was the dress she'd be buying today, even if the main reason was comfort.

"Get out here, Jess!" Hadley called.

Jess stepped out of the dressing room and turned to her friends. It didn't matter what they said. This was the dress.

"Oh, yeah. That's the one," Everly said.

"Definitely," Thea added.

Jess crossed her arms over her chest, already wondering if she could get one of those shawl things. Being pointedly looked at always made her want to cover up or disappear. "Have you decided on one?"

Hadley held up the pile in her hands. "I'm about to try these on."

"I have some too," Thea said before disappearing into a stall.

Everly sat on a padded stool beside the mirror. "I already have a dress."

Jess locked herself back in the dressing room and took a deep breath. She tilted her head to the side as she studied her reflection. The dress hugged her curves around the waist but flared out a little over her hips. It was just fitting enough to accentuate her figure without making her feel overexposed.

Another flurry of feelings rose in her middle, and she latched onto the one that roared the loudest.

Hopefully, Linc would like the dress too.

CHAPTER 7

LINC

L inc parked the truck facing Jess's place. The single-story house was as plain as they come. Brown roof and brown shutters. Wooden planks painted the color of clay, and a small porch on the front.

It fit Jess, and even though she didn't talk about her house much, he knew enough to see the excitement in her eyes whenever someone brought up that she had her own place.

Real estate was top dollar this close to the national parks, and Jess had probably worked hard and saved harder to be able to afford the small house.

It was one of the things he admired about her. There was a long list, but the fact that she'd been smart enough to afford a house in her early twenties didn't escape him.

He adjusted his tie as he walked to the door. Everly had suggested navy, and he'd purposely not questioned the unsolicited advice.

Knocking twice, he let out a deep exhale and looked around. Jess had briefly talked about her neighbor, Ms. Landry, but Linc had yet to see her. He'd only been over a few times, but the reclusive neighbor had avoided him.

The blinds on the window facing Jess's place moved, and Linc remembered why he hadn't seen Ms. Landry. Jess said the woman was a busybody who told all of her friends about the things she saw going on outside her window. She kept her little group of friends updated about the birds and squirrels.

Apparently, he'd just bought himself a substantial portion of the rumor mill. It wasn't often a well-dressed man showed up at Jess's doorstep.

The door opened, and Jess looked around, brushing a hand over her wavy hair and the other over her dress. "I can't find that stupid purse thing that goes with the dress."

What was she talking about? Linc's brain had just exploded at the sight of Jess.

Good grief, why did she have to be drop-dead gorgeous?

Everly's navy suggestion was on point. The dark dress painted Jess in a perfect silhouette, and her light hair fell in big waves over one shoulder.

Torture. Jess in a dress was pure torture.

Jess held up a finger. "One sec. Let me check the laundry room."

Linc rested a hand over his eyes and counted backward from a hundred. Watching her walk away would be like pouring gasoline on the flames.

When he made it to zero, he shook out his hands.

She's beautiful. You knew that. Get it together.

Jess appeared in the doorway and held up a little blue purse. "Found it. Let's go."

She locked the door behind them, and he stopped at the three steps leading off the porch. Holding a hand out to her, he waited as she pulled her skirt to the side as she walked down the stairs.

In those heels, she had an extra few inches to meet the ground if she took a tumble.

Jess looked at his hand for a second before switching the purse to the side bunching the skirt. Her soft hand settled in his, and he fought his reaction to the contact. He'd made a point not to do any touching with Jess, but it was the gentlemanly thing to do to help her down the stairs.

Unfortunately, having her small hand in his was a wildfire he wasn't prepared to face, and when she reached the bottom of the steps, he released his grip so he could breathe again.

He opened the passenger door for her and, once again, offered his hand.

He had to tell her. His feelings were growing stronger by the day. By the minute. Jess appreciated honesty.

But she wouldn't appreciate his feelings if she didn't return them. Then, they'd be stuck working together.

If she'd give him one sign, he'd take the leap. He had a whole evening to hopefully get a signal.

That was it. Linc would make a decision by the time he dropped her off after the wedding. Surely, she'd give him a clue before the end of the night.

As the miles and minutes passed, neither of them spoke. It wasn't abnormal. In fact, they often went whole days without saying much, and Jess never let on if it bothered her.

They drove slowly through the ranch to the event venue. He'd attended half a dozen weddings in the last few years, but he never got used to the upscale gathering scene.

He was made for hay and horses, not champagne and caviar.

Jess sat up straighter in her seat. "Ready to stick out like the *Beverly Hillbillies*?"

"Ready as I'll ever be."

He helped Jess out of the truck. How women managed to walk around on little sticks, he'd never know.

The arbor, draped in white, stood tall on the southern side of the building. Chairs were neatly lined up in front of it, and more than half the seats were already taken.

A few groups of people standing and talking near the back noticed them and waved. He recognized many faces from town, but there were just as many he hadn't seen before.

Jess leaned close as they walked. "You ever get the feeling you're being watched?" she whispered.

A single chuckle reverberated in Linc's chest. "They're not looking at me. They're looking at you."

Jess stiffened. "Why?"

Oh, he'd set himself up for that one. Now, he had no choice but to be honest. "You're beautiful."

Instead of cooing some sweet thanks, Jess stayed quiet.

Oh, well. At least he'd tried. Would she clam up if he told her how much he liked her? Would she stop talking to him altogether if he got the guts to ask her on a real, official date?

A lot was at stake here, but no pressure.

He followed Jess to a pair of open seats near the back. She would be just as reluctant to socialize as he was. They just might get through the evening without incident.

"Jess!" Mrs. Scott hustled over with her arms open.

"Hey." Jess stood but didn't assume the position for a hug.

Mrs. Scott didn't take the hint and went in for a full-on hug. Jess's body tensed.

He'd noticed Jess wasn't much of a hugger. The ladies at church hadn't gotten the memo. He'd seen her offer a hand to shake, but hugging always drew her up short.

"Hanson told me he had a great time on your date. Did you have a good time too?"

Great. Now it was Linc's turn to tense up.

"I liked hanging out with him, but we decided it wasn't going to work out."

At least she'd cleared that one up before Linc had an aneurysm. He wiped his sweaty palms on his pants and stretched his neck in the tight collar.

"Oh no. I'm so sorry," Mrs. Scott crooned. "That's too bad."

"Don't worry. He won't have trouble finding a good woman. And he said he'd like to be friends."

"Oh, good. You know, he's supposed to be here."

Jess straightened. "Really?"

"Yes, he's on his way." Mrs. Scott leaned around Jess and waved. "Hey, Lincoln. How are you today?"

Mrs. Scott was as nice as they came, and despite her tendency to matchmake whenever she could, she'd never set her sights on him.

He'd briefly wondered if it was because he was a lost cause. Not that his feelings were hurt over it. The nice older woman would clutch her pearls if she knew half of the crimes he'd committed.

Probably best she didn't try to set him up anyway.

Mrs. Scott looked back and forth between Jess and Linc. "Are you two here together?"

"We rode together," Jess said quickly.

"Oh, well. You two have a nice time," Mrs. Scott said, clearly not understanding Jess's non-answer any more than he did.

He'd been the one to backpedal when Jess asked if this was a date. It was his own fault if she told people they just "rode together."

"Bye, Mrs. Scott," Jess said with a wave.

Linc fidgeted in his seat. Was it getting hot?

No, it wasn't anywhere near warm. It was April in Wyoming.

Jess sat beside him and leaned in. "I hope she doesn't tell her friends."

Linc swallowed and leaned in. Anything that brought him closer to Jess was a gift. "Tell her friends what?"

"That I'm still on the market. My first date crashed and burned. It's so stressful. I don't know how some people do it all the time."

Soon, everyone started calming down and finding seats. Whispers buzzed as Ridge took his place at the arbor.

Weddings were a circus. Linc would rather get kicked by a bronc than stand up in front of a hundred people. Being the center of attention had never been his thing.

Cheyenne appeared in the back, and everyone turned to see her.

As awkward as it was to be at the front, the bride might have it worse. People came to see the bride in her ridiculously expensive dress.

Spending a month's worth of paychecks on a dress wasn't his idea of romantic, but he seemed to be in the minority.

"Good grief. Look at the shine on that thing," Jess whispered beside him.

"Trust me, I noticed. I think they caught the glare in Cody."

"I don't want to know how much that dress cost. I might throw up."

Linc suppressed a chuckle. Jess wasn't flashy, and while she wasn't a penny pincher, she wasn't extravagant with her finances either. He hardly ever saw her with something new.

Even the dress she'd worn was understated. The navy hung in folds, but the neckline and even the slit were modest.

It was the perfect dress for her. She didn't need flash to draw attention or look good.

There were prayers, verse readings, and vows exchanged. Sniffles peppered the air, and boxes of tissues were passed down the rows.

Ridge and Cheyenne made a good couple, but they hadn't always been that way. After Cheyenne sold Ridge out for a hefty check, they'd all thought the two were really finished.

Apparently, love was stronger than hurt, and the two mended their fences. They'd been inseparable ever since.

If Ridge and Cheyenne could go from dislike to love, who was to say he and Jess couldn't move from friends to more? Even Colt and Remi had figured out how to turn their friendship into a romantic relationship.

He glanced over at Jess to find her eyes were dry. That hadn't surprised him much. She wasn't a crier. In fact, he'd only seen it once, and that was after he'd gone with Brett to help save Thea from her demented family.

Jess had shed a tear, then she'd frowned and tried to make him promise not to scare her like that again.

He hadn't made the promise. If someone needed help, he'd do everything in his power, and that might mean facing the front lines. If push came to shove, he'd stare down the barrel of a shotgun again.

When the newlywed couple kissed, everyone clapped. Another thing he couldn't imagine doing in front of a crowd was kissing. It seemed like a private thing, and while it was expected at a wedding, he still didn't think he could do it.

He glanced at Jess again. Would she want a wedding? She wasn't the type to make a fuss, and she didn't like it when people touched her. It would be hard for her to get on board with all the congratulatory hugs.

"Yessss!"

Linc turned just in time to see Abby, little and cute, dressed in what looked like a tutu, running wild down the aisle in front of the newlyweds.

Cheyenne laughed, and the crowd gave a collective laugh once they knew the bride wasn't upset about the excited outburst of a four-year-old at her wedding.

"You think she's celebrating her freedom?" Linc asked.

"Definitely. I wonder how long she's been standing still for photos. Everly said the wedding party had to be here early this morning."

"For a wedding at six in the afternoon?"

Jess nodded. "Sounds crazy to me too. It might just be me, but so many wedding traditions seem ridiculous. I mean, I get that the couple wants photos on their wedding day, but help me understand throwing the garter or not seeing each other the day of the wedding?"

"I'm no help at all because I feel the same way," Linc said.

"Don't get me started on toasts. It's almost a guarantee that one of the bride's parents is going to make an inappropriate joke."

"Eh, probably not Ridge and Cheyenne's families." Ridge had awesome parents. Cheyenne's mom still suffered from symptoms of a stroke she had years ago, and her dad had only found out recently that he even had a daughter.

Jess brushed her hands down the front of her dress as they waited for everyone to file out of the rows. "I guess it's a good thing to have parents who are alive and actually support your happiness. A few jokes aren't so bad."

Linc froze. Jess never talked about her parents, but Linc knew enough to know why. Her mom was a psycho, and her dad was murdered.

Enough said. No wonder she didn't give them two seconds of her thoughts.

Jess looked up at him with her brows drawn together. She opened her mouth like she was going to say something, then closed it.

He had a brief history of Jess's family, but she knew nothing about his.

For a reason.

No one wanted to hear about the abused kid who found his way into foster care before he was a year old. No one worried about why he lived his life like parents weren't a real thing.

Because for Linc, all those things were a nightmare, and he woke up a long time ago.

He could let it be his excuse. He could milk it for all it was worth.

Or he could turn the tables. He'd chosen to do just that.

Well, Mr. Chambers hadn't given him much of a choice, but Linc had accepted his new path. He was on the straight and narrow now.

They followed everyone inside the event hall where tables were covered with white tablecloths, twinkle lights hung from the rafters, flowers grew out of nowhere, a waterfall cascaded in one corner, a five-foot-tall ice sculpture dominated the other side of the building, and a massive cake stood front and center against the far wall.

"Wow," Jess whispered beside him. "This is fancy."

"That's what I was thinking," Linc whispered back.

"Where is your seat?" she asked. "You know they gave us assigned seats, right?"

Linc pinched the bridge of his nose. "I forgot about that. Um, I think my invitation said table five."

Jess looked around the room and pointed to one to their left. "That's my table too."

Interesting. They hadn't told anyone they were coming to the wedding together until this week, but the seating arrangements had been made for months. Whoever decided on seats must have known to put the two of them together.

"You're beside me," Jess said. "That's a good

thing because I would have tracked someone down to swap so I could be beside you."

Linc crossed his arms over his chest. "Really?"

Jess shrugged. "Of course. I'm not sitting by a stranger all night. And why would I sit with anyone but you?"

Linc looked at their place cards and grinned. "You want anything to drink?"

"Punch?"

Linc pulled Jess's chair out for her. "I'll get it."

He hurried through the drink line and came back to find Tracy talking to Jess. The owner of the bakery in town was one of the sweetest women Linc had ever met, but she had a fierce loyalty that came out harsh sometimes.

Linc hadn't ever been on the receiving end of Tracy's rants, but he'd heard about them. Apparently, Tracy didn't like to see people taken advantage of. She'd named herself their official spokesperson.

"Don't tell me you came here lookin' like that without a date tonight," Tracy said.

Jess looked over her shoulder just as he handed her the cup of punch. "Oh, no. I'm here with Linc."

Tracy's eyes widened. "Are you two together?"

CHAPTER 8

LINC

Linc's throat closed up. Oh, boy. Way to draw out the truth.

"No, ma'am. We're just friends," Jess said sweetly.

Linc tried to inhale a full breath after that gut punch, but his lungs refused to cooperate. If he'd wanted a sign, there it was, flashing bright and bold.

Just friends.

He'd known men in the friendzone. Sometimes, they clawed their way out of it.

Sometimes, they didn't.

But would it be so bad to be just friends with Jess? They'd been friends the whole time they'd known each other.

Yet, every day he wanted more, and she wasn't willing to give it.

Resignation sat heavy in his gut. Jess always spoke the truth, and she said they were friends.

So, that's what they would be. She didn't see him as more, and he could bow out gracefully.

Maybe not gracefully. It did more than sting.

"Really?" Tracy drawled. Her gaze zipped back and forth between Jess's blue dress and Linc's matching suit and tie. "Hmm. Could'a fooled me."

He knew he liked that woman.

The songs started, and the lights dimmed. Ridge and Cheyenne had their dance, and Linc spent most of the time sneaking glances at Jess.

How was he going to get over her?

He wasn't. Plain and simple. He hadn't intended to fall for her, and he also didn't plan on falling for anyone else in his life.

After the official dances were over, the DJ welcomed everyone else to join the bride and groom on the dance floor.

Someone grabbed his arm, and he turned to see Stella tugging him up from his seat.

"On your feet, cowboy. I wanna dance."

And he was being pulled away from the table. He looked back to see Jess chuckling.

Oh, she'd get her dance too. He'd make sure of it.

Stella whirled him around in the middle of the dance floor and rested her hands on his shoulders. "So, heard any good news lately?"

Stella and her husband had been regulars at the

ranch until her husband died. After that, Stella came to Wolf Creek and never left.

They all needed the ranch in one way or another. For Stella, Linc guessed it was about keeping her husband's memory alive.

Linc searched the older woman's face for any clue. "Um, the Rockies might beat the Marlins tomorrow."

Stella furrowed her brow and pursed her lips. "I'm talking about Jess's date."

"I *don't* want to talk about Jess dating," Linc said. Hopefully with enough finality that Stella got the picture. "And how do you even know about it?"

"I heard she didn't click with Hanson," Stella said quietly.

"I don't know what clicking is, but I'm glad it didn't work out."

Stella leaned in. "Listen, if you're gonna make a move on that girl, you better do it before she finds someone else who will."

"She doesn't like me like that," Linc said. "Now, will you please stop talking about Jess, and dating, and anything else that gives me heartburn?"

"No, this is serious. Jess is a little rough around the edges, but she's a good girl."

"Agreed," Linc said.

"But I don't think she needs to be looking for her next date," Stella said slowly.

"I don't know what she should be looking for, and I'm not in the mood to talk about it."

Stella pointed one finger at Linc. "Put on your big boy underwear and ask that girl out," she demanded.

"I just heard her tell someone half an hour ago that we were friends. Do you know what that means?"

"It means you haven't told her that the two of you are more than friends yet," Stella said.

"No, it means Jess thinks I'm just her friend. If she wanted to be more, she would have said it."

Stella looked at him and slowly shook her head. "You're thick-headed, boy."

"Thanks. It saved me from a few concussions."

Stella sighed and looked over Linc's shoulder. Jess was back there, and Linc knew what Stella was seeing—a beautiful, smart, brave woman who deserved more than an ex-convict.

Stella's shoulders slumped. "That girl doesn't know what love is. Nobody told her. I've noticed a change in her. She knows something is happening, but she doesn't know what to call it."

Linc stared at Stella. What if she was right?

But what if she was wrong?

"Thanks for the advice. I'll give it some thought."

Stella patted his shoulder as the song ended.

"That's about as much as I can ask for. You be good to her."

"Always," Linc promised.

"Now, go dance with her before some of Ridge's pro football player friends get there first."

Linc rolled his eyes. He wasn't built like a pro football player, but he could hold his own. He had a feeling that wasn't Jess's type.

"Fine. I'll ask her. But it's not because you told me to. It's because I want to."

"Whatever floats your boat, cowboy," Stella said with a wave as she walked off.

Good grief, that woman was determined. It was a good thing he didn't have a mother. Stella might just push her to the side and demand the title.

Jess was already getting to her feet when he made it back to the table. "Please dance with me," Linc said, offering her his hand.

"You took the words right out of my mouth."

Jess took his hand, and her small fingers slid perfectly between his. He'd only been thinking about leading her through the crowd of people, but the way she clung to him was better than he could have imagined.

When they were lost in the sea of people, Linc turned to face her. Jess rested her hand on his shoulder and took his hand in the other.

Linc put his hand on her waist. He'd made a

point to keep his hands to himself in the past, but Jess didn't seem to mind the contact.

It was a good thing because his palm might be forever glued to the soft curve of her waist.

"Did Stella boss you into something?" Jess asked.

Linc bit the inside of his cheek as he contemplated his answer. "She tried."

"She'll manage your whole life if you let her," Jess said with a grin.

"Trust me, I know." Though, he couldn't help but wonder if her way was the right way. She had a good forty years on him. Maybe she was older and wiser.

Stella didn't understand the precarious line he walked around Jess. One wrong step, and his whole world could come crashing down.

Jess spotted Ben and Abby dramatizing a slow dance on the other side of the room. "Those two are so happy. I kinda wish I had that."

"Had what? Kids?" Had they jumped topics and he hadn't realized?

"No, that carefree joy."

"They're kids. They're supposed to be like that."

Jess looked up at him. "I wasn't like that. Ever."

Her words brought up the few things she'd mentioned about her childhood, and Linc's hand tightened on her waist without his consent. "Are you happy now?"

"I am, but I still never look giddy or smiley like some people."

"You don't have to," Linc said. "Just be you."

"But everyone is always asking me why I look mad and what I'm upset about."

"Who cares what they think?"

Jess shrugged. "I've been told I *should* care what people think."

"Don't change. You're perfect the way you are."

Jess stared up at him for half a second, and panic rooted in his stomach. He'd said too much, and she was going to backpedal.

Instead of putting distance between them, she rested her head on his chest and whispered, "Thanks."

"Jess?" a man's voice said beside them.

Linc looked over as the guy smiled at Jess.

Jess lifted her head. "Hanson. Hey, it's good to see you."

Linc gave him a once-over. Hanson's face was a little too friendly for someone who got turned down for a second date.

"Good to see you too." Hanson looked at Linc and raised his brows. "You must be Linc."

Linc turned to Jess. How did this guy know him? Had Jess talked about him after he ran into her at the steakhouse?

Jess's mouth opened and closed before she tried again. "Um, yeah. This is Linc."

Hanson's expression hardened, and he looked Linc up and down before extending a hand. "I heard about you."

Oh, really?

Linc took the hand and gave it a firm grip. "I heard things didn't go your way Monday night. Better luck next time."

Jess jabbed her elbow into Linc's side, but he didn't take his attention off the guy.

"You win some, you lose some. Jess gets to break another heart."

Jess dramatically rolled her eyes. "Stop it."

Little did this guy know, she'd done that very thing less than an hour ago.

"I'm just messing with you. No hard feelings," Hanson said. "Well, I'd better get back to my aunt. She's been trying to set me up with someone else here. Half of my house is still in boxes, and she thinks finding the love of my life is at the top of my to-do list."

Jess laughed. "I don't envy you."

Linc didn't envy the guy either. Blind dates sounded about as appealing as getting a shot in the eye.

"I might sneak off to go fishing and stay gone for a while," Hanson said. "Maybe she'll forget I'm the lonely new bachelor in town."

Linc chuckled. "You could come on a pack ride with us and disappear into the wilderness."

"Linc, behave," Jess seethed.

"I meant that in a good way. Not like I wanted him to get lost."

"Kinda sounds like a good idea, minus the horses." Hanson grimaced.

Linc hooked a thumb over his shoulder at Hanson. "This guy doesn't like horses?"

Jess nodded. "They have big eyes," she explained.

Everything clicked into place. Jess and Hanson had found some common ground in that they didn't like being set up by the town, but Jess's heart for the horses and Hanson's dislike drove a wedge between them.

"Ah. Too bad, man," Linc said.

"I'll be fine. You two have a nice night," Hanson said with a wave.

Jess smiled as she waved, but it faded as soon as she turned back to Linc. "What was that?"

"What?"

"You were trying to intimidate him like you were my protective big brother or something."

Ouch. He'd been demoted from friend to big brother all in a few hours.

"Just looking out for you."

Jess propped her hands on her hips. "I can look after myself."

Linc put his hands in the air. "I know you can."

Jess's shoulders sank, and her hands fell from

her hips. "I have no idea what I'm doing when it comes to dating, but I know I don't need your help scaring men off. I do a pretty good job of that on my own."

Linc hung his head. "I'm sorry. It won't happen again."

Jess nodded once, accepting his apology. "Thanks."

An upbeat mainstream song blared through the speakers, and everyone around them started jumping.

"Okay. I think that's my cue to exit stage left," Jess said, pointing toward their seats.

"I'll join you." Linc wouldn't be caught dead bouncing to pop music.

Jess smoothed her dress before sitting down. As much as she claimed she wasn't the classy kind, she sure did look the part tonight.

Classy or not, Jess was perfect, in Linc's opinion.

Jess propped her chin in her hand and rested her elbow on the table. "I think I've had enough weddings to last me a lifetime."

"What about your own?" Linc asked.

Jess cut her eyes to him. "That's so far away, it might as well be a dream."

The sadness in her voice said she cared that marriage wasn't on the horizon for her. He'd always thought Jess was happy the way she was, but maybe her new peek into dating life was making her think about what she was missing.

"Is it a dream? Your dream? Do you want to get married?"

He ignored the way that last question had a completely different meaning if asked on its own. Right now, he just wanted to get to the bottom of the upset look on her face.

"I don't know. It doesn't matter." She waved a hand in the air. "Any chance you'd want to get out of here?"

Linc stood and offered her a hand. "I'm way ahead of ya."

They said a few goodbyes on the way out and congratulated the bride and groom.

Jess clutched the little purse she had in both hands, and she looked left to right as they stepped out into the twilight. "I don't think I'll ever get used to the dark out here."

Linc knew what she meant. It was one thing to be scared of the dark in your bedroom when you were a kid. It was another to have a healthy vigilance this close to the wilderness.

Linc walked close enough to Jess's side that their shoulders brushed together. "Don't worry. I won't let the monsters get you."

Jess looked up at him and grinned. "I didn't think you would."

The ride to Jess's house was quiet, but Linc

hadn't expected anything else. He parked in front of her house and shut off the truck.

"You don't have to walk me to the door," Jess said.

"What would Ms. Landry say if she reported I picked you up earlier and then dropped you off in the driveway." Linc clicked his tongue behind his teeth. "I'd get a bad reputation around town."

Jess laughed. "We don't care what my busybody neighbor thinks."

"Good, but I'm walking you to the door anyway."

He followed Jess to the porch with his hands in his pockets. He'd hoped the night would end with some relationship-defining revelation, but he'd heard enough this afternoon to know Jess either didn't share his feelings or she wasn't ready to hear about them yet.

"Thanks for the ride," Jess said as she reached for the doorknob.

"Jess."

She turned, and the dim porch light shone on her downcast expression. He'd give anything to wipe the sadness from her eyes.

"Promise me something."

"I'm gonna need to hear the request before I promise anything."

Linc took a step toward her, and she let her hand fall from the doorknob. She looked up at him, and he could've sworn there was a small spark in her eyes. "Don't ever change. Not for a man or anyone. You're perfect just the way you are."

A small smile turned up her lips. "I'll promise. Only if you promise to stay the same too."

Linc pulled a hand out of his pocket and offered it to her. "Deal."

When she took his hand, there was a slight tug on her end.

Linc didn't stop to think about what she might be doing. He pulled her in and wrapped his other arm around her. Something in his chest kicked, hard enough to hurt, as her head rested below his jaw.

He released the hug just as quickly as he'd started it. With a step away from her, he let her hand slip from his. "Good night, Jess."

"Good night, Linc."

Pushing his hands back into his pockets, he glanced at Ms. Landry's house and waved at the skewed blinds.

In the quiet of his truck, he pushed his hands through his hair and rested his forehead against the steering wheel. How was he going to get over Jess? It didn't seem possible.

His phone buzzed in the console, and he picked it up. A text from an unlabeled number jumped his heart rate from resting to running.

I'm out. Where are you?

CHAPTER 9
JESS

Jess measured out feed for Star and Burgundy. The perfect amount for each.

Numbers she could handle. Feelings? Not so much.

Thea closed the lid on one bin and opened another. "I know you probably don't have anything to say, but how did things go with Linc last night?"

Most people at the ranch hadn't thought twice about Jess showing up at the wedding with Linc last night. They were usually stuck together anyway.

Jess's sister-in-law, Thea, knew about the small "not a date" aspect of the evening, which meant there were unwelcome follow-up questions.

"Things went well. Same as always."

Linc had held her hand a few times, and she could still feel the echo of that tingle in her palms.

Then, he'd danced with her. She wasn't much of

a dancer, but being that close to Linc hadn't locked up her muscles the way she'd expected. No, she'd been hyperaware of every inch of her skin that touched his.

Memories kept her up half the night, and this morning, she still wanted to bring back that bubbly feeling that had covered her from head to toe when they'd danced.

And his hug? Yeah, she'd remember that until her dying day. She was definitely rethinking her aversion to touching.

Yet, Linc was the only person who'd ever conquered her avoidance of physical contact.

Her rational brain said it was ridiculous, but her heart wanted more.

So much more.

"Really? You two looked cozy dancing. You sure things didn't heat up?"

Jess straightened, holding onto the handle of a bin lid. "Things did not heat up. I don't know what you mean by that."

Thea tilted her head and narrowed her eyes. "Are you sure?"

"I'm sure. Nothing happened. He took me home, walked me to the door, and said good night."

Oh, and they'd hugged, but that wasn't the juicy gossip Thea wanted. No one else thought hugging and handholding was big news.

Except Jess. It was big news to her. Ground-breaking.

"Hm. That's strange. I could have sworn he was into you."

Welcome to the club, sis.

Jess went back to measuring feed. "Well, he isn't. Time to move on."

"Maybe he was distant because you didn't say it was a date."

"Why did I have to be the one to say it? He was the one that brought it up and then didn't want to say it was a date."

This was the reason she hated vagueness. Just say what you mean.

"He said it would be what you wanted it to be. Did *you* want it to be a date?"

Jess huffed, unhappy with the swirl of indecision in her head. "I don't know. All I do know is that we're fine the way we are."

"But are you really fine with it if you're stressing over it?"

Jess straightened. "I'm not stressing over it. You're the one trying to talk about it."

Thea put her hands in the air. "I get it. We don't have to talk about it. Just know, I think he does like you as more than a friend. He might be too scared to tell you."

Well, that made two of them. "Thanks, but if he liked me, he would tell me."

"Like you told him?"

Jess slammed the lid down. "Are we still talking about this?"

"Nope." Thea grabbed the buckets she'd filled and headed out of the feed shed.

Jess growled. She wasn't ever scared to say how she felt. Why was it different now that she suspected she had feelings for Linc?

Because she wished they were more than friends. Because he was the only man she'd ever met that she truly trusted. Because he understood her odd behaviors and never turned up his nose when she said something sharp. Because things progressing to more with Linc was terrifying.

If she could just get a glimpse of what it would be like, just a taste, maybe she'd know if this was the path they were meant to be on.

Thea poked her head back into the shed. "Have you prayed about it?"

Jess didn't turn around. "No. God doesn't care about my boy problems."

"This isn't a boy problem. This is your happiness."

"I'm happy enough."

"You don't look it."

Jess sighed. "This is just my default expression. I'm happy on the inside."

"Liar."

Jess whirled on Thea. "Will you get back to work?"

"Will you promise to pray about it?"

Jess gritted her teeth and took a deep breath. "Fine. I'll pray about it, but I won't expect an answer."

"Good enough."

They both stood still for a moment, and Jess sighed. "Why do you even care?"

Thea huffed. "Because we're family. But not just that. I love you and care about you and want you to be happy."

Jess couldn't look at Thea. There were too many things she didn't understand. Love being the first one.

Thea disappeared out the door, leaving Jess to put out the fires in her head.

Prayer was the last thing on her mind, but she closed her eyes and tried to block out the nervousness that had her heart beating like a drum. The familiar grainy feed smell slightly calmed her, and she focused on the simple words she needed.

Lord, help me understand. I don't know what Linc is thinking, but I want to know. Should I just tell him? Should I wait for him to make the first move?

Make me brave, Lord. Please.

She opened her eyes, and everything was as it should be. The feed buckets waited on her, and she did the only thing she knew how to do—her job.

Taking the buckets to the stables, she greeted Burgundy with a hand outstretched toward her nose. "Hey, girl."

Burgundy pressed her cheek into Jess's hand.

"You're not gonna try to make me talk about my feelings, are you?"

Jess's phone vibrated in her back pocket, and she answered it without taking her attention off Burgundy.

"Jess? It's Julia Letterman. How are you?"

Julia? She owned one of the flower shops in town, but they rarely spoke outside of church. "Hey, Mrs. Letterman. I'm fine. How are you?"

"Pretty good. I meant to catch you at church this morning, but you snuck out too quickly. Listen, Betty told me you went out with her nephew last week."

Oh, joy. The news was spreading. "I did."

"She told me things didn't work out between you two, but that y'all seemed to get along well enough at the wedding last night."

Okay, so the whole story was public knowledge. At least she wasn't being painted as a heartless man-eater.

"That's about right."

"Well, my grandson is coming to town this Thursday. He's with the rodeo in Cody, but they're having a small rodeo here this weekend. I mentioned you when he said he was coming to town, and he said he'd like to meet you. I thought to myself, Julia, those two would really hit it off, and I think I'm right."

It was good to know Julia held meetings with herself. If she could keep her thoughts quiet, maybe Jess wouldn't end up in awkward conversations like this.

"It's nice that you thought of me, but I don't think I'm ready to go on more dates."

"Oh, sweetie. How are you going to find the love of your life if you don't put yourself out there?"

That was a good question—one Jess didn't like asking herself.

Julia was right, but Jess really didn't like staring the truth in the face sometimes. Hence her silence.

"Okay. I guess I could meet him."

"Good! I'll give him your number."

If she was lucky, the guy would conveniently forget to call her. "That's fine."

"How's your brother doing? Loving married life?" Julia asked.

Considering Jess never asked Brett how he was doing, she didn't know the answer. "I'm not sure."

Julia laughed. "Oh, you're so funny. I'll see you next week. Have a good day."

"Bye."

Jess ended the call and stared at her phone. She'd prayed for guidance, then she got a phone call about a date.

Was God being funny? Or was He telling her to move on?

CHAPTER 10

JESS

Jess grabbed the big pink box out of the passenger seat of her truck and bumped the door shut with her hip.

Abby wanted a princess castle, and she'd get a princess castle.

In the form of a tent.

The kid always seemed happy and entertained. Jess could show up to the birthday party with a cardboard box and still get a massive thank you.

Linc pulled up in his truck and parked beside hers. She stopped on the steps leading up to the dining hall. When Linc stepped out of his truck, it was instinct to stare.

His boot hit the ground hard, and he grabbed his hat off the dash. The brown shirt was the color of his dark eyes, and his jeans fit him just right.

Was he moving in slow motion? Was this the equivalent of the *Baywatch* run?

Snap out of it!

She shook her head and continued up the stairs. She'd be sighing like a schoolgirl when he walked by if she didn't get her head in the game.

"Wait up!" Linc yelled behind her.

She stopped on the porch and turned. Linc wasn't doing the *Baywatch* run anymore. He was pulling a long, flat box out of the backseat of his truck.

"What did you get her?" Jess asked when he made it to the steps.

"Bow and arrow."

Jess's jaw dropped.

"What?" Linc asked, looking confused and handsome at the same time.

"She's gonna love that."

"I know. I got one with a low draw weight. She should be able to use it."

"Drat," Jess whispered.

"Why? What did you get her?"

"A castle," Jess mumbled.

"A castle? Like a stone fortress?"

"No, a castle like a tent."

Linc clicked his tongue behind his teeth. "That'll get you mediocre points compared to my gift."

"Shut up," Jess said as she pushed the door to the dining hall open with her hip.

Inside, Remi pointed up at Colt, who stood on a ladder with his hands above his head. A pink piñata hung from the rafters.

Remi waved her hand. "A little lower."

Linc huffed softly beside Jess. "A piñata. That's pretty cool."

"I know. I never had a piñata at a party when I was little."

"Me either."

Jess looked up at him. "I never even had a birthday party."

Linc's dark eyes locked on her, and warmth brushed down her spine. If anyone understood how hard it was when your childhood was dead on arrival, it was Linc.

They hardly ever talked about the past or their families, but people who grew up in abusive homes had a different look about them. There was a spark missing in their eyes and a hardness about their shoulders.

Linc had jumped headfirst into her family's dumpster fire when Thea had been in trouble. Brett needed help, and Linc didn't ask why. He just got in the truck.

They'd talked about what happened that night a total of zero times, and Jess wasn't going to ask about it. At least not yet. Knowing multiple people had come out with holes in them did nothing good for her imagination.

"Me either, but I think we turned out okay," he whispered.

Jess swallowed, but the tightness in her throat persisted. "That's up for debate."

"Not in my world."

How did he do that? Erase the hurt of the past with just a few words. If he talked enough, she might forget all the bad stuff.

Remi spotted them and pointed toward a table on the far side of the room. "Gift table is over there. Abby should be here any minute."

They put their gifts on the table where Everly organized the boxes, bags, and cards. A full spread of breakfast foods filled the serving counter, and everyone from the ranch plus a few more familiar faces hung around in clusters, mostly separated by gender.

"Jess, come here!" Hadley hollered from a nearby table.

"I guess this is where we part ways," Linc said before walking over to join the men.

All the women huddled around Ava, who sat cradling her stomach with a broad smile on her face. Everyone at the ranch had gotten a front-row seat to Ava's pregnancy woes. She'd been through the wringer since the day she found out she was having a baby.

"Twenty-six weeks. I feel like your pregnancy has flown by," Cheyenne said.

Ava huffed. "It's different when I've been sick every day of those seven months."

"I don't know how you do it," Hadley said.

Jess seconded Hadley's statement. Ava's sickness had been hard to watch, but she kept her chin up, even when it was obvious she was exhausted or feeling bad.

Babies rarely crossed Jess's mind, mostly because they weren't on her radar.

Yet.

She'd like to get married and maybe have kids, but the opportunity definitely wasn't presenting itself. She had one suitor lining up for a date, and they hadn't even met face-to-face.

Ava chuckled and rubbed her bulging belly. "What choice did I have?"

"You're gonna be a great mom," Everly said. "And this baby is already so loved."

Vera clasped her hands at her chest. "I can't wait to hold him." The sweet-as-pie kitchen manager at the ranch loved Abby and Ben. You could see it in her eyes that she had a heart for children, but she'd never had any of her own. Or a husband.

Ava's eyes widened and she reached for Vera's hand. "Want to feel him kick?"

Vera's smile fell, and she didn't move to take Ava's hand.

"You don't have to, but he's being active right now."

Vera snapped out of her frozen state and offered her hand.

Ava guided the hand to the right side of her belly and moved it around a little.

A low gasp escaped Vera's lips. "That's him?"

Ava nodded, and her teeth showed through her smile. "That's him."

Vera's eyes turned glassy, and she raised her other hand to her chest. "I've never felt that before."

Jess's chest gripped. Vera didn't have much family to speak of, and Jess got the feeling they were a lot alike in that they'd adopted the ranch family as their own.

"Feel mine!" Remi said as she walked up rubbing her smaller belly. "It doesn't kick as much, but it's still so cool to think there's a baby in there."

Jess pushed her hands into the back pockets of her jeans. Remi was right. It was cool to think about babies growing, but feeling a baby kicking in its mother's womb was a little more than she could wrap her head around.

Motherhood hadn't been romanticized for her until a few years ago. Her mother hated her kids, and nothing the woman had done even hinted at love.

Abby and Ben came to the ranch last year, and Jess got to see what it was like for kids to grow up with guardians—not even biological parents—who cared for them.

It was a game changer–night and day from what she'd always known.

Now, seeing Ava and Remi about to become mothers, the whole idea of one day having kids of her own wanted to take root.

Again, she stomped the stupid hopes down. She was going on her second first date ever soon, and she was far from baby talk.

Jess watched Vera whose mouth still hung open. What if she ended up like Vera in her fifties with no husband and no kids? Would she be okay with that? She might have to be, whether she liked it or not.

Jess took a deep breath. Twenty-two was young. She had plenty of time.

The door to the dining hall opened, and Abby jumped through the doorway. "I'm here!"

Everyone shouted "Happy birthday!" together and ran to hug the birthday girl.

Everyone except Jess. She was still stuck in the pit of woes wondering why all of her co-workers and everyone she spent her time with had happy families, but she didn't.

She might not ever.

Jess shook off the gloomy mood and made her way to see Abby. The little girl twirled from one friend's arms to the next, shouting thanks and giggles.

Jess crouched and held out her hand for Abby to slap. "Happy birthday, slugger."

Abby slapped the hand as hard as she could before lunging herself toward Jess. The little arms latched tight around Jess's neck, and she buried her nose in Abby's soft hair.

Why did she want to cry?

She gave Abby one last big squeeze before releasing the hug. "You're pretty awesome, you know that?"

Abby leaned in and pecked a kiss on Jess's cheek. "I know. You're awesome too."

With that gut-punching compliment, she skipped off to the next admirer.

No one ever told Jess she was awesome. Or even nice. Except Linc.

She wanted to be nice. It was hard to know how. She appreciated her friends, she cared about them, but the sweet sentiments were difficult to put together.

Jess stuck to Linc's side, and whether he noticed her silent panic or not, he didn't mention it.

Thankfully, because she had no idea how to explain what was wrong. Nothing was wrong. She was just being emotional for no reason.

One of her least favorite things about being a woman with hormones–feelings. Complicated, messy, irrational feelings. Feelings didn't make sense.

After they'd eaten cake and ice cream, Linc

looked at his watch. "I need to head out. See you at the stables later?"

She'd love to. Except she had other plans.

Linc's hair was just long enough to fall down in the front, creating a messy look that he rocked as if he were Elvis himself. She was staring, and staring was impolite.

Or so she'd been told.

"Actually, I have a date tonight."

No matter how many times she said it, the whole dating thing was not sinking in for her. Why wasn't there a way to skip the awkward dating part?

Oh, there were mail-order brides. Were there mail-order grooms? It was a stupid thought, but she might actually contemplate it if it meant she got to bypass dating.

Linc froze halfway between sitting and standing. His hands were planted on the table beside her, giving her a front-row seat to his thick forearms and biceps, since he'd rolled up the sleeves of his flannel shirt during the piñata bashing.

Those have practical uses, Jess. They're not for ogling.

"Pardon?" Linc asked, slow and deliberate.

Why did she like it when she made him do a double take?

"Mrs. Letterman called and said her grandson or something was coming into town for a rodeo. I'm going out with him tonight."

Linc sat back down and stared at her with a blank expression she couldn't read. "Where?"

"Ha. Nice try. You're not showing up for this one." He'd done the protective friend thing before, and she hadn't made up her mind on how she felt about it.

Scratch that. She had, and she just didn't like the outcome. Having Linc ride to her rescue, even when she didn't need it, was nice. More than nice. It was like a safety net.

No one had rushed in to save her before, and she liked it when Linc showed up, even when she didn't need saving.

"What if you need help? Someone should know where you are."

"If I need help, I'll let someone know where to find me."

Linc straddled the bench seat and faced her. His shoulders rose in a deep swell. "I don't like that."

Jess shrugged. What did he expect her to do about it?

He sighed and brushed a hand through his hair. He really needed to stop drawing attention to the parts of him she liked most. "Just let someone know where you're going, please."

"I don't know where we're going. He said he wanted it to be a surprise."

Linc scoffed. "Now I'm not worried at all. Jess,

you need to drive yourself so you can leave if you need to."

"I drove myself to the date with Hanson, and he turned out to be a gentleman." She'd been overly cautious with Hanson because he was pretty much her first date ever, but she'd probably been wrong to put up a ton of walls before giving him a chance. "This guy seemed like he really wanted to pick me up like it was a *real* date."

Had her emphasis on the word real been intended? Yes. The least Lincoln could have done was identify the short amount of time they'd spent together at the wedding. If he'd just said it was a date, she wouldn't be waffling over everything right now.

Linc clinched his jaw and turned toward the door. His Adam's apple bobbed, and he pressed his lips together.

Ugh. She hadn't thought about his lips until they had the kissing talk a few weeks ago. Why had she brought it up? Now she thought about kissing whenever he was around.

Did he have to have such great lips? It was distracting in a way she didn't need.

He finally swung his gaze back to her, but he wasn't taking it easy on her. His look said he would give it back to her as fast as she'd give it to him.

Was she ready for that?

"What did you learn from the last date?" he

asked in a whisper. It didn't help that his words had been so low she'd been forced to read his lips.

Why was he questioning her? She might not like the whole dating thing, but she could do it on her own. She didn't need his pushback. "That I know what I *don't* want."

Linc's dark eyes held hers. "What's that?" The small wrinkle in his brow said he was very interested in her answer.

Oh, no. She hadn't expected him to actually ask her what that was. She wanted to back the truck up and erase that part.

"Jess, what *do* you want?" There was no joking in his question. This man wanted the truth, and he wanted it straight.

She wanted a man she was sure about. If she was going to add love to the mix, it had to be worth the risk. It needed to be epic and life-changing.

Jess froze, staring at Linc as he waited on her answer.

Maybe she didn't want life-changing. Maybe she wanted what she already had.

Lincoln North.

No. He wasn't *hers*. He was her friend. Her co-worker, even. That was different. It wasn't romantic. It was the definition of platonic.

Her carefully constructed walls started cracking. Linc wanted an answer, and she wasn't capable of lying. She never had a problem being honest with him.

Why was it difficult right now? She could usually speak her mind, but not about this. Not when Linc might look at her differently if she said something that changed the dynamic of their relationship when he wasn't on board.

She still hadn't answered him, and he was looking at her like he was ready to set up a tent and camp out until she came clean. Heat rose under the collar of her shirt and spread up her neck. She had to say it because it was the only response she knew.

I want you. Why wouldn't the words come out?

Lincoln broke his stare, and Jess inhaled like she hadn't taken a real breath in years. He hung his head before looking back up at her. "Just be careful, okay?"

Jess nodded. A lot. She kept nodding until he stood.

He rapped his knuckles on the table. "Call me if you need me."

Turning the words over in her head, she watched him walk out of the dining hall. What constituted need? Did that require an emergency?

Was she looking for an excuse to call him?

Emerson stepped over the bench and sat in the seat Linc had just vacated. It was probably still warm, but Emerson was replacing that coziness with ice.

Jess gave Emerson a side glare. "What?"

Emerson scoffed. "Hey to you too, sis."

"I'm not your sis," Jess said before turning back to her empty cake plate. There weren't even any crumbs to play with while she pretended she had something more important to do than talk to her long-lost sister.

"Yes, you are. It doesn't have me jumping for joy either, but even you can't deny the genetics."

Emerson didn't look like Brett or even their dad, and Jess wasn't ready to check those similarities in the mirror. The color of Emerson's eyes matched Brett's perfectly, and the shape of her nose was one she'd recognize as a Patton anywhere.

Jess stabbed at a pretend crumb on her plate. Brett and Emerson had taken a genetics test. Good for them, but Jess wasn't ready to embrace and have a sleepover.

Emerson cleared her throat. "So, how are the horses and stuff?"

Enough was enough. Emerson could be her sister all day long, but it didn't mean Jess had to make friends. "I don't want to talk to you."

Emerson slapped her palms on the table. "That's not news. Let's cut to the chase. Linc. Is he single?"

Jess's grip on the fork tightened, and her head snapped up faster than a bucking bronc out of the chute. She pinned Emerson with a stare that could melt glass. "That's none of your business."

Emerson laughed. Actually threw her head back and laughed like something was funny.

Nothing about this unwelcome conversation was even remotely humorous, and the pounding in Jess's ears was loud enough that it almost drowned out Emerson's laughter.

Emerson made a show of wiping tears from her eyes as her cackling subsided. "Easy, drama queen. Don't claw my eyes out. I wasn't staking my claim."

More pounding. The plastic fork in Jess's grip snapped in two. "Don't even think about it." Each word was carefully articulated, so Emerson would have no trouble getting the message.

Emerson narrowed her eyes and flashed a fake smile. "I just asked a question, and I got my answer."

Jess broke her stare and dropped the broken fork. She shouldn't care if Emerson was interested in Linc, but she *did* care. She cared a lot.

CHAPTER 11

LINC

Linc pushed crates against a wall, sending dust and dirt flying. The tack room saw plenty of action, and Jess always got tense when things were out of order.

He arranged the medications in a blue crate and huffed. He wasn't doing this for Jess. He was rummaging around in the tack room after dark because it was his job. There wasn't anything wrong with getting a jump on things.

Who was he kidding? Linc was on this cleaning and organizing steam train to take his mind off Jess's date.

It wasn't working.

Everything in the barn reminded him of Jess. This was her world, and he was just lucky enough to get to see it. She loved and cared for the horses like they were her babies, and everyone else stayed out of her way.

Linc got a swift punch in the gut every time that woman whispered to a horse or wrapped her arms around one. If he was jealous of the sweet pieces of Jess that the horses got, the news about her date turned him into an ugly green envy monster.

His phone dinged, and another ding followed right after. Twisting to pull it from his back pocket, he hastily cradled it in his hands as if it held the cure for the clawing in his chest.

The screen showed an unknown number, and he didn't need to see a name to know the face behind the words.

Come on, man. I'm headed north.

Where are you?

Linc shoved the phone back into his pocket. No way was he letting Ryan anywhere near this ranch. After crawling out of prison, the last place Linc would ever go was back inside those walls.

Ryan was a fast pass to the lockup. Never again.

There were a few years of Linc's life that got constantly kicked into the gutter of his memories. He'd stolen everything from guns to cars. He'd thrown countless rocks through windows. He'd picked off mailboxes with a bat until his arms were sore.

He'd burned every bridge he set his sights on,

and he hadn't just lit them on fire, he'd blown them up in a red-hot puff of smoke.

Okay, so the bridges were metaphors, but the rest was real. When he met Ryan in Memphis, they'd been a matching pair with a thirst for destruction. The cops knew their descriptions and their aliases, but it took the law three years to catch them.

That's when the real fires started. Literally and figuratively.

Linc slammed the side of his fist against the wall. The old wood pounded but didn't budge. Ryan was out, and Linc knew exactly what the guy wanted. It wasn't a meetup for old time's sake.

No, Ryan had a reason to come after Linc, and it had nothing to do with chatting over a beer like old times.

Linc looked around the tack room. Everything was in its place, and this chore wasn't holding his focus anymore.

The rumbling of a truck outside had him raising his chin. It was a diesel, but it wasn't Jess's. Linc turned off the light and locked up. He'd just opened Jess's office door when Brett walked in.

"What are you doing here so late?" Brett asked.

It wasn't unusual for Linc to be at the barn well after dark, but Brett had been spending more time at home in the evenings since marrying Thea. He couldn't blame the guy. Linc would probably stay home more too if he had a wife.

Too bad that kinda life wasn't in the cards for him. Getting married, settling down, and even having a family sounded like heaven these days.

"Just cleaning up the tack room. I'm headed out."

Brett jerked a thumb over his shoulder. "I'll lock up the office when I'm done. You go home."

Linc studied Brett for a second. "What are you doing here?"

"Thea thought she left an email unsent this afternoon from Jess's address. I told her I'd check it since it was a feed order."

"Right. Speaking of Jess, have you heard from her tonight?"

Brett whirled around and narrowed his eyes at Linc. "I wasn't talking about Jess. I was talking about Thea and Jess's email."

"You said Jess." Linc wasn't prepared for Brett's mind games tonight, and he'd walked himself right into a trap with that one.

Brett slowly turned and headed into the office. "I haven't heard from her. She asked Thea to wrap things up because she was going to Cody for something. Why?"

Linc averted his eyes. Brett would know something was up if he dug around too much. That guy saw everything, and Linc had promised not to tell anyone at the ranch that Jess was dating.

He'd never betray her trust. If she didn't want

word getting around, Linc would lock it all up and throw away the key. Zip his lips. Cross his heart. All the things.

"Just wondering. See ya later."

"Good night. Sweet dreams!" Brett shouted from the office.

The night was pitch black without a moon in sight. The ranch was eerily quiet in the off season. He didn't have any love for the crowds, but he liked escaping into the mountains with just the horses and a handful of folks for a few days. It had been months since he'd been on a trail ride, and the wilderness was calling his name.

Linc closed himself in the cabin and hung his hat and coat by the door. The cabin was quiet since Brett moved out, and it was the kind of peace that dreams were made of.

After showering, Linc went straight to bed. He'd gotten up early and worked well over twelve hours. Sleep should come as quick as a wink.

But this was the longest wink of his life, and staring at the ceiling was incredibly boring. If he just had some kind of confirmation that Jess made it home from her mysterious date okay, he could shut the engine down.

For once, he wished he was a part of Ms. Landry's phone tree. Half the town probably knew Jess's date's height and hair color, as well as the make and model of his truck.

She might even have the license plate number.

Linc flopped onto his side and stared at the wall. This was ridiculous. He had no reason to care if Jess hit it off with the guy on her date. It wasn't his business.

But making sure she made it home safely was a legit concern. He sat up and rummaged on the nightstand looking for his phone. Where'd he put it?

Throwing the covers off and launching out of bed, he checked the pockets of his jeans until he found it. The screen lit up the dark room. No messages.

He opened the text app as he sat back on the bed. It was almost eleven. She was probably asleep.

But if she wasn't home yet, then he actually had a reason to worry. He tapped out a message.

Linc: You make it home okay?

He pressed send before the fire burning up his throat made him sick. Maybe the indigestion wasn't the issue. Now, he had to wait for a response.

What if he didn't get one? Did he call her brother or the sheriff first? Would Brett help him ride around town looking for her in the middle of the night?

Definitely.

"Come on, Jess. Give me something."

Staring at the phone was going to slowly burn him alive. He flopped onto his back and rested his forearm over his eyes and started listing all the reasons why he shouldn't be worrying about her.

She's smart. If the guy was a creep, she'd let him know and then call for a ride home.

She's scrappy. She could probably take the guy in a fist fight if it came to throwing hands.

She was–

The phone rang in his hand, and he was sitting up in bed before the first chime faded. Jess's name lit up the screen.

"Hello."

"The date was a short one. I've been home for a while."

Linc fell back onto the bed like a blue whale breaching. A short date was good news. Well, good news for Linc, at least.

"What happened?" He asked the question before stopping to consider whether or not he actually wanted to know the answer.

There was rustling on Jess's end of the call, and Linc imagined she was wrapping the blankets around her and getting comfy in bed.

Time out. He was not allowed to think about Jess in bed.

She was in the living room. No. She was probably in her kitchen. He couldn't think of any reason she'd be in the kitchen this close to midnight, but it was much safer than the image of her in bed.

Jess sighed. "He took me to Little Italy."

"In Cody? But you don't like Italian food."

Linc had picked up on that little tidbit about her years ago. She always went home for a sandwich at lunchtime if Vera was making pizza or pasta.

"Yeah. He didn't care. Also, he was a little bit wrapped up in himself. I was glad I didn't have to do a lot of talking, but I was also disappointed that I couldn't just chow down while he was boosting his own ego."

"What a tool," Linc whispered. These guys were making him look better by the day.

Jess yawned, and her voice changed to a low, tired tone. "I thought we would connect over horses, since he's with the rodeo. No luck there. He's a bull rider and thinks he's better than the bronc riders, barrel racers, and calf ropers."

"He's probably been hit in the head one too many times."

Jess chuckled, and Linc closed his eyes as the sweet sound sent a tingle down his arms and legs all the way to his fingertips and toes.

"You're probably right. It wouldn't have worked out anyway. He's with the traveling rodeo."

"I'm sorry it didn't go well," Linc said, and to his surprise, he really was sorry. Jess deserved a man who would wake up and put her in his top two most important things every day.

"I'm starting to think dating isn't for me," she whispered.

That soft broken sound did some damage in his chest. She'd been overlooked her whole life, and how many people had stopped to tell her she was amazing?

"You went on two dates. Don't give up on finding love because two losers happened to cross your path first."

"I wouldn't say Hanson was a loser," she said.

"Hanson wasn't a total loser, but he doesn't like horses, so he gets points knocked off for that."

She chuckled again, and Linc decided sleep was for the weak. If Jess kept talking and laughing, he'd gladly get shocked by her lightning over and over again.

Linc cleared his throat, trying to weigh the pros and cons of telling the truth, the whole truth, and nothing but the truth.

"Jess, don't give up. You're amazing. Someone is going to see that, and that guy will move mountains for you."

Linc's heart thudded like the bass in a hard rock song. He'd put a little bit of his heart on the line, and while he didn't expect her to do anything with his confession, he also didn't want her to run for the hills.

Jess sighed. "We'll see."

"Take my advice or not. Just don't settle."

"I'm not really the settling type. I might fall in love with a guy who gets tired of my sassy mouth and decides I'm not worth the trouble. Let's face it, that's the most likely scenario."

"If he lets you go, you're better off without him."

Jess hummed low and yawned again. "Thanks for the pep talk. Pretending to care about some guy's bull riding stats is exhausting, so I'm going to bed."

"Good night, Jess."

"Good night, Linc. Sweet dreams."

She didn't need to worry. His dreams would be sweet, as long as she was happy.

CHAPTER 12

JESS

J ess stared at the verse she'd written on the board yesterday. It could stay another day. Mostly because she hadn't figured out its meaning yet.

The Lord will fight for you; you need only to be still. — *Exodus 14:14*

The words seemed simple enough, and she knew all of their separate meanings. It was the overall concept that stumped her. Was the verse about patience or faith? Maybe hope?

She'd ask Vera about it later. She checked the time on her phone and called over her shoulder on her way out of the barn. "I'm headed to the garage!"

Brett shouted back. "What for?"

"My truck has a light on. I want Linc to check it out."

Brett didn't respond, which meant he must be

really busy in his office. Though, she had no idea what he did in there. She took care of all the schedules and appointments. He much preferred the physical labor to the paperwork.

The sky was overcast, and the wind stung against her cheeks as she dashed to the truck. Spring was taking its precious time coming this year, and if the snow on the mountain didn't melt soon, they'd be forced to push back the first trail rides of the season.

She started the truck, and that pesky light came on. There were few things she couldn't do on her own, and for some reason, the mechanics of vehicles had always stumped her. She hadn't even owned a car until she moved out of her parents' house.

The check engine light was something she did know. It had been staring at her since yesterday, and she'd finally worked up the courage to ask Linc if he'd take a look at it.

Linc's truck was already parked outside the garage when she pulled up. She hadn't seen much of him the last few days with things ramping up at the ranch. They didn't have many more weeks before the guests started arriving, and everyone was working overtime.

Jess pulled into the open bay and left the truck running. Linc stepped out of the supply closet shoving a rag into his back pocket. His hair was tousled as if he'd been wearing a hat all day, and the sleeves of his flannel shirt were haphazardly rolled up on his forearms.

The tingle that started in her chest and spread out all the way to her fingertips was unnerving. She'd seen Linc a thousand times, and that initial sensation whenever he walked into a room these days was frustrating.

She stepped out of the truck but didn't move as he approached her. Her breaths turned shallow, and she watched every step with a captivated appreciation.

Linc knew how to walk like a man. He had a commanding presence that made him the most dominant man in every room.

Too bad he was always trying to blend into the shadows.

"What's the problem, miss?"

Jess took a step back and waved her hand toward the driver's seat. Linc leaned inside and inspected the dash.

"Check engine. That's never a good sign." He popped the hood and walked around to the front. With the hood up, he rested his hands on the frame as he looked around.

His thick forearms were front and center, and she averted her gaze. Staring at him wasn't going to make things easier. "You see anything?"

He shook his head and reached into the complicated machine. Jess couldn't name a single thing under the hood, but Linc worked like he knew the code to solve the Rubik's cube.

Jess rested her elbows on the side of the truck and watched Linc's silent assessment. He walked to the toolbox, grabbed a few things, and returned to the truck.

Jess didn't know how to sit around. If she wasn't sleeping or eating, she needed to be moving and working.

Watching Linc work could convince her to take a break. He looked at the parts under the hood as if they were talking to him, telling him what to do and how to fix it. As much as she wanted her truck patched up and ready to roll, hanging around while Linc worked on vehicles wasn't a bad way to spend an afternoon.

He unscrewed the oil cap and pulled out the dipstick. "Low oil."

"But it's not time to change it," she said.

"You're burning oil. I'll have to keep a check on it to see if it keeps happening."

"How long will it take to fix?"

He wiped his hands on the rag. "Not long. You got somewhere to be?"

Ugh. She'd hoped to get out of this visit without talking about her plans. "I have a date later."

"Same guy?" he asked.

"No. Another first date."

Linc turned his attention to the rag in his hands

and kept wiping, tensing his jaw the entire time. "Is there a chance you'll tell me where you're going this time?"

It was a simple enough question, but there was a low-boiling warning behind it. Linc was holding back, and she probably didn't want to hear the rest of his thoughts.

"He's taking me to The Barn."

Linc's brows quirked up, but he didn't say anything before walking over to the toolbox.

She hadn't been exactly thrilled about the guy's date destination choice. Barn Sour was one of her favorite places to hang out, but she usually went with the others at the ranch. The place often had live music she enjoyed, and dancing that she steered clear of at all costs.

This guy was probably banking on dancing tonight, and she wanted to kick up her heels about as much as she wanted to jump off a cliff.

Linc didn't talk while he worked, and Jess didn't have anything to say either. After their little chat about kissing a few weeks ago, she couldn't talk to Linc about her dates. That conversation had started the confusing sensations whenever Linc was around, and the last thing she wanted was more complicated feelings.

"What's his name?" Linc asked out of nowhere.

"Jason. He's from Colorado, so I don't expect it

to end in a second date, but..." Jess shrugged. "You never know."

"He lives in Colorado?"

"Yeah. He's in Cody helping a friend get his farm ready to sell."

"Then he'll head back to Colorado?"

"I assume."

Linc seemed to hang on to that one little piece of information.

The low commitment possibility had been the main factor when deciding whether or not to go on the date. They would need to both have a strong, instant connection to consider making it a long-distance relationship, and Jess's hope was the size of a sunflower seed that they'd end the night with that kind of confirmation.

"Why are you going, then?"

"I figure practice makes perfect. At least I'll get some experience under my belt. Dating is tough. There should be clear-cut rules, and everybody is so opinionated. Plus, there are no absolutes, which bothers the stew outta me. Don't get me started on the whole 'I'll call you' trend. I hate all of it."

Linc didn't look up from his work. "If you hate dating, why are you doing it? Why now?"

Jess rested her chin on her hand. "I'm never gonna meet someone if I don't try."

Linc closed the hood and leaned his hip against it. With his arms crossed over his broad chest and his shoulders tense, he had the stern look of a man who made people ask "How high?" before he even said "Jump."

Not to Jess. Linc had never scared her, and every time he gave orders without room for negotiation or stood up for what he believed in, her respect for him grew.

He kept his stare locked with hers for a few seconds, and she didn't cower. In fact, she stood and pushed her shoulders back.

"I have some advice for you," he said before looking down at the dirty rag. There was just as much grease on the rag as there was on his hands.

He took a deep breath and looked up at her. "I don't know everything about what you went through growing up. Brett told me enough to know your parents weren't in the running for mom and dad of the year."

Something inside her wilted. Every time she thought about the quiet, terrified kid she'd been, the fear rose inside her, as clear and intense as ever.

"You don't have to tell me anything," Linc whispered. "My life wasn't a bed of roses either, so I'm going to give you a few pieces of advice your parents should have told you but probably didn't."

She tried to think of any warnings or advice her parents ever gave her, but as much as she scrambled through her thoughts, she couldn't come up with anything good.

They'd pitted her against Brett, locked her outside all day, and told her to walk to school when she missed the bus, but all of those things didn't seem like golden parenting moments.

Linc looked her up and down as if trying to decide where he should start. "First, don't take rides from strangers."

"But he has to pick me up."

"Why? Your truck is ready."

Jess groaned. "He said he wanted to pick me up, and I said he could."

Linc pinched the bridge of his nose and closed his eyes. "Next, don't do anything I wouldn't do." He raised his head. "Better yet, don't do anything Mr. Chambers wouldn't do."

"Well, that rules out going on a date with a guy," Jess said. "I don't think your advice is hitting like you planned."

"Just don't do anything stupid."

"Are you saying you've never done anything stupid?"

Linc stared at her and swallowed hard. "Forget that one. Just..." He sighed and looked around as if help might jump out from behind the nearest tractor. "Just don't give up the milk until he buys the cow."

Jess stared at him. What did he say? "Explain, please."

Linc's shoulders fell. "Don't make me spell it out."

"You don't have to spell it. Just say it in a way I can understand."

Linc rubbed his chin. He was cute when he was thinking hard. There was a small wrinkle between his brows, and whether he meant to be flexing or not, his strong arms were on full, beautiful display.

"Okay. You know how we talked about not kissing a guy on the first date?"

"Yeah." How could she forget that interesting conversation?

"Don't do anything else either. You should probably not hold his hand either. Just to be on the safe side."

Jess tilted her head as she assessed his words. "I–"

"I'm not trying to tell you what to do. Just consider not giving him all of the benefits before you know if he's worthy."

Oh, Linc was trying to tell her not to have sex with the guy.

Cue her flaming embarrassment. Her throat swelled and closed as heat bloomed on her chest and face.

Now she knew what people meant when they claimed to die of embarrassment. She was definitely having trouble breathing.

Linc twisted the rag in his hands. "You know

what? I'm just gonna pretend like you're not going out. It's better for my sanity."

"Um, that's not gonna happen. You can calm down."

Linc pushed a hand through his hair and whispered, "He could be a killer. Not a mass murderer. Just a casual killer."

Jess reached out and took the poor rag out of his clenched fist. "You have got to stop worrying. I'm going. I'm gonna eat dinner. He's gonna take me home. And there's a good chance that'll be it. Plus, you forget I know how to defend myself."

Linc nodded but kept his gaze on the floor. "Okay. I'm sorry. Have fun, but just be careful."

Jess crouched and tilted her head to get in his line of sight. She grinned up at him and tried to transfer comforting thoughts to him. Linc was having a harder time about the dating than she was.

"I'll be careful," she promised.

His eyes turned to her, and his shoulders relaxed. "I know you will."

She straightened and pointed a finger at him. "I'd appreciate it if you didn't go to Barn Sour tonight and hang over my shoulder staring at my date. I can't tell you not to go out, but I can ask."

He took a deep breath. "Okay. But it's not far away. You'll call me if you need me?"

There was that pesky ambiguous word again. What constituted a need again?

"Or if you just want to," he added, so low and husky that the words vibrated in her veins.

Oh no. She could think of quite a few reasons to want him.

This was bad. Really bad.

She wanted to call Linc. She'd always called him when she had a reason—mostly work-related—but he'd given her permission to call him if she wanted.

Did it matter what she wanted? Linc was off-limits. He was her co-worker. He was older than her measly twenty-two years. He was closed off and tough. He was honest and selfless.

This was really bad.

She wanted Linc.

CHAPTER 13
LINC

Linc pried open another crate of supplies, but the contents were a blur.

Paul leaned over his shoulder and pointed to the opposite side of the pack shed. "Tarps go there."

On any normal day, working with Paul meant Linc hit the jackpot. The older cowboy wasn't much for talking, and neither of them were tempted to chitchat. That was one thing he liked about Paul. He only spoke when he had something meaningful to say.

"Leave them in packs of three," Paul said before moving back to his own crate.

Work should take Linc's mind off Jess and her date, but this evening, he wasn't having any luck pushing those unwelcome thoughts away.

He should just tell her. On the bright side, she might have feelings for him. It wasn't likely, but a guy could dream. On the downside, things would get awkward, and he'd lose her.

For every way they were alike, there were three ways they were different. They'd both grown up in poverty and abusive homes, but Jess reacted differently. She'd lifted her chin in the air and decided to be better than the lousy hand she'd been dealt. Linc had rebelled and tried everything in his power to burn the world to the ground.

Literally, he'd set fire to anything that would burn. He had multiple arson charges on his record to prove it.

Jess spoke her mind, but Linc had to keep his mouth shut. He'd learned that lesson too many times. No one wanted to hear what he had to say, and he dug a nice hole for himself every time he thought it was okay to talk.

Jess tried everything in her power to put on a strong front, but her actions spoke louder than words. She was nurturing and caring with the horses, she was honest with her friends, and she had a deep-rooted responsibility to do right by everyone.

Linc had lied, cheated, and stolen whenever he got the chance. He'd used everyone who crossed his path. Foster parents, old friends, women–they were all fair game.

He rested his hands on the side of the wooden crate and hung his head. He hated the things he'd done. It was hard to look anyone he respected in the eye. Mr. Chambers, Paul, everyone at church–they'd be disappointed and ashamed of him if they knew half of those things.

"Where's Jess?" Paul asked.

So much for not thinking about her tonight. Linc grabbed the top bags of tarps out of the crate and stacked them on the shelves. "She had a date."

Jess wouldn't care if Paul knew. There was zero chance he'd tell anyone about her date.

"Hm." Paul didn't look up from his work. He kept stacking rope in the corner like he hadn't just thrown a wrench into Linc's wayward thoughts.

"What?"

"Nothin'. I just thought you two had something going on."

Linc stopped and propped a hand on the shelf. If Paul had noticed that Linc liked to hang around Jess a little too much, who else had noticed. "Really?"

"I just assumed."

Piling the tarps in his hands, Linc got back to work. "No, there's nothing going on. She just started dating, and she doesn't want anyone to know right now."

"I won't say anything."

If things worked out between Jess and one of her dates, she'd be telling people at the ranch soon. Then everyone would see Linc's pouting because he was pretty sure he wouldn't be able to hide that lost puppy frown.

What if he never moved on? What if this was it, and he'd missed his shot? What if his happiness was walking toward someone else?

Telling her how he felt would only make things worse. She deserved better. She'd probably avoid him like the plague if she knew about his past.

"Knock, knock," Hadley said as she rapped on the wooden doorframe. "I have goodies. Vera sent old bones for Thane, apples for the horses, and dinner for the two of you. Don't get the bags mixed up."

Paul reached for the bags. "Thanks, and please tell Vera we appreciate it."

"I will." Hadley took her time looking around the room. "What do y'all do in here?"

"We pack bags for the longer trips. Some of the supplies will stay at the camp sites, but some things we need to bring with the group," Paul explained.

"Cool. I hadn't ever been around horses until I came here, and I've definitely never been on a long ride. It sounds fun though."

Fun wasn't the way Linc would describe it. The long pack rides were his favorite, but they were more relaxing and calming than fun to him.

Hadley's phone rang, and she answered it while she peered down into the crate. "Hello." She straightened and moved toward the door. "Of course. I'm on my way."

"Everything okay?" Paul asked as Hadley ended the call.

"Jess is at Barn Sour and needs a ride home."

Linc jerked his head up. "Why? What's wrong?"

Hadley shrugged. "I don't know. She said she was on a date, and he can't drive her home." Her brows furrowed. "I didn't realize she was dating."

Linc tossed the bags onto the shelf and started for the door. "I'll go get her."

One big question flashed in his mind. Why hadn't she called him?

Hadley stepped in front of Linc, looking up at him like she wasn't sure getting in his way was a good idea. "Wait, did you know she went out?"

Answering that question would betray Jess's confidence, something he wasn't about to do. Stalling here wasn't an option either. There was a red tinge coloring the outside of his vision, and his body was heating from the inside out. "I need to go."

"Is she okay?" Hadley asked as she stepped to the side.

"She better be." The words came from low in his chest, releasing a warning meant for a loser at Barn Sour.

Hadley followed him out. "Linc, do you think she's in trouble?"

"Like I said, that would be dangerous to the guy's health." If he found out someone had hurt her, there was a chance Linc would find out if the Black-water jail looked like all the others he'd been in.

"Will you tell her to call me?" Hadley asked as she quickened her pace to keep up with him.

"Sure."

"And, um, she sounded kinda upset."

Great. Now his fingers were tingling, itching to meet the guy's face.

Patience, Linc.

"I know she called me, but you're probably the better choice to pick her up. She seems more comfortable with you when she's not in the mood to talk."

They didn't have to talk. He probably didn't want to know the details anyway. He'd check on Jess, introduce the guy to his fist, and take her home.

"I'm worried," Hadley said as they reached his truck.

"Don't be. I'll take care of her." That was a promise he could make with all certainty. He started the truck and made a swift three-point turn. He could be at the Barn in five minutes if he doubled the speed limit.

He twisted his hands on the steering wheel, and the burn in his palms was the only thing keeping him from screaming on the drive to Barn Sour.

It was everyone's favorite place to go out besides the dance hall at the ranch, and there was a differ-ence knowing Jess was there with her friends who didn't drink and would leave before people got drunk and hearing that her date tonight couldn't drive her home.

Couldn't or wouldn't? Did it matter? Either way, the guy had a big red target on his nose.

The gravel parking lot was packed, and the crunch of rocks beneath his tires didn't drown out the steady roar in his ears. He didn't bother looking for a parking spot. He stopped the truck in front of the entrance where Jess sat on the top step with her knees propped up and her chin in her hands. The bright lights streaming from the glass doors behind her painted her in shadow, but he didn't need to see the whites of her eyes to know she was upset.

Linc jumped out of the truck and left it running. When he made it to the entrance, Jess was getting to her feet.

"I thought Hadley was coming," she said quietly. So quiet, the music from inside almost drowned out her words.

"I thought you were going to call me," Linc said, fighting the urge to reach for her.

Her shoulders sank. "This is embarrassing."

Linc jerked his head toward the door. "Show me who he is so I can embarrass him."

"Wait. Don't do that."

Her hands wound around his bicep, and as much as he wanted to storm inside and stomp his boot into the guy's face, he couldn't move while Jess was touching him.

"Why not? He deserves it."

Jess shook her head. "I just want to leave."

Linc kept his eyes locked on hers, dim and sad in the faint light. Her hair was loosely braided and fell over one shoulder, and she was wearing new boots– not even the nice ones she wore to church on Sundays.

Seeing how she'd tried to impress this loser clawed at his insides. She was so much better than this. What guy in his right mind wouldn't want to do right by her?

It took a dozen painfully tense seconds before Linc's fury started to subside. He wanted to teach someone a lesson and defend Jess's honor.

But that wasn't what she wanted, which meant his intentions needed to change.

When his vision cleared and he could think straight again, Jess was still watching him like he might make a run for it.

Linc nodded toward his truck. "Let's go."

Jess held onto his arm and tucked her body to his side as they walked down the steps. He opened the door for her, and she climbed in.

On his way around the front of the vehicle, he decided he would follow her lead. If she wanted to talk about it, they would. If she changed her mind and wanted the guy to bleed a little, Linc would make it happen.

He settled into the driver's seat and rested his hand on the gear shift. "I'm sorry," he whispered.

Jess slumped against the door and crossed her arms over her chest. She looked like a tired kid, and she wore that innocence so easily.

When she didn't respond, Linc headed toward her place. In the darkness, it was easy to focus on the small area in front of them lit by the headlights, but he was intensely aware of the woman wrapped up in the seat beside him.

As hot as his anger burned a minute ago, all of that fury had morphed into something that tore in his chest.

He didn't want to punch the guy. He wanted to hold Jess.

When he pulled up in front of her house, he shifted into park and rested back against the seat. "I bet Ms. Landry is going to have the whole town talking. One guy picked you up and another brought you home."

Jess chuckled, and while it sounded like a genuine laugh, there was a sad sigh behind it.

"Thanks for bringing me home," she whispered.

"Anytime."

Jess rested her hand on the door and looked toward her house. After a few silent seconds, she turned back to him. "Will you come in? I don't want to be alone right now."

Linc stared at her in the darkness, thankful once again that she always spoke her mind. She wanted him here, and she'd been brave enough to ask.

He shut the truck off and got out. Despite the terrible evening they'd both had, there was still time to turn it around.

CHAPTER 14

JESS

Dragging her feet, Jess unlocked the front door and stepped inside. She turned on the lights by the front door and headed straight for any other light switches in sight. Lots and lots of light was needed if she was hanging out with Linc.

Not that she would be tempted to make out in the dim light. The brightness was just to pump up her mood.

Though, having Linc in her house was oddly comforting. He was familiar and safe. She clung to both of those things as if she needed a shot of happiness.

"Make yourself at home," she called over her shoulder. "You want something to drink?"

"Water, please."

She grabbed two glasses and filled them with

ice, then water from the sink. "Sorry, I don't have the fancy bottled stuff."

Linc chuckled and took the glass. He looked around as he took the first drink. "Nice place."

Jess put her glass down and flopped back onto the couch. It was her favorite furniture. She'd splurged on the pillowy-soft piece, and she fell asleep on it more nights than not.

"Thanks. I don't spend a lot of time here, but I'm secretly a homebody. If I'm not at the ranch, this is the only place I want to be."

Linc walked around for another minute before taking a seat on the far end of the couch. "Nice neighbors too."

Jess rolled her eyes and flopped her head back. "Ms. Landry leaves me alone most of the time. Though, one time she called to let me know there was a mountain lion in my yard. She also advised that I never go outside again."

Linc's eyes widened. "Ever?"

"Ever. She doesn't leave her house much. I think she's afraid of life."

Who could blame her? Jess wasn't afraid of life, but every time she stepped outside, there was a chance she'd get hurt, say something stupid, or just forget to put on the placating face she wore for the world.

Linc hummed deep in his chest. "I didn't know

we could just quit. I might have done that years ago."

The sadness in his voice choked her.

"I'm sorry. My bad mood must be rubbing off on you." She pointed at the small TV on top of a squatty bookshelf. "I don't have cable. Just local channels."

Linc rested his arm on the back of the couch, and the heaviness she felt earlier eased enough for her to inhale a full, deep breath. Why did seeing him relax in her safe space make it easier to breathe?

He pinned his gaze on her. "What would make you happy right now?"

Happy? The irritation from her dumpster fire of a date was already dissipating. She was well on her way to content, and happy wasn't far behind.

"I like hot chocolate. And popcorn."

"You have those things here, or am I making a store run?"

Her mouth tugged in a smile. Why did she want to smile and cry at the same time? "I have them. You want some?"

"I'll share some popcorn with you."

He started to stand, and she jumped to her feet. "I'll get it. You just...wait here."

"Where is your bathroom? I need to wash my hands."

She pointed to the hallway. "First door on the left." She darted out of the room in desperate need of a minute alone.

Standing in the kitchen, Jess leaned back against the counter and took a few deep breaths. Those pesky emotions were taking over again.

After a few seconds alone, the grip on her throat loosened. She shook out her hands and got out the things she needed for hot chocolate. She preferred the powdered mix, but only in the off-brand. The perfect hot chocolate also included milk, not water.

The pantry was small, but it was plenty big enough for everything she needed. Grocery shopping was formulaic. Jess liked certain things and rarely ventured out of that box. She didn't need extras, the newest flavors, or anything special.

Enough was as good as plenty. What was the point of having lots of options when she already knew what she wanted?

By the time the popcorn was in the microwave–butter lovers only–her mood had shifted to happy. Maybe even a little excited. The date had been a bust, but Linc was here, and the smells of her favorite snacks tingled in her nose.

She propped her hands on the counter and stared at a crack while the pops in the microwave slowed. Hanging her head, she said a silent prayer of thanks that Linc showed up tonight. Hadley was a good friend, but she wouldn't have had the same calming effect as Linc.

Jess wouldn't have invited Hadley in either because girl talk gave her hives.

With a mug of hot chocolate in one hand and a bowl of popcorn in the other, Jess padded back into the living room where Linc rested his head back with his eyes closed.

Jess handed him the bowl as he raised his head. "Sorry it took so long."

"Not long at all. I called Paul and apologized for running out on him."

Jess winced. "Sorry. I didn't mean to pull you away from work." In fact, she hadn't called him at all, but he'd come running anyway.

"No problem. I wasn't getting much done anyway." He shoved a handful of popcorn into his mouth and hummed. "This is good."

"Butter lovers."

Linc picked up another handful. "I think I'm going to devour this bowl. We might need another one in about three minutes."

"There's plenty. Are you hungry? I can make you something?"

Linc shook his head. "This is good." He pointed to the TV. "Are we watching something?"

Jess grabbed the remote. "What do you want to watch?"

"I have no preferences. My cabin doesn't have a TV."

"Your choices are an old western, an evangelical talk show, and *Jeopardy*."

Linc chewed popcorn like someone might steal it

from him if he didn't eat it fast enough. "Which do you prefer?"

"*Jeopardy*. I've tried to watch the westerns, but it's a little confusing."

Her heart beat violently at that tiny confession. Jess hated admitting all the things she didn't understand that other people seemed to grasp so easily, but Linc never made her feel stupid.

When he didn't laugh in her face and question her intelligence, she kept going. "I have trouble with most movies. I don't understand why most people do the things they do, and trying to work out how one person can act in multiple movies and have different personalities every time I see their face on TV is just..."

"Confusing. I get it," Linc said. "I bet it's because you're so honest with people, so you expect them to be honest too. Acting goes against that."

She'd never been able to put her finger on the reason why movies made her so uncomfortable, but Linc's words made sense. Something unfamiliar bubbled in her middle. She cleared her throat and stared down into the dark drink she held in one hand. "Maybe. I also have a hard time watching the shootouts. I know it's not real, but my brain doesn't get the memo and it's awful watching someone die, even if it's all pretend."

Linc pulled the popcorn bowl closer, hugging it

to his chest like a kid holding a stuffed animal. "You any good at *Jeopardy*?"

Jess chuckled. "Not really."

"Me either. I never got any awards for being smart."

Her lips tingled and tried to turn up in a smile. If anyone had asked her an hour ago if she'd be smiling, she wouldn't have believed it.

She chose *Jeopardy* and put the remote down. Tucking her legs underneath her and cradling the warm cup of hot chocolate with both hands, she settled in while commercials played.

"I really want to go back and deck that guy," Linc said, not looking away from the TV.

"Don't worry about it. I'm over it. Plus, you'll be happy to know my reflexes are fantastic. I dodged like it was a horse hoof flying at my face instead of a guy's lips."

Linc sat up straighter, still hugging the bowl with little crumbles of his favorite snack in the bottom. "He did what?"

"He tried to kiss me, and I maneuvered my way out of it. I guess that's why he told me to find another ride home and started throwing back whiskey shots."

Linc stared at her with wide eyes. "Why didn't you tell me this while we were there? Jess, that's not okay!"

"He got the message. He didn't need to hear it

again from you." Her body heated, and she huffed. "Well, I said I was over it, but it does make me mad. He didn't say three nice words to me the whole night, then he put his arm around me and thought we were going to make out in public or something. He didn't even know my last name, and he didn't open the door for me or anything."

Yeah, the more she thought about it, the more she liked Linc's idea to go back and teach the guy some manners.

She shook her head and put the mug down on the end table. "But what do I know? That could be the norm on dates these days." Her mood was declining again, all because of that stupid guy. She was so mad she couldn't even remember his name. "Why am I mad?"

Her first instinct was to burn with anger. Always. Shouldn't she be sad or disappointed? The guy didn't give two thoughts about her.

Maybe she didn't know how to truly be sad when anger had always been her best friend.

"Because he didn't respect you. At all. And that's never fun." Linc sat up, moving the bowl to the end table. "You know what would be fun? Watching my fist meet his face. Let's go now, and you can film it to watch again later. We could have more popcorn. I bet Everly could make it into a gif. He could be internet famous by tomorrow morning."

Linc's idea was half appealing, half funny. The

humor won out, and Jess pinched her lips together to hold in a laugh.

"You think I'm joking." He stood and reached a hand out. "Come on. Let's go."

Jess set the laugh free and swatted his hand away. "Thanks for the offer, but you don't have to duel for my honor or anything. My first kiss has yet to be claimed."

Linc's brows rose, as he lowered back to his seat. He sat closer to her than he'd been before, and the heat of his stare burned her neck.

She shouldn't have said that.

"What?" Linc asked, slowly and clearly.

Oh, the control in that tone said there were dozens of words waiting behind the one he'd chosen, and Jess squirmed in her seat.

She finally let it slip that she'd never been kissed before, and now Linc was going to look at her differently.

Just as she'd feared.

CHAPTER 15
LINC

Linc stared at Jess as she lowered her chin. Did she say her first kiss, or did she mean her first kiss with that jerk?

Jess was in her early twenties. How had she gotten this far in life without kissing anyone?

And why did that revelation both excite and terrify him?

Keeping her head down, she whispered, "You're being weird."

"No, I'm not."

He *was* being weird, but his brain hadn't caught up yet.

"Are too."

Linc cleared his throat and reached for the popcorn bowl. *Don't be weird. Don't be weird.* "Speaking of weird, my snack seems to have disappeared."

Nice save, idiot.

Jess grabbed for the bowl. "I'll get you some more." Half a second later, she was dashing out of the room.

Linc sat forward, propping his elbows on his knees and resting his head in his hands. Jess was going to be the death of him. Write it in stone. He had massive feelings for her, and he had no idea what to do with them.

There was no way he could tell her that now. Not only was she sweet, caring, and strong in a way he respected and admired, she was completely innocent.

Linc was not.

Kissing had never been one of those sweet, romantic things for him. In fact, he'd done a fantastic job of avoiding it during his meaningless hookups.

Now, after seeing what it meant to Jess and imagining what it might be like to have the kind of amazing, pure connection Jess could offer, his chances of being a man worthy of her were non-existent.

A proud grin spread on his face thinking about Jess dodging a kiss from the loser who took her out tonight. He'd almost recovered his good mood when Jess walked back in. She handed him the bowl and took her seat on the couch beside him. At least she faced him this time.

"What are you smiling about?" she asked. The little wrinkle between her brows said she had no idea what to make of his expression.

"I was picturing you ducking and swerving away from fast lips tonight."

She rolled her eyes, but a smile lit her face too. "It was probably a funny sight. I almost knocked my drink over."

"Would have served him right if it ended up in his lap."

Jess tucked her feet under her and wiggled a little as she got comfortable. "I thought things were gonna be weird now."

Linc reached into the bowl and grabbed a handful of the warm popcorn. "Not weird. I'm still processing. Is there a reason why you haven't kissed anyone before? No judgment."

She scoffed. "Do I look like the kind of woman a man wants to kiss?"

Linc had a very strong answer to that question, but he kept his mouth shut as she went on without missing a beat.

"The answer is no. Guys seem interested at first, but they all run away screaming as soon as I open my mouth. I'm too outspoken. Too honest. Too assertive." She shook her head. "Men don't like that."

Linc shoved popcorn into his mouth. This was

Jess's turn to talk, and he was about half a second away from setting her straight.

Because he definitely liked a woman like that. He liked everything about Jess. All those things she'd just listed were his favorites. What was wrong with a woman who knew what she wanted and stood by her convictions?

Nothing. If no one else saw the value in those things, they were the ones missing out.

Linc offered her the popcorn bowl. "Don't ever be anyone but yourself. If a guy doesn't like who you are, then he's not the guy for you."

Jess glanced at him so quickly he almost wondered if he'd imagined it. If she didn't look him in the eye soon, he'd crack and challenge her to a staring contest just to see the full beauty of those green eyes.

They were the color of early summer grass. He'd memorized the color a long time ago and searched months before he found anything that rivaled the vibrance.

She ate one tiny bite of popcorn. Then another. There were hundreds of differences between them, and knowing they didn't even eat popcorn the same way just made that list longer.

"Jess?"

She looked up at him, finally pinning him with that beautiful stare. "What?"

"You okay?" The words were almost a whisper.

She nodded. "I'm over it now."

She probably wasn't, but Linc would die before pointing that out. "I just want to remind you that you deserve better than that. A whole lot better."

Jess rolled her eyes, but a true smile played on her lips.

Lips he shouldn't be thinking about. At all.

"Next you'll be telling me I'll make a wonderful wife someday."

"You will. True story."

She looked around the room, and Linc followed her gaze. "In case you haven't noticed, I like things a certain way. Having a boyfriend, getting married, sharing a life with someone–it means I'll have to be able to change and compromise, and half the time, I don't know how to do that."

"I guess none of us do at first, but you've had roommates before."

"Yeah, but that wasn't a lifetime commitment. Remi was here about as little as I was, and she didn't move things around. I never said anything to her about my weird quirks, but I'm sure she noticed and just didn't care enough to make a fuss out of it."

Linc was in over his head. Talking about marriage and getting along was rich coming from him. He'd annoyed Brett on a regular basis just by staying quiet. The guy liked to talk way too much, and Linc didn't have two things to say most days.

"I guess when you find the right person, all that stuff works out."

"Or the two of you have to work it out," Jess said. "I never got good grades on group projects in school because I don't work well with others."

Linc gasped. "You don't say."

Jess chuckled and brushed a hand through her long hair. "I know that's no surprise."

He knew why she had all the doubts. Growing up the way they had would do that to the best of them. They had to sort through a lot of lies to get to the truth, and determining one from the other was never easy either.

It still crushed his heart a little bit every time her chin fell. He watched her closely while she stared at her hands in her lap. Her eyes were usually so bright and fierce. Seeing her like this was like listening to mournful music.

Sitting up straighter, Linc cleared his throat. "It'll all work out. You don't need to stress about it."

"You're right." She pushed her hair back and lifted her chin, seeming bolder and more confident already. "Listen, what I said about kissing. Could you not tell anyone?"

Linc nodded. "I'll keep your secrets if you'll keep mine."

Jess handed the popcorn back to him with a whispered thanks, and the urge to pull her in tingled in his hands. But Jess wasn't the touchy-feely kind.

He wasn't either, but something about Jess made him wish for more than he had any right to want.

She turned the volume up on the TV. "It's a new round. Want to make it a competition?"

Linc rubbed his jaw. "I usually don't get into fights I know I can't win."

Jess scooted closer to him, and his throat locked up. She'd never been this close for any extended period of time. In fact, no one liked to be around him that much. He didn't have to growl and bare his teeth for people to keep their distance. There was probably some instinctual warning he put off.

But Jess was moving in, and he wanted to meet her halfway, or all the way. He wanted more of her like he wanted water on a scorching hot day.

Wait, that was a need. Maybe he needed her.

But he couldn't have her. Basic human rules said that two loners didn't make a right, so he put the thought behind him as they settled in to watch the show.

They both tanked at *Jeopardy* to the point that it was sad and funny. With one correct answer each, Jess declared it a tie for last place.

But Linc didn't mind being a loser, as long as he got to sit at the losers' table with Jess.

Jess rested her cheek against the back of the couch beside him and yawned. With her legs curled up on the couch, she looked like a little bunny cuddling up to sleep. "Want to go another round?"

Linc grinned. She was beautiful all the time, but she was adorable when she was tired. There wasn't any hardness in her expression. Her skin was smooth without a single furrow between her brows. She wasn't putting on a brave face for the world; she was just hanging out with him.

He wanted to be the only one who made her feel safe like this. He wanted the secret moments when she revealed her true and vulnerable self and trusted him to keep the inner workings of her heart to himself.

"You sure you're not ready to call it a night?" he asked as her eyes slowly drifted closed before opening again.

"Not yet."

She stopped adding her answers before the commercial break, but Linc kept watching the game show. If sitting with her had made her feel better after the bad date, he didn't want to leave without making sure she was truly good for the night.

When she rested her cheek against his shoulder, his work was done. Soft snores lifted to his ear, and he turned down the volume. Better be safe than sorry and stay for another episode.

He blinked up at the clock on the wall. How was it eleven thirty?

The ache in his back said he'd fallen asleep with Jess slumped against his side, which meant Ms.

Landry was going to have plenty to talk about tomorrow. She might even call the preacher.

Linc looked down at Jess. She was sound asleep with her cheek pressed to his shoulder. He rubbed his eyes and turned off the TV.

After a deep breath that would hopefully wipe out his groggy thoughts, he wrapped an arm around Jess and gently eased her down until her head was lying on a couch pillow. He grabbed a blanket and covered her up.

The next step was to walk away. She didn't need him anymore, and he didn't have an excuse to stay.

But why were his boots glued to the floor?

He knelt down beside the couch and took advantage of the chance to admire Jess. Had she ever looked this peaceful? Would he ever see her this uninhibited again?

Linc made a bold move and leaned in to press a kiss to her hair. "Night. Sweet dreams."

He stood and turned off the light, locking up as he left. Every movement between the door and the end of the porch creaked, but the night was pitch black and silent. The cold hit him like a punch from reality. The warmth of snuggling up next to Jess was only a memory by the time he reached the truck. She wouldn't remember any of it tomorrow.

Oh, but he would. The press of her up against him would stick with him until he was old and gray.

The truck door creaked and groaned loud

enough to wake the neighbors as he tried to make his stealthy exit. If Ms. Landry had fallen asleep on watch, she was sure to be up now.

His phone rang loud, and he grabbed for it like the noise might still wake Jess.

"Hello."

A constant roaring filled the background of the call as a familiar voice shouted to be heard above the racket. "There you are. I was starting to think you were doin' time too."

Linc's hand tightened around the phone. "What do you want?"

"I'm out. Where are you?" Ryan yelled.

"Middle of nowhere."

Ryan had never been patient, and the fact that Linc had ignored him for so long meant the call started off with the carefully controlled tension they both used to survive when it came to trusting–or not trusting–on the streets of Memphis.

There was a charged pause on Ryan's side of the call, but Linc knew better than to get his hopes up. Once Ryan dug his claws in, he didn't let go until he drew blood.

"I thought you were avoidin' me," Ryan said. Though, the statement held a clear question.

Did you do it?

The record had been sealed when Linc came forth as an informant, but Ryan had ways of finding out things no one else could. He had "friends" all across the States. His friend list consisted of people who had either screwed him over or been framed for screwing him over, and he had a memory like a lock-box. He remembered everything, and he used it for his gain when he wanted favors.

"What do you want? Sorry, but I'm not in the game anymore. I don't have contacts."

Ryan laughed. "Hard to believe the fire king has fallen out of favor, isn't it?"

"Nope. I got caught just like you, and I didn't see the point in gettin' another sentence. I've had enough ham sandwiches to last me a lifetime."

"Aw come on. It wasn't that bad. Where'd you end up?"

Nope. Exchanging facts with Ryan was sure to put a target right on Linc's back. It had taken years to assimilate back into society. Funny how it only took one year to set his reformation in place.

"Listen, I've got a job now, and my shift starts in a few hours. Have a nice life."

He ended the call and looked up at Jess's house. Releasing a sigh that did nothing to release the strain in his shoulders, he started the truck and backed out.

His past couldn't lay a finger on his future. One brush with the old days would send any semblance of his normal life up in flames.

CHAPTER 16

JESS

Jess led Thunder from the barn, walking backward and maintaining eye contact with the dark horse. "Come on, buddy. I'm nice enough. I swear. Your sister likes me." She ducked her head to the side, trying to keep Thunder's attention on her. "Linc likes me. At least, I think he does."

It was a topic that hadn't left her thoughts since he stayed with her after that disaster of a date. She'd woken up on the couch the next morning with a smile on her face. The text message waiting for her only served to add gasoline to the already burning fire in her middle.

Linc: You fell asleep. I'm the Jeopardy champion. Better luck next time.

Not once had he brought up the bad date, or the cuddling they'd done on the couch, or her humiliating confession. Any mention of those might shatter her carefully held-together sanity.

One thing that continued to knock her off-kilter was her new and bold attraction to Linc. Knowing he was the strong silent type was one thing, but knowing he was sweet and caring on top of his endless understanding was just too much to ignore.

She sensed him every time he walked into the barn. Her neck and face heated and her palms tingled, begging to reach out to him.

But he'd been nothing but gentlemanly. Platonic described his treatment of her. He'd said hello. He'd asked her about the barn chores. He'd brought her lunch as usual.

Nothing had changed, and that realization was both comforting and disappointing.

"Hey, Thea!" Jess shouted over her shoulder, keeping her gaze on Thunder.

"Yeah?"

"Can you bring Lightning out?"

"Be right there!"

Jess steadied Thunder as he shifted, turning his left side away from her.

"I'm not going to bother your leg. We're just trying to see if you're ready to go back to the big leagues."

Jess kept up the casual conversation with Thunder while they waited for Thea and Lightning. Well, it wasn't a conversation if it was one-sided, but Thunder was a lot like his rider, Linc. They were both stoic and observant. Thunder had his guard up like the enemy army was going to ambush the ranch at any moment.

Thea led Thunder's sister out into the late-afternoon sun. It was still unseasonably cold for late April, but new snow hadn't fallen in almost a week. The break had given everyone the energetic boost they needed to work the long hours leading up to the tourist season.

There was still so much to do, and it was only a few weeks before opening. Jameson and Ava had hired a couple more hands this week, and hopefully more would be coming soon enough to get them trained before the guests arrived.

The horses were ready, and Jess was right there with them. She didn't care for all the strangers, but she enjoyed sharing her love of horses. The guests always seemed captivated during the lessons, and she'd never get tired of recognizing that happiness.

"Let's take them on the Thunder Creek Trail." Jess turned her attention to Thunder as she brushed a hand over his cheek. "No, we didn't name it after you. Get over yourself."

"I've never been on that one," Thea said as she pushed up onto Lightning, who was looking around, wondering why Jess wasn't her rider today.

"It's the shortest trail, but we need to start him slowly. Linc and Thunder need to be able to go out on the trails three times a week, and Thunder might not make it back to the longer trails until a few weeks after opening."

"Lead the way," Thea said as she settled in the saddle.

Jess gave Thunder a nod that she hoped he interpreted as assurance. "You can do this," she told him again before lifting onto the saddle.

Thunder was a beast. There wasn't any better way to describe the massive stallion. He'd given them all kinds of fits when he first came to the ranch, and between Jess and Linc, they'd gotten him trained to the trails. Now, he was one of the best leads they had.

The trail was a little more than an hour long, but it was plenty of time for Jess to clear her head. Except riding on Linc's horse was a constant reminder of him. Thunder had given up complete control to Linc, but he still gave a few fits for Jess.

The ride back was worse than the ride out. Thunder bumped from side to side, getting antsy after the ride.

"I don't think he's ready," Jess said. "We need to get the vet back out to check for infection." She hadn't seen any of the signs, and the wound looked great. Best-case scenario, Thunder was just acting out because Linc wasn't around.

When Thunder tensed even more, Jess

dismounted. "Okay, buddy. That should be better. We don't have much more to go, and you can rest."

Thunder sidestepped, pushing Jess a few steps back. She gave more slack to the lead. "Easy, boy."

Thea led Lightning over and leaned around Thunder's backside. She was still a few feet away when she asked, "You okay?"

Thunder sidestepped again, pushing Jess back.

Trying to keep her footing and give Thunder his space, Jess told Thea, "Move back."

Jess was on Thunder's wounded side, and he wasn't happy. Thea led Lightning around Thunder's other side, giving him a wide berth.

Dividing only made Thunder's panic rise. He jerked his head back and forth, trying to watch both sides.

"Easy, boy." Jess backed up until they were well off the trail. Checking over her shoulder, she moved around to Thunder's front.

Once he stopped crowding her back, she backed up to give him an extra few feet of space.

Thunder stopped, but his head continued to jerk to one side and the other.

"Jess!"

Thea's shout came too late. Jess's heel caught on something hard behind her, and she released the lead as she fell. She hit the ground hard, jabbing something into her left side just before a sharp pain burst in the back of her head. She gasped at the stabbing in her side, but the punch to her head had the air stalling in her throat.

"Jess!"

She rolled to her right side and tried to breathe. A cold sweat tingled over her shoulders and down her back. The edges of her vision turned black, and a heavy exhaustion weighed her down.

Thea slid to the ground beside her. "Jess, talk to me. Oh, shoot. You're bleeding."

Jess braced herself on one hand and tried to push up.

"Whoa, whoa, whoa," Thea said. "I'm calling someone."

Bile rose in Jess's throat, and panic wasn't far behind. She couldn't afford an injury right now.

"Hey, Jess is injured. How fast can you get to the mouth of the Thunder Creek Trail?"

CHAPTER 17

JESS

Jess heard Thea's words, but they were distant and muffled. She rested back down on the ground and fought the nausea. No, no, no. She didn't want this. Fighting to push away reality, she silently prayed.

God, please let this be nothing. I need to get up. I have things to do. I have responsibilities.

"Jameson is on his way," Thea said. "Oh, you're bleeding pretty bad."

"The horses," Jess said as the dizziness subsided enough to think. She didn't want to ask about the blood. She didn't have a problem patching someone else's wounds or tending to the horses, but seeing her own blood always made her sick to her stomach.

"Got 'em."

A few deep breaths told her she probably had a

few ribs bruised or broken, and she likely had a concussion too.

By the time the engine roaring reached her, Jess had opened her eyes and sat up. She turned her head to the side and rested her temple against a tree.

Boots hit the ground as Jess opened her eyes. Instead of Jameson, Linc was running toward her. He slid to his knees beside her and gently rested a hand on the side of her head.

"Jess, talk to me."

"I'm not suddenly mute. I can talk." Though, she wasn't ready to admit that her jaw was heavy and every breath sent a stinging and constant pain to her side.

Linc lifted his hand from her hair, and the color drained from his face. His palm was splotched with blood. "Jameson!"

"I'm here." Jameson crouched on Jess's other side with a bag. He started pulling things out and ripping plastic.

"What happened?" Linc asked quietly.

"Thunder," Jess said. She meant the word to come out sounding comical, but the humor fell flat.

Linc jerked his attention toward his horse.

"He's fine," Jess assured.

"I'm not worried about him. I'm worried about you."

"I think he's gotten so used to you that he didn't trust me on his left side. I was backing up to give him some space, and I fell over a rock. He didn't do anything wrong."

She closed her eyes against the blinding light. Stringing the words together drained all of her energy.

Jameson readied his pen light. "Look at me."

She winced as the light sent a jolt of pain throbbing in her head. "That hurts."

"We need to bandage your head and get you to a doctor. I'm almost positive you have a concussion, and you might need staples for the head wound."

"Is it bad?" Jess asked as she reached up to feel the back of her head.

Linc's big hand gently wrapped around hers. "It's not good, but it'll probably hurt worse if you touch it."

Her hand relaxed in his, the warmth spreading like slow-moving lava up her arm. "Okay."

Jameson put the bandage on the sore spot on her head and wrapped a band around her entire head. Once it was secure, he packed up his bag. "We should go ahead to Cody. If you need staples, they'll send you there anyway."

"Brett is meeting us with my truck at the trailhead," Linc said. He was still holding her hand.

Jameson rested a hand behind her shoulder and offered his other for her to take. "You think you can stand?"

"Yeah." She took Jameson's and Linc's hands and

pulled while the men supported her back. Gritting her teeth together and squinting her eyes, she sucked in a slow breath on the way up.

"Is anything else hurt?" Jameson asked.

Jess pointed to her side. "I hit something."

Linc helped her pull her shirt up, but she couldn't twist to look at the damage. His quick inhale told her all she needed to know.

Jameson nodded to Linc. "We need to get her on the road." He looked over to Thea. "Call Ava and tell her to get the ambulance on its way."

"Ambulance? That's overkill, don't you think?" Jess asked.

"Not if you have internal bleeding," Jameson said as he guided her toward the side-by-side.

"I'll take Jess with me if you'll bring Thunder," Linc said to Jameson over his shoulder.

Jess held onto the handle in the front and the back of the seat. For once, she was thankful she didn't have to mount a horse. Even with that mercy, she wasn't looking forward to the ride. If her side hurt when she walked, bumping down the rest of the path was going to be horrendous.

Linc rested his steady hands on her waist as she climbed in. Even with a head injury, she wasn't immune to his touch. She'd have to be dead not to feel the fire whenever Linc touched her.

By the time she was settled in the passenger seat, each breath was labored, and she was panting like she'd just run a marathon. Linc ran around the vehicle like he was a firefighter on his way to put out the flames.

He had the opposite effect of putting out a fire, and she didn't hate the sparks that kindled in her middle at the mere thought of Lincoln North. Her attraction to the man beside her was keeping her mind off the damage to her broken body.

Linc turned the vehicle around and grabbed for her hand as they drove down the slant at the base of the mountain. "You okay?"

"I'm okay." She infused her voice with all the assurance she could muster because each bump in the road made her want to scream.

Brett waited at the edge of the forest in Linc's truck, but Linc waved for him to follow. They were making it just fine on the side-by-side, and if the ambulance was coming, she didn't need a truck.

Her head swayed as if her neck couldn't hold it up anymore. Oh no, she was going to puke her guts up if he didn't hurry.

"Stop." She'd meant to shout so he could hear her over the engine, but it came out more like a whisper.

He must have heard her because he pulled the side-by-side to a stop. She leaned over the side just as everything she'd eaten today came up.

Linc grabbed her hair into his hand, pulling it

back. "Brett, get to the entrance and lead them out here."

She barely heard the truck pass, but it had to be close as its shadow rushed by the edges of her vision—a vision that was shrinking into darkness.

"Hang in here, babe. They're coming as fast as they can."

Jess puked again and slumped forward with a groan. The pain in her head needed to ease up. She teetered on the verge of passing out and puking again, until Linc grabbed her shoulders and slowly eased her to sitting.

Upright again, he guided her to rest her cheek against his chest. Her world was spinning, but Linc was solid and strong, holding her steady like an anchor to her storm-tossed ship.

Closing her eyes, she wrapped her arms around him. His hand cradled the side of her head, careful to stay away from the bandage. "You're gonna be fine."

"How can you say that? I don't feel fine at all."

Linc chuckled, and the humming in his chest vibrated against her cheek. "I think it'll take more than a bump on the head to take you down."

"I hope so, but I'm so dizzy. And tired."

"Concussion. I've had a few of those in my day. It's never fun."

"What did you do?" she asked, her eyes already too heavy to keep open.

"Football in high school. Got hit by a line drive in a baseball game in middle school. A few fights."

Fights? She wanted him to elaborate, but she didn't have the energy to ask. Instead, she rested against him, letting him hold the weight of her body. It was what she'd imagine swinging in a hammock would be like. Comforting, cradling, and weightless.

Linc lifted his head at a noise, but Jess didn't open her eyes. "They're here. Just hang tight until they're ready for you to move. Maybe you won't get sick again if we move you straight to the gurney."

That sounded like a good plan, so she waited for someone to tell her to sit up. Resting against Linc was the only thing keeping her from toppling and tossing her cookies.

"I don't have inside bleeding," she whispered. Was that what it was called? "It only hurts when I move or breathe."

Linc tensed against her. "That's not a good sign, babe."

Jess grinned, but she didn't open her eyes. "Babe. I want to laugh, but it'll hurt."

It could have been a minute or an hour before the ambulance pulled up beside them. Thankfully, there weren't any sirens wailing. She puked once during the move to the ambulance, and the nausea seemed to settle when they put the IV in her arm.

Everyone around her was talking, but she

couldn't pay attention to any of the conversations. Icy cold slid into her arm and up to her shoulder. A shiver tensed her muscles, and the hand that clasped hers tightened.

"She's cold," Linc said.

"It's the saline in the IV," another man said.

A blanket spread over her body, but it did nothing to help the cold. It was inside, and the shivering was uncontrollable.

She heard enough to know they were arriving at the hospital. The dizziness was subsiding, and the shivering had stopped. The EMTs were preparing to transfer her to the hospital staff, and a warm hand continued to hold hers.

"How's she doin'?" Brett asked.

Linc's hand slipped from hers. "About the same, I think."

Jess opened her eyes and gave her brother a quick grin. "Hanging in there. Someone needs to be at the stables. Thea can't get Lightning and Thunder in by herself."

Brett stepped closer to her side. "I'll stay." He pulled his keys from his pocket and handed them to Linc. "Take my truck."

Linc stared at her with silent indecision in his expression. She wanted him to stay, but saying it would make her sound needy. Plus, nobody wanted to spend time at a hospital unless it was necessary.

"Neither of you have to stay with me. You can't do anything."

"I'm not leaving you," Brett said with his arms crossed over his chest. "Especially since we don't know what's wrong yet."

"Concussion and bruised ribs. You're free to go," Jess said.

"Nice try, sis," Brett said with a playful grin. "You're stuck with me."

Linc nodded and took a step back. "I'll get Ridge to help Thea until I get there. Call me when you know something."

"Ten-four," Brett said as he slapped a hand on Linc's shoulder. "Thanks for staying with her."

Linc locked eyes with her again, and the words almost slipped out. She didn't want him to go, and maybe she was imagining it, but he didn't look like he wanted to go either.

Linc took one step back, then another. "I'll call you."

"Thanks, man," Brett said with a wave over his shoulder.

Jess turned her head to watch him leave, and the pain in her head and side wasn't what brought tears to her eyes.

CHAPTER 18

JESS

Jess groaned and squirmed in the hospital bed with a wince. After almost twenty-four hours confined to one spot, she was ready to claw out of her skin.

"You want to walk again?" Linc asked from the recliner beside the bed.

Brett stayed with her until they got a report. Concussion and two bruised ribs. No internal bleeding, and no lung damage.

Linc showed up before the sun, saying he'd taken the day off. In the years she'd worked at the ranch, she'd never heard of him taking off for himself. He'd taken some time off when Brett needed his help dealing with Thea's family, and he'd cut his shift short by a few hours to come rescue her from a bad date.

Never for himself. Now he was cutting out

precious pre-season hours for her, and despite her arguments, he was staying.

"She told me to give it a rest. I don't want to rest. I want to get up and walk around by myself."

"The nurse didn't mean that you couldn't walk anymore. She was just concerned you were going to overdo it."

Jess threw her hands in the air. "How can I overdo it when I'm not doing anything?"

Linc rubbed a hand over his mouth, trying and failing to hide his smirk. "You don't quit, do you?"

"What does that even mean? Why would I quit anything?"

Linc leaned forward, propping his elbows on his knees. "I mean, you don't rest. Do you ever get tired? Overworked?"

She gave him the courtesy of actually taking a second to think about his question and her answer. "I get tired, but I like what I do. I'd rather be working than sitting around wasting time. What about you? You're cutting hours right now."

Linc rubbed his hands together. "You know, I don't like resting either, but you need a ride home."

Jess sighed and gave up the fight. "Thanks for coming to get me. I know you don't like missing work, and I don't either. Mr. Chambers is lucky to have us."

"We get some time off work, and we want to go back," Linc added. "We're quite a pair."

Jess laid her head back onto the pillow. Being told to quit or give less than her full effort went against her instincts. Her legs itched to be up, but not just walking. She wanted to be helping, doing.

Everyone else knew how to relax. Why didn't she understand it?

"When I first came to the ranch, Mr. Chambers invited Brett and me to church. I didn't want to go at first. Mostly because I was so angry."

"You? Angry?" Linc said.

She swatted at him and missed because she couldn't actually bend her body to reach him. "I finally went, and I met some nice people. I started listening, but I had so many questions. Mr. Chambers set me up with a Christian counselor. We talked about my faith journey, but she also helped me work through some of the problems I was having with my family. Brett and I had pretty much moved out once his trial was over without saying 'have a nice life.'"

"How anyone could think Brett was capable of killing someone is beyond me," Linc said.

"Yeah, but our uncle was a lot older and more convincing than Brett when we were just teenagers. There were times when I thought they'd find Brett guilty."

It had been a long time since the trial, and Thea busting into their lives recently brought back all of that anger and helplessness. Jess had moved past the anger, but the injustice of what her family had done and continued to do her whole life still sparked memories that made her hair stand on end.

"One of the things the counselor told me was that people who have been in situations where the basic human needs weren't met sometimes have trouble taking time off work. She said the fear of falling behind if you don't work hard enough just pushes you to the edge and makes you stay there because if you stop working, you might run out of money again. No money means no food. The stress of working non-stop is better than the stress of living paycheck to paycheck."

When Linc didn't say anything, she glanced up at him. His jaw moved from side to side as he stared at the floor. His scruff was a little longer than usual, and there was a tiredness in his eyes. She was responsible for that, and her own exhaustion didn't mean much in comparison.

"I think that's true to an extent," Linc said.

There was a quick rap at the door before a nurse with short dark hair entered. She went straight to the computer and started clicking. "You ready to go home?"

"Can I go now?" Jess asked.

"You sure can. You need help getting dressed?"

Jess sat up slowly, holding back a wince, and moved to the side of the bed. "No, thank you. I can handle it."

She'd better be able to handle it. There was no

way on earth she was letting anybody think she needed help with basic things like getting dressed. The people at the ranch would have someone at her house constantly hanging over her shoulder asking if she needed anything every five minutes.

The nurse handed her a set of papers. "They'll be around in a minute with your wheelchair."

Jess's eyes widened. "I don't need that."

The nurse waved like she was swatting a bug. "Standard procedure. Just roll with it. Pun intended."

Jess looked to Linc for help, but he sat relaxed in the chair with his arms crossed over his chest and a grin on his face. At least one of them was going to enjoy the ride out of the hospital.

Getting dressed was painful, but she managed it on her own in the small bathroom. She stopped to check her reflection in the mirror and grimaced. She couldn't see the back of her head where they'd shaved the hair to put in the staples. A nurse had attempted to wash her hair last night, but there were still traces of red near the roots.

Who had time to sit around and be injured? She'd lost a full day and a half of work, and even knowing Thea, Ridge, and Cheyenne were making sure things at the barn were getting done, the urge to be back at work tingled in her legs as if she needed to run all the way to the ranch.

Linc was attentive yet silent as they left the

hospital. "You okay over there?" he asked as they neared her house.

"Yeah. Just...thanks again."

Linc kept his attention on the road. "You said that already."

"I know. I just needed to say it again."

He glanced over at her, but the look lasted only a split second. "I'm happy to help. You need anything in town?"

"I don't think so. I got the prescriptions filled at the hospital, but I hate taking that medicine."

"Is it not helping?" Linc asked.

Jess pressed two fingertips into her temple. "I guess it is. I just don't take a lot of medicine, and it makes me feel different. Not necessarily bad different, but..." What was she trying to say?

"It's different, and you don't like change."

Jess snapped her fingers. "That. That's probably what it is." She rested her head against the window. "I have two days off. What am I going to do? I can't even drive."

"I can drive you to the ranch and back, but you probably do need to rest. Maybe just hanging out with the horses and not working would be good for you."

"I'd like to try that. I haven't enjoyed just being around the horses in a long time. I mean, I love taking care of them, but it would be nice to hang out."

"I'm sure they've missed you," Linc said.

Jess tilted her head. "You think they do? I mean, do you think they miss us like we miss them?"

"I don't know, but I know I miss you when you're not around. I assume your four-legged friends feel the same."

Jess's shoulders sank like melting butter. The messy feelings she was having toward Linc grew messier every time he said sweet things. Why couldn't he be unlikable and ugly? Then she wouldn't be battling confusing feelings about her co-worker.

Decoding other people's feelings had always been difficult for her. Understanding Linc had always come easy. Now, she spent most of their time together overthinking every word and move he made.

Linc pulled the truck into her driveway and shut it off. His leg bounced in a quick rhythm. "Do you mind if I come in?"

There he went again, surprising her and throwing all of her expectations into chaos. "Sure, but you don't have to. I'm feeling okay. I'll probably just take a nap."

"I'd like to."

Jess slowly tilted her head toward the house. "Then let's go. Fair warning, I'm not up to entertaining."

Linc chuckled. "Am I the kinda guy who needs to be entertained?"

He wasn't. He was the same Linc as always–no changes–and if he didn't want to be here, he wouldn't have asked to stay.

Jess opened the door. "Let's go then."

"Let me help you." Linc dashed around the truck to her side and held out a hand to her.

Using the door and his hand, she slowly lowered from the truck. "I'm gonna need a lower vehicle."

"I'll ask Hadley if I can borrow her car to pick you up next time," Linc said as he kept a hold of her hand.

At the front door, she reluctantly released his hand to unlock the door.

Linc shouted behind her, "Hey, Ms. Landry."

"You like taunting her, don't you?"

"Oh yeah. She's probably told everyone in town that you've let a rogue stay over way too late. If we're gonna cause a stir, we might as well make sure the rumor is worth her time."

Jess turned around and glared up at Linc. "A rogue? Are we living in the eighteen hundreds?"

"It's better than some of the names I've been called," Linc said, and despite his joking tone, he wasn't kidding.

She'd been called her fair share of names, and most of them were accurate. She'd never given off friendly vibes, and she tended to make a terrible first impression.

Pushing the door open, she said over her shoulder, "You're more of a scoundrel."

Inside, Linc stayed by her side, hovering close enough that their arms brushed against each other. "Something like that."

"I'm going to the bathroom. Make yourself at home."

"You want me to make something for dinner?" he asked.

She stopped to think. "Soup sounds good. There's some canned chicken noodle in the far right cabinet. The one by the laundry room."

"Chicken noodle it is," Linc said as he disappeared into the kitchen.

Linc was always efficient and helpful, but having him focus his efforts on her only made the warm and fuzzy feelings grow. Still, she couldn't gather the nerve to tell him to quit. She liked having him around, even if it meant she'd owe him one in the future.

When she made it to the kitchen after a touch-and-go experience in the bathroom, her limbs and eyelids were heavy.

Linc turned around with a steaming bowl of soup in his hands and set it in front of her. "Dinner is served. I slaved over it. Feel free to compliment my efforts."

His joke livened her tired body, but her mind was still fogging up. The warm vapors from the chicken broth had her mouth watering. "It smells delicious. Much better than the tasteless stuff they gave me at the hospital."

Linc reached for his hat and hesitated when he realized it wasn't there. He gave her a little grin. "Habit."

It was a habit she'd picked up too, though she sometimes favored a ball cap instead of a cowboy hat. If it was hot enough that she needed her hair pulled up into a ponytail, she found herself wishing ball caps were approved in the ranch uniform.

Linc bowed his head and propped his elbows on both sides of his bowl of soup. "Thank You, Lord, for always providing the things we need. Thank You for this food, and thank You for Jess's healing. I pray You would give her body the strength she needs. Amen."

It took extra effort to open her eyes when they wanted so badly to stay closed, but the savory smell of the soup had her stomach growling. The first mouthful hit the spot, heating her insides into blissful contentment.

"I don't want to feed your ego, but this is the best soup I've ever had," Jess said after a few bites.

"I know. I really outdid myself," Linc said with a wink.

Her head rolled to one side, then the other as she

finished the soup. "Okay, I can't keep my head up any longer."

Linc stood. "Are you finished?"

"Yeah." The exhaustion was pulling on her hard enough that she didn't want to fight it anymore.

Linc was by her side in seconds. "Let's get you to the bed."

"Couch. I like it better."

Linc kept his steadying hands on her shoulders as he guided her to the living room. If she had an ounce of energy, she'd tell him to quit coddling her, but right now, she preferred his hands on her. Knowing he was here gave her that extra dose of comfort that pushed her over the edge into sleep as soon as her head hit the pillow.

Little clinks drifted from the kitchen, slowly dragging her out of sleep. After opening and closing her eyes a dozen times, she tried to sit up. Her side stabbed in pain, but she pushed through it. Better get used to that nagging discomfort that would be with her for a while.

Rubbing the weariness from her eyes, she stood and waited a few seconds to make sure the dizziness was gone. More clinking in the kitchen drew her toward it.

She stepped quietly into the room to find Linc with his head in her dishwasher. A handful of tools were scattered on the floor at his side.

"What are you doing?"

Linc grunted and backed out of the dishwasher. "It wasn't working, so I fixed it. I'm just cleaning up."

Jess looked at the clock on the microwave. "Have I been asleep for four hours?" It couldn't have been that long. It was the middle of the day.

Well, now it was evening. She'd slept the day away.

"Yep. Feeling okay?" he asked as he gathered his tools.

Jess rubbed her fingertips over the back of her head. "I think so."

"Brett came by and brought the part I needed. He said to tell you to call him if you need anything."

Her brow furrowed. "Did he come in?"

"Only for a little bit."

"And I didn't wake up?"

Linc rose to his feet. "Nope. You were out cold."

She looked around the kitchen. Other than Linc's tools, everything was clean. "I could have fixed the dishwasher. I just haven't been home a lot lately."

Linc put his tools on the counter. "Are you ever home much? You always work long hours."

"I like the long hours, but Jameson said they'd be a little less now that we have Thea. And he'd planned to hire another ranch hand before the season specifically to keep the stables clean and stocked."

"I'm sure you could have figured it out on your own, but I didn't have anything else to do. Besides, you were getting your beauty sleep."

Jess playfully kicked the side of his leg. She wasn't the princess type, especially not Sleeping Beauty. Linc never looked at her like she was a pretty princess. In fact, he treated her like an equal in most situations. He saw her need to do the work, and he let her do it.

Tonight, he'd been taking care of her instead, and that wasn't like him.

"I'm okay, you know. The doc said to take it easy for a few days, but I'll be fine."

Linc leaned back against the counter, propping his hands on the edge. "I know. You just scared me."

She'd been scared when she hadn't been able to fight the dizziness or exhaustion, but what did it mean that he was scared? This was one of those times when she wished she understood other people. If she didn't know her own emotions, how could she interpret anyone else's?

Linc cleared his throat and stood. "Want to watch some *Jeopardy*?"

Jess sighed, thankful that some things never changed. "It doesn't come on for another half hour, but *Family Feud* is on. Want to share popcorn with me?"

"It's a deal." Linc went to the pantry and found the popcorn.

"I'm gonna change clothes." Remi had brought her jeans and a flannel shirt to wear home from the hospital, but if she dozed off on the couch watching game shows again, she wanted to at least be sleep ready.

Linc walked into the living room at the same time she did. Carrying a bowl of popcorn, he looked like the answer to all of her prayers.

He gestured to the couch, silently asking her to choose a seat first.

Forcing his hand was fair play, wasn't it?

Jess sat in the middle of the couch and pulled a blanket over her legs as she curled them onto the seat.

Now what, buddy?

Without hesitating, Linc took the seat on her left, resting his arm on the seat behind her and positioning the bowl between them.

Hmm. So he didn't have a problem sitting close to her. Interesting, but what did she do with that information?

She found the remote and turned to the local channel that favored game shows in the evenings. Her head was still foggy, and she might not guess any of the right answers, but she'd try her best if Linc would hang around a little longer.

"Any more dates on the horizon?" Linc asked.

"Nope. The season is about to start, and I won't have time to date anyway. Plus, Bethany started back to work this week, and she told this horror dating story at breakfast on Monday. The guy invited her to his place after they went out—"

"Do I want to hear this story?" Linc interrupted.

"Just listen. And he showed her his pets. He sells exotic pets online, and he had whole rooms full of spiders and snakes!"

Linc's brows furrowed. "That's a real thing?"

"Apparently. She said the house smelled terrible, and she had to call her sister to come pick her up."

"Did she know about the pets before she got to his place?"

"I'm guessing she didn't. She said he tried to sell her a tarantula the whole time. He said they made good practice pets."

Linc's eyes widened. "I think a fish is a good starter pet. I'd rather not fall asleep anywhere near a pet that could eat my fingers off."

Jess shivered and groaned. "I'm not afraid of a normal spider, but I don't like that they're sneaky. They never announce their presence!"

"You think a spider should give you a heads-up?" Linc asked with a wide grin.

"It would be polite. If they could talk," Jess added.

Linc covered his face with his hand and laughed. "You're killing me."

"I am not!" Why would he say that?

"It's a figure of speech. Not literal."

"Oh, well don't say things like that." She'd never understand some of the things people said that didn't have the same meaning as the actual words.

"Yes, ma'am." His chuckles died, but commercials still played on the screen. "Between your recent date problems and Bethany's exotic pet dealer, I'm glad I'm not worried about dating."

Jess's smile fell. He'd brought up his dating life. Now she had a free pass to talk about it. Wasn't that how conversations worked? "You don't want to date?"

He looked down and brushed at the knee of his jeans. "Nah. It's not for me."

"Why not?"

Linc shrugged, and she loved being this close to him. She could study every move and every expression. Maybe she'd figure out what made him so appealing.

"Just never thought I was the kind to settle down and have a family."

"Why not?" Maybe if she kept asking that question, he'd keep talking. She could hang on to his every word and forget about the throbbing that was starting to build in the back of her head.

"It's a long story," he said, looking everywhere but at her.

"I've got time."

CHAPTER 19

LINC

F amily. Yeah, he wasn't the family type. In fact, he thought the whole concept of a group of people who shared blood and loved each other was a myth, until he saw Ava come to the ranch and go through so much in the name of family.

Ava was a special case. She wasn't the norm. Most people wouldn't have been nearly as forgiving as she was. Her mother had lied to her. The man she grew up calling dad was only kin to her by marriage. She spent her first summer at the ranch with her real dad without knowing it.

Linc couldn't understand half of the lies Ava had believed her whole life. Thankfully, he didn't have any false truths to debate.

"I don't have a family. I can't really be a good husband or dad when I don't even know what that looks like."

Jess rolled her eyes. "That's not true. We see Mr. Chambers be a good dad to Linda every day, even after she was so horrible to him. And Colt and Remi are good parents to Ben and Abby when the kids aren't even theirs." The steady boldness in her voice said she truly believed it.

She was right. The people at the ranch knew how to do the whole family thing. Why did the thought of family still leave a sour taste in his mouth?

"I don't know who my parents are or when they gave me up. For all I know, Child Services could have made the decision. I was a toddler when I started getting passed around in the foster system."

Jess's brows furrowed. "I don't understand why anyone would give up their kid, or be mean to them, or not take care of them."

Despite Jess's terrible parents, she somehow ended up with a strong sense of responsibility and a kind heart. Most people would have used their upbringing as an excuse to live a selfish life. That's exactly what Linc had done.

"You're a rule follower. Your own parents were terrible to you, and you still think parents are supposed to be good to their kids."

Jess shrugged. "Well, yeah. If you have a baby, you should love it and take care of it."

Linc held up a finger and started ticking off reasons. "Some parents are young and ignorant.

Some parents are selfish. Some are addicted to drugs or alcohol. Some can't afford to raise a kid. Need I go on?"

The deep wrinkle between her brows said she was still thinking and trying to understand. Jess's heart was loyal and determined for good. If she had a kid, there wasn't a doubt in his mind that she'd do her very best to be a good mom.

"I guess you don't know anything about your parents?" she asked.

"Not a thing. I know I was a stupid kid, and I got into trouble constantly. None of the foster families wanted me."

Funny, the truth didn't sting so much anymore. He finally had a job where he felt wanted and respected. His co-workers trusted him to get the job done and do it right.

And Jess. She never looked at him like he was a screw up. She never pushed him away. She never treated him like he was a disappointment.

When she looked at him, he wanted more than anything to be wanted, and that was a dangerous desire.

"Why did you get into trouble?"

"I did things that were bad." Why was this so hard to explain? He didn't have any reasons other than he'd been an angry and confused kid.

"I don't understand. I mean, why did you make bad choices?"

Linc sighed. The guilt was building, adding brick on top of brick until it was too heavy to carry. "And I'm glad you don't understand. I didn't have any excuses for my actions back then. It doesn't make sense. It's just what I did."

"Okay," she whispered, seeming to accept the explanation, even though she didn't understand it.

"I got caught on a few petty crimes when I was younger. I beat up a kid once when I was in middle school."

"Why?"

Linc huffed. "No reason. I was mad, and he was the closest punching bag. That one landed me in alternative school. When I was of age, I still did the same stupid stuff, but the punishments were worse."

Now that he'd made it to the meat of the story, he didn't want to keep talking. Telling her the extent of his crimes would make her pull away from him, and despite the urge to come clean, he couldn't risk losing her. She'd run for the hills as soon as she found out how stupid he was.

"What does that have to do with wanting a family?" she asked.

Right. He'd been giving her reasons why he didn't deserve a happy life with a wife, two kids, and a dog in the suburbs. "Because I have years of bad decisions following me around. No one wants to start a family with that cloud hanging over their head."

Jess's brows pinched together.

"What I mean is, women don't envision marrying a guy with a past like mine."

That past had been trying to creep into the present lately, and the last thing Linc wanted to tell Jess about tonight was Ryan and that whole fiasco.

"But it's the past," Jess said. "Whatever you did couldn't have been that bad."

A snarky chuckle escaped before he could rein it back in. "I bet I've spent more time locked up than Cain, Tommy, and Bruce combined."

Jess's eyes widened, but she quickly tried to mask the surprise. Unfortunately, the eyes didn't lie.

"Oh," she said slowly. "Are you sure about that? Because between the three of them, they have about four months of just one-night lockups."

Linc's fist clenched on the back of the couch. Why'd he have to bring it up? Why was he telling her when it would push her away for good?

"I'm sure," he said, sealing Jess's idea of him as a broken criminal.

He'd seen it hundreds of times. When someone found out about his time in prison and the charges, there was a quiet fear in their eyes from that point on. How could he be trusted?

As much as the counselors had tried, prison reform wasn't on his record. Mr. Chambers took a big risk on Linc, and as much as he wanted to run from the past and never look back, the guilt still hung around, coloring everything in gray.

When he looked up at Jess, she was staring blankly back at him. "I did not expect that."

Linc pushed a hand through his hair. "I made a lot of mistakes."

"But we all have," Jess said.

Linc clicked his tongue behind his teeth. "Not like me."

Jess opened her mouth to speak, then closed it again. The second time, the words came out. "I believe you, but I also...don't want to. Everyone deserves a second chance."

"You can't deny the truth. Mr. Chambers helped...is helping me turn things around. He gave me a job when he probably shouldn't have, and it came with one condition."

"That you don't do anything stupid?" she guessed.

Linc thought back to the first time he met the old man. He'd just gotten released and hopped on a bus to Wyoming. He wanted to be as far away from Memphis as possible, and Cody was the cheapest ticket.

After a week back in the real world, Linc still hadn't found a job or a place to live. He knew next to nothing about the area, and housing was sky high.

Still, he ran out of money in Blackwater and

happened to stumble into Deano's Diner around the time the morning crowd started showing up.

Linc ordered a cup of coffee and a biscuit with bacon just as Mr. Chambers walked in.

Mr. Chambers looked like your average grandpa with gray hair sticking out from underneath his worn cowboy hat. His flannel shirt was neatly tucked into his jeans around his bulging belly, and his boots had seen better days.

Linc hadn't given him a second look.

"You new 'round here?" Mr. Chambers asked behind him.

"Just passin' through."

A beat later, the man behind him asked, "You sure?"

Linc turned and gave the old guy his attention. "Why?"

"You don't look like a tourist."

A woman set an empty Styrofoam cup on the counter and pointed toward the coffee maker. "Help yourself."

"I'm not a tourist."

"Then what are you doin' here?"

Mr. Chambers had rushed the words "what" and "are" together until it sounded like he'd said water, and Linc rubbed a hand over his face to try to hide his grin.

When Linc didn't answer, Mr. Chambers stuck a hand out. "I'm Ronald Chambers."

Linc shook the hand. He had a firm grip for an old guy. "Lincoln North."

Mr. Chambers jerked a thumb over his shoulder. "I have a dude ranch up the road, and I'm lookin' to hire a few new hands. You in the market for a job?"

All traces of laughter faded away. He wanted a job, and this guy was just giving one away. It seemed too coincidental.

"I am."

Mr. Chambers looked him up and down. "Where are you stayin'?"

Linc looked around. He'd slept outside a package store the night before till the owner ran him off. He'd been walking since before sunup.

Mr. Chambers didn't wait long for an answer before holding up a finger, telling Linc to wait. He ordered a coffee and asked for a lid. The waitress filled Mr. Chambers's cup and secured the lid before picking up the empty cup she'd left for Linc and filling it too.

With coffee in hand, Mr. Chambers nodded toward the door. "Take a ride with me, son."

The memory of laughing at Mr. Chambers that day was still fresh. "I thought he was some backwoods pawpaw who wanted me to shovel horse manure for him when he said he had a job for me."

"The joke was on you," Jess said, lifting her hands and shaking them. "Surprise! He owns a multi-thousand acre ranch right beside two huge national parks."

"I definitely didn't see that one coming, especially not after I told him about my past."

"So, he knows?" Jess asked.

Linc nodded. "I thought about lying, but I liked him so much I didn't want to start things off on the wrong foot."

"I bet that was a tough conversation," Jess said, leaning back against the couch.

"It wasn't easy. And he had one condition."

"You had to promise not to steal anything?" she asked.

"I didn't say my sentencing had anything to do with theft."

"I know. I was guessing."

Of everyone in his life, Jess deserved to know the most. Hiding it from her was just as bad as lying.

"He said I had to go to church every Sunday."

"Oh, I should have guessed that," Jess said. "You know why he did that, don't you?"

At the time, Linc hadn't had the slightest clue why the old man wanted him to go to church. He'd stuck out like a sore thumb those first few visits, but he figured it out soon enough.

The people there hadn't looked at him like he was garbage that belonged in the dumpster. They'd welcomed him in and decided he was one of them. He hadn't gotten a say-so in the matter.

"He wants me to believe in God," Linc said.

Jess tilted her head, and that wrinkle between her brows was back. "Are you saying you don't? I thought you did." She brushed a hand over her forehead. "I also thought you went to church because you wanted to."

"I do now. Back then, I had no intention of believing in Christ or acting like a Christian, church or not. But now I get it. Mr. Chambers knew I would see the difference in the way those people treated me. He knew they'd see the potential in me that he saw."

"Good. I didn't get into church until after Brett and I left home, but I hate that we spent all those years without hope. I think God was the only thing that could have pulled me out of all the anger. I'm still a little mad about what our family did, but now I know there are good things in life that I couldn't see before."

That was one thing he hadn't figured out about God. The forgiveness. "Have you forgiven your parents?" he asked.

Jess huffed. "Not that they care, but yeah. I think I have. I don't understand why my dad had so much hate in his heart, and I don't know why my mom still carries it around, but I needed to separate myself from that, and I couldn't do it until I forgave them."

"Doesn't it bother you that they'd probably treat

you the same way again if they got the chance?" Linc asked.

"Yeah, but I can't spend all my time worrying about that. I've made peace with them...mostly. And I know better than to give them another chance to hurt me."

Linc searched Jess's eyes for any hesitation, but there wasn't any. She'd really forgiven them. "I don't understand the forgiveness."

"Welcome to my world," Jess said. "I spent weeks in counseling only talking about forgiveness. I have a hard time understanding why people do the things they do on a good day. Understanding why people do terrible things was beyond me. I had to learn to focus on what I could do instead of what they were doing. I still haven't mastered it, but I feel better with the progress I've made so far."

Linc nodded. "It seems like such a stretch. You do something wrong and you just have to ask for forgiveness and you get it. It can't be that simple."

"But it is," Jess said. "We all make mistakes. God forgave the Israelites lots of times when they wandered in the wilderness. Every time they turned away from Him, He always welcomed them back when they repented."

"That was a million years ago," Linc said. "It doesn't apply now."

"Thousands," she corrected. "And it does apply. We're still messing up every day, and He still wants to save us. We should let Him. Stella told me it's as easy as believing, confessing, and repenting. Over and over until you die."

Linc chuckled. "You really know how to sell it."

Jess lifted one shoulder. "I believe it. And I believe it for you too. You're not a lost cause. You might have done some bad things in the past, but that's not the life you're living now. That's one step closer to embracing God's love."

Linc worked his jaw from side to side as he stared down at the bowl of popcorn they hadn't touched. Jess talked about the Lord with such passion. She made him want to believe what she was saying and dive in headfirst. She was so certain, and he'd been resisting because it sounded too good to be true.

Was he afraid that the God of forgiveness wouldn't be able to forgive his major wrongs?

Jess nudged her shoulder against him. "You think you can't be a good man because you didn't come from a good family? You think you can't be a good husband because you didn't have a good dad? Do you hear how ridiculous that sounds?" she asked.

"Kinda," Linc whispered.

"You don't know your parents, but I know mine. I came from bad who came from bad who came from bad. But I don't want to be bad like them, and I don't hate people the way they do. You can reverse the curse."

"You're better than me," Linc said.

Jess laughed. "Not at all. We're all the same. It took me a while to understand that one too. It's been especially hard while I'm trying to accept Thea and Emerson. I've spent so much time pushing family away that it's my first instinct."

The opening music of *Jeopardy* started, and Jess reached for a handful of popcorn. "Want to make it a competition?" she asked.

She was talking about *Jeopardy*, but Linc was ready to accept her challenge for his life. Jess made him want to be a better person and erase the mistakes he'd already made.

He couldn't make his past disappear, but he could ask for forgiveness and make the decision to change his future.

CHAPTER 20
JESS

Jess sprayed the soap out of the sponge she'd just used to wash Star. She'd been following the vet around while he did checkups on the horses all day, and the lack of actual physical labor had her fingers tingling.

She turned over her wrist and checked the time. Ten minutes before she had to leave.

"Hey, Thea. Can you put Star up? I need to head out."

Thea stepped out of the tack room and wiped her arm across her brow. "Sure. It's getting stuffy in there anyway."

Jess put away the soap, sponges, and brushes before heading for the big sink. She had suds up to her elbows when Thea walked up.

"Where are you going?"

Jess focused on scrubbing her hands and arms harder than necessary. "I have a date."

Thea gasped. "Really? Who is it?"

The last thing she wanted to do was leave work on time for a date with a guy she'd never laid eyes on. "I don't know. Mrs. Huntington set me up."

"Jill Huntington?"

"Yeah. She cornered me at church. I tried to tell her I wasn't interested in dating, but she'd already heard about the other dates I'd been on lately. It seems everyone is up-to-speed on my social calendar."

"Why didn't you just tell her no?" Thea asked.

Wasn't that the question of the day? "I tried, but she said he's a nice guy–her nephew or something–and he's really eager to find a good girl. Of course, Mrs. Huntington thought of me first. Isn't that just ridiculous?"

"Not really, but I can tell you want me to agree with you," Thea said.

"Well, I think it's ridiculous. I have the shortest and worst dating record, and she thinks I'm the woman destined for her nephew."

Thea didn't say anything while Jess dried off her hands and arms. When she looked up, Thea had a confused look on her face. "What?"

Thea shifted her weight from one foot to the other. "Does Linc know?"

There it was–the cause of all her confusion. Why was she so against dating anymore?

It was guilt. She had feelings for Linc, and dating somehow made her unfaithful, even if she didn't have a reason to be loyal to Linc. They weren't even thinking about dating, but everything inside her said it wasn't fair to date when her heart wasn't in it for a reason.

"Um, no. And I'd rather not tell him. It's point-less anyway. I've come to my senses. Dating is a waste of time."

"If everybody thought like that, no one would live happily ever after."

Jess narrowed her eyes at Thea. "Maybe happily ever after isn't for everyone."

She was coming to grips with that idea. Sure, most people dated for years before they found "the one," but if Jess wasn't willing to put in that kind of determined effort, maybe that meant she should forgo it altogether. Her heart wasn't in it.

"I'm surprised you didn't stand up to Mrs. Huntington."

"I would have if she hadn't seemed like she was asking me for a favor and I was denying her."

Also, peer pressure was still very much a thing in her twenties. Instead of people in high school trying to get her to smoke or drink, old ladies were asking her for favors.

It was much harder to stand up to an old lady than a popular kid.

Thea stretched her arms over her head and yawned. "Well, have fun. I'm going to get some coffee before getting back to cleaning out the tack room."

Jess hung her hat on the hook inside the office and headed home. She could make it through one more date. It was only a few hours.

T he Basket Case was busier than usual. Just as she got used to the slower pace of the winter months, the tourist season ramped up again.

Jess looked around the laid-back restaurant. It wasn't Italian food, and it wasn't a bar setting. This date was already shaping up to be better than the others. The Basket Case was more her speed.

Jeremiah stood from a table by the window. She'd taken all the precautions on this date. She'd asked for a photo before meeting him so she could look him up on social media, and he seemed perfectly normal.

She even gave herself a pat on the back for meeting him at the restaurant. Lesson learned there.

Jeremiah waved and smiled as he approached her. He was tall. Really tall. He had a lean build and dark hair. Overall, he was the definition of an average American guy in his twenties.

"Jess?"

"Hey."

She waved, but Jeremiah extended a hand.

Shaking hands wasn't as bad as hugging, but getting away with a wave would have been fantastic. She shook his hand and noted there wasn't any unnecessary squeezing.

Jeremiah kept his bright smile and waved for her to follow him. "Come on. I got us a table."

She followed Jeremiah to the table where a basket of fried pickles waited. He held out an appetizer plate. "You want some? We can get a different appetizer if you want something else."

Slowly taking the seat in front of him, she accepted the plate. "Thanks. This is fine." She wasn't a big fan of pickles, and she didn't normally spring for an appetizer before a meal. If he was paying, she didn't want to order excessively. Enough was as good as a feast, in her opinion.

"So, I'm glad you agreed to come out with me." Jeremiah put a few pickles on his small plate and poured out a dollop of ranch dressing from a cup.

"Mrs. Huntington is convincing."

Jeremiah picked up the menu and looked at it for a few seconds before putting it back down. "You know what you want to order?"

"I usually just get a burger."

"Oh, theirs are the best here. I like the veggie burger myself. Never tried one with meat."

Jess fidgeted with her fingers in her lap. "Are you a vegetarian?"

"Not really. I eat chicken and seafood, but beef is just gross. I tried it when I was a kid and found out it's not for me." Jeremiah's nose scrunched up until his teeth showed.

That wasn't a big deal. So he didn't like red meat. She didn't care for salad or carrots. Maybe he wouldn't tease her about her dislikes either.

The waitress came around with a bright smile. Her light hair was purple at the ends, and she chatted with Jeremiah as if they knew each other.

Was that the way naturally friendly people acted? Like strangers were friends? As hard as she tried, Jess didn't have that naturally friendly personality that made a friend of everyone she met.

The waitress finally left when someone at another table shouted for her attention, and Jeremiah rested his forearms on the table, hands clasped, looking at her expectantly.

Was she supposed to say something? *Your people skills are great. You really understand how to be friendly. I'm glad you know how to talk to strangers.*

A bead of sweat slid down her back. Why hadn't she just told Mrs. Huntington to cut the matchmaking?

"So, what do you do?" Jeremiah asked.

What did she do when? Before work? After church? When she didn't understand first-date questions?

Her hesitation must have lasted long enough that Jeremiah took pity on her. "I work at the chicken processing plant. We cut up chickens for parts."

Jess inhaled a deep breath through her nose. So his aversion to red meat wasn't a moral issue. "Oh. That sounds...bloody."

"It's not terrible. I do the same thing every day, so it's a little boring at times."

Cutting up chickens was boring. That was good information to know in case she ever found herself jobless.

When Jeremiah launched into a long and descriptive explanation of the chicken processing assembly line, Jess hung onto the water the waitress dropped off like a lifesaving device. If she kept the water going down her throat, maybe she wouldn't vomit while Jeremiah separated poultry drumsticks and thighs.

When their food arrived, Jeremiah held his hand palm up for her to take. "I'd like to bless the food."

That was good news. He was probably a Christian and not ashamed to pray in public.

Major points for Jeremiah, even if she reluctantly put her sweaty hand in his. His prayer was short but vehement, and he released her hand without lingering.

Jeremiah talked between bites, and Jess enjoyed her food. Maybe she'd been approaching the dating thing all wrong. It wasn't so bad if she just listened to someone else talk.

Her phone vibrated in her pocket, and she wiped her hands on a napkin before checking it. A text from Linc waited, sending her heart rate from resting to running without her consent.

"Please excuse me," she said as she slid out of the seat. Stella had pointed out Jess's rude table manners a few years ago, and she tried to keep them in mind ever since.

Manners hadn't been on her parents' list of things to teach her and Brett, so Jess's journey to politeness was fairly new.

That saying about teaching an old dog new tricks was true. She wasn't a dog, but twenty years of not caring what other people thought was a hard habit to break.

In the bathroom, she read the text.

Linc: What did you feed Applejack today?

She typed out a quick message and stuck the phone back in her pocket. Oddly enough, Applejack didn't like apples or most treats, for that matter, and she did better on her usual diet.

By the time she got back to the table and Jeremiah, her phone was vibrating again. She pulled it out and checked the text.

Linc: *Did anyone else feed her something different?*

She responded and left her phone on the table. Something had to be up with Applejack.

"Who are you texting?" Jeremiah asked. His tone wasn't accusing, just curious.

"Sorry. It's work, and I might have to respond."

"You never told me what you do."

Oh, that was what he'd meant. What she did for work. "I'm the barn manager at Wolf Creek Ranch."

"Oh," Jeremiah said. That one sound hung in the air between them.

Great. She had a feeling this guy was going to confess his fear of horses like Hanson had. How many people around here didn't care for horses?

Jeremiah leaned forward on his arms. "What are you doing this Saturday night?"

Jess leaned back in her seat. Was he asking her out on another date? The better question would have been "Do you want to go out again on Saturday?"

"I'm probably working." Her phone vibrated again, and she checked it.

Linc: *She's restless and chomping at her side. You want me to call Tucker?*

Jess inhaled a breath, but the air was thick. It settled in her lungs like lead. Linc was thinking about calling the vet.

"Any chance you'd like to go with me to my ten-year high school reunion?" Jeremiah asked.

Jess gave him her attention, but her mind was stuck on Applejack. She couldn't even spare a second to consider his question. "I'm not sure."

Jeremiah fidgeted in his seat. "Listen, I've sort of told my old friends that I'm a little more successful than I really am. If you could just come with me and pretend to be my wife, I'd be so grateful."

Wife jerked Jess out of her thoughts faster than a bucking bull out of the shoot. "What? That's ridiculous."

"I know, I know. I just don't want them to think I'm a loser because I process chickens and live at home with my parents."

Good grief. Jeremiah had seemed so normal, but his secrets were falling out like a waterfall now. "Having a job and a place to live doesn't make you a loser. Lying kinda does."

The phone buzzed again, and she remembered Applejack—the most important thing right now.

"Please, please," Jeremiah begged. "I'd owe you forever."

Jess read the text.

Linc: Tucker is helping with a breech foal right now. It'll be a while before he can get here.

She texted back.

Jess: I'm on my way.

Jeremiah had his hands clasped at his chest.

"Please. And if you could pretend to have a good job, like an accountant or something, that would be great."

This guy. What was he even talking about? "Listen, I have to go. Sorry to cut the dinner short, but there's a horse in trouble at the ranch."

Jeremiah grabbed her hand and tugged her toward him. "Please, Jess. I really need you."

She jerked her hand out of his grasp. "Don't touch me. Dude, this is crazy. Have you thought about what you're asking? You want me to lie. Flat out lie. I don't do that. I'm also not interested in finishing a date with a guy I can't trust." She pulled a few bills out of her pocket and threw them on the table. "Have a nice life."

Jeremiah sighed and let his head fall to the table, but she didn't care if he was upset.

Leaving Jeremiah behind and marking the night off as a bust, she headed back toward the ranch. She had bigger problems to take care of right now.

CHAPTER 21

LINC

Linc led Applejack around the indoor arena. Every step was touch-and-go as the horse's gait lumbered. She was definitely restless, but there was a chance it wasn't colic.

At least, he had to hope there was a chance. He'd seen colic take some good horses in just a few hours, but he'd also seen some recoveries.

Thankfully, Applejack wasn't trying to lie down. If he could keep her on her feet, he'd feel a lot better about the odd behavior.

He turned one side of the loop and saw Jess coming in, walking with a determination that sent his heart racing.

He should be relieved she was here. She was much better at taking care of the horses, but the pounding in his veins was far from relief.

Her hair was down, flowing behind her as she

strode toward him. She wore a red-and-blue flannel shirt and dark jeans. When she got closer, he did a double take. Was she wearing earrings?

She didn't slow her stride until she was right on him. "How is she?"

Jess was wearing earrings and makeup on her eyes. Since when did she do that?

Apparently, since this morning, which was the last time he'd seen her.

Jess was still looking at him like she was waiting for him to countdown to a race or something.

"What?" Linc asked.

"How is Applejack?"

Linc looked at the chestnut horse. She was still antsy. "Um, I don't know. If it's colic, it isn't severe yet."

Jess had her hands on the horse's side, feeling over her belly. "When did she start acting differently?"

He needed answers too. Like when did Jess start wearing makeup? "I got here about an hour ago."

"What's the ETA on the vet?"

"Still on another call. I've been texting him updates, and he said he'll be here as soon as he can."

Jess lifted Applejack's lip and examined her gums. "Did anyone else say they fed her something? When was the last time she was out?"

"Thea fed her at the same time as always today, and she says it was the proper measurement and feed. Applejack was in the side pasture earlier, but she didn't have a rider."

Jess took the lead from him and led the horse to the grooming area. "Can you get her some water?"

Linc did exactly as he'd been told and worked to dislodge the rock in his throat. When he returned to the grooming area, he watched Jess nurture the horse. She had a way of comforting that he'd never possess. Applejack calmed under her touch.

"Were you busy? I didn't mean to mess up your plans," Linc said.

Jess sighed. "I was on a date."

There it was, the shot straight to his heart.

What could he say? Sorry I interrupted? He wasn't really sorry. Selfishly, he wanted her with him instead of some other guy.

His stomach knotted. Maybe he was getting colic too.

"It wasn't working out anyway." A grin lifted the corners of her mouth as she continued to study Applejack. "It's kinda funny, actually."

If she was about to go into detail about how funny this guy was, Linc would definitely lose his breakfast.

"He seemed like a normal guy." She covered her mouth as she laughed.

Okay, now he was invested. He wanted more of whatever was making Jess Patton laugh.

She shook her head and tried to calm her laughter. "He wanted me to be his date to his high school reunion."

Linc blinked a few times. "Why would anyone want to go to a high school reunion?"

Jess pointed at him. "Exactly. That. But he wanted me to pretend to be an accountant and act like he was my successful husband."

A rogue chuckle ripped from Linc's chest before he could stop it. "He was that big of a loser?"

"He works at a chicken processing plant, which isn't terrible, but he wanted me to be an *accountant*. Can you imagine?"

Picturing Jess sitting behind a computer all day or doing paperwork was a huge stretch. She passed off all barn finances to Brett like money might burn her hand.

Jess pressed her ear against Applejack's side. "You know, he's the second date who wasn't impressed with my job."

"They're in the wrong. You're great at your job."

She raised her head and ran her hands over the horse's back. "Thanks. I don't have any plans to change careers."

Linc took a half breath. "So, you're saying he's a jerk?"

"Yep."

"I thought you weren't dating anymore," he said low, half hoping she wouldn't hear him.

Jess rolled her eyes. "Mrs. Huntington cornered

me at church last week. To be fair, her nephew was nice before he started asking me to lie."

Linc's phone chirped, and he read the text. "The doc wants an update."

Jess gave Applejack a once-over. "She seems okay for now, maybe a little uncomfortable. I'd rather be overly cautious than disregard her change in behavior."

Linc typed out the response and pocketed his phone. "Did I interrupt you before you got to eat?"

"No. I had a burger. You need something to eat?" she asked.

"I ate before I came." The thought of another guy buying her dinner didn't sit well with him, even if the guy ended up being a jerk.

He had to man up and tell her how he felt, or he'd have to be content watching her find her happily ever after with someone else.

But could she have a happily ever after with him? He didn't have much to offer, and he wasn't oozing charm or romantic vibes. What made him a good choice for her?

They took turns monitoring Applejack and doing other menial chores around the barn. As much as he loved the trail rides, working in the stables with Jess was a much better job.

Jameson walked in with a determined stride. The foreman had his hands in everything at the ranch, which was normal, but his attention had been focused on his wife lately. Ava's pregnancy had been rocky from the start, and she and Jameson had been spending a lot of time at medical appointments.

"Heard about Applejack," Jameson said as he nodded at the horse.

"Tucker is on his way," Jess said. "I'll stay with her tonight to make sure she's okay."

"I can stay. I'll let you know if things change," Linc said.

Jess shook her head. "I can't leave."

"Then we'll both stay." He wasn't leaving Jess alone, and he didn't want to. If she was going to dedicate her night to watching Applejack, so was he.

"Looks like the two of you have this covered. Call me if you need anything," Jameson said with a wave as he headed toward the exit.

Linc sat on a bucket next to Jess. "You can go home. I promise I'll let you know if anything happens."

Jess shook her head. "Not getting rid of me."

Linc rubbed a hand over his jaw. "In that case, I'm going to the kitchen to see if Vera has any leftovers. If we're gonna be up all night, we don't have to starve."

"Can you bring me a Coke?" Jess asked.

"I bet Mr. Chambers has coffee."

The widening of her eyes was subtle, but Linc noticed.

"So, coffee?" he asked.

"Coffee, if it's not too much trouble."

Linc headed for the dining hall with one thing on his mind. A night in the barn didn't sound too bad if he got to spend it with Jess.

CHAPTER 22

JESS

Jess pressed the stethoscope to Applejack's side and closed her eyes. Somehow, it helped her hear better. There were a few intestinal sounds, but was it enough to alleviate her concerns?

Linc had been gone for a while. Maybe he decided to stay home and get some decent sleep. She wasn't going to be worth two cents tomorrow if she stayed up all night watching Applejack.

Spending the night with Linc was the last thing she needed. Curbing her confusing feelings for him should be a top priority, but not one part of her wanted to let it go.

The heaviness in her chest was back. If she didn't get a handle on her reactions to him, she'd just have to live with this pressing weight. They'd been working together for years, but how could she pretend like she didn't care when he'd tended to her so sweetly when she was injured and been there to turn her mood around when her dates had been busts?

Being with Linc right after those dates had been a bad idea. She couldn't go from being treated badly to being held by Linc and not see the contrast. She knew better than anyone that most things in life were confusing, but the difference between other men and Linc was black and white.

The barn door creaked, and Linc entered with his arms full. Rushing to help him, Jess took in the things he carried. Pillows and blankets. She darted behind him to close the door and followed him to the office.

And following him was a bad idea. He'd changed into a white thermal shirt that hugged his broad shoulders, putting the muscles in his back on full display. Thankfully, the flannel shirts he usually wore hid that definition. She'd never get any work done if Linc's muscles hogged all of her attention.

The gray sweats he wore didn't help either. And did the bottoms have to be messily tucked into his work boots? It was as if he knew what kind of bait to use to catch her attention.

So unfair. She looked like she'd just rolled out of a dumpster in her night clothes. Linc looked like every woman's fantasy.

Jess rubbed her eyes with the back of her arm.

No more ogling. She couldn't spend the night hours with him if she was lusting after him.

"How's our girl?" he asked.

The kick in her heart when Linc called Applejack "our girl" was unmistakable. Why did her entire body warm when he loved the horses the way she did?

"She's okay. No change. I'm hoping we're being overly cautious."

Linc put the pillows and blankets on top of her desk. "Better safe than sorry. I brought a few things in case we're actually here all night. Pillows and blankets. I figure we'll use the cots in the storage room." He picked up a wad of clothes and handed them to her. "I stopped by Remi's and got you some comfortable clothes."

Jess's eyes widened. "What did she say?"

Linc opened a brown paper bag and pulled out a pack of microwave popcorn. "Nothing. She knows you wouldn't leave a sick horse. Don't worry. I stopped by before I changed."

Jess studied the clothes in her hands. She'd been dreading the sleepless night, but carrying her worry for Applejack didn't seem so bad when Linc was doing everything to make her comfortable. "Thanks for all this."

"No problem. I'm going to put the popcorn in the microwave and check on the other horses."

As soon as he stepped out of the office, she

darted for the door, locking it in one quick turn of her wrist. Pressing her back against the door, she took a few deep breaths.

She should go home. Spending more time with Linc was a bad idea. He could take care of Applejack. Well, even though they'd been at the ranch close to the same amount of time, she'd seen more colic than he had. Still, he could just call her if something went wrong.

But time was an illusion with colic. Things could go south in a hurry.

Deciding to stay and quit flip-flopping, Jess changed into the pants and long-sleeve shirt Remi had sent. They closed the barn doors at night, but it wasn't much warmer than the night outside. She stuck her feet back into her boots and pulled her hair into a ponytail. She was ready for work with a side of comfy.

She walked out of the office tugging on the sleeves. Jess was a little bigger than Remi, but not enough that the clothes didn't fit.

Linc walked out of Applejack's stall and halted when he saw her. His intense stare made her skin burn beneath the cotton of her shirt.

"What?"

Linc shook his head. "Nothing."

Jess looked down at her clothes. Oh, Remi's shirt was a little tighter than she'd realized. It hugged her curves well, and while it wasn't revealing, it did draw attention to her very feminine shape.

That didn't stop her heart rate from ticking up. On the one hand, if he was going to wear sexy PJs, he should be subjected to her voluptuous curves too.

On the other hand, there was already a lot of tension crackling around them, and she didn't need any more. She turned on her heels and shouted over her shoulder, "I'm going to change!"

"You don't have to do that," Linc said behind her.

She didn't stop as she marched back toward her office.

"I have an extra shirt in there. Just wear that," he shouted behind her.

Not a chance. She'd wear the shirt she'd worn on her date and like it. She needed zero more things that would keep her mind on Linc tonight.

She closed the door and locked it behind her. Picking up her shirt, she spotted the one Linc mentioned. It was a dark-blue T-shirt that would look amazing on him.

No, Jess. Stop it!

But she couldn't help reaching out to touch it. Why did it have to be soft? She picked it up and let the shirt in her other hand fall. Pressing his shirt to her face, she breathed in the clean smell that had her chest aching. Linc usually smelled like a horse, and she didn't mind it, but his clean shirt was the stuff men paid big bucks for in a bottle.

"Ugh. This is crazy," she whispered to herself. Why did Linc have to be handsome, thoughtful, and smell amazing?

Making up her mind, she pulled off Remi's shirt and picked up Linc's. She wanted to wear his shirt, and that was all there was to it. It didn't have to mean anything.

Except it did mean something–to her.

When she stepped back out of the office, Linc had set up the cots just outside Applejack's stall. A bag of popcorn sat on one of them and two bottles of water lay on the other.

Linc stepped out of the stall and hung the stethoscope around his neck. He stopped short when he spotted her, just as he'd done the last time. This time, his mouth turned up in a tiny grin. "Feel better?"

She did feel better, especially after seeing Linc's smug grin. He liked seeing her in his shirt. She could feel it in her bones. "Much."

He handed her the stethoscope. "I'm going to get the pillows and blankets. The vet is on his way. He'll be here in about fifteen minutes."

Jess took the stethoscope as the worry knotted in her gut started to relax. "Good."

She wasn't naive enough to think the vet's gold star meant nothing would happen to Applejack, but knowing they would get another opinion did make her feel a little bit better.

Jess rubbed a hand over Applejack's nose. "You okay, girl?"

The horse shifted a little. She didn't seem to be in pain, but she was definitely restless.

"Want to take a walk?" Jess asked. Knowing there wasn't an audible answer coming didn't stop her from waiting for some kind of response.

Applejack turned and nipped at her side.

Jess's chest tightened. Okay, maybe she was being appropriately cautious asking the vet to drive out here at eleven at night.

She grabbed the lead and coaxed Applejack into the indoor arena. Linc was replenishing the hay in some of the stalls.

"I'm taking her for a walk," Jess said over her shoulder.

They'd made quite a few rounds by the time the vet showed up. Tucker Lawson wore the same gray slacks he always wore, but his usual button-up was replaced by a "Blackwater Animal Clinic" sweatshirt.

"Any update?" he asked.

Linc shook his head. "About the same."

After giving the vet a thorough history on the horse, Jess stood with her hands on her hips watching everything he did, while Linc paced back and forth behind her with his arms crossed over his chest. Nervous energy radiated from him, pressing into her back and shoulders with every pass.

"Can you stand still?" Jess asked.

Linc let his arms drop and fisted and relaxed his hands. "I'll be in the feed room."

She expected some relief when Linc left, but the worry didn't leave, pinching the back of her neck and holding on.

Tucker gave her a few updates during his assessment and finally propped his hands on his hips. "The colic is mild, and it could resolve on its own. You know what we're looking for. Her gums are fine, and abdomen sounds are normal, and her heart rate is great right now. I don't think she's in enough discomfort to tube her yet."

"Right." Thankfully, the vet seemed to share all of Jess's opinions.

Tucker handed Jess a syringe and a bottle along with a printout. "Call me if things turn south."

"Thanks. I'll try not to bother you unless it's an emergency."

"I'm going to give her a pain reliever, but that means you'll need to observe her through the night." Tucker raked his gaze down her oversized shirt and pajama pants. "I'm going to assume you're staying."

"I am. Linc will be here too. We'll let you know if anything happens."

Tucker pressed his lips together and wiggled his

mustache. "Good. I'll give her this pain reliever and be on my way."

Jess walked Tucker to the door and came back to lead Applejack into her stall. She seemed to have calmed considerably over the last hour, and the pain reliever hadn't taken effect yet.

Jess wrapped her arms loosely around the horse's neck and closed her eyes. She said a silent prayer that the Lord would lay His hand on all three of them throughout the night.

Lifting her head, Jess looked up at Applejack. "You're gonna be okay, girl. I'm here." She leaned in to whisper, "So is Linc. He acts tough, but he's a softy. He loves you too."

When she turned around, Linc was propped in the doorway. His face was darkened by shadow, and everything about him should have told her to keep her distance, but she couldn't do it. She wasn't strong enough to push him away, and she didn't want to.

She had a night alone with Linc ahead of her, and despite the heat that had been building under her skin all evening, there wasn't anywhere else she'd rather be.

CHAPTER 23

JESS

Jess bunched the blanket in her hands as she stared at the barn's ceiling. She'd stayed up with a horse before, and it was never fun. Over-worrying about the horses was her default. Add in a lack of sleep, and she was guaranteed to be a wreck.

The one o'clock alarm had just gone off, and Linc, who had been pretending to sleep in the cot beside her, got up without a sound and checked on Applejack.

She'd been doing her part at pretending too. They'd been lying in the cots just outside Apple-jack's stall for over an hour, but sleep was the last thing on her mind.

She was still counting the wooden beams holding up the roof when Linc stepped out of the stall. Trying his best to be quiet and stealthy, he slid into the cot beside hers.

Having him so near in the dark had every nerve ending in her body firing. They weren't touching, but his heat radiated against her left side.

"You awake?" Linc whispered.

"Yep." So much for battling her thoughts alone.

Linc reached up and rested an arm behind his head. "She's gonna be okay," he said softly.

"I know." Jess had seen enough colic to know this was a minor case. She hadn't crossed out all of her worries, but she was fairly confident Applejack would pull through.

Linc turned his head toward her and let out a long exhale. "Go to sleep."

"You go to sleep," she quipped back.

Linc chuckled. "Fair enough."

Applejack might be fine, but Jess was sleeping within inches of a man for the first time in her life. She'd been on plenty of multi-day trail rides, but she always had her own tent. No boys allowed.

Being this close to a man–physically and emotionally—stirred up feelings she'd never wanted before.

But she wanted Linc. She wanted to be closer, and that simple thought had her bones buzzing beneath her skin, pulling her toward him without words or movement.

She turned over and grabbed her phone from the bucket she'd made into a nightstand. "I'll take the next watch."

"Just sleep, Jess." Linc's words were deep and heavy in the dark night, but every word tingled in her ears.

"I can't sleep," she whispered.

"That makes two of us."

Jess huffed. "If we're not going to sleep, you should just go home."

"No, ma'am," Linc said, quick and sure.

"Why not?" She didn't appreciate the constant temptation he presented. Being next to him for this many uninterrupted hours bordered on torture.

"I don't want to," he said matter-of-factly.

Jess turned to stare at the dark where he lay only a few inches beside her. "Why not?"

Linc shifted beside her. "Because you're here."

Oh no. She was in so much trouble. Something was growing inside her, and she didn't know what to call it.

Some people claimed to *fall* in love. The action described was scarily accurate. Someone could have pushed her off a cliff and she wouldn't have been nearly as terrified as she was right now.

"Tell me something about you," she whispered. "Something about your life before you came here."

Silence. It wrapped around her and choked the breath out of her chest.

When she'd waited long enough, she whispered, "Linc?"

"I'm thinking." He sighed. It was a painful sound, and she regretted ever asking the question.

"I can't think of anything good to tell you," he admitted.

She curled in her shoulders against the ache in her middle. As much as she wished Linc's childhood had been full of games and fun, it wasn't. She had a feeling his upbringing was a lot like hers, and if so, no wonder he didn't have anything good to say.

He shifted again. "Yeah, I don't have any stories. Sorry."

"Have you ever been happy?" she asked, terrified of his answer.

He clicked his tongue behind his teeth. "Yes."

Her breaths grew shallow, and her throat constricted. "When?"

"I'm happy right now."

Right in this moment with her, or since he came to Wolf Creek? It didn't matter because she got to have happy Linc beside her.

"Good. Tell me something else about you."

A long string of silent seconds told her he'd turn her down again. Jess hadn't ever been an open book, and she only gave what was honest, but she wanted to collect little pieces of Linc like people collected thimbles or snow globes.

She bit back the urge to ask him again. If he didn't want to tell her, she couldn't force it out of him.

He sighed and rubbed his hands over his face. "There isn't anything good about me, Jess. Sorry to disappoint you, but my life isn't exactly a bedtime story. In fact, you'd probably hate me if you knew half the truth."

Heat crept up her neck and face. The warmth was vaguely familiar as the precursor to her anger, but she wasn't mad. What was it? Defiance?

"I want to know."

"I don't want you to know," he retorted quickly.

She swallowed the lump in her throat. "You really think I'd do that? Just stop talking to you and forget about you because of something that already happened and no one can change?"

"Yes."

Jess scoffed. "The only thing I hate is how little you think of me."

"Jess–"

"And above all things, have fervent love for one another, for love will cover a multitude of sins," Jess quoted.

"What is that?"

"1 Peter 4:8. Do you want me to repeat it?"

"No. I don't know the Bible that well, so forgive me if I don't recognize the scriptures."

There was a bite in his tone she wanted to bristle against. "I don't know a lot, but I know what it means. God wants to save you. Let Him!"

Linc rested back against the pillow. "I'm sorry. I–"

"You don't have to tell me if you don't want to. But know that if you did, I could handle it."

She rolled over and pulled the blanket under her chin. He really didn't have to tell her, but she needed him to know she wasn't the kind of person who didn't forgive wrongs. Sure, she'd given Thea a hard time, but she was moving past it, and Thea had been patient.

Linc sighed. "Jess, I'm sorry. That's not what I was trying to say."

"I know," she whispered. "I've earned my reputation. There's a reason everybody thinks I'm heartless."

"I don't think you're heartless."

Jess flopped onto her back. "But I am. I don't always understand why people say the things they say or react the way they do. And when I look confused, people think it's because I don't care or I'm judging them."

Linc's breaths were audible, hanging in the air between them like a roaring wave crashing against a rocky shore. He swallowed hard before speaking.

"I burned things."

Jess's brows furrowed, but thankfully, Linc couldn't see her confusion in the dark. "What?"

"I burned things. When I was young. Well, it started when I was really young, and things got worse when I was in high school, which I didn't finish, by the way."

Fire. Burning. Destruction. She wasn't afraid of fire, but she'd always had a healthy fear of its capabilities.

Fire was devastating, and there wasn't anything that could erase that destruction.

"What?"

Linc huffed. "That's how I ended up in jail. Well, most of the time it was arson. There were a few other things that got me arrested. Theft. Vandalism. Destruction of property. I have two DWIs."

"What's that?" Jess asked.

"Driving while intoxicated."

Drinking and driving? It didn't sound like Linc. Yet, she had to believe what he was saying.

The pressing weight in her middle rose, clogging in her throat. None of it sounded like the man she knew.

Because it wasn't. He was different from the boy he was describing. Everything she knew about him added up to good. Not bad.

"Okay," she whispered.

"See? It's not a pretty list. In between nights in jail, I was doing the same things without getting caught."

Jess played through her memories of Linc. She'd never seen him do any of those things. In fact, he did more good on a regular basis than many people she knew.

It didn't make sense. Which was why she chose to erase it. Those crimes didn't get to hang out in her assessment of Linc. His past wasn't his present or his future.

"It's still okay," she said. "You did bad things. You paid the price. Now, you don't do those things anymore. It's over."

"I burned buildings," Linc said, not bothering to whisper now. "I burned entire buildings to the ground. I've destroyed more than I've built."

"And now you've done so many good things that I'm having a hard time believing what you're saying. That counts for something. You're moving in the right direction."

Who was she to talk about the right direction? She didn't know where she was headed either. All she knew how to do was the same thing every day. She knew how to go to work, care for horses, go to church on Sunday, and repeat.

Where was she going?

"I messed up. A lot. No one wanted anything to do with me," Linc said. "But I had a friend who was even worse, and knowing I wasn't the worst person in the world was my way of justifying everything. If I burned a dumpster, he wanted to burn the building. If I busted out the windows of cars, he wanted to steal everything inside."

Jess pressed her eyes closed. She couldn't see much in the dark, but she wanted to block out everything Linc was saying. Too bad she couldn't will her ears closed. "I get it. You did bad things."

"I don't think you do." He sat up and turned toward her. "I can't take back what I did. I hurt people. I stole things they'll never get back. I–"

"I do get it!" Jess sat up too, squaring off with his shadow. "I'm not stupid. I know people make mistakes. But I know forgiveness. I've struggled with it for a long time. Do you know how hard it is to walk into a church every Sunday knowing I had dreams about giving my family what I thought they deserved? Do you know how bad I hated them?"

"I don't blame you!" Linc said, throwing his hands in the air.

"But God does blame me." Jess stabbed a finger at her chest. "I'm not supposed to hate. I'm supposed to forgive, but it's so hard when I don't understand why they hurt me. I don't understand why they liked hurting others. I don't understand why some people got to have loving parents while mine starved me as a punishment!"

Linc stilled, staring at her as his shoulders rose and fell with his deep breaths.

She'd said too much. She hadn't said the right things. She never knew what to say, and her misspoken words always had a price.

He sighed and hung his head, pushing a hand

through his hair. When he spoke, his words were calmer. "I don't like hearing about your parents."

"Well, I don't like hearing about your past, but it's a part of you, and I can't pick and choose the truths I want."

Linc lay back and released a deep breath. "I'm not the guy you should be focusing on, so just forget you ever thought it was me."

There was a stalling in Jess's chest. The rhythm of her heart was off, and it pulled the air out of her lungs. How many times would broken kids grow up into broken adults just because they'd been told they were worthless all their lives?

"People change. You did," she whispered.

"I don't know if I've changed enough."

"You have." Her voice broke on the last word, and she hated that little hiccup. Hated how it betrayed her, laying out her fear for him to see.

"Good night, Jess."

She threw the blanket off and stood, picking up the lantern and turning it on. "I'm going to check on Applejack."

She couldn't stay next to Linc. Not when he was pushing her away.

If she stayed, she'd be tempted to beg him to let her in, and that was one decision he had to make on his own.

CHAPTER 24

LINC

Wℎat was ringing, and why wouldn't it shut up?

Linc pressed his eyes closed as the noise kept stabbing at his head. Whoever was calling could wait until morning.

A man cleared his throat, and Linc's eyes opened wide. Every muscle in his body stiffened as he slowly turned toward the source of the sound.

Blinking away the fog in his vision, Linc frowned at the two people standing at his feet.

Right. He'd slept in the barn last night.

He'd slept in the barn with Jess.

She was still curled up beside him. She might have been on a separate cot, but Linc's arm was still draped over her.

Oh, great. He'd cuddled her in his sleep. He'd never hear the end of it.

He pulled his arm away, reluctantly, because apparently, even his sleeping brain wanted to be closer to her. She'd probably never let him touch her again.

Last night's conversation came back to him in pieces. He'd pushed her away. He'd done the right thing, but he'd pretty much let her know nothing was happening between them.

That was probably the reason he wanted to lean over and puke his guts up. She'd gone to sleep mad, and he couldn't blame her. At least she got the memo that he was a jerk.

Linc sat up and stretched his neck from side to side. "What's up?"

"What's up?" Brett repeated. "That's what I wanna know."

Brett's voice was already an octave too high, which meant he was reading way too much into the compromising position Linc had been tangled in with Jess. "I've been awake for a total of ten seconds. Let me catch up."

"Take your time, sleepyhead," Brett said before chomping into the side of an apple.

Thea's hand hadn't moved from where it covered her mouth, and Brett continued to stand there with his arms crossed and a goofy smile on his face.

Thane walked up beside Jess and pressed his nose to her hand that was hanging off the side of her cot. She groaned and rolled onto her back. "Leave me alone," she grumbled without opening her eyes.

Brett chuckled. "Good to know she's grumpy all the time. I thought it was just me she didn't like."

Thea slapped Brett's chest. "She likes you, and she's not always grumpy."

Brett gestured to where Jess lay still sleeping. "Looks like she likes Linc too. We caught them canoodling in the barn!"

Linc propped his elbow on his knee and pointed his finger at Brett. "Don't tell a soul."

"No dice," Brett said. "I'm telling everyone. Her reputation will be ruined. The whole county will force you to marry her. It's shameful, Linc."

Linc dropped his head into his hand. "I'm too tired to fight with you today."

Thane licked Jess's face, and her nose scrunched just before her eyes opened, blinking a few times against the morning light. "What are you..."

Her eyes widened, and she bolted upright. She looked from Brett and Thea to Linc and back again. Then, remembering she was wearing his shirt, she jerked the blanket up to her chin.

Brett coughed on a bite of apple he'd been chewing. "I was just joking, but you two look guilty."

Thea seemed to snap out of her daze and grabbed Brett's arm. "Maybe we should come back after breakfast."

"No. No. No," Jess said quickly. "Nothing

happened. We were just keeping an eye on...Apple-jack." Jess looked around, still getting her bearings. "Oh! Is she okay?"

Linc rested a hand on Jess's shoulder. "Relax. She had a bowel movement around three this morning, and she's been fine ever since." He'd never been excited about horse poop before, but there was apparently a first time for everything.

He'd been up every hour, careful not to wake Jess. She'd been pushing herself hard these last few weeks trying to make sure everything was ready for the season. On top of that, she was still healing from the concussion and bruised ribs.

Apparently, he'd been too exhausted after the last check-in to set another alarm. At least he'd thought to text Jameson at three to let him know Applejack was out of the woods.

Jess frantically rummaged through the blanket. "Where's my phone? What time is it?"

"Teatime, sis," Brett said with that smug grin still on his face.

"Can you maybe give her a second?" Linc didn't even try to keep the growl out of his voice. Clearly, Jess didn't think this was as funny as her brother did.

Brett held up his hands, one still clutching the apple. "Fine. I'll give you some privacy." He crossed his arms and shook his head. "Shame on you. Right in front of the horses."

"Brett!" Linc and Jess shouted at the same time.

Thea was trying her best to hold back a laugh as she dragged Brett away by his arm. "Quit pestering them."

"But it's so much fun," Brett said as he followed his wife out of the barn.

Thane still sat beside Jess's cot waiting for attention. She pointed at him and said, "Don't look at me like that. We just slept together. I mean, we slept next to each other."

When Thane continued to stare, Jess sighed. "It was for Applejack!"

Linc rested a hand on her shoulder again. "Jess, you don't owe the dog an explanation."

She jerked her attention to him, eyes wide as if she'd forgotten he was there. "Easy for you to say. You didn't wake up being judged."

Linc looked around. "Pretty sure I did."

Jess's shoulders sank. "Okay. I just need a minute to wake up." She rubbed her eyes and let out a long breath.

Linc stood and stretched. "I'm going to check on Applejack."

"I will," Jess said through another yawn. She threw off the blanket and slid her feet into the boots beside the cot.

And he'd forgotten she was wearing his shirt. A light buzzing started under his skin, reminding him to keep his distance.

But he wanted her. Selfishly, unapologetically. He wanted every smile, every look, every second of her time. He wanted the pain and the past. He wanted the future with every up and down along the way.

His palms tingled with the need to touch her and pull her in, but he couldn't. He'd spent a good part of the night explaining just why he couldn't have her. Too bad his base desires didn't get the cease-and-desist letter.

Jess stomped over to the stall before turning to him. "Why didn't you wake me up?"

Linc shrugged. "I must have forgotten to turn on the alarm."

Or he'd slept through the alarm because he was cuddled up with Jess. He hadn't meant to oversleep either way, but he couldn't regret it too much. Those last few hours were some of the best sleep he'd ever had.

Waking up next to Jess was officially one of the best moments of his life, and he had zero apologies.

Jess turned on her heels with a huff and disappeared into Applejack's stall. Maybe he had a few regrets. She didn't seem happy about their early-morning snooze fest.

Linc rubbed his hands over his face. What a morning. The hangover from the midnight conversation with Jess had his stomach in knots.

He put away the cots, called Jameson with

another update on Applejack, and went home to change clothes. After stopping by the kitchen to get two breakfast plates, he went back to the barn. He put Jess's food in her office and grabbed a few pieces of bacon to eat while he got started.

Jess kept a list of barn chores tacked to the information board, but something else drew his attention. The quotes and verses she wrote on the board always stopped him short. It was almost as if he got a peek into her head when she changed the board.

Today's verse was meant for him. It was a direct stab to his heart.

Above all, love each other deeply, because love covers over a multitude of sins. 1 Peter 4:8

The words seemed simple enough, but surely there was some other context that caused the verse to mean something else. He didn't know much about the Bible–only what he'd been taught at church–but he knew enough to know the whole thing went straight over his head.

Love. He didn't know anything about love, so how could it have any effect on the mound of sin he carried?

Linc studied the chores list and started at the top. It was half an hour later before he saw Jess again. She'd changed back into her clothes from the night before and started working. He fully expected her to go home, but the stern look on her face said she was going to be stubborn and put in another shift despite her exhaustion.

He was one to talk, since he was back at work too, but he couldn't sit at home. Not when the only thing he had to do was think about Jess and how she seemed to be going out of her way to avoid him now.

He'd known telling her would push her away, but he'd done the right thing. She'd been misled, and he'd set the record straight.

Thea strolled back into the barn after breakfast and looked around. "Where's Jess?"

Linc pointed toward the shower area where she was giving Jethro a bath.

"Thanks," Thea said over her shoulder as she headed that way.

Linc went to the storage room to get a few things he needed for his next horse when he heard part of Jess and Thea's conversation.

"How'd your date go last night?" Thea asked.

And that was his cue to leave. He'd heard enough about Jess dating, and if he ever had to hear about it again, it would be too soon.

Before he could get the things he needed and get out, Jess answered.

"Not good. I'm done with the whole dating thing."

Thea whined. "Don't do that. You have to go through a bunch of bad apples to find a good one."

"What does any of this have to do with apples?" Jess asked.

He smiled involuntarily. Jess never understood figurative speech, and he loved that she preferred plain language. She kept things straight and to the point, just as they should be.

"It's fine. The season is starting, and I don't have time to waste on dates that don't work out. I'd rather be working anyway."

Linc gripped the lead rope in his hand. He'd missed his chance. Not that he'd had one in the first place.

Jess and Thea moved their conversation away from the storage room, and Linc slipped out. He worked through chore after chore, focusing on the work instead of Jess.

Who was he kidding? He kept one eye on Jess the whole morning. Thankfully, she didn't notice.

Around noon, she walked out of her office and said to no one in particular, "Going to lunch!"

Linc relaxed when she left, working harder without the distraction wandering around the barn. He'd skip lunch and get ahead on some chores, but after a while, he started to imagine the horses were judging him. They'd heard the rough conversation last night, and they all seemed to be looking down their noses at him.

Great. Now he was assigning human thoughts to horses. Mr. Chambers would be extra proud of him.

Linc stopped with the rake he'd been using to muck stalls hanging in the air.

That's what he needed. A talk with Mr. Chambers. It had been a while since he'd visited his boss.

Jess walked back into the barn, continuing to ignore him as she passed.

Linc propped the rake against the wall. "I'm going to the main house."

"Kay!" Jess shouted back. Clearly, she didn't care one bit whether he went to visit his boss or jumped off a cliff.

Linc shook his head. It was for the best. He was bound to ruin anything good anyway.

Just as he'd expected, Mr. Chambers sat in his usual rocking chair on his back porch. He raised his mug of coffee as Linc approached.

"Look what the cat dragged in. Coffee's hot."

Linc walked inside and filled a mug. He didn't drink a lot of coffee these days, but having a cup with Mr. Chambers always seemed to bring back memories of the day they'd met.

One cup of coffee led him here. Mr. Chambers changed Linc's life that day.

When he stepped back outside, he took in the view. All of this belonged to Mr. Chambers, and the guy deserved it. He'd worked hard his whole life, and he deserved to sit on his back porch and rest.

Linc would be paying dues until the day he died.

It was only fair. He'd destroyed more than he could rebuild in a lifetime.

"You makin' it this mornin'?" Mr. Chambers asked.

"Barely. I stayed at the barn last night. Applejack gave us a scare."

"Jameson told me she's fine. That still the case?"

"Yep."

Mr. Chambers rocked for a few more seconds before speaking. "I saw another truck at the stables last night."

Their boss didn't miss a thing. He might spend his days at the house, but he had his finger on everything going on at the ranch.

"It was Jess."

"She can't leave a sick horse," Mr. Chambers said.

The statement didn't require a response. Jess might be rough around the edges, but she had a tender heart. She'd deny it until her dying day, but she cared more than seventy-five percent of people in the world.

"She can't leave a hurting man either," Mr. Chambers added as he took another sip of his coffee.

Linc kept his attention focused on the mountains in the distance. The pain in his chest grew from kindling to a roaring fire. "She should have better sense than that."

"You've come a long way, son, but you're not

ready yet."

Linc knew the truth when he heard it. Even Mr. Chambers knew he wasn't good enough for her. "I know."

"You can change that. It's up to you."

Linc shook his head. "There isn't anything I can do to change the past, so I guess this is as good as it gets for me."

Mr. Chambers scoffed. "You're stupider than you look."

Linc chuckled. "Thanks."

"You're missing something. Something you need."

"Need for what?" Linc asked.

"Something you need before you're ready to let her in. She knows what she wants—a man who can look to God first. A man who believes. You're not there yet."

Linc stared down into the dark coffee and swallowed the thickness in his throat. He knew there was a God. There had to be. His hang-up was on the forgiveness part. If Linc couldn't see anything that could make up for his sins, it didn't exist. If there wasn't atonement, there wasn't a way to erase it. "You're right."

"Of course I'm right, dummy. You miss one hundred percent of the chances you don't take. You're sitting around like you can't leave the pity party and fix it."

Linc looked up at his boss. "I can't fix it. I hurt a lot of people. You know that. I can't just give them back what I took."

"That's not what I'm talking about, and you know it."

"No, I don't. You don't know what it's like to have a massive list of sins."

"Oh, I don't? If you believe that, you're even stupider than I thought."

Linc huffed. "You and I aren't the same."

"We're not the same, but the Lord can look at us like we're the same. As soon as you get your head out of your behind."

Linc huffed a long exhale. The old man didn't understand. They weren't even in the same league. "If you say so."

"I do. I've got a few wise years on you. Just clean your ears out and listen this time."

"I've been listening to you this whole time! You told me to go to church, and I go."

"But you're not listening."

"I have been. I just don't get all of it. I didn't finish high school. Cut me a break. The Bible is big and confusing. You can't expect me to understand it."

"No, but I expect you to get the basics. You don't need to know every how and why. A lot of it takes a level of faith that you haven't accepted."

"I have faith," Linc said.

"You have *some* faith. So far, it's not enough. Maybe if you keep spending time with Jess you'll get it. It's black and white for her–just like she likes it. If she can get it, you can too."

Linc worked his jaw from side to side. He trusted Mr. Chambers, and he trusted Jess. Why couldn't he trust God?

"I'll work on it. Just–"

"Don't give up on you. I know. Been holding on for years. I'd like to see you come around before I kick the bucket."

"You're not–"

"I'm not dying any more than you are. But we all have an expiration date. It'd do you well to remember that you don't have forever to come around."

Linc propped his elbows on his knees and leaned forward. "I haven't had enough sleep for this conversation."

"Go rest. The work will be here waiting on you tomorrow."

Linc looked up at Mr. Chambers. "With all due respect, Jess is still working, and she'll just have more to do if I leave now."

"Then go. Just remember what I said."

Linc stood and headed for the kitchen to leave his cup. "I always do."

CHAPTER 25
JESS

Jess walked into the church stifling a yawn. A full twelve hours of sleep hadn't been enough to catch up, and she prayed her morning caffeine boost would kick in soon. Falling asleep during the church service was the last thing she needed.

The first thing she needed was to set things right with Linc. They'd avoided each other for a whole day, and she didn't want to miss her friend anymore.

She'd done her part, but he had to figure out forgiveness and repentance on his own. Hopefully, she'd at least gotten through to him a little bit.

Paul and Vera sat on the far end of a pew on the right side of the sanctuary, and Jess headed toward them. They were the only two people who hadn't been giving her unsolicited dating advice, and she appreciated the break.

Today, she didn't want to talk to anyone about anything. She'd done enough hemmin' and hawin' over Linc, and Sunday was a day of rest.

Paul and Vera were a lot like Linc and Jess. They enjoyed each other's company, but everyone at the ranch wondered if the two had more than friendly feelings for one another. If they did, neither had spoken up about it. They seemed to just like being around each other.

Jess took the seat beside Vera who said a friendly good morning and nothing else.

Jess's shoulders relaxed. She might just get some peace.

Then a tingling in the back of her neck made her turn around. Linc was walking in wearing his Sunday best–a nice shirt, dark-wash jeans, and his good boots.

Drat. Of course, he looked well rested and handsome.

When he looked up, his gaze locked with hers, and she froze. Why did she have such drastic reactions to him? He walked in a room and her adrenaline spiked enough to trigger her freeze response.

And of course he was headed her way. She couldn't be lucky enough to spend a day without thinking about him. He was everywhere she turned. In the barn, in the dining hall, at church.

She liked having him around, but she was also

still confused about their conversation in the barn. Why couldn't he see himself the way she saw him?

She'd had plenty of time to think about what he told her, and while he'd confessed to stealing, lying, and burning things down, the unknown that surrounded his confession made her mind wander to the worst things. If he'd been in prison, there had to be a major crime attached to it.

When Brett heard Thea was in trouble with her family, Linc had jumped in the truck without a second thought. Knowing Thea's family didn't play games, he'd gone accepting he might have to stare down the barrel of a gun or choose to pull the trigger himself.

Had he pulled the trigger before? Not for practice or sport but for evil or self-defense?

Linc took the seat beside her and whispered, "Good morning."

"Good morning."

"How are you feeling?" He pointed to his side.

"Better. It only hurts when I cough or sneeze now."

Linc nodded. "It took me about a month to get over it when I bruised my ribs."

Jess tilted her head. Now he was offering free information. What changed?

"How did you get hurt?"

The music minister approached the podium and

addressed the congregation. "It's a beautiful day to be in the Lord's house."

Linc turned his attention to the front of the room, and she'd never know whether he'd meant to tell her or would have avoided her question had the service not saved him from the talk.

Trying her best to listen to the message, she found herself praying for guidance. Linc was right beside her, and she wanted to help him see his worth, but no one could make him do it.

She'd considered smacking some sense into him, but violence wasn't condoned by the church.

After church, everyone from the ranch met at the dining hall for lunch. Jameson and Ava were the only ones missing, and they hadn't been at church either.

Jess had just finished her chili when Hadley stood and clinked a fork against her water glass. "May I have your attention please. If your name isn't Remi or Colt, please meet me in the dance hall in fifteen minutes."

Colt whined. "Why am I not invited?"

Hadley made a gesture of zipping her lips.

Remi rested a hand on her belly and elbowed Colt. "They're planning us a baby shower."

Colt's eyes widened, and he mouthed "Oh."

Jess took her plate to the dump tray and headed for the door in the back of the dining hall leading to the dance hall.

Hadley whistled loudly, turning everyone's heads. "Lincoln North, get your broody behind to the dance hall."

Everyone chuckled as Linc stood in the doorway. He was probably contemplating how far he could get before Hadley caught him.

"Now!" she said, pointing toward the other door.

Jess found a seat in the dance hall. Hadley had gone all out for the planning meeting. The chairs were placed in rows in front of a white board on an easel.

Linc took the seat beside Jess but didn't say anything as Hadley went over the dos and don'ts of the combined shower for Jameson, Ava, Colt, and Remi. They'd all decided to move up the timeline for the shower, since Ava had been put on bedrest and was now considered high risk.

"Is everyone clear on the expectations and duties?" Hadley asked.

"Yes, and now I'm hungry again," Brett said as he stood and headed back toward the dining hall.

Linc stretched his legs out beside Jess. "I'm headed to the pack storage room. You want a ride if you're headed to the barn?"

Jess stood and stretched her back. "Sure, thanks."

Maybe things weren't changing, but the urgency she'd been feeling lately was only heightened by Linc's confession. It was one thing to assume he was okay, but now that she'd had a glimpse of his internal struggles, she couldn't just ignore it.

She followed Linc to his truck and got in. They'd driven the stretch from the dining hall to the barn dozens of times without speaking a single word. This ride wasn't any different, until he parked at the stables.

Instead of getting out, he shifted into park and sat there. "I don't have to go, do I?"

"To the baby shower? You definitely do. If I have to go, you'd better be there."

Linc chuckled. "Maybe it won't be so bad knowing I'm not the only one suffering."

"And you'll have another wallflower to hang out with."

Thankfully, a baby shower wasn't a social event where people were expected to show up with a date. If Linc asked her to go to another event like Ridge and Cheyenne's wedding, she'd have to tell him no.

They weren't on the same paths, and acting like they were would only make things harder later.

Linc grabbed his hat off the dash. "Brett is going to pester me to death if I go."

"I don't want to hear your complaining. He's my brother, which means he bothers me ten times more than you."

Linc looked out the front window of the truck.

"Hmm. Guess it's a good thing I don't have to worry about that."

"You don't have siblings?" Jess asked.

"One that I know of, but probably more."

The answer had come so easily. Maybe Linc shared information better in small doses.

"Really?"

"We were separated in the foster system. Last I heard, he was in jail in Atlanta." Linc clicked his tongue behind his teeth. "It runs in the family."

"You're not like that."

Linc's jaw tightened, and he didn't agree with her or deny it.

"You might end up with a secret sister like I did. I have to say, Emerson is not the sister I would have ever expected."

"The two of you are a lot alike," Linc said.

Jess opened her mouth to protest, but he was right. Emerson was as hardheaded as Jess was, and it was one of the things that Jess liked about her new sister. She didn't pretend to be anything except what she was. Take it or leave it.

Jess reached for her own hat in the seat beside her and didn't look up at Linc. "You know, she asked about you. She wanted to know if you were single."

Linc turned to look at her, but she didn't look up. She couldn't. He'd see the truth.

"And what did you tell her?" he asked.

"I don't remember. I was too busy seeing red."

There. She said it. It was the truth, but she didn't know what it meant. If she didn't know, then neither would he.

Linc propped an arm on the steering wheel and the other on the seat beside her. "Why would that make you mad?"

Why did it make her mad? She didn't know because it didn't make sense. "I'm not good at piecing out my emotions," she finally admitted. It was the truth, but would he accept it?

Linc leaned back in his seat. "Fair enough." He put his hat on and opened the truck door. "Let's get to work."

Breathing a sigh of relief, she got out of the truck. Finally, something she understood.

CHAPTER 26

JESS

J ess walked Liberty around the indoor arena. The dapple gray was fairly new to the ranch, but her training progress had been better than expected.

"You're a really good listener," Jess whispered.

The horse followed until Jess stepped to the side. With clicks and commands, Liberty completed every training exercise.

Thea walked up and propped a hand on her hip as she reached out to stroke Liberty with the other. "She's a really good one."

"I think she'll be ready for the trail rides. Mr. Chambers said a new wrangler starts next week. I'm hoping he'll be a good match for her."

"You think she's strong enough to carry the packs?" Thea asked.

"She will be. Once the weather warms up, I'll up her training."

"We only have a few weeks," Thea said.

"Why does it feel like this season is rushing toward me?"

"Because you took almost a week off when you got injured. Well, I'm not sure showing up at the barn and giving orders is exactly taking off, but you didn't do much physical labor."

Jess huffed. "Don't remind me about that." Those few days of "rest" were tough. She liked working, and being told to stay away from work went against her instincts.

Footfalls behind them made both women turn. Jameson walked toward them with a tablet resting on one arm.

"Just the people I wanted to see," Jameson said. "And the horse."

"What's up?" Thea asked.

Jameson unlocked the tablet. "We need to send out a clean-up crew to the Red Canyon campsite. Jess, I need you and Liberty. You still think she's ready?"

"I do."

"We were just talking about that," Thea added.

"That means you and Brett will need to stay to get things ready here. It'll be a sixty-hour week for both of you."

Thea nodded once. "We can do that."

Jameson poked at the tablet with a stylus. "Jess, you'll take Liberty. Linc will have Thunder. Paul will have Bolt. I think you'll need two or three pack mules, but I'll verify that with Paul."

Jess gasped a little at Linc's name on the list. It had been a while since she'd been on a trail ride with Linc, and only Paul had been to the Red Canyon site. It was secluded, and they'd dropped it from the trail ride schedule a few years ago when the last foreman retired. Jameson had been overwhelmed when he took over, and the best thing to do had been to minimize the workload.

"Is Thane coming?" Jess asked, trying to push Linc from her mind.

"I assume he will. Do you think Liberty will have a problem with Thane?"

Paul's wolf dog was as gentle as they come, but the best horses could get spooked by a dog that big if he got riled up.

"I think it'll be fine. I'll ask Paul to bring him around more while I'm training Liberty."

"Good. Things should be thawed from the last freeze, but we'll give it a few more days. You think you can be ready to leave Monday morning?"

"Yep."

Jameson locked the tablet. "Great. I'll get this on the schedule."

Thea waved as Jameson left and whispered, "Ava must be bad off if Jameson is making the schedule."

"I don't want to think about it," Jess said. Worrying over Ava during the pregnancy always seemed to make her hands sweat and breaths come quicker. They were two of the signs her doctor told her signaled an anxiety attack, but whatever it was, she didn't like it.

Thea hummed. "Okay then. Let's talk about you and Linc."

Jess tugged on Liberty's lead. "Nope."

Thea fell into step beside the horse. "I'm serious. You think this is a good idea? I've noticed some tension between you two."

"There's no tension."

Lie. Lie. Lie.

"I know you two don't talk a lot as a rule, but you've been antsy, and he's been broodier than usual."

"I'm not antsy, and he's not broody. I don't even know what that means."

Thea observed Liberty as they kept walking. "If you say so. I'm here if you need to talk."

Jess scrunched her nose. "I don't like talking."

"Ha! That's not news, but sometimes it helps."

Pushing Linc out of her mind was more difficult than usual. She wanted to focus on Liberty, but Linc kept taking over her thoughts.

"It's not like this is the first trail ride I've been on with Linc. We've been doing this for years, and we work well together."

"No one is questioning that," Thea said. "I know it's hard for you to name your feelings, and I'm sure sorting through whatever this is with Linc is extra tough."

"There's nothing going on with Linc," Jess whispered, painfully aware that there truly wasn't anything going on.

Thea sighed. "I know you've done this before, and I know you've done it with him. But the two of you will be in close quarters for an extended period of time. You think you can do that without sharing the truth about your feelings?"

"Yes. I do it all the time, and I can't speak for his emotional state, but I've got mine covered."

"Both of you are emotionally constipated," Thea said.

"I am not constipated," Jess retorted. "Why are we talking about bowel obstructions?"

Thea chuckled. "You and Linc are so much alike."

Jess clicked her tongue and gave Liberty another command. They were a lot alike. They'd grown up not knowing love and rebelling against the injustice of the world. They'd handled their anger differently, but they'd both made mistakes and ended up here. "That's not a bad thing."

"It's not. It's a good thing. I love how you two understand each other, and you don't even have to say much to communicate. It's like the two of you have mastered the art of communication."

Oh, how wrong Thea was. Jess was intentionally hiding her growing feelings for Linc, and Linc was doing everything he could to keep her from knowing things about his past.

He had every right to keep things to himself, but it still hurt that he didn't want to let her in.

Maybe she had to give more of herself. If she told him about her past, he might feel better about talking to her.

"Hey, don't worry about it," Thea whispered. "You'll figure things out. I'll be praying about it."

"The Lord doesn't care about my emotional constipation," Jess said.

"See, that's where you're wrong. He does." Thea waved a hand over her head as she turned and headed toward the tack room. "See you tomorrow."

Jess offered Liberty a treat and led her back to the pasture. Burgundy trotted over and nuzzled her, begging for a treat too. Jess handed one over and smoothed a hand over her side.

"I can go on a trail ride and not do something stupid. Right?"

Even Thea knew something was up, and Jess had known her the least amount of time. Surely, the other workers on the ranch had noticed her feelings too.

If she'd been walking around while her friends whispered behind her back, did Linc know too? How could any of them know when she didn't even know what she was feeling?

Maybe she needed to take Thea up on the offer to talk. As soon as the thought entered her mind, her stomach revolted.

No. No talking. At least not with anyone except Linc.

They had things to do. The season was almost here, and they had more work to do than they had hours in the day. She didn't have time to date, but she didn't have time to lose her mind over Linc either.

Too bad her mind didn't get the message to calm down. She needed to figure everything out before Monday morning.

CHAPTER 27

LINC

The frozen ground crunched with every step of the horses as they climbed the steady hill. The edge of Red Canyon peeked through the mix of bare and evergreen trees to their right. They'd been traveling for hours, and for once, the silence was heavy, despite the forest sounds.

"See? It's really pretty up here."

Jess had said the same thing in different words three times already, but she wasn't talking to him. Once, she addressed Liberty by name, so neither Linc nor Paul had responded to her comments yet.

He didn't blame her for favoring a chat with a horse over him. He had things to say, but none of them were about the scenery.

I miss you so much it hurts.

You're so much better than I am.

I'm not worthy, but please love me anyway.

Linc let his shoulders sag just an inch. That last one would go over really well. What kind of woman wanted a begging wimp?

He'd never been that guy, but everything was different with Jess. Thankfully. Thoughts of how he'd treated every other woman who had crossed his path between the ages of fourteen and twenty-one made the hair on the back of his neck stand on end.

"I met with a couple of the new guys yesterday," Paul said, throwing them into a conversation out of the blue. "Wes Jenkins is coming in from Texas. He has plenty of experience, so he shouldn't be hard to train. Austin Roberts is off the rodeo circuit. Said he's gettin' too old to keep gettin' bucked."

"I don't blame him. You couldn't pay me to get on a bronc or a bull," Linc said.

Paul scoffed. "I know what you mean. Not even in my younger days."

"I heard Bethany is coming back," Jess added.

Bethany had worked the check-in office last year, and Linc avoided her at all costs. She talked more in a minute than Jess did in a week.

"We're getting a new evening activities director too. Any news about that one?" Jess asked.

Paul hummed like he was thinking. "No, but I think Everly and Linda are in charge of those interviews. I heard they're getting a few new assistants to help with the weddings too."

Paul's phone rang, and he answered, "Hello."

Paul was quiet for a while before grunting something that sounded like an acknowledgment. When he hung up the call, he stayed quiet.

A quarter of a mile up the mountain, Paul finally spoke. "Ava's having contractions."

Jess's low gasp behind Linc confirmed his fears.

"It's too early," Jess said.

"Jameson said it could be a false alarm or Braxton Hicks contractions. I don't know what that means, but he said if it's that, then it's okay."

None of it sounded okay to Linc. "Do you need to go?"

"Jameson said he'd keep me posted."

"Glad we brought the satellite phones so we could get phone calls," Jess said quietly.

No one spoke again until they reached the first site. Aside from basic assignments, they didn't talk much through the rest of the day either.

The first campsite was in fairly good shape. The Red Canyon trail was a four-day ride round trip, and Blake and Ridge had cleared the trail to the first site last year. They'd passed a few obstructions on the way in, but nothing more than they could handle.

The clearing where they'd be setting up camp was another story. The forest had reclaimed the land, and a dead tree had fallen across the entrance.

Paul and Linc got to work clearing the tree first, moving sections of the trunk to the tree line. Jess picked up sticks and fallen branches after rebuilding the fire pit with the old stones.

Once the fire she built was tending itself well, she grabbed two buckets. "I'm going to get water."

Linc watched her disappear into the trees and brush heading west. Fisting his hands at his side, he pushed against the urge to follow her.

"She'll be fine," Paul said. "I think we all learned a lesson after Ava fell in the creek a few years ago."

Linc let loose the heavy breath he'd been holding. Jess was smart. She could handle herself in the woods for a few minutes.

"How's she doing?" Linc asked as he picked up the ax.

"Jameson messaged and said things are still the same. They're still at the doctor's office." Paul worked for a few more minutes before propping his ax next to a stump. "Keep her in your prayers."

Linc nodded. "I'll do that." He'd already made a commitment to pray and study the Bible more. Mr. Chambers's kick in the pants had knocked something loose in Linc's brain.

If he wanted to understand God, he had to put in the legwork.

Jess came back and gave the horses water and tended the fire before making another trip to the creek. She had water boiling within the hour and had oatmeal ready soon after.

Linc's stomach growled when the warm maple smell hit his nose.

Paul rested his ax over his shoulder. "I think that's our cue to stop for dinner."

Jess was washing a bowl of blueberries when Paul and Linc put their tools away. She pointed to a bag next to her. "Can you give the horses and mules some carrots?"

Linc picked up the bag and headed for the horses that grazed on the far side of the camp. Thunder tried to knock him over to get an extra carrot, and Liberty hesitated before accepting hers. She was a well-trained horse, but she'd gotten so close to Jess that she was wary of anyone else.

When he returned to the fire pit, Jess handed him a bowl of oatmeal along with a plate of blueberries and beef jerky.

"Thanks," Linc said as he took the food. He didn't have anything against Vera's cooking, but he hadn't been this hungry in a while, and the smell of Jess's oatmeal had his nose tingling.

She jerked her head to the chairs she'd set up. "Take a load off."

They ate in silence until Paul's phone rang. He put the empty bowl aside to pull his phone out of his pocket.

Linc gripped the bowl in his hands like it was a lifeline. Knowing Ava and the baby might be in trouble had stirred up an uneasiness in him. He'd be losing his mind if he was in Jameson's shoes, or Paul's, or Mr. Chambers's.

He listened as Paul gave grunts and asked simple questions. Linc purposely avoided looking Jess's way. She had to be upset, and he didn't know what to do to help her or anyone else in this situation.

Paul hung up the call and rubbed a hand over his face. He'd aged ten years in the last six hours. "She's still at the hospital. They admitted her to keep an eye on her condition. They've given her steroids that are supposed to help the baby's lungs develop in case..."

Jess stood and walked to Paul, who kept his head down. She knelt at his feet and bowed her head. Linc couldn't hear her words, but her whispered prayer sent chills up his arms and neck.

Life was hanging in the balance, and there wasn't anything he or anyone else could do about it.

Jess's prayer got louder. Her bold words were so sure.

Of course, she would stand firm when things were crumbling around her. She had the faith he needed.

Mr. Chambers's words came back to him. He had to learn from Jess. She knew what she was doing.

And so did the Lord. Jess didn't pray for everything to work out perfectly. She prayed His will would be done and they'd all have the strength to endure it.

It was the most selfless thing he'd ever heard in his life. When he wanted to scream and demand things go the way he wanted, Jess anchored her feet in her faith and doubled down.

When she finished the prayer, she stood and patted Paul's shoulder. The older man wiped his eyes.

Paul cleared his throat and stood. "I'll start on the tents."

Linc and Jess gave him a few minutes alone while they finished eating. Jess cleaned up dinner while Linc picked up with Paul as they set up the second tent.

Jess returned from the creek when Paul and Linc finished up.

"Thanks for putting up my tent," she said. "I'll make breakfast in the morning."

"I won't say no to that," Paul said. His words were low and drawn out. They'd all had a long day, but Paul had to be feeling the worst of it.

"Night," Jess said as she slung her pack over her shoulder and ducked into her tent.

Linc doused the fire and locked up the food before grabbing his pack. He didn't mind sharing a tent with Paul. He'd expected complete silence, but he might get more than he bargained for tonight.

Once Paul had changed into his night clothes, Linc took his turn getting ready for bed.

They made up their bedding and got settled

before Paul grabbed the lantern. "You mind if I leave this on low for a little bit?" He held up a Bible in his other hand.

Linc kicked off his blanket. "Go ahead. I'll get mine too." He reached into his pack and grabbed the heavy Bible. It was an old one Mr. Chambers had given him when he first arrived, and he hadn't spent much time with it since.

Linc sat up and opened it, flipping through some pages looking for a place to start. The passages he paused on all seemed too complicated, so he kept flipping.

The verse Jess had written on the board last week jumped into his mind. What was it? 1 Peter? He flipped to that book and scanned until he found the verse. Then he started at the beginning of chapter four.

Jess knew what she was doing. This was exactly what he'd been looking for. He'd never heard sin explained in terms of the flesh and the world that way.

Atonement, repentance, redemption. It was all here, and it made sense.

He'd been judged by men, but he had judgment from God to look forward to, and for once, it wasn't so scary. If the Lord knew his heart, maybe he was on the right path.

Love covers a multitude of sins. It made sense now. Linc was making changes in his life, but that wasn't the end of the story. He had to let the Lord make changes too.

Mr. Chambers said the same thing. Linc didn't have all the time in the world to fix things. He had to start today.

CHAPTER 28

JESS

J ess poured hot water over the coffee grounds. The smell would definitely wake the men.

Then again, they'd worked until the sun went down yesterday. It wouldn't be bad if they slept in.

What was happening to her, and why was she getting soft?

There was stirring in the men's tent, and she turned at the zipping.

Oh no. She shouldn't have done that.

Linc stepped out of the tent wearing nothing but his jeans and socks.

Yes, his abdomen was on full display, and it was glorious.

Jess jerked her attention away. What was she doing?

Coffee!

She snuck a glance his way because she was only human. He stuck his feet into the boots right outside the tent and raised up, stretching his arms over his head.

Jess growled. Actually growled. Why did he look like a perfectly sculpted male model two minutes after rolling out of bed?

Not even a bed. He'd slept on the ground. He'd probably had rocks sticking in his back like she had, but he looked as fresh as a daisy.

At least, she thought that was how the figure of speech was supposed to be used. She had no idea if daisies were fresh or not.

Linc was not enticed by the smell of her coffee. At least not yet because he walked straight into the woods behind the tent.

Half a minute later, Linc returned and slipped back into his tent. He reemerged pulling a shirt down over his abs.

Great. Now she wouldn't blubber like a fool when he greeted her.

"Morning," he said with a grin as he leaned over the pan of bacon by the fire. "Smells good."

Note to self: Bacon is effective Linc bait.

"Good morning."

Paul emerged from the tent and whistled for Thane. The wolf dog sprang from the trees at his friend's call.

"You ready for a walk?" Paul asked.

"I think he's already been walking this morning," Jess said.

"I need a walk." Paul stretched his back from side to side. "I'm getting too old to sleep on the ground."

"Breakfast is ready when you are," Jess called to him as he started jogging down the trail they'd taken yesterday.

"You think he's okay?" Jess asked when he was out of earshot.

"Don't know. He seemed okay when we went to bed last night."

Jess sighed. "Has he heard from Jameson this morning?"

"Probably not or he would have filled us in."

"Maybe that's why he needed a run. To get his mind off of it."

"No, he runs with Thane every morning."

Jess's eyes widened. "Every morning?"

"Unless the snow is too deep. I've seen them running in the rain and snow before," Linc said as he poured a cup of coffee.

"Wow. That's intense."

"Probably why he's still fit for a man pushing fifty."

"Probably why he hasn't throat punched some of the stupid wranglers he has to work with."

Linc coughed as he took the first sip of coffee. He chuckled as he wiped his mouth. "Ain't that the truth. I gave him my fair share of grief when I started too."

"You mean to tell me you weren't perfect." Jess placed a hand over her heart. "I had no idea."

Linc rolled his eyes, took another sip of coffee, and hummed. "Hey, this is really good."

"You sound surprised."

"I'm not. You're good at almost everything."

Jess held up a hand. "I'm not good at making polite conversation."

"Are you saying our conversations aren't polite, Miss Patton?"

Oh no. Why did his voice change? Why was he looking at her like that?

Was he flirting?

Her lungs froze, and every muscle in her body tensed. Despite the fear of passing out due to oxygen loss, Jess couldn't help but bask in the warmth of Linc's stare.

"I don't think either of us have been accused of being too polite," she finally said.

Linc rubbed his jaw and looked up at the bare trees. "Polite. I'll have to give that a try sometime."

"Don't hurt yourself," Paul said as he jogged back into the clearing.

"That was fast," Jess said, offering him a mug.

Paul held up a hand to decline it. "I just heard from Jameson. They can't stop her labor, and they're preparing for her to deliver."

Jess stood. "Now?"

"Soon," he said. "I might be able to make it back if I leave now."

Linc stood and set his coffee on a rock. "I'll ready the horse while you pack up."

"I'll put some food together for you to eat on the way," Jess said.

They had Paul ready to go within the next half hour. They'd have to leave some things behind at the campsite in order to make it to the next stop. Thankfully, they'd have a cabin to sleep in next, but the state of the cabin after years unattended promised plenty of work.

Linc and Jess watched Paul ride off with Thane leading the way.

"Looks like it's just the two of us now," Linc said.

Jess tilted her chin up to glance at him. "We can handle it."

"That's not what I'm worried about," Linc said before turning around and heading for the tent. "I'm going to finish clearing the tree line."

What had Linc worried? She didn't even know what was gnawing at her insides, but it was something between worry for Ava and the baby and spending unsupervised time with Linc. They didn't have a buffer anymore, and their journey promised plenty of opportunities to mess things up.

"I'll take the horses to the creek," Jess said as she headed for Liberty.

One horse at a time. Liberty was new and needed the most guidance, so they set out first.

She crouched on the bank and filled the bucket she'd brought along as Liberty drank. A knot twisted tighter in Jess's stomach. What would happen if Ava had the baby too early? She knew little to nothing about babies and pregnancies, and the unknown only served to fuel her concerns.

After ten minutes, the sounds in the woods changed. The birds quieted, and even the sounds of the bugs died.

Jess reached for her bear spray. They were coming out of hibernation now, and a creek was a prime meeting spot for wildlife.

She'd just settled her finger on the trigger when the crunching of leaves revealed Linc and Thunder coming out of the trees.

Jess breathed a sigh of relief. "You scared me. I thought you were working at the campsite."

"Yeah, well I got worried about you."

"I'm fine. I have the bear spray."

"Bear spray doesn't ease my concerns when you're involved," he said as he led Thunder to the creek. His left hand gripped a shotgun at his side.

Jess sat on a boulder, and Linc crouched beside her, resting the gun on the ground.

"I can't stop thinking about Ava," Jess finally said.

"They'll let us know if anything happens. Paul said he'd keep us updated."

"Paul is probably gonna be promoted to foreman until all this stuff with Ava and the baby is settled. Mr. Chambers could do it, but he's not getting around too well right now. The season is starting in a few weeks, and we need all hands on deck."

Linc hung his head. "All this is hitting at once."

"Maybe we can get some friends from town to come help when they can."

Rubbing his jaw, Linc sat quietly for a moment. "I bet Asa would help. Maybe Dawson Keller too."

"What about Beau Lawrence?" Jess asked.

"Yeah. Maybe we can get the preacher to announce it at church that we need some extra hands."

"I'm sure they'll all want to help as soon as they find out about Ava," Jess said.

Liberty and Thunder stopped drinking and stared at the forest on the other side of the creek. Jess looked around. The noises hadn't returned since Linc and Thunder arrived.

Linc slowly stood. "Something's out there."

Liberty pushed off with her front legs and darted up the path behind them. Thunder stepped back and threw his head around.

Jess scrambled off the rock to run after Liberty, but Linc gripped her arm. "Don't move."

The heavy beat of a drum pounded in her ears as

the grass on the other side of the creek moved slightly. Something crouched in the thickets.

"Mountain lion," Linc whispered as he stepped in front of her, blocking her view of the predator.

He'd barely got the words out when the big cat pounced, clearing the creek with its focus locked on Linc.

CHAPTER 29

LINC

L inc raised the shotgun and fired straight at the mountain lion, praying the shaking in his hands didn't cause him to miss.

The animal continued rushing toward him, and Linc stepped to the side just in time, swinging an arm behind him to push Jess out of the way too.

The mountain lion landed on the edge of the bank and didn't move. Jess let out a strained gasp behind him.

"Is it..."

"It's gone," Linc said. The electricity pulsing in his veins didn't let up, even though the danger was over. The arm outstretched in front of Jess shook.

It had come too close. Linc had been too close to losing her. He'd been in his fair share of life-or-death situations, but none of them had shaken him like this.

Understanding dawned on him. He'd felt an undeniable urge to follow Jess to the creek. Had God led him here with a purpose?

Jess's breaths came in a quick, shallow rhythm. "I can't believe it."

Linc looked over his shoulder and turned to her, dropping the gun beside him. "Are you okay?"

"Yeah. I'm fine. Thanks to you."

She was shaking too, and he didn't hesitate as he wrapped his arms around her shoulders. Her arms slid around his waist, and he tightened his hold.

He wasn't sure how long they stood there, but he didn't loosen his grip on her until her shaking stopped and her muscles relaxed.

"Are you okay?" he asked as he slid his hands down her arms.

"Yeah. Just shaken up. Whew." She blew out a long breath.

Linc turned around to look at the cat that almost got them. "We'll have to get rid of that. It'll lead other predators here, and it's too close to the camp."

Jess wiped her eyes and cleared her throat. "Probably need to burn it."

Linc nodded. "I'll take care of that."

She propped her hands on her hips and stared at the path where Liberty had made her escape. "Looks like we're up a creek without a horse."

"It's up a creek without a paddle," Linc explained.

Jess tilted her head and furrowed her brow. "Why would we need a paddle?"

Linc grinned and picked up the gun. She was so cute he wanted to squeeze her again. He'd never thought of a grown woman as cute before, but Jess had an innocent quality that made it impossible not to like her.

"If you'll take Thunder back to camp, I'll be there shortly, and we can go look for Liberty together."

Jess nodded and reached for Thunder's lead. "Be careful."

"You too."

After what just happened, he didn't want her walking away from him again. He wanted her in his sights at all times. Two were better than one, right?

When he returned to the camp, Jess had lunch ready. They'd planned to be back on the trail in the early afternoon, but that timeline didn't look promising.

She lifted her head when she heard him coming. "Any news?"

Linc shook his head. "Maybe no news is good news."

"I hope so," Jess whispered. "I hate not knowing. And I hate having so many…emotions about it." She waved her hand in the air like emotions could be swatted away.

Linc knelt by her seat and rested a hand on her knee. "It's okay to be upset, but they might be fine.

We don't need to break down before there's something to break down about."

The little crinkle between her brows eased. "You're right. It's silly to worry this soon."

"No sign of Liberty?" he asked.

"No, and I want to go looking for her as soon as possible. I didn't want to set out on my own."

"That was a good idea. I think we should stick together out here. We'll go look for her as soon as we eat."

They ate quickly and set out on foot looking for the stray horse. They followed the path they'd already taken, hoping she'd stuck to familiar trails.

Jess stepped lightly behind him. "I thought she was ready," she said.

"She is. Almost any horse would get spooked by a mountain lion."

"Yeah, but on a trail ride, we don't usually have extra men to go out looking for a horse. She needs to be more reliable."

"And she's pretty stuck on you," Linc pointed out. "You think she'll trust anyone else enough to take her out?"

"Maybe. We just have so much to do before the season starts."

"When it rains, it pours," Linc said.

"What does that mean?" Jess asked.

"That when things get bad, they tend to get worse."

Jess hummed. "I don't like that saying."

Linc chuckled. "That makes two of us, but it seems to apply to us right now."

Jess stopped, and Linc stopped too. He turned to watch her. She tilted her head to the side before turning it to the right. "That way." She pointed to the east.

Linc led the way, and they found Liberty standing calmly beneath a Douglas fir tree.

"She looks like she didn't mean to worry us sick," Jess said with plenty of sass.

"We found her. That's all that matters." There had been a good chance they wouldn't have found the horse, but he didn't point that out.

Jess reached for Liberty and hugged her. "Don't run off again, okay?" She whispered lower, "Linc will protect us if we stay with him."

Hm. When Jess said nice things about him, his chest started to warm from the inside out.

He was also in danger of following her around like a puppy for the rest of his life, but that was a secret he planned to keep.

"Let's get back to camp. Looks like we're spending another night here," Jess said.

"Sorry. I know you're looking forward to the cabin."

"Just sturdy walls around while I sleep. After seeing how big that mountain lion was, I might not sleep tonight."

He hadn't thought about the lasting effects of the attack. A tent flap separating Jess from danger like that didn't make him happy either.

They both stayed busy until sundown, and they made good progress on the things they'd planned to do on their return trip. At least the time wasn't wasted.

When they finished dinner, Jess disappeared into her tent and came out with a blanket over her shoulders. The chill of winter hadn't relinquished its hold to spring yet, and the nights were harsh.

She handed him a blanket too, and he took it, moving to a seat closer to her beside the fire. They sat quietly for a few minutes, watching the crackling and sparks in the fire against the darkness that surrounded them.

Linc stared at the flames wondering why he'd used them so irresponsibly in the past. Fire had its purposes, but he'd wielded it all wrong.

"I need to know about Ava," Jess finally said.

Linc pulled his phone from his pocket and dialed Stella's phone number. He put the call on speaker before she answered.

"Hey! You okay?" she said in greeting.

"We're fine. I'm out on the Red Canyon Trail with Jess. Any update on Ava and the baby?"

Stella sucked in a breath before answering. "She had the baby."

"She did?" Jess asked in a high-pitched voice. "Is he okay? Is she okay?"

"Ava's fine. She's shaken up, but she's physically fine. The baby is stable for now, but he has quite a few medical issues to work through."

Jess rested her hand over her mouth, so Linc picked up the conversation to give her a few minutes to herself.

"Did Paul make it back in time?"

"He did, but no one has been allowed to see the baby yet. He's in the NICU."

"I don't know what that is," Linc said.

"Intensive care for babies," Stella explained.

Linc hung his head. "What are the doctors saying? What are the odds?"

"They keep saying they don't know yet. They're still trying to make sure he stays stable."

"Does he have a name?" Jess asked.

"They said his name is Ronald James. They want to call him Ron."

The firelight lit up Jess's smile. "They named him after Mr. Chambers."

"Yep. And James is Paul's middle name. I think Ava struggled a lot with that one because she loved the man who raised her too. But Paul missed out on Ava's life, and she's grateful Paul gets to see her kid grow up."

"It's a good name," Jess said.

"Agreed." Hopefully, they'd get to meet the little guy soon.

"Paul is gonna pick things up around here for Jameson and Ava. He's interviewing four more hands in the morning. People are coming in looking for seasonal jobs."

"Good. We need all the help we can afford," Linc said.

"We'll handle it," Stella said. "Times are testin' us, but we'll make it through. You two say your prayers. We need 'em."

"Yes, ma'am," Linc said. "Will you keep us updated?"

"I sure will. You two just stay safe out there."

Jess's gaze locked with his. They'd keep the mountain lion encounter to themselves for a while. "Thanks."

They sat in silence for a few minutes before Jess started laughing. She tried to control it at first, then the sounds bubbled out.

"What are you laughin' about?"

She wiped her eyes and gasped for breath. "I was just thinking about naming my son after my dad."

"I thought you didn't like your dad." At least she hadn't had anything good to say about him. And thinking about Jess with a little boy was treading into dangerous waters.

"I couldn't stand him. I would never name my

kid after him. I couldn't call my kid Oscar with a straight face."

Linc sat up straighter. "What's wrong with Oscar?"

She shook her hands. "Nothing. It just sounds like an adult name. People like to give babies nicknames, and I have no idea what cutesy name they'd come up with for Oscar."

"I didn't know your dad's name," Linc said.

Jess's giggles were wearing off. They were probably induced by lack of sleep. "I don't like talking about him."

Linc didn't blame her. He'd heard a few stories, and none of them were good.

"He thought I was a waste of space because I was a girl. He wanted boys for free labor. He had half a dozen illegal side jobs, and he needed the extra hands. He did get some use out of me. I was his punching bag when he got mad."

She said the words like she was detailing the weather forecast, but all of the blood drained from Linc's face. "He what?"

"Brett always tried to help me." She scoffed. "How do you think he learned how to fight? He wasn't scared of anything, even back then."

"I'm glad he's dead," Linc said through gritted teeth.

"You and me both. Apparently, he was cheating on his wife too because I have a sister to show for it.

He was just a terrible man. He thought the world was his playground."

Linc felt that stab like it was meant for him. He'd treated the world like it was his in the past. He knew how easy it was to fall into the arrogant idea that he ran the place and no one could stop him.

The stupid ideology of a kid with too much anger and a big imagination.

"I don't know my dad's name," Linc said to change the subject.

"Really? Not at all?"

"Nope. I don't know my mom's either."

"Do you wish you knew?" she asked.

"What would it matter? They didn't want me, so I figured it wouldn't do me any good to want them."

Jess leaned forward, propping her elbows on her knees. "What was it like in the foster system?"

"That's not a fair question because I abused it as much as I could. I knew all of those families were either in it for the check or really trying to make a difference in kids' lives, but I treated them all the same. I did everything I could to make their lives harder."

"Why?" Jess asked quietly.

He didn't miss the note of sadness in her voice, and his confession felt more like a slow and painful death. "I didn't understand love, and I didn't recognize it when it was standing in front of me. Every time the families were good to me, I assumed they would be the ones to hurt me the most. I didn't trust anyone, and it was easier to push them away than sit quietly and get hurt again."

Linc huffed, and his warm breath billowed out like a cloud into the cold night. "I know you don't get it. I don't either. I was always mad, and it felt good to let the anger out."

"I've been angry," Jess said. "A lot. Mostly at myself. I don't know when I can trust people, so I keep testing them, but the tests never end and sometimes the trust never comes, even if they do everything right."

Linc looked up at her. She was bundled in a blanket near the fire, and he imagined her as a kid asking a grown-up to explain trust. It wasn't one of those black or white concepts that Jess understood.

He hadn't gotten it either back then. He didn't even entertain the thought of trust until Mr. Chambers picked him up at Deano's that day. If the man hadn't been so patient, Linc might still be screwing up lives every chance he got.

Jess yawned. "I think I'm past ready for bed."

Linc stood and offered her a hand. The second her warm hand touched his, all of the turmoil in his chest settled, quieting to a sedated state.

He cleared his throat and dropped her hand before he did something stupid, like latch on and never let go. "I'll put out the fire."

Jess wrapped the blanket tighter around her neck. "Good night."

"Good night." Why was his voice so low? It was like his throat wanted to close, delaying the end of his time with her.

Linc watched her until she disappeared into the tent. He had at least three more days and nights alone with her, but no amount of days with Jess would ever be enough.

CHAPTER 30

JESS

J ess sighed and tugged the blanket tight under her chin. Exhaustion sat heavy on her shoulders, but as much as she wanted to drift off into sleep, slumber was just out of reach.

After spending her life keeping people at a distance, somehow the people here had slipped their way past her barrier. Now, Jess couldn't get Ava and the baby she hadn't even laid eyes on out of her head.

How was it possible to care so much for someone who was only a few hours old? Jess didn't have any relation or real ties to the kid. Every time the worry choked her, she tried to swallow it down.

Leaves rustled outside the tent, and she squeezed her eyes shut. Too bad the darkness couldn't hide the flashback of that mountain lion pouncing at them.

She hadn't actually seen the cat flying through the air. Linc had stepped in front of her, protecting her with his broad shoulders.

But she'd seen its eyes as it crouched to pounce. The predator locking in on its target would haunt her for a while.

Jess squirmed beneath the blanket and silently prayed.

Lord, help me find peace. Help me to rest. Help Ava and the baby. Please. Please.

After holding her breath for ten seconds, she let it out. She wasn't going to be much help to Linc if she didn't get to sleep soon.

Rolling onto her back and staring up at the tent ceiling, she sighed, hoping this was the position that would allow her to relax.

"Are you huffing to get my attention?" Linc asked from the tent beside hers.

"No. Just can't sleep. Sorry."

"They're gonna be okay."

Jess scoffed. "How do you know? It sounds serious. Sometimes, things happen, and we can't stop them."

There was a beat of silence before Linc whispered, "I know."

Pinching her eyes closed, Jess tried to breathe evenly. "I hate feeling helpless. I hate...feeling."

There was rustling in Linc's tent, then soft footfalls outside. "Can I come in?"

Jess's heart pounded. Everything inside her said she trusted Linc, and her chest expanded as she took her first full breath in hours. "Yeah."

He unzipped the tent and crouched to dip inside. He carried a pillow and blanket under one arm and a lantern in the other. He set the light at her feet, casting shadows around them.

Linc tossed his pillow down beside her and spread out the blanket before lying next to her. Not one part of their bodies touched, but there was a humming warmth emanating from him as he settled beside her.

When he stopped rustling, he lay on his back just like her. After a few seconds, he turned his head toward her. The shadows distorted his features, but she could fill in the blanks. She knew his face better than she knew her own.

Linc's first words were a deep whisper, floating through the night like an early-morning fog. "Do you want me to pray?"

The breath she'd been inhaling hitched. She hadn't known what to expect, but it hadn't been that. She'd been so tied up in knots all day thinking about Ava and the baby, she hadn't stopped to wonder if he'd been worried too.

"I'd like that," she whispered back.

Linc turned toward the ceiling and closed his eyes. Jess did the same as he started to speak.

"Lord, I don't know what Ava and the baby need,

but You do. I hope they're okay and that everything gets better for them."

He paused, not daring to move for a few seconds as he gathered his thoughts. "But I know You have a plan, and we're supposed to trust it. If Your plan is different from what we want, then I'd like to ask for the strength and understanding we'll all need."

No. No. No. It couldn't happen like that. She couldn't handle it.

But Linc knew that, and he was being braver than her. They'd both seen things go wrong at different times in their lives, and it was easier to brace for impact and prepare to fall apart than ask for strength and the tools to face what was coming.

Linc swallowed hard. "And can You please give Jess some peace and let her rest?"

Oh, no. A tear snuck out and slid down her temple and into her hairline. She'd been battling the exhaustion, but Linc knew to pray.

He said a quiet amen and waited an extra beat before speaking again. "I need to get better at that."

"At what?"

"Praying. Remembering to do it when things get tough."

"You will. It took me a long time to get used to talking to God." She chuckled. "I don't like talking to anyone, but talking to someone who doesn't talk back or look down on me is...oddly comforting. It's like having a conversation with my heart."

Linc chuckled. "I like that." He nudged her shoulder. "You okay now?"

Jess nodded, shifting the shadows in the small tent. "I am. Thanks for praying."

"Anytime. You're a good influence on me. Thanks for that."

"If I'm your good influence, we might be in trouble." She rolled over onto her side, facing him. "Good night."

He sat up and fanned out his blanket before gathering it into his arms. "Good night. Don't let the bedbugs bite."

"Or the spiders, or the snakes, or the bears."

He tucked his pillow under his arm. "I'm going to pretend you didn't say any of that."

"They're probably still in their winter states," she reasoned. "But I don't care where they are. I don't want any of them."

Linc crouched at the tent opening and turned back to her. "I'll protect you. Sleep tight."

She'd been joking about creepy critters, but Linc's sure, masculine tone chased away all of her laughter. He *would* protect her. He'd already done it, though she'd never asked him to.

"I mean it," he said. "All joking aside, I would protect you with my life, so don't worry about anything, and get some sleep."

Jess's "Okay" came out weak and shaking. Linc didn't have any obligation to her, yet he'd already proven he could be trusted. He put himself in the line of fire to make sure she was safe.

He cared when he didn't have to–something her own flesh and blood hadn't done.

As he slipped out of her tent and settled into the other one, Jess bundled the blanket against her chest and prayed, daring to hope that the Lord had a plan for her that included Linc by her side.

CHAPTER 31

LINC

L inc managed to work with Jess the entire next day without revolving around her like a satellite. They didn't say much the whole day, but he didn't get the feeling she was pulling away. Instead, her small smiles were silent assurances that she was okay, and that was all he really needed.

He'd even managed to stay away from her tent the entire night. He deserved major points for that, since having Jess right next to him made him want to drift closer.

The draw toward Jess was like an addiction. He had to keep his guard up at all times if he had any chance of resisting her.

Reading the Bible he'd brought along helped keep his mind off her. He understood about every tenth sentence, so he had to really focus to study.

His eighteen-year-old self would have burst into

a fit of laughter if anyone told him he'd be studying the Bible one day. Still, every time he thought about that guy and the things he'd done, a wave of guilt rushed up, hot and boiling as it climbed up his neck and face.

He wasn't that kid anymore. He was better. At least, he was trying to be.

The next morning, Jess woke first, and her rustling pulled him from sleep. The ache in his back pushed him out of bed, and he nodded once to Jess before disappearing down the path leading back toward the main part of the ranch.

The walking helped, and he headed back to the campsite ready to get moving to the cabin.

Jess handed him a bowl of oatmeal as she set her empty one to the side. She started packing up her tent as he scarfed down breakfast. Five minutes later, he was packing up the tools and tents while Jess strapped the bags to the mules and horses.

They hardly spoke until they were on the trail leading to the cabin. It was amazing how easily they worked together. The only other person Linc could work with in silence was Paul. Everyone else liked to chat, and while Linc didn't have anything to contribute to most conversations, he enjoyed the time without expectations.

They stopped around noon to let the horses rest and eat a quick lunch.

Jess looked around as she fed Liberty a treat.

"How far is the river?"

Linc turned his head, listening for the sound of running water. "Maybe an eighth of a mile," he said, remembering the map he'd studied before the trip. "If we keep going another quarter of a mile, it gets closer to the trail."

"Trail. That's a loose term," Jess said.

"Blake and Ridge have their work cut out for them clearing this section." The forest had encroached on the path, leaving little to go by.

Jess wiped her hands on her jeans before propping them on her hips. "You ready?"

"Ready as I'll ever be," Linc said as he mounted Thunder.

They continued on until they heard the river to their left. Tying the horses and mules to trees, they each grabbed a bucket and headed off the trail toward the water.

"How much longer do we have?" Jess asked as she pushed briars away from her legs.

"A couple of hours. Not long. We should have time to get settled before supper."

His phone dinged in his pocket, and he switched the bucket to his other hand to check the message.

"It's Stella. She said Ava was discharged, but the baby has to stay."

Jess turned to look at him over her shoulder as she walked. "For how long?"

"She didn't say."

Jess walked on for a few minutes before turning to him again, "I just hope the—" Her words cut off with a gasp as she slid, falling into a ravine and out of his sight.

"Jess!" he shouted, dropping the bucket and lunging for her as her head disappeared. He grabbed the edge of the ravine and scanned the rocky expanse for her blonde hair. His heartbeat pounded in his ears.

She lay in a crumpled heap about fifteen feet down, unmoving.

"Jess!" he shouted again as he turned and lowered himself onto the closest rock.

No. No. No. No. Please. Please. Please. Please.

He gripped a rock with one hand and searched for a foothold beneath him. "Jess, talk to me!" He didn't bother to stifle the panic in his voice. She still hadn't answered him.

Looking over one shoulder, he risked a big final leap to the bottom and braced for the impact. The ground was slanted, sending him crashing into the rock wall to his right. The pain in his shoulder didn't stop him as he scrambled toward her.

"Jess," he said as he crouched beside her, frantically assessing her for any injuries.

She slowly lifted her head and groaned. "Ouch."

"Don't move yet. Let me check you out." He rested a hand on her shoulder, easing her back down to the ground. "Easy, easy."

He brushed her hair away from her face first, then rubbed his hands over her head. No bumps, and no grunts of pain. After that, he let his hands roam over her shoulders.

"Ow. That's it," Jess said, sucking in a breath through gritted teeth.

"Your left shoulder?" he asked. "Anything else?"

She pointed. "My leg."

Her jeans were torn just below her knee, show-casing a bloody scrape on the outside of her right leg.

Linc pulled his flannel shirt over his head, then pulled off the under shirt before wrapping it around her leg. It didn't look deep enough to need stitches, but the blood was really flowing.

Jess winced a few times, and he whispered apologies over and over. Why did it have to be her who got injured? Why couldn't it have been him instead?

When the leg was wrapped, he buttoned his flannel shirt back up. Standing, he looked down the ravine both ways. "It looks like it gets shallower that way. Let me check it out, and I'll come back for you."

"I'll go with you," Jess said, trying to push up onto her arms.

Linc crouched beside her and rested a hand on her back. "Please just stay here. I can carry you."

Her left eye squinted as she eased the weight off her left arm. "Okay. You win."

If Jess was going to let him carry her, the pain had to be bad. "I'll be right back."

Linc carefully stepped through the ravine until he found a spot where it was shallow enough that he could reach to lift her out. When he got back to Jess, the color was fading from her cheeks, and her eyes looked dark.

"Stay with me, babe. I'm getting you out of here."

She didn't protest as he positioned his arms behind her back and legs, and she held on with her right arm as he stood. She really wasn't heavy. It would be easier to lift her out than he'd anticipated.

Linc found the shallow spot again and hefted her up. The edge was low enough that he could just rest her on the ground. He climbed out in a few quick movements and lifted her back into his arms.

The walk back to the trail was slow. He focused on keeping his footing while trying not to jostle Jess in his arms. He hugged her tight to his chest until they reached the horses where he set her down on the path and went to grab the first-aid kit from one of the packs.

They didn't speak when he returned. He rolled her pants up as high as he could so he could disinfect and bandage the scratch on her leg. Once he was sure the blood wouldn't soak through the bandage right away, he searched through the kit for something to make a sling for her shoulder.

"This is just great. Now I'm useless," Jess said.

Linc shook his head as he dug some strapping from the kit. "You're not useless. We'll just head back and get you checked out. Are you sure you didn't hit your head?"

"I didn't hit my head, and we're not going back. We've come too far to turn around now. We won't have time to get the cabin ready before the season."

Linc tied the sling together, focusing on anything to keep his hands from shaking. "I don't care about the cabin. You might need stitches."

"I don't need stitches. The scratch is long, but it's shallow. I've healed from worse without stitches."

"I don't want it to get infected."

Jess picked up the bottle of disinfectant and shook it. "Good thing we have something for that."

Linc wrapped the sling around her neck and fit her elbow into it. No amount of concentration could stop his hands from shaking now. "I think we should go back."

"I think we should go to the cabin," Jess said.

Linc stopped and looked her in the eye. "Please?"

"No," Jess said. "But I do need help getting on my horse."

He hung his head in his hand for a minute before offering her his arms. Protecting her injuries, he helped her to her feet.

"Are you sure about this?" he asked.

"Positive. As long as you'll take care of the scratch when the bandages need changing and let me help out during the day."

"I don't want to do that," Linc said.

"You don't want to help me?"

"No. I don't want you to help me."

"Well, tough," Jess said. She squirmed a little before Linc realized she wanted to cross her arms but couldn't.

"What about you take care of meals, and I'll do all the rest?" he asked.

She sighed, and her shoulders dropped an inch. "Fine, but only because I like doing it."

"It's a deal," Linc said before pulling her close. Careful not to touch her injured shoulder, he wrapped his arms around her and whispered, "Stop scaring me."

"I'm not scaring you," she said back. "People get hurt sometimes, and it's no big deal."

He wanted to argue with her on that point. It *was* a big deal, if only to him. The image of Jess lying lifeless in the ravine would haunt him for a while.

"Did you lose consciousness when you fell?" he asked.

"No. I just needed a minute to wrap my head around what was hurting. And I prayed a little. I wanted to be prepared for whatever injuries I had."

He ducked his chin and rested his jaw against

her hair. She was so much stronger than anyone gave her credit for.

"I prayed for you too because I knew you were going to freak out," she said.

"I didn't freak out."

"You did. A little bit."

Linc chuckled once. "Okay, maybe a little." He was still freaking out on the inside, but she didn't need to know how much the fall had shattered him.

She pulled back enough to look up at him, and her small smile had his heart racing for a different reason. She'd been drifting closer over the last few weeks, and the change between them was becoming impossible to ignore.

And he didn't want to. From the look on her face, she didn't want to fight it either.

Assured her injuries were tended and that she wasn't in too much pain, Linc released her and nodded his head toward the woods. "I'll go get water. Are you okay to hang out here for a few minutes?"

"I'm fine. I'll just be spoiling the horses," she said.

Good. Knowing she was happy and willing to take the rest she needed, Linc set out for the creek, making a note to mark the ravine on the map as soon as they reached the cabin.

CHAPTER 32
LINC

Linc sat with his back against the headboard of the twin bed. The cabin was small, but it didn't need nearly as much work as he'd expected. He'd clean out the chimney tomorrow, pull up some broken boards on the front porch, and cut some firewood.

They'd made it to the cabin a little later than they'd planned. He rebandaged her leg when they arrived, and Jess had seemed content to rest most of the evening.

It was a good thing because Linc couldn't do anything without messing something up. His hands continued to shake, causing him to drop things and spend way too much time trying to untie the knots and buckles holding the supplies in the packs.

Now, his hands had stopped shaking, but his

thoughts were still swirling. The words on the pages of the Bible were small and blurry.

He glanced over at Jess in the other twin bed. She lay on her side, facing him, but her eyes were closed in a peaceful sleep. Her light hair spread out over the pillow, and she tucked the blanket close under her chin.

His chest tightened as the fear from earlier rocked through him again. He'd never been scared of anything until Jess came along. Now, she could get a papercut, and he'd fall apart.

She was doing a really good job of acting like nothing had happened. Her breathing was even, and there wasn't a single wrinkle on her face. Her eyelashes lay peacefully against her cheeks.

Linc grinned, knowing few people got to see this side of her. This wasn't the tough barn manager, or the stern trainer, or the abrasive woman the world saw.

This was the Jess he knew—peaceful and vulnerable. She could put on a show and act like she knew the answer to everything. That's why everyone who had business at the barns at the ranch respected her.

But inside, she cared so much. He'd been staring it in the face these last few days while she worried about Ava and the baby.

He'd seen it the night he'd left with her brother too. Thea was in danger, and when Brett jumped in the truck, Linc hadn't hesitated a second before following him. No one got to harm a woman and get away with it. At least not on his watch.

There'd been a pleading in her eyes that day. He'd only caught a glimpse of it because he'd turned away as soon as he could. He couldn't see that broken and scared look on her face.

That was the day he started to wonder if she cared about him. There hadn't been any signs before that, but she'd cried for him the same way she cried for her brother, and he knew she cared about Brett.

His phone rang, and he quickly silenced it. Closing the Bible, he left it on the bed and walked as lightly as he could across the creaking wooden floor.

He stepped out onto the porch and closed the door behind him just as the phone stopped ringing.

Ridge. No one would send straight-forward Ridge to deliver bad news, so Linc returned the call and rested onto the top step on the porch.

"Hey, man. Y'all makin' it?" Ridge asked.

"As best we can. Jess took a tumble today, but she wants to finish the work here. I'm planning to hit the ground running in the morning, just in case she changes her mind when the pain comes back."

"You sure she's okay?" Ridge asked.

"No, but have you ever tried to get that woman to do anything she didn't want to? It's a firm no from her right now."

Ridge laughed. "You're right. I wouldn't go toe-to-toe with Jess. Glad to hear she's okay."

"What's the word on Ava and Ron?" Linc asked. Calling the baby he hadn't seen before by a name made everything seem even more real.

"He's hanging in there. Ava is a nervous wreck. Jameson is trying to hold it together. Paul and Mr. Chambers are holding down the fort. We took on three wranglers and another stable hand. Everly and Linda hired an assistant to help with the weddings, and Cheyenne and I got a helper for the youth program."

Linc whistled low. "That's a lot."

"We need more. The ranch is booked out. It'll be our biggest season yet."

"Are you trying to tell me we have a lot riding on getting this cabin ready?" Linc asked.

"Pretty much. I'm calling for the supplies list."

Linc pulled a notebook out of his chest pocket. "Get ready. It's a long one."

It should've been reassuring knowing Ridge and Blake could finish up any projects Linc didn't get finished, but they were running out of time. Pushing the deadlines to the last minute wasn't ideal, but it was all they had at this point.

"How's the roof?" Ridge asked. "There's a storm heading your way. It doesn't look like anything we need to worry about, but keep your eyes on the radar."

Linc pinched the bridge of his nose. "We'll hunker down. When's it supposed to hit?"

Ridge was quiet for a moment before answering. "Tomorrow afternoon, if things don't change. I'll ask Cheyenne to keep an eye on it for you. She'll give you a call when it gets closer."

"Thanks, man. I appreciate it. I better get going. Sounds like I have wood to chop as soon as the sun comes up."

"You need me to ride out? I can be there in a couple of days."

"I can handle it. Thanks for the offer though."

"Take care, man."

Linc slid the phone into his pocket and rested his head in his hands. If they had a storm coming, it might bring sleet or snow at this altitude. They needed a functional fireplace ASAP. The wood stove would be fine until tomorrow.

Jess was counting on him. The ranch was counting on him. His friends were counting on him.

The pressure should have been crushing, yet having people around who trusted him to do his job and take care of things that mattered meant he had something worth fighting for.

That's what had been missing in his life before coming here. He'd lived a life looking out for himself. He'd choose this life over the old one every time.

The scare with Jess earlier left something unsettled in his chest. She was fine. Why couldn't he convince himself to relax?

Because the nagging feeling wasn't just about Jess. It was a call from his heart.

Good grief, he was turning into a sap, but at least he was a sap who knew a call when he heard it.

Leaving his head in his hands, he whispered into the quiet night. "Okay, God. You have my attention."

He sighed and let the pressure ease as he submitted to the Lord. "You have my attention. Sorry I didn't listen before." He swallowed hard. "But You got me by the throat today. I'm glad You saved Jess because I don't know what I'd do without her. She's the woman I want in my life, but I guess You had that planned. I have to say, I like the way You work things out sometimes. She led me here.

"I've been running, but I don't want to anymore. I know You're here. I know You know better than I do, and I want that. I want to trust what You have planned for me. I want to do better. I've done things all wrong, but I want to change that."

Linc rubbed his hands over his face and clasped them in front of him. "I hear You know how to forgive people, but I've done a lot. I guess You know that. I'm ready to own up to all those things and ask if You can really forgive all that I've done. I want You in my life."

Linc sat there for a moment, breathing through the resignation taking root in his life. He wanted to hand it all over–his life, his trust, and his soul–to the Lord.

Finally, he whispered, "I'm not worthy, but please love me anyway."

He bit the inside of his cheek and lifted his head. The forest was still dark, and the air was still icy. Nothing around him had changed, but everything inside him had shifted, welcoming a new alliance with the One who had his best interests in mind.

CHAPTER 33

JESS

I t had been a full twenty-four hours since she decided to fall off the face of the earth, and someone had apparently sewn Linc's mouth shut because he'd been quieter than usual.

What was quieter than quiet? Lincoln North.

Jess stared at him across the fire where they'd been eating lunch for the last ten minutes. The only reason they were still sitting was because Linc had gone for seconds of her less-than-stellar oatmeal.

She'd watched him for the entire ten minutes, and he hadn't looked at her once. Oh, he'd thanked her for cooking, which had been a real feat with only one working arm, but other than that, the entire day had been silent.

Her nostrils flared as the pressure in her gut built. It was probably impolite to just outright ask him what was wrong, but she didn't like knowing that *something* was bothering him.

Linc stood and held out a hand for her bowl. "I'll clean up. You go rest."

"I've done nothing but rest, and I need to do something."

Linc shook his head, still averting his gaze. "I don't know what's wrong with your shoulder yet, but using it might do more harm than good."

"Jameson said it was probably just bruised. I'll be fine. I just hit a rock the wrong way."

He looked up at her then. "Is there a right way to hit a rock?"

Jess pinched her lips together, determined not to let his lighthearted comment distract her from the confusion that had kept her company all morning. "I don't think so, but that's all it was. I've been hurt worse before."

Linc held up the hand that wasn't carrying the bowl. "I don't like hearing about you getting hurt."

"But I'm okay now. What does it matter if it's in the past?"

"I don't know, but it makes me sick to think about," Linc said sharply.

Jess sat up straighter. "Is that why you've been avoiding me? Because I got hurt?"

"I don't want to avoid you. You scared me!" He held his hands out like that was a perfectly reasonable explanation for acting like a toad all day.

Maybe it was, but she'd never been good at determining how other people's minds worked.

And that reminder steadied her frustration. Maybe he didn't know why he was avoiding her. She didn't know why she did half the things she did either.

Linc sighed. "I'll finish this up, but you need to get inside. The storm will be here soon, and I want to make sure the horses are okay."

Jess nodded, but he'd already turned away from her. Her shoulders sank as she watched him disappear into the woods toward the creek.

Inside, she readied the fireplace and brought in enough wood for the night. At least that was something she could do one-handed. She'd had enough of the helplessness.

Linc walked in an hour later with his head still down. Was he mad or upset? Why couldn't she ever tell?

Unable to stand another minute in the terrible unknown, she walked straight over to him and grabbed his hand. It was freezing, but the strength in his grip was an anchor she needed to say what was on her mind.

His head jerked up to her and gave her his attention for the first time all day. His frown softened as he registered her confusion, her hurt, and her remorse.

"I'm sorry," she said softly. "I'm sorry for whatever I did, and I hate it when things aren't good between us."

Linc looked down at their clasped hands and tightened his jaw. He stayed there so long she wondered if he was going to keep up the silent treatment.

Finally, he whispered, "You didn't do anything."

There was a crack in one of the words that proved he was lying. "I feel like I did," she said.

He rubbed a hand over his face. "You didn't do anything bad. I got scared yesterday. That's all."

"I'm fine," she said, squeezing his hand as proof of life.

"But I can't shake it. I know it's stupid to worry over something that didn't happen, but if I lost you... if anything happened to you...I couldn't live with myself."

Jess's chest ached, squeezing as if someone had it in their grasp. Was that what Linc had been feeling all day?

She stepped forward and wrapped an arm around his waist, pulled toward him like a horse that knew the way home when the sun started to set.

Linc's strong arms wrapped around her back, and she rested her head against his chest. He smelled like a working man, and she smiled at the comfort of his scent. He'd never smelled like a bottle from a department store. They'd been on the trail for days, and neither of them had gotten a proper shower.

Still, she'd always choose to step into his comforting arms. It was better than the mist after a summer rain. It was better than the crisp fog on a cool morning. It was better than the dust that billowed under a horse's hooves.

It was better than home.

He squeezed her tighter until a traitorous grunt escaped when the pressure on her shoulder sent a pain shooting down her arm.

"I'm sorry." He loosened the hold but didn't let go. "There's something I want to tell you."

"What's that?"

His lighthearted grin had the tension in her shoulders easing before he spoke. "When I said you scared me yesterday, that was an understatement. I spent most of the night shaking in my boots."

"Your boots were by the door," she pointed out.

"It rattled me, and that prompted a little talk with the Man Upstairs."

Jess's eyes widened. He'd prayed for her?

"Anyway, amongst the many thanks that you were okay, I decided to let the Lord handle the things I can't. I've been holding back, but not anymore."

The air in the small cabin thickened. "Really?"

"Really. I haven't always been good, but I want

to do everything I can to make things right. I'll need the Lord for that. And you, if you'll keep me in line."

Jess lunged at him, wrapping her uninjured arm around his neck and pressing her body against his. "That's the best news I've heard all week."

Linc's arm pressed against her back. "It wouldn't take much. It's been a week for bad news."

Linc's phone chimed in his pocket, and they jumped apart like they'd just been caught doing something they shouldn't. He checked the screen and held up a finger.

"Hello."

She watched him pacing around the small room, hoping it was news about Ava and the baby. Or at least good news about the storm headed their way.

"I'm sorry. I'm out on a ride, and I won't be back for a few days. I'll let Asa know and send him out there."

Asa? Who would call Linc when they needed the police?

"Everything okay?" she asked as he ended the call.

"You know Mrs. Grant?"

"The elderly lady from church?"

"Yeah. She has a leaky pipe."

Jess narrowed her eyes. "And she called you?"

"Is that so hard to believe? Mrs. Grant loves me."

Jess chuckled. "I'm sure she does. I just didn't

know you were a handyman for the elderly on the side."

"I only do it for her. We go way back."

Jess crossed her arms as much as she could. "Please tell me a story."

Linc rubbed the back of his neck. "It's a long one."

Jess waved her arm in the air. "I've got all night. It's not like we're going anywhere."

Linc gestured to the small table and chairs in the corner, and Jess took a seat.

"You're making me think this isn't the funny story I was expecting."

"It isn't. At least it isn't if I start at the beginning." He sat and planted his boots shoulder-width apart. "You know I was in prison for a while."

Oh, this was *that* story. "Um, yeah."

"My attorney was Mrs. Grant's grandson. He was in the process of moving out of town, so he asked me to look after Mrs. Grant."

Jess tried to hide her grin. "That's precious. You've been taking care of an old lady." She pushed his shoulder, but he barely budged. "I always knew you were a softie."

Linc pointed at her and fixed her with a stern expression. "I'm not a softie."

"Why do you hide it?" she asked.

"Am I supposed to tell everyone when I do a

good deed? That's stupid. No one cares if I fix someone's appliances."

"It's just so sweet. And humble."

Linc scoffed. "I haven't always been humble. It's
new for me."

Jess rolled her eyes. "I doubt that's true."

He leaned toward her, resting his elbows on his
knees, and locked his gaze with hers. "Gangs wanted
to recruit me when they heard about the terrible
things I did."

All of the air whooshed out of Jess's lungs.
"What kind of things?"

"I'm not telling you that."

"Were you ever part of a gang?" she asked,
gently toeing the line.

"No. I didn't like authority."

"So, you did all of those bad things just because
you wanted to."

Linc shrugged, as if the truth spoke for itself.

"But you said you had a friend," she said.

"And he ended up worse off than me."

"Worse than prison?" What could be worse than
prison?

"He just got a longer sentence, and something
tells me he isn't trying to turn things around like I
am. Ryan needed violence like he needed air."

Jess stared down at her boots. Linc could have
easily chosen to stick to what he knew. If he had,
they wouldn't be here right now. He wouldn't have

given his life to the Lord. He wouldn't have risked his life to protect her.

But something about Linc made her trust him, and that trust had come early. That had to mean something.

"I'm glad you turned things around. Mrs. Grant is lucky to have you. And...so am I."

A loud clap of thunder jerked her attention away from Linc. So much for good news about the storm.

Linc stood and pulled his phone out of his pocket. "I need to call Asa, then check on the horses. I'll be right back."

Jess nodded, suddenly aware of the knot in her throat. She'd never been afraid of storms before, but the danger felt closer this high on the mountain.

CHAPTER 34

JESS

Thunder rumbled outside, and Jess tried to focus on the mug in her hand. The thing was dry as a bone, but she kept rubbing the dish towel over it. The dishes were clean, but she needed something to keep her mind off Linc and the storm. He should have been back by now.

What if one of the horses got spooked? What if he got stuck or ran into a wolf or a bear?

Of course, the storm was bringing out all of her worst fears, and the terrible thoughts kept swirling and growing into bigger and worse scenarios.

"Come on, Linc," she whispered. She needed proof of life soon, or she was going to brave the storm herself.

She reached up with her good arm to put the mug on the top shelf when Linc's boots pounded quickly on the porch. The door flew open a second later before shutting out the storm.

Linc stopped just inside the door, dripping wet. He toed off his soaking boots as he pinned her with a stare. "What are you doing?"

Apparently, worrying about him amped up the urge to wrap him up and cling to him. And did he have to look so good after working in a thunderstorm?

"Just putting away some dishes."

That sounded normal. Right?

Linc crossed the room in quick strides, keeping a stern expression on his face that would have intimidated a grown man.

She didn't recoil as he stepped up behind her and grabbed the old coffee mug from her hand. He pressed closer against her as he reached over her and set the mug neatly on the top shelf.

She turned to face him, craving his presence after worrying about him for so long. His body shadowed her as he rested his hands on the counter on both of her sides. He was twice her size, but relief settled over her as she looked up at him.

Now, the nearness had her head buzzing. No. Her whole body was buzzing. Water dripped from his hair and face, but the heat of his body radiated around her.

Breathe. Breathe.

Linc took a step back, swiping his sleeve over his dripping face. "Sorry, I–"

"Don't." She grabbed his arm and pulled him back toward her. Her heartbeat pounded in her ears as she waited to see what he would do next.

She didn't even know what to do next, but she was counting on him to take the lead this time.

It was a bold move, but she couldn't hold it in any longer. Whatever she felt for Linc was big and scary, but she couldn't dance around it anymore.

He tensed, and his shoulders rose and fell in deep waves as his gaze locked with hers. "I'm soaking wet, Jess."

Despite his warning, she kept pulling him closer. "I don't care." The words were barely a whisper, but at least she got them out. She didn't care about the storm or anything except following the brave hope that Linc would understand her silent plea and meet her halfway.

Linc closed the distance between them as if the rope holding him away from her snapped. His strong arm wrapped around her waist, while the fingers of his other hand brushed gently against the side of her neck, leaving a freezing trail in their wake.

Her hands splayed against his wet shirt before moving to his sides. She'd spent her whole life pulling away from every touch, but it was different with Linc. Her skin burned like fire whenever they connected, but it was a slow burn that seeped down to her bones, warming her from head to toe, despite the cold water dripping off him.

Oh, boy. She inhaled a deep breath. She'd never been this close to a man before, and her heart thought she should be running for her life.

No. Not from Linc.

He pulled her closer, tucking her beneath him as he looked down at her.

Linc knew she hadn't kissed a man before, and she trusted him to guide her through whatever was happening between them. She couldn't breathe, but he would understand everything she wasn't saying.

"Are you sure?" he asked.

She had expectations for her first kiss. After waiting this long, she wanted it to be perfect.

And it would be. With Linc.

She reached up and wiped the rain from his brow, letting her hand slide down his face and jaw.

"I've never been more sure of anything," she whispered. Her words were quiet, but they held a resolution she prayed he noticed.

Her hand trailed down the front of his wet shirt, but it wasn't the cold that had her hand shaking.

He lowered his head until his forehead rested against hers. She closed her eyes, praying her pounding heart would settle. It was hopeless this close to Linc, but maybe if she filled her lungs full enough, she'd stop gasping for air.

"Slow," he whispered, lifting his hand to trace her jawline with the pad of his thumb. His fingers slid into her hair and cradled the back of her head.

His lips hovered just above hers. The heart in her chest would burst if he moved even an inch.

"Linc?" she breathed softly.

He pressed his mouth gently against hers. She gasped as he moved painstakingly slow, drinking her in, whispering silent promises.

It was only a second before she came to life, strengthening her hold on him. She tried to hold the slow pace, but his hand tightened in her hair, urging her to follow his every deliberate movement.

She was weightless, flying. Breathless and dying.

He pulled back, gasping for air. She did the same, blinking through the haze in her thoughts. There was nothing there except Linc.

She looked up at him and saw a mirror of the shock running through her own veins. His mouth hung open slightly, and he stared down at her, blinking slowly.

She knew this feeling. It was like she'd been sucker punched and couldn't catch her breath.

Linc was a force stronger than anything she'd ever been hit with.

His gaze dropped to her lips, and oh how that one little tell lit up her insides.

"Linc?" she asked.

He swallowed hard before giving her a quick, "Yeah."

"That was... Is it always like that?" she asked, unsure of her words.

Linc shook his head, keeping his gaze locked on hers.

Is every kiss life-altering?

Is it ever like two magnets clicking into place?

Is it something that could cause cardiac arrest?

"No. That was different," he said.

She followed the trail of her hand as it moved along his wet shirt and up his chest. The cold rain seeped into her clothes, but she couldn't bring herself to care. It was insignificant when Linc was holding her so close. "I don't know how to describe it."

"Welcome to my world," he said as he brushed his fingertips over her brow and back into her hair.

Complete. That was the word that kept pushing to the front of her thoughts.

"I know your first kiss meant a lot to you, but it was just as special to me. I want you to know that."

She nodded. "I do. I can...I can feel it. It's like seeing color in a world that has always been black and white."

Linc looked down at her, letting out a slow breath. "I want this. I want us. I've wanted to tell you for a long time, but I didn't think I deserved you."

She opened her mouth to protest, but he kept talking.

"I've been stuck in the past with my mistakes, but I don't have that hanging over me anymore. Whether I deserve you or not, I want to try. And I promise to do everything I can to be good enough for you."

She'd tried the dating thing, and while she knew those men weren't right for her, she was sure Linc was different.

"Are you sure I'm the one you want?" she asked.

"I'm sure I want you to be the woman for me. If you don't think so too, then it doesn't matter what I think."

Jess huffed out a quick breath. "I don't know what I'm doing."

"Me either. I was hoping we could figure it out together."

He lifted a hand and grasped one of hers that rested on his chest. He straightened his fingers, opening his palm flush against her hand. His fingers fell into the spaces between hers and rested perfectly together–intertwined and stronger together.

"I want that. I want you," she said.

He dipped his head to hers and smirked. "Say it again."

"I want us."

Thunder boomed loud enough to shake the

floor, and the horses cried outside.

Linc focused his attention back on her. "I need to get dry." He looked down to where the rain had seeped into her shirt. "You do too."

She tilted her chin up to him with a silent plea for another kiss–another awakening that could trap her in an addiction she didn't want to give up.

Linc lowered his mouth to hers. He moved slowly at first, but their movements quickly grew as his lips danced across hers. She clung to him, breathless and wild, as he guided her through every move.

When he pulled away, she gasped as if she'd been underwater the entire time.

Linc took two steps backward, locking her with a hunter's stare. "We can't do that all night."

She knew what he meant. It would be easy to want more, but that wasn't what she wanted. Kissing was new and safe. Anything else was off-limits.

"You're right."

He pointed toward the door. "I'm going to check on the horses again. And...probably sleep outside."

With that, he pushed his feet into his boots and ran back out into the storm.

Jess stood in the kitchen, soaking and freezing, with a shaking hand over her mouth. She'd just kissed Linc, and everything between them about to change.

CHAPTER 35
LINC

Linc lay on the hard wooden floor of the cabin and stared up at the sheet suspended above them. "I can't believe you built a blanket fort."

Jess slapped his chest. "It's cold in here, and we need to harness the heat." She pointed to the wood burning stove. "And you said we couldn't cuddle."

Linc scoffed. "I didn't say we couldn't. I said we shouldn't. There's a difference."

"Whatever. You sound like we need a chaperone."

She could joke, but that was too close to the truth. Having Jess laughing and happy beside him was the basis of all his dreams, and it was hard not to keep kissing her like he'd done earlier.

He hadn't attempted to kiss her again. The first two had nearly lit him on fire.

"Okay, I need another story," Linc said, hoping to distract his thoughts from kissing.

Jess hummed as she thought. "You want to hear about the time I broke my collarbone?"

"No. Not that one. I don't like it when you're hurt." It turned his stomach in funny ways to think about Jess in pain. Funny how things changed since he used to go looking for a fight on the streets almost every day.

"It's a funny story," she promised.

"I somehow doubt that, but tell me if you want to."

She wiggled closer to him. She'd been doing it for the last half hour, thinking he didn't notice that her little shimmies were covert moves to get closer to him.

He still thought cuddling was a bad idea. Hence his insistence on lying on the floor by the heat source. Maybe if he was uncomfortable enough, he'd stop thinking about being alone with Jess during a thunderstorm twenty miles out in the wilderness.

"Well, it was all Brett's fault."

"That doesn't surprise me," Linc said.

Her little finger brushed against his hand as she spoke. The woman was intent on getting close to him, and he both loved and hated it.

"We'd had a ton of snow, and Brett said Dad had a piece of metal in the shed we could use to sled down the hill behind our house. I was maybe eight."

Linc wanted to slap young Brett upside the head. Sledding was generally harmless, but knowing Jess was about to get beat up in this story had Linc bowed up and ready to knock her brother silly.

"We went up and down that hill all day, but I ended up flipping on the last ride down. Brett thought we should try a different hill. I slid right into a tree at the bottom. I guess I hit it with my shoulder first, but I really don't remember."

"Brett is getting my fist in his face when we get back."

Jess laughed. "He made up for it. He took care of me the whole time I had to wear the sling. I think it was the one time I can remember when he didn't pester me. Back then, I didn't know why he was being nice to me. Looking back, I bet he felt bad. There's a lot of things I didn't understand when I was younger."

"There's nothing wrong with that. Kids don't understand a lot."

"What about adults? I still don't know how to interact with people ninety percent of the time."

The hint of sadness in her words had Linc's chest tightening. Jess was different, but there wasn't anything wrong with her, and he hated to think she'd spent her life thinking she wasn't normal.

He wrapped his pinky around hers, sensing she needed reassurance. "It's okay if you don't understand. We're not supposed to always know why people do the things they do."

She turned to face him, and her grin was solemn. "I love that you don't look at me like I'm stupid when I don't understand things. I love that you explain things plainly, but you don't talk to me like I'm a kid. I love that you see and know things about me, even if I don't say it out loud."

Linc swallowed hard, but the words he needed to say came out in a rush. "I love you just the way you are."

Jess gasped, and her eyes widened. She sat up a little and stared at him, frozen with her lips slightly parted.

The confession was only half out, but he was committed now. She deserved to know the whole truth. He sat up, propping on one arm and facing her. "I'm going to tell it to you straight. I love you. I think I've always loved you. Everything about you."

He was fighting for each breath now as the heat from the stove melted his skin. Or maybe it was the fear of what Jess would say when he finished his confession. He was ready to cut himself open so she could see the mess inside.

"You're strong. You're not afraid to tell me like it is or kick me when I get out of line. I love that you have my back, and I have yours."

He brushed a thumb over her cheek, craving the softness of her skin against his calloused hands. "I love that you're so beautiful I can't think straight. And you don't even try. I love that you make me want to be a better person because you deserve the best."

Jess stared at him, completely unmoving. Since he'd decided to lay it all on the line, he might as well get it all out there or die trying.

"You've been dating, and it's been tearing me up to see you with anyone else. I know what I want. I want you and only you. No other woman on earth could turn my head. If I have you, I have everything. If I don't have you, I'm lost."

He'd said more in the last two minutes than he'd said in the last month, and if Jess's unmoving stare was anything to go by, she was completely lost.

She closed her mouth, then opened it again. "That makes sense," she whispered. "You're the only thing that makes sense."

Linc wrapped an arm around her, pulling her to him where she could rest her head on his shoulder. "That's quite an honor."

She nestled closer and relaxed against him. "I never thought I'd love anyone. I'm not sure if this is love, but I think it has to be. I can't imagine living my life with anyone but you."

Linc pressed a kiss to her hair and rested his cheek against her head. "I haven't felt it before you either. I just hope I get this right because I don't ever want to lose you."

"We'll figure it out together."

"It might take a while. We're both stumbling in the dark," Linc said.

Jess sat up, propping on her arm to look down at him. Her blonde hair draped beside him, and he brushed a hand through the soft waves.

"I love you too," Jess whispered.

Linc watched her mouth as she formed the words, but he knew exactly what it felt like when Jess didn't understand things. He was having a hard time comprehending what she'd just said.

"Say it again," he said, finally coming out of the fog.

"I love you."

Her words were sure this time, and the meaning hit him like a ton of bricks to the chest.

Sliding his hand into her hair, he gently pulled her down to him and kissed her again.

He had one thing figured out. He'd do whatever it took to make sure she was happy with him for the rest of their lives.

CHAPTER 36
JESS

J ess blinked through the fog in her head as light shone brightly through the cabin.

The cabin. She was on a work trip.

With Linc.

She pushed up onto her elbows and stretched her aching neck. She'd fallen asleep as soon as the storms passed, but her body was heavy with the need for more rest.

Her head spun, and she propped a hand against it, closing her eyes to block out the light. She was supposed to be up early. Her shoulder was feeling well enough that she could help Linc get things finished up here and they could ride out by mid-day.

A groan slipped out, releasing only a small bit of the heaviness in her shoulders. Had she been hit by a truck last night?

No. She'd spent the evening lying on the floor by

the wood-burning stove and talked with Linc until the storms faded into the distance. Then, they'd talked about their plans for getting everything done at the cabin and went to bed.

Everything about the evening was perfect. She'd finally been honest with Linc about how she felt, and the tension that had tangled up in her gut for weeks was finally gone.

Except there were new aches and pains now that had nothing to do with harboring secret love for Linc.

Love. Even the thought of the word filled her stomach with flutters.

Linc loved her, and she loved him. It was something straight out of one of those sappy romantic comedies or made-for-TV Christmas movies.

Jess was one of those love-struck women with hearts in her eyes, and as much as she wanted to scoff at her own goofiness, she decided to wallow in the happiness of her new relationship instead.

If only the pounding in her head would stop bugging her.

Linc's twin-sized bed beside her was perfectly made, and the cabin was quiet.

How long had he been up? Why hadn't he woken her? She never slept in.

Water. She needed to hydrate. She'd experienced altitude sickness a few times, and she wasn't

looking forward to dealing with the irritating symptoms again.

Slipping out of the bed, she stumbled to the
small kitchen area and opened the cooler. They'd
been boiling water and storing it in a cooler until
Blake and Ridge came to test the well. She did *not*
want to be the guinea pig for strange mountain well
water.

After gulping down half a glass, she slowed
down, remembering drinking too quickly would
probably have her throwing it right back up in a few
minutes.

The haze didn't dissipate as she inhaled deep
breaths. Great. The sickness was here to stay.

Deciding to do the best she could despite feeling
like a wet saddle, she reached for the coffee Linc had
brewed.

The carafe was half full, but the coffee she
poured into the cup was cold.

What time was it? She searched for her phone
and gasped when she saw the time.

"Ten o'clock!"

She'd never slept that late in her life.

A thud outside caught her attention, and she
changed into jeans and a flannel shirt. After braiding
her hair, she slipped on her boots and ran out the
door, heaving the whole way.

Linc was chopping firewood, and he didn't look
up until she was right beside him. His lips turned up

in a smile that had her pulse thundering in her chest.

"Hey, are–"

"Why is it so late?" she interrupted. "Why didn't you wake me up? We have so much to do." She was panting like she'd just ran a marathon instead of twenty yards.

Linc's smile fell, and his stare stayed locked on her. "Are you okay?"

"Yeah. Why?"

Linc reached for her hand, and she gave it to him, too tired to protest.

"You look pale," he said, leading her to sit on the stump he'd been using to chop wood on.

"I'm fine. Probably altitude sickness. I'll drink a bunch of water." She looked up at him, and the movement rattled her brain inside her head. She reached up and pressed her whole hand against her temple to stop the throbbing. "We have so much to do."

Linc crouched in front of her. "Relax. I'll handle it. I'm actually almost finished with our list for the day. I just need to clean out the chimney, but I was waiting for you to wake up." He tilted his head as he examined her. "Do you want to head home?"

Home. She'd never longed for home as much as in this moment. She wanted her soft bed, her warm shower, and lots of over-the-counter meds that would at least treat these irritating symptoms.

"But I didn't do anything I was supposed to today," she said feebly.

"I did it." Linc pressed the back of his hand to her forehead, and his brows pinched together. Those soft lips she'd kissed last night were thinned into a stern line. "I think you have a fever."

"What? I don't get fevers. I haven't had one since I was a kid."

Linc stood and offered her a hand. She took it and stood, not liking the way everything swayed around her.

"Let's check anyway. I'll get the first-aid kit and meet you in the cabin."

Jess walked back inside, frustrated that she was slowing things down instead of helping. They were on a timeline, and she'd thrown a wrench in everything.

She sat in one of the chairs in the kitchen just as Linc came in with the bag. He set it on the table and started rummaging through it.

Jess, on the other hand, couldn't tell which way was up, much less find whatever she needed to cure the all-over sickness.

Her head slowly lowered until it rested on her arm against the table, and dang it, he was right. She could feel the heat from her head radiating into her arm. Exhaustion wanted to take over, but a nagging discomfort clouded everything, preventing any kind of rest.

"Hold still," Linc said as he pressed the thermometer to her ear. A few beeps later, and he checked the screen.

But he didn't say anything.

She lifted her head. "What does it say?"

The mask he'd thrown up to hide his concern was paper thin. She saw right through his attempt. "It's a little high."

Jess reached for the thermometer and read it. "A hundred and three!"

Linc was already opening a small pack of fever reducers. He reached for the glass she'd drunk from a minute ago and handed both of them to her. "Take this."

She did as he said, then let out a groan. "I can't be sick."

Linc pushed stray strands of her hair back and brushed his thumb over her forehead. "You *can* be sick, and it'll be okay. I'll take care of you."

She let her head rest in his strong hand. Letting Linc take care of her sounded like a dream come true right now, but she wasn't the damsel in distress type, and she didn't want to start now.

"You're so good to me. What would I do without you?"

Linc huffed, and his smile rose on one side. "Be lonely and grouchy."

She let her head loll to the side. "I'm glad I have you then."

He rubbed a hand over her back, and she let the soothing motion calm her. "I'll be okay. The meds should kick in soon."

Linc pulled his phone from his pocket. "I'll call Jameson and let him know we'll be at least a day behind."

Her head jerked up. "No! I can help." She stood and gripped the back of the chair to steady herself in the spinning room.

"It's okay. I'm saying I think you need to rest. You don't look up to riding half a day tomorrow."

Jess shook her head. "Then we won't get all the things done here."

"I've almost finished everything we planned to do today. Blake and Ridge can handle the rest when they get here."

Hanging her head, Jess sighed. "We can start heading back today and at least make some progress. I might not be able to go far, but progress is progress, right? I'll get the chores done in here while you finish the firewood. Then, we'll pack everything up and be on the trail in an hour."

Linc wrapped an arm around her and pulled her to him. She made the mistake of sinking into him like melted butter, and no amount of willpower would make her lift her head from his chest. It was the pillow she'd been craving since she crawled out of the bed, and she didn't care that it was hard as a rock. She was going to sleep right here and enjoy every second of it.

"Just relax. The guys know what they need to do when they get here. Paul is hiring a bunch of hands, and they're probably already starting training. Everything will get done, and you don't have to kill yourself to do it."

A traitorous sniffle snuck its way out. "Are you sure?" Man, she hated being sick.

"I'm positive. Your health is the most important thing right now, and I bet everyone back at the ranch would agree with me."

Jess tried to shake her head, but Linc held her closer.

"You know I'm right," he whispered.

"Fine. I'll do the bare minimum and call it resting."

Linc kissed the top of her head. "I'll take it."

He released her and gave her a once-over before heading out the door. Why did he have to be so reasonable when she tried to just will things into being the way she wanted? She didn't want to be sick. She wanted to be helpful and strong.

At least he knew she'd rather be doing her part. Linc had never coddled her, and even now, he saw her struggle to push past everything for her responsibilities.

An hour later, they were wrapping things up at the cabin, and Jess was gasping for every breath.

Before they loaded up the water, she splashed a handful onto her face. The shock of cold pushed some of the exhaustion back, but the ache in her head was getting stronger.

Linc stepped up beside her as she readied Liberty for the ride. His heat pulled her in, and she finally gave into the urge to look up at him.

She'd expected pity, but the tightness of his jaw held concern. Did she look that bad?

"We can stay another day so you can rest."

Jess shook her head before he finished the sentence. "No. We need to go. We can at least make it to the nearest campsite today."

Linc's fingertips brushed over her temple and the rough pad of his thumb grazed her cheek. "I hate seeing you like this. I just want to help."

She leaned into his touch, craving the warmth and comfort he promised. "I'll be okay."

It was all she had right now, and she prayed it was enough to get them down the mountain.

CHAPTER 37

LINC

J ess swayed in the saddle again, and Linc gripped the reins. He'd held with his tight fists long enough that his fingers were numb, and there wasn't any sign of letting up his grip.

Thunder kept nervously stepping out of line. The horse could probably sense the storm in Linc's head. Whatever Jess had was severe, and he didn't like the helplessness that taunted him.

Was this what it was like to love someone? The worse Jess got, the worse he felt, but his ailment wasn't a sick fever. It was an echo of her pain in his bones like someone had tied him up and made him watch her suffering.

The clearing for the campsite opened through the trees, and he'd never been so happy to see a patch of dirt in his life. He pulled Thunder to a stop and dismounted in one swift movement. Rushing to

Jess's side, he coaxed Liberty to a stop. "How do you feel?"

A low groan released from Jess's chest as she stretched her back to one side. "Really glad we're here," she said heavily.

"I know." Linc reached for her waist and lifted her off. Liberty was a smaller horse, and Jess didn't give him any push-back as she rested one boot in the stirrup. When her feet were on the ground, he turned her toward him. Sweat beaded on her forehead, and the hair at the nape of her neck was damp.

Linc pressed his hand to her forehead, and the heat surged the fire in his middle. Her skin burned, despite the cold sweat on her brow.

He pulled her to him and pushed past the panic, willing his stupid head to stop spinning enough to think.

Jess raised her head and pushed stray hairs away from her face. "I hate this," she groaned.

"That makes two of us," he said, cupping the side of her face in his hand. Now that he was free to touch her, he didn't want to stop. His hands tingled constantly, begging to brush against the softness.

"Let me get you some more medicine. Stay right here." He lifted her hand and placed it on Thunder's side. "Don't move."

He jogged to the mule that carried the first-aid

kit and unstrapped it, pulling out another pack of the pills she'd taken earlier.

She stood where he'd left her with her hand on Thunder and her head hanging low. She lifted her chin as he approached, but her eyes barely opened. "I'm so tired," she whispered.

"I know, babe. Take this, and I'll put up the tents." He handed her the pills and the canteen of water.

Jess took a few sips and looked around before sitting down on the ground right where she'd been standing "Okay. I'll be right here."

Linc untied one of the packs and laid it on the ground beside her. With his hands on her shoulders, he slowly led her to lie down and use the pack as a pillow. Her eyes closed immediately, and he felt her head again. Still hot.

Don't panic. Don't panic. She just has a fever. It could be the flu. It could be altitude sickness.

Pulling out his phone, he called Jameson. He rested it between his shoulder and ear as he found a rag and drenched it with water from the canteen.

Jameson answered on the fourth ring, giving Linc plenty of time to sweat. "Hello."

"I know you have a lot going on, but I need some help. It's Jess."

"What's wrong?" Jameson sounded tired but eager to help.

"We're still on the mountain, and she's got a

fever." Linc glanced over to where he'd left her. She'd rolled onto her side and tucked her knees to her chest. "It's bad."

"How long has she had it? How high is it? Is she drinking enough? How far are you from the main house?"

Apparently, Jameson's mind was firing on all cylinders just like Linc's. "Since this morning. A hundred and three. Drinking a lot of water. We're at least half a day's ride away, but she can't go any further right now."

Jameson huffed and didn't speak for a minute. Linc knelt beside her and rested the rag above her brow while he waited for some kind of hope from the other end of the call.

"I'll send someone to meet you with meds for her. Have you given her anything?"

"The fever reducers in the first-aid kit. We don't have many more."

"Anything else you need while I'm sending help?" Jameson asked.

"Prayers and water," Linc said resolutely. "How's the baby?"

"We had a scare earlier, but he's looking stronger now."

Linc stared at Jess, and his chest ached. "I hope he pulls through this."

Jameson let out a long breath. "Thanks, man. Keep us in your prayers. Jess is in good hands."

Linc readjusted the rag on her head, and his worry mounted. "I hope so."

"Let me make some calls and get someone headed toward you."

"Thanks." Linc hung up the call and tossed the phone to the side. He unpacked the tents and worked to get them up as quickly as possible. The ground was still soft from the storm the night before, and his boots slid in the mud every time he moved.

His phone rang on the ground beside Jess as he tossed blankets inside. Scrambling for it like a life-line, he answered before the second ring.

"Hey."

"I'm headed your way," Brett said.

"Who else?"

"Blake and Patrick. He's a new one, but he has paramedic experience."

Linc hung his cowboy hat on the top of the tent and pushed a hand through his hair. "Just get here as fast as you can."

"You know I will. Is she okay?" Brett's usual joking tone was nowhere to be found.

"I don't know. I'm not sure the meds are working much."

"Take care of her. I'll be there soon," Brett said before abruptly ending the call.

At least Linc wasn't the only one willing to do

anything for Jess. Her brother would push the limits to get here. Linc would bet his life on it.

Hopefully, no one's life was at stake here.

He crawled into the tent and spread out the blankets and pillows. Jess was miserable, and Linc was grasping at straws to make her comfortable any way possible.

After arranging the bedding, Linc stepped back outside. Jess lay in the same position he'd left her in, cuddled to the pack under her cheek. Even in sleep, her brows wrinkled, and her fists clenched to her chest.

He'd done plenty of praying on the ride this morning, but Jess's fever wasn't ready to let up. Squatting beside her, he brushed a hand over the side of her face. The wrinkle faded, leaving her features relaxed.

Gently, he slid his hands beneath her and lifted her into his arms. She didn't stir, even as her head lolled against his chest.

She was so small in his arms, but it wasn't hard to remember the fiery woman who managed one of the most important parts of the ranch with a fierce determination that had even men a decade her senior snap to attention.

He ducked to step into the tent and gently laid her on the blankets. She rolled onto her side instantly, and he tucked the thin sheet around her.

Kneeling at her side, he hung his head. He

wanted to pray or ask or beg, but the words wouldn't come to him. Everything in his head was a war of worry and desperation. What could he do with that? Panic?

Finally, he found the simplest request. It summed up everything she needed.

Help her. Please.

He found a canteen and propped it beside her head and closed the tent behind him as he stepped out. After the horses were taken care of, he'd spend the rest of the day by her side.

The phone in his pocket rang as he plopped the bucket of water beside Liberty.

The name on the screen conjured up a turmoil inside him.

"Everything okay?" Linc asked.

"The path is blocked near the base of the mountain," Brett said. "Ridge is coming with chainsaws so we can get it cleared. It's a full tree, so it might be later when we get to you."

Linc glanced at Jess's tent and back at the trail. "Just hurry. She has meds through the afternoon."

"I'll be there as fast as I can," Brett said before ending the call.

Linc rubbed a hand through his hair and headed for the tent.

CHAPTER 38

JESS

Jess squirmed, wrapping the blankets tighter around her. A groan escaped as she stretched a leg out.

"Jess?" Linc whispered beside her.

"Yeah." She rested a hand against her head, willing the pounding to stop.

"Are you okay?" he asked.

Jess blinked and looked around. Darkness covered everything. She was in the tent.

And Linc was with her–lying beside her in the blankets she'd rumpled up.

That was...unexpected.

"How is it nighttime?" she asked, squinting into the darkness.

"You've been asleep for hours." He leaned over her, reaching for something beside her. "You need to drink."

She sat up, propping on her hands. "I have to go to the bathroom."

Linc unzipped the tent and the shadow of his hand reached out to her. She took it, moving slower than dried tree sap as she crawled out of the tent.

Jess slid her feet into her boots. They had the equivalent of outhouses set up at all the campsites, and it was her least favorite part of camping.

Uh-oh. She'd gone all day without having to pee until now. That was probably a really bad sign.

"I'll be right here," Linc whispered as he planted his feet shoulder-width apart and crossed his arms over his chest.

She got a chance to look him up and down in the dark. She liked it when he was attentive and protective. He probably couldn't see the grin spreading on her face, but why should she care anyway?

Linc was her *boyfriend*, and she would be doing a happy dance as soon as her head stopped swimming.

Having a boyfriend was going to be fun...as soon as she got up the nerve to tell anyone about their new relationship status.

All the mean girls in high school could have a good cry now while she pranced into the woods protected by the incredibly hot and broody Lincoln North.

Well, there wasn't any prancing going on, but as

soon as the stupid fever broke she would get right to it.

And apparently fevers made her woozy because she'd had dreams about calm waves brushing over her hair and face while Linc whispered sweet things to her.

Except, Linc didn't seem like the kind to wax poetic or sit at someone's bedside and nurse them back to health.

Fever dreams were weird.

Stumbling back to the tent, she spotted Linc pacing in the clearing.

Could she just run up and hug him? Squeeze him a little? That would be fun.

She stepped on a branch, and Linc's chin lifted. His attention locked on her, stopping her in her tracks.

Oh, that look was not good.

Or it was very good. Confusion was her friend tonight.

He took long strides toward her, pinning her with his gaze.

She blinked, and he was in front of her, holding her waist and caressing her cheek.

Just like in the dream.

Jess lifted her chin to look up at him. The forest shadows were splashed across his face, but his eyes were bright–focused on her and unwavering.

"Are you okay?" he asked, deep and hushed in the cold breeze.

"I'm okay. Still stumbling around a little," she managed to croak out.

She hadn't gotten used to being in Linc's arms. Would she ever?

"You need to drink. A lot," he said, just as he turned away from her, leaving a chill with more bite than the Wyoming night.

He ducked into the tent and emerged with the canteen. "Drink. Please."

She took it from him without a fight. Her bones were thirsty, and she'd made it through a few gulps before Linc rested his hand on her wrist.

"Not so fast." He gently tugged her toward the tent. "You need to eat."

"I can't eat. I'm not hungry."

"You should be starving. You didn't eat all day." He rummaged through a pack they always carried on the pack rides. Finally, he pulled something out. "Crackers?"

Jess plucked them from his hand and sat on the ground beside the tent. "Yes. I'll take that." She ripped open the paper and closed her eyes as the crunching swamped all of her other senses.

Then Linc was by her side again, handing her something else. "Take these."

More medicine. When would this stupid fever

give up? "Thanks." She swallowed them, washing them down with water and more crackers.

Linc crouched beside her and trailed his fingers over her face. Her eyes drifted closed, and she rested her heavy head against his hand.

"You're so good to me," she whispered.

She heard the words as they left her mouth, as if they hadn't stopped to ask for permission before escaping.

Linc huffed, and his warm breath puffed in a cloud between them. "I don't think I'm doing enough good. Tell me what I can do. How can I help you feel better?"

She reached up and slid her hand over his, marveling at the ease with which they touched. "You stayed with me?"

"Of course."

She looked at the tent they'd slept in. They'd been side-by-side, just like the night in the barn, but she'd missed it this time.

"Stay with me. Again?" she said. Hoping she'd correctly formed that as a question instead of a command.

Linc nodded once and rose to his feet. He opened the tent flaps and moved to the side, allowing her to go in first.

Jess kicked off her boots and climbed into the tent. It was about ten degrees warmer inside, but the temperature rose even higher when Linc ducked in behind her.

She focused on adjusting the blankets just the way she wanted them while Linc waited, unmoving, by the exit.

"What?" she whispered.

"Are you finished making your bed, princess? Is there a pea in there somewhere?"

She scoffed. "I have leaves in my hair, and I haven't showered in days. I can hardly qualify for princess status. And I don't want to think about what little critters might be hiding in these covers."

Linc leaned in and pressed a kiss to her forehead. "Take all the time you need."

Oh, great. Now he was going to start doing that knee-melting forehead kissing thing, and she was going to turn into a complete sap in front of everyone at the ranch.

Whatever. It wasn't as if she could change it. If she wanted to bask in Linc's attention, she'd do it and dare anyone to say a word.

She plopped down onto her back very ungracefully and pulled the thin blanket over her. Once she was settled, Linc slipped beneath the covers beside her.

"Are you sure this is okay? I can put up another tent."

"It's fine. I haven't brushed my teeth today, and I have zero fears you'll want to take advantage of this mess." She waved a hand in the air, gesturing to her whole body.

Linc laughed, and the sound was so new and sweet she wanted to reach out and catch it. "Whatever you say."

He settled on his back beside her, and they both stared up at the tent ceiling. The soft night sounds filled the air around them, almost lulling her back to sleep.

"Thank you," she whispered.

"For what?"

"For staying."

Linc's fingers brushed against hers, and he slowly opened her hand. Their palms slid together before their fingers locked into the empty spaces.

He lifted their clasped hands and stared at the link they'd created. "I could never leave you." His head turned to face her, and the deep timbre of his confession vibrated over her skin. "Ever."

Jess inhaled a deep breath through her nose, grasping for an evenness that was slipping away. "I always have to prove that I'm strong," she whispered. "I don't look strong."

"You do to me," Linc said.

"I'm little. I'm blonde. I'm a woman. Respect is hard to come by, and it didn't help that I came from the second worst family in the county."

"It's only because my family doesn't live here," he said.

"Where is your family?" she asked.

"Don't know. Don't care," he said quickly.

Jess turned to face him, imagining a little boy without parents. "You had a lot to prove too," she whispered.

"You don't have to prove anything to me," he said.

Those old insecurities rose to the surface, choking the joy out of her. "I had to do more than everyone else. I couldn't stand the thought of Mr. Chambers giving me a job because he felt sorry for me. Because of where I come from."

Linc squeezed her hand. "I get it."

"You do. And I don't have to prove anything to you. I don't have to fight for your respect, and that's...nice." She finally let the breath out she'd been holding for what seemed like years. It was better than nice. It was essential to her now.

Linc lifted their hands and pressed his lips to her knuckles. "Get some rest. Brett, Ridge, and Blake will be here in the morning. They got stuck by some downed trees on the trail."

"Good night, Linc," she whispered as she rolled toward him, chasing his warmth.

"Good night. Don't let the bedbugs bite."

Jess closed her eyes, and the darkness hid the smile on her face.

"What do you think you're doing?"

Her brother's shout cut through the grogginess in Jess's head. Rolling onto her back, she groaned. Sunlight filtered through the tent, and she blinked through the haze.

"I don't think it's your business what I'm doing," Linc said, much lower than Brett's shout.

"Oh, it's my business when it's my sister you're shacking up with."

Jess lay still, trying to piece together what was going on outside.

Linc huffed. "I'm not shacking up with Jess. She's sick, nitwit."

"This isn't the first time I've found you two together," Brett spat.

Good grief. Jess propped up on her elbows, wincing at the pull in her shoulder. Breaking up a scuffle was the last thing she wanted to do. Especially when her brother *was* being a nitwit. The pounding in her head hung on the edges, but her skull didn't feel like it was about to implode anymore.

She stretched her aching neck and climbed out of the tent. Sure enough, Brett was about three inches from Linc, looking like a rubber band about to snap.

"Can you two shut up?" she said as she reached for her boots.

Brett threw his hands out to the sides. "What's going on, Jess? You snuck away to cuddle up in the mountains?"

"Linc said it's none of your business."

Brett's lips tightened into a thin line, and his jaw tensed. "You've got to be kidding me."

Jess stood with her boots on and looked down at herself. She really needed a change of clothes. She'd slept in jeans, for goodness' sake.

When she faced Brett, she fought the urge to thump him in the forehead. "I'm sick, your voice is getting on my nerves, and we aren't cuddling in the mountains. You make it sound like we're on a romantic honeymoon. I've been half-alive for the last twenty-four hours, and Linc has been pretty great at making sure I don't wither up and die. You owe him an apology and a big thank you."

Brett crossed his arms over his chest and glared at Linc. "But I don't wanna."

Good. If Brett was joking about it, then he'd already decided to let it go.

Jess pressed a hand to her forehead and closed her eyes against the pain. "Where is the thermometer?"

Linc stepped around her to the tent and emerged with it a second later. Instead of handing it to her, he checked the temperature himself.

"Ninety-nine. Much better than yesterday," he said, offering her a soft grin.

"Do we have anything I can take for the headache?" she asked low, making it clear she was on friendly terms with Linc and not her brother.

Brett picked up the bag at his feet and rummaged inside until he produced a pill bottle. He handed it to her, and she took it without meeting his gaze.

"You need to drink a lot of water too," Linc added.

"Jameson sent these drinks," Brett said, pulling out a few drink bottles.

"Thanks." She accepted a bottle and opened it.

Brett propped his hands on his hips and stared at the ground. "Sorry I came at you, man."

Linc didn't look away from her. He watched as she took a few drinks, searing her with his intense stare. "You're forgiven."

Wow. That was more than she'd expected Linc to give. Especially since she wanted to stew over her brother's stupid assumptions a little longer.

Brett pushed the dirt at his feet with the tip of his boot. "Sorry for waking you up, Jess. I hope you're feeling better."

"I am. Thanks." Her irritation was slowly dampening. She didn't have the energy to stay mad.

Brett jerked a thumb over his shoulder. "I'll get some water for the horses."

"Thanks," Linc said, finally turning to Brett.

Her brother slipped off onto the trail where the

horses waited, giving Jess and Linc the privacy she'd been craving.

"He's lost his mind. I guess this is one of the first times he's ever seen me with a guy," she said as she pulled her hair out of its braid and ran her fingers through it.

Linc took a step toward her and slipped his arm around her waist. "I—"

Jess pushed him back. "Oh no. I haven't brushed my teeth."

Linc chuckled. "Hurry. I want you all to myself before he comes back."

Jess ducked into her tent, grabbed her toiletries, and disappeared into the tree line. Ten minutes later, her hair was in a new braid and her teeth were sparkly clean.

Linc tended a new fire, and she had a small second to watch him work. He'd done so much over the last few days, and he hadn't complained a bit about having to do double the work while she was sick.

She reached his side, and he rose to his feet. Sliding her arms around his waist, she rested her head on his chest. "Thank you."

Linc wrapped her up, pulling her tight against him. "I don't know what you're thanking me for, but you're welcome."

"I don't know what I'm thanking you for either,

but it's a lot." She looked up at him and smiled. "This is my favorite."

Linc gave her a playful grin. "What's your favorite?"

"This. Being close to you."

He brushed a hand over her forehead and let it slide over her hair. "The feeling is mutual."

He dipped his head and pressed his lips to hers. A flash of light and heat exploded inside her. Linc's kiss was soft and slow, but the pressure in her chest rose until it pressed against her ribs and sternum.

She'd wondered a few times over the years what it would be like to kiss a man, but nothing had prepared her for Lincoln North.

He pulled back slightly, pressing a few small kisses to her lips. "You should get some more rest."

"I don't want to rest anymore. I'm tired of being tired."

Linc chuckled. "I'm not sure that makes sense."

"It does." She closed her eyes and thought back over the day she'd practically missed. "How's the baby?"

"Good, last I heard."

"How are things at the barn?"

Linc pulled his phone from his chest pocket and looked at it. "I haven't gotten a call about an emergency today. I'm sure Thea is managing."

Thea knew her way around the stables, but she hadn't been through a tourist season at the ranch yet. Knowing the huge list of things that needed to be done this week, Jess reached for her own phone. "I'd better call her."

Linc jerked his chin toward the tent. "Rest while you do it. We have three more people helping now. We'll be out of here right after lunch."

Jess looked around, making sure the campsite was clear. "I hate that I was half-conscious last night," she whispered.

Linc smiled and the playful expression was so new to her that she couldn't get enough of it. If she could just snap a photo and keep it in her pocket, she'd spend half of her working hours daydreaming about the cute smile on the tough-as-nails cowboy.

Then the joyful expression morphed into something else. Desire?

Oh, no. That look would get her in trouble. When his gaze lowered to her lips, her heart rate skyrocketed.

Maybe she should put some distance between them now that the fever that had made her say and do crazy things was gone.

His lips brushed over hers again, and she let him lead her through another whirlwind of emotions. Would he always have this effect on her? Would she ever be able to breathe when he adored her?

He pulled away just enough to speak. "I don't want to fight your brother." Linc kissed her again. "But I want more of this."

Jess nodded, shaking her head up and down rapidly in agreement.

"Go check on Thea," he whispered.

"Okay." That one word took way too much effort to get out.

She stepped away from him, and his hand slowly slipped from her waist.

Did they really have to part? Linc was going to be terrible for her work ethic.

"Where is that first-aid kit?" Brett shouted as he entered the clearing. "I think I just rubbed my cheek against some poison ivy."

Jess looked at Linc as she pressed her lips together. Was she laughing about Brett's dilemma or the fact that they almost got caught kissing? "How'd he get it on his face?"

Linc shook his head. "I'm not asking." He jerked his head toward the pack by the tent. "There's a cream for that."

CHAPTER 39

LINC

L inc untied one of the mules from a tree and wound the rope around his arm. Every muscle in his body had relaxed since Jess's fever had gone down. She'd been up all morning working around the campsite. Hopefully, she wouldn't get tired again now that it was time to leave.

Passing Liberty, Linc brushed a hand over her mane. "Listen, I need you to be extremely good today and get my girl home safe."

The horse had gotten over her timidness on the trip. Maybe the horse got the memo that they were both trying their best for Jess.

"Who are you talking to?" she said as she walked down the slow rise, bouncing with each step.

"My new friend. Liberty says she's gonna be good today."

Jess gave Liberty a bright smile. "Of course she's

gonna be good. She probably wants to be home as much as I do."

"Are you ready to be home because you've been sick, or are you ready to be home because you're homesick?"

Jess tilted her head as she rubbed a hand over Liberty's nose. "Both. I used to love trail rides. I still do, but I like the shorter ones better."

"Because you actually have a home now."

She looked up at him, and a small wrinkle made a line between her brows. "I've never thought of it like that, but yeah, I think you're right. I know my place isn't much, but it's home. I feel safe there."

Linc pressed a kiss to her forehead. "I'm glad. I can't wait to get you home. Ms. Landry is probably gathering a search party for you."

"Oh no. She tried that once. Now I always tell her when I'll be gone for a few days."

Linc chuckled. "I was joking, but it's good she won't be stirring up trouble."

"Don't underestimate that woman," Jess said. "You ready to get on the road?"

"Yep." Linc reached out and grabbed her waist, pulling her in for a quick kiss.

Well, he'd intended it to be quick, but it was hard to pull away when her soft body melted into his. Her hands rested on his shoulders, then slid up the sides of his neck and into his hair.

He pulled away, gasping for air and words. Jess

had always shied away from touch, but it seemed she'd gotten over that aversion.

"Wow."

She tilted her head back and played with his short hair. "You're always running your hands through it, especially when you're stressed. I've been wondering if it was as soft as you make it look."

A punch could have hit Linc square in the chest, and he still wouldn't have been able to move from that spot. Jess was showing him how to open up, and he liked every step they took together.

"Cheese and grits. What is the world coming to?" Brett asked as he stepped down the small hill, catching Linc and Jess wrapped up in each other.

Jess chuckled. "I guess we should just tell him."

Linc shouted over his shoulder, "Hey, Brett. Jess and I are together. This is your fair warning that kissing is bound to happen."

Brett reached them, shaking his head. "I kinda saw it coming, but not really."

"That makes no sense," Jess said as her brother reached them.

"You're just so...similar," Brett said, waving his hands in the air. "I also thought you were both too dense to see the potential."

Linc straightened. "Be honest, man."

"Just calling it like I see it," Brett said.

Jess tilted her head from side to side. "You're probably right."

"Well, I guess this is congratulations." Brett stuck his hand out to Linc.

"Thanks, bud," Linc said as he accepted the hand.

Brett turned to Jess. "You feeling up to the ride?"

"I can't wait another minute," she said, mounting her boot in the stirrup and swinging a leg over Liberty.

"See you back at the ranch. Ridge and Blake should be making progress on the trail. You'll probably run into them on your way back." With that, Brett waved a hand over his head as he trudged up the hill back toward the camp.

Liberty stepped anxiously from side to side. Jess reined her in, leading toward the path. "Let's go home."

The lights of the main house and dining hall lit up the darkening sky as they left the woods behind. Linc gripped the reins, understanding Jess's pull toward home. He'd moved around to a few different cabins on the ranch and switched roommates more than once, and no matter where he was at Wolf Creek, it had the welcoming sense that settled the restlessness inside him.

"I'm officially done," Jess said as she brushed her arm over her brow. "I think the fever is back."

Linc dismounted and quickly made his way to Liberty's side. "You want to go to the clinic? I'll drive."

Jess shook her head as she carefully climbed down from the horse. "No. I just need to go home."

Linc helped her to her office. "Just sit and drink some water while I put the horses up."

He didn't want to push, but maybe she'd be more open to letting him take her to the clinic in the morning if she wasn't feeling better. The complete exhaustion that overtook her was enough to keep him on a worry roller coaster.

"Can you give Liberty some of the treats in the blue box?" she asked, cradling her head in her hands.

"You got it. I'll be right back." He pressed a kiss to her forehead and sighed. Her skin was warm again. He didn't want to leave her. Not for a second. He could call Thea, but she'd already worked longer hours with Jess and Brett gone.

As soon as he walked out of Jess's office, Paul and Thane showed up.

"Everything okay?" Paul asked. "Saw y'all ride in."

"Jess is sick, but everything else is fine. Can you give me a hand putting these two up and unpacking? I want to get her home as soon as possible."

Paul gave a casual wave. "You go on. I'll take care of this."

Linc propped his hands on his hips. "How's Ava and Ron?"

"They both seemed better today. I saw the little guy this morning." Paul pulled his phone out and showed Linc a picture of a tiny baby in a clear case-looking thing. He had a tube coming out of his nose and stickers and wires on his abdomen. His expression was serene like he was sleeping through sweet dreams.

"He looks good, man. Congratulations again."

"Thanks." Paul stared at the photo, completely mesmerized by the kid. "I just can't wait till he gets home."

Linc slapped a hand on Paul's shoulder. "Hang in there. He'll be home before you know it."

"I hope you're right." Paul jerked his head toward the office. "Take her home. I've got it here. Trying to stay busy so I don't worry."

"I appreciate it. I'm hopin' she'll let me take her to see the doc in the morning."

"Good luck with that. She's a stubborn one," Paul said.

Linc glanced back at the office. "Yeah, but I don't mind it. She knows what she wants."

Paul nodded. "Take care of her, son."

Linc narrowed his eyes at Paul. "Who told you?"

"Nobody had to tell me. If you don't already know it yet, you love that woman."

Chuckling, Linc rubbed his chin. "Thanks for the heads-up. I figured it out."

"Good thing you didn't wait around too long. I started sweating when she kept going on those dates."

"You knew about those too?" Linc asked.

"I think everybody in the county knew she was dating. Word gets around."

"You're tellin' me. I figure everyone will know our little secret soon."

As much as Linc wanted to shout it on the mountaintop that Jess was giving him a chance to love her, he also didn't want to let the world in to corrupt the new relationship.

They'd just have to handle things as they came, and that didn't sound like a bad plan when Jess was by his side.

"Don't let it shake you." Paul jerked his chin at the office. "Take her home."

Linc tipped his hat at the older cowboy. "Yes, sir."

He turned on his heels and went after her. In the office, she was slumped over the desk, exactly where he'd left her.

Brushing the back of his hand over her brow, he tried to gauge her fever. It didn't feel warmer than earlier, which might be a good sign. The last round of fever reducers should be starting to work.

"Hey, babe. You ready to get outta here?" he whispered.

She stirred and lifted her head slowly. "Yeah," she groaned.

Her movements were slow and dragging. As soon as she was on her feet, he rested a hand on her back.

"You want me to carry you?" he asked, hoping she didn't punch him for insinuating that she couldn't take care of herself.

She hesitated only a beat before nodding, and her compliance both thrilled him and terrified him.

Jess wouldn't let someone help her like this if she wasn't feeling really bad. He prayed she was just tired from being sick and not getting worse.

She looped her arm over his shoulders, and he lifted her into his arms. It would be a whole lot better if he was carrying her under different circumstances.

Jess's body melted against his, and the heat from her head seared against his neck.

"Are you sure we can't go see the doc?" he asked.

"I'll be fine. I'm just tired," she whispered.

Darkness had fallen, and he carried her out to his truck. He settled her in the passenger seat and rounded the truck to the driver's side. If she wasn't going to let him take her to the doctor, his goal was to get her home and comfortable as quickly as possible.

She sat up more on the ride home. He'd offered her a thermos of water that she sipped on during the drive. By the time they pulled up at her house, her eyes had more life in them.

"The water made me feel much better," she said as she reached for the door handle.

"Let me come get you," Linc said. He raced around the truck, but she was already stepping out by the time he got there.

"I'm okay. I'm really feeling better." She stretched her shoulders back and her arms up with a yawn. "I need a shower."

"That makes two of us," Linc said, relaxing a fraction after seeing Jess more alive.

He followed her to the porch and waited while she unlocked the door.

"Will you come in?" she asked.

"I was going to ask if I could. I don't want to leave you when you're sick."

She pushed open the door and took a deep breath. "If I don't feel better by morning, you can take me to the doctor." She turned around to face him and gave him a once-over. "You can get a shower if you have something clean to change into."

He started stepping back toward the truck. "I have a change of clothes."

"Good. I definitely don't have anything you can wear."

There was a warmth in the grin on her face that eased some of Linc's concerns. "I'll be right in."

"I'm going to get a shower. Make yourself at home, then you can get clean."

He grabbed the bag from his truck and jogged back to the house. Ms. Landry was going to have a juicy story for her gossip group tomorrow.

He left his duffle bag by the door and toed off his boots. Jess's place wasn't big or fancy, but it had a warm home feel. He completely understood why she loved it. A big beige rug covered most of the floor in the living area. A stone fireplace was the centerpiece of the main wall.

His favorite part? The furniture. Her sofa was older, but he'd melted into it like slow-moving tree sap the last time he'd been here.

It was a good thing it was comfortable because he might end up sleeping there tonight if Jess didn't show signs of improvement.

He wandered around the room, taking in Jess's secret spaces. What did she need to beat this sickness?

"Hey, Jess?" he shouted toward the hallway.

"Yeah?"

"You want me to make you something to eat?"

There was a pause before she said, "That would be great."

Good. He wasn't sure when she'd get her

appetite back. She hadn't eaten much of anything in two days. "What do you want?"

"I think there is bacon in the refrigerator. And eggs."

Linc headed toward the kitchen. "Breakfast it is."

Jess's place was still pretty new to him, but he found things easily. She wasn't one for extras, so the kitchen was stocked with only the essentials. No wall hangings. No decorative vases. No figurines. It was a functional space.

He could get used to this. Maybe she'd agree to let him come over and cook breakfast for the two of them instead of going to the dining hall every morning.

He was already trying to get more alone time with Jess. He'd never been drawn to someone before, and the need to keep her close was new, but it didn't scare him. They'd been living in each other's worlds for years. The progression seemed natural. Expected.

Twenty minutes later, he had bacon, eggs, and toast plated. Jess walked in as he was washing the dishes. Rubbing a towel over her hair, she let out a heavy sigh when she saw the spread of food.

"Wow. I doubt I can even make a dent in this. I hope you're hungry," she said as she eased to his side.

"I'll accept your best effort." He pulled her close

and pressed a kiss to her hair. He would never get tired of these easy moments with her.

He took a step back, still holding onto her arms. "I haven't had my shower yet."

She rolled her eyes. "It's not like I didn't smell you all week." She eyed the food. "I think my fever is down. I actually want to eat."

Linc guided her to a chair at the table. "Dinner is served."

She chuckled and sat. The smile on her face hadn't faded when he finished the blessing.

"What are you so smiley about?" he asked before he took the first bite of the scrambled eggs.

"Just thinking about how different this is from the dates I went on before. It was all so formal, and the expectations weren't clear. This is so much easier."

He reached over and laid a hand on top of hers. "I'll take you on real dates."

"No, you won't. I mean it. I like this better. Dates are about getting to know someone who is usually a stranger. You're constantly straightening your shoulders and trying to say the right thing. At least that's what I was doing. This is so much better. And besides, we already know each other."

"I know that I love you," Linc said. "I like you too most of the time."

She chuckled, and the sound sent a tingle of happiness up his spine. If he could wrap up in the joy of that sound, he'd sleep soundly for the rest of his life.

They ate in silence for a few minutes before she spoke again. "I like that you know me and still like me."

Linc lifted one eyebrow. "What's not to like?"

Jess shrugged. "Lots, I guess."

"You got it all wrong, but it's fine. I'll make you see the truth."

A knock at the front door had them stopping short.

"Who could that be?" she whispered.

Linc lifted his hands. "Don't look at me. I'm not expecting anyone at your place."

Jess stood and went to answer the door. Linc followed a few steps behind, just to make sure everything was okay. If he had his way, he'd stand by her like this for the rest of his life.

That revelation hadn't been a stretch after he'd confessed to loving her. She was different. She was the one. Nothing was holding him back now.

Jess rested a hand on the door and said, "Who is it?"

Good, at least she hadn't just opened it.

"Nathan. I'm Wes's friend," a man replied.

Jess looked at him and squinted. "Who is Wes?"

Linc shook his head. The name didn't ring a bell.

Jess's eyes widened, and she snapped her fingers. "The new guy. From Texas."

"If he's from Texas, how does he have a friend here?"

Jess lifted her hands and shoulders. "Beats me."

She opened the door, revealing a familiar face that made Linc's blood turn cold.

Ryan stood in the doorway with his hands in his pockets. The guy looked like he'd aged ten years, and the shadows that fell across his face only made him look older.

The cocky grin was all the warning Linc needed. He put an arm in front of Jess and gently pushed her behind him.

Ryan pulled his hands from his pockets and spread them wide. "I thought I'd find you here."

CHAPTER 40

LINC

L inc stared at Ryan and forced his breaths to come even. "What do you want?"

Ryan scoffed, but the malicious smile he wore didn't falter. "Long time, no see, friend."

The emphasis on the last word wasn't lost on Linc. He had no idea if someone had confirmed what he'd done to Ryan or not, but the look on the guy's face said he knew.

Ryan folded his arms over his chest and spread his feet to shoulder-width. "I knew you'd get a real job when you got out. I wasn't surprised when I heard you were a cowboy." He chuckled and shook his head. "How wholesome."

Ryan's attention turned to Jess. She was standing somewhere behind Linc with a hand resting on his shoulder blade, but he didn't dare take his gaze off Ryan.

If only he could tell her to hide somewhere in the house. He'd feel a lot better about facing the enemy if Jess was somewhere safe.

"Looks like you found a woman too." Ryan made a show of trying to get a peek at her. "She's hot."

Fire surged in Linc's middle. Jess wasn't a part of this fight. He raised a hand and pointed a warning finger at Ryan just as Jess spoke.

"Shut up and go home," she said with enough bite to let Ryan know she wasn't one to play games.

Linc leveled his stare at Ryan. "Leave her out of this."

Ryan raised his hands in mock surrender. "Sorry, man. Just trying to catch up."

"How'd you get here?" Linc asked.

"There are a lot of cowboys in town. I had no idea this was a hub for summer cowboy jobs." Ryan laughed. "Cowboys! Can you believe it? Anyway, all those kids at the bar in town like to talk about their new jobs. There's not much else to do around here."

"That's a good reason for you to leave. Or you can wait until I escort you out. Take your pick," Linc said in a low warning.

Ryan chuckled. "Nah. I think I'll hang around. Those guys at the bar are funny. They told me all about you. Did you know they're all scared of you? Half of them haven't even met you, but they've heard about you."

"We're done here," Jess said. "Get off my property."

Ryan jerked back like he'd been slapped in the face. "Where'd you find this one? She's mouthy."

"Leave," Jess said again, enunciating the word.

"Better do what the lady says," Linc added, hoping Ryan picked up on the warning in his voice.

Ryan tilted his head back and forth. "I don't like taking orders. It's a whole thing." He waved his hand in the air like he was swatting off a fly. He looked at Jess and jerked a thumb at Linc. "He doesn't like taking orders either. He tell you about that?"

"That's none of your business," Jess spat back. "He told me enough about you."

Great. She'd picked up on who their visitor was. Hopefully, she remembered all the things Linc had told her and would proceed with caution.

Ryan tightened his arms over his chest and settled his wide smile on Jess. "He tell you about the woman he killed?"

Linc's breath stopped in his throat. Ryan was going to tell Jess before he had a chance to explain.

"He tell you about the building he burned down? And the woman in it?"

"Shut up," Linc said.

"You didn't tell her?" Ryan asked, playing coy. "He tell you he only got a year, and I got five?"

The blood pulsing in Linc's ears drowned out all

sound, and the edges of his vision started to blur. He hadn't told Jess. There wasn't ever a good time to tell someone you'd been partially responsible for someone's death.

He didn't want to see her face right now. Not when it was probably dawning on her that he was worse than she'd feared–that he was every bad thing he'd warned her about.

"I didn't do it," Linc said.

"But you made sure they knew that I did. How convenient. Don't lie to yourself. You were just as responsible as I was."

Linc slowly shook his head. "I didn't mean for anyone to die."

Ryan shrugged. "Like it or not. It was bound to happen sooner or later. I didn't think you'd care so much."

"You didn't think I'd care? You knew she was in there?" Linc narrowed his eyes at Ryan, reassessing everything that had happened that night.

"Of course not." Ryan huffed, and his sinister smile was back. "I bet you've convinced everyone you know here that you're just a quiet, decent guy. We used to destroy anything and everything we wanted."

"That's the past," Linc said. "I don't live there anymore."

"Life doesn't work that way, *partner*. You don't

get to walk around pretending you didn't kill someone."

"I didn't kill anybody! *You* killed her. I tried to stop you."

"That's what you told the cops too," Ryan said, monotone and sinister. "How convenient that you just absolved yourself of that guilt. It just vanished." He lifted his hands, waving them like a magician ending a trick.

It wasn't magic. It was regret, remorse, and God. Linc had done terrible things. He'd burned plenty in his day. His destructive streak had been a mile wide.

But he valued human life. He wouldn't have killed someone. Ryan hadn't cared if someone was in the building, and he'd already stoked the flames by the time Linc ran inside to check.

Memories of the headlines flew through his mind. Things said in court still haunted him.

He hadn't been able to save that woman, and that regret spread and painted every single thing he'd done up to that point in red.

Ryan looked behind Linc. "What do you have that he would want?" His gaze scanned over Jess from head to toe. "Linc doesn't do anything unless he can get something for himself."

"Get out," Jess sneered from behind Linc.

"Time for you to go. We're done here," Linc said, pushing the door closed.

Ryan slipped his foot through the small opening, preventing the door from closing completely.

Linc tensed his jaw and leveled Ryan with a hard stare. "Move your foot, or I'll cut it off."

Ryan lifted his hand, aiming a gun at the center of the door.

A cold wave ran down Linc's spine as he registered the trajectory of the bullet. Jess stood on the other side of the door and couldn't see the threat waiting for her.

The playful smile on Ryan's face was gone, replaced by a sinister stare. "Let me in, or I'll blow her head off."

CHAPTER 41
JESS

J ess froze at Ryan's words.

I'll blow her head off.

Linc hadn't moved either, and she took her cues from him. He knew Ryan, and she had to trust Linc's judgment on this.

She still couldn't piece together what they'd been talking about. Linc had killed someone. A woman. Was Ryan telling the truth or just trying to get her to do or say something stupid?

Either way, Linc hadn't denied that a woman was dead, and a cold foreboding rushed down her spine. It didn't make sense. She didn't understand.

Confusion always kindled her anger, and here it was, right on time.

Blow her head off. Ryan had a gun, and from what she'd heard about him, calling his bluff wouldn't turn out well for her. She was close enough that a bullet would go straight through the door.

Run. Fight or flight?

Stupidly, her body chose to freeze. Ugh, that wasn't what she wanted. She wanted to punch Ryan in the face, but her limbs wouldn't move, and every breath was harder to take in than the last.

Linc stared out the small opening in the door, and she watched him for any signs. What should she do?

Please, God. Help us. Help us. Help us.

Then he moved. Linc's hand gripping the door twitched and his finger pointed. He wanted her to sneak away.

Okay. No more freezing. Linc said to move.

But she couldn't leave him. She couldn't save herself and leave him in Ryan's crosshairs.

The air in her chest whooshed out. She couldn't leave him. He could die.

"Last chance," Ryan said.

Linc's finger flexed again, pointing adamantly toward her safety.

She had to move. Linc was asking her to, and she had to trust him. She *did* trust him.

Slowly, she took a measured step to the right. Then another. With the next step, she crouched and crawled toward the sofa. Scanning the room for anything to use as a weapon, she came up empty.

Drat. Now would be a great time to have a pointless figurine or a candle at least.

"You were always selfish," Ryan said. "You should have been upfront with her about that."

The shot rang through the house. She covered her ears and ducked her head as pieces of the door went flying.

Her heart pounded, and she reached for the phone in her pocket. She pressed her back against the sofa and looked from left to right as she typed out a message.

Jess: Help. Call 911. My house.

There was a thud behind her followed by scuffling. All the movement meant Linc hadn't been shot, but her panic didn't ease.

"Where is she?" Ryan grunted like he was straining.

"Let her go. She doesn't have anything to do with this," Linc said.

Jess risked a peek over the sofa. The door was open, but Linc and Ryan must have been fighting on the porch because she couldn't see them.

"She does now!" Ryan shouted. "You took everything from me. You ratted me out!"

The phone in her hand vibrated.

Brett: Done. On my way.

Jess gripped the phone, and her head spun. How long would it take for help to arrive?

She had to help. *Think, think, think.*

She had a pistol. In her bedroom. She'd have to cross the room, putting her in full view if Ryan decided to look up.

There wasn't time to weigh the options. She had to go.

Easing around the sofa, Jess kept her attention on the door.

Ryan spat, "You got me a sentence I couldn't get out of. You're the reason I spent all this time in max security!"

Jess took a deep breath and made a run for the hallway, praying she'd make it back in time to help Linc.

She ran straight to the bookshelf where she kept the gun on the top shelf. Sliding to a stop in front of it, she grabbed the gun and magazine. Her hands shook as she loaded it.

The gun had sat on that shelf for years, and she'd never needed to use it. Now, she might have to. Linc needed her, and there wasn't time to think. Her head spun from the fever, and the pounding behind her temples was back. Her heart pounded so hard, she wasn't sure if she could hear it or just feel the thumping in her veins.

Jess rushed back into the living room. The remains of the door were swung open, and she could see out onto the porch now. Linc and Ryan were landing blows back and forth. They were too close for her to get a shot at Ryan.

The gun was heavy in her hand–a weapon in more ways than one.

Running out onto the porch, she zeroed in on Ryan and raised the butt of the gun. Putting all of her strength into it, she swung down, landing a hard blow to his head.

Ryan covered his head, and she'd caught him off guard enough for Linc to secure the upper hand. He let his fist fly, and Ryan lost his balance, falling to his hands and knees on the wooden porch with a thud.

When he looked up, his stare locked with Jess's. Dread washed over her like a wave.

Ryan broke the stare and reached to his right. When he stood, the gun was back in his hands, and he pointed the barrel at Linc. Scrambling back a few steps, Ryan pierced Linc with a warning glare.

"I don't have anything left to lose because of you." Ryan's attention turned back to Jess. "But you do."

"What do you want?" Linc said, staying bent and ready to make a move on Ryan if he got the chance.

"Money. And suffering."

Linc laughed. "I don't have any money."

"Fine." Ryan shrugged one shoulder. "Then I'll settle for double the suffering."

Ryan turned the gun toward her. She didn't have time to catch her breath before he fired.

CHAPTER 42
JESS

Jess dove through the open front door, but a sharp pain pierced her arm. She hit the floor with a thud and immediately crawled around a corner, propping her back against a wall and tucking her knees to her chest.

Seconds ticked by as the ringing in her ears continued. Panic hung on the edges of everything as numbness covered her whole body.

"Jess!"

The scream was far away and muffled.

"Jess!"

The second shout was clearer, and the pounding of her pulse filled her ears.

The ringing faded, and the blurriness cleared. The doorframe was shattered. Pieces of wood and Sheetrock littered the floor. She reached for her shoulder. There was tingling but no pain.

She hadn't been shot. Debris must have hit her. Too bad her adrenaline hadn't figured it out yet.

Leaning against the wall, Jess huffed for breath after breath.

"Jess!" Linc screamed amidst a struggle.

Think. Think. Think. She had to distract Ryan or get him away from Linc.

"Don't move, or I'll kill you too," Ryan seethed.

Linc's footsteps pounded on the porch. "Jess!"

Another shot rang through the house. Jess pressed her hands over her ears and tucked her shoulders in. A thud shook the floor beneath her, and she let out a sob.

Keeping her eyes squeezed closed, she prayed frantically.

What do I do? What do I do? What do I do? Please, God. Help!

A groan and a huff from Linc told her he was still alive.

She opened her eyes, and her gaze landed on her gun. She'd dropped it after Ryan shot at her.

Grabbing it, she tucked back against the wall. With a deep breath, she peeked around the busted corner.

Ryan stood over a writhing Linc with the gun in his hand pointed down.

Linc's teeth were gritted, and his eyes were squeezed closed as he gripped his upper arm.

No. She couldn't lose him. She had to help him. Had to save him.

She lifted the gun and looked at it. When she peeked again, Ryan was crouching over Linc. They were too close, and she didn't trust her aim with shaking hands.

She had to get Ryan away from Linc. Knowing what she had to do, she stepped out from behind the wall.

"Ryan."

He looked up at her, but there wasn't any fear in his eyes. His bland expression made it seem like she was insignificant. He stood, holding the emotionless look on his face.

Surprise. It was the only advantage she had. She lifted the gun from behind the corner and steadied it with both hands before pulling the trigger.

Ryan's left side jerked back, pulling him to the floor with a thud.

She'd done it, and the implications hit her square in the chest. Her hands shook, but she held tight to the gun in her hand.

Ryan groaned and twisted.

Linc pressed up onto his hands and moved toward Ryan. A trail of blood followed.

Jess spotted Ryan's gun on the floor and ran for it, grabbing it before he'd even had the chance to get up.

Linc was beside her, panting and slumped. "Nice shot."

Jess held the guns with shaking hands. Linc's side was covered in blood, but he wrapped her in a quick hug with his other arm.

"You okay?" he asked.

"Yeah. I'm fine. What about you?"

"Don't worry about me. Go to the neighbor's house."

"I'm not leaving you. The cops are on their way. So is Brett," she said. The words gave her a surge of hope that they'd make it through this.

Ryan tried to push up onto his elbows, and Linc crouched next to him. "Give me something to tie him up with."

Ryan spat and shouted through a string of curses as Linc pinned him to the ground.

Jess ran to the laundry room where she kept all of the odds and ends. She stood in the small room and stared at the cabinets on one side. "Come on, come on, come on," she mumbled.

"Zip ties." She tucked one of the guns under her arm and pulled a pack of them out of a cabinet. She darted back to the living room where Linc fought to contain Ryan while he thrashed.

Ryan's teeth were bared, and his eyes were wild. With the next jerk, a flash of silver caught Jess's attention.

"No!" she shouted as she lunged for the two men.

Linc seethed when the tip of Ryan's blade cut into his side. Losing his grip, Linc fell to the floor.

Jess jerked to a halt, dropping the zip ties and one of the guns.

No. Not Linc. They'd just found each other. They were about to start something new.

Heat boiled in her middle. It was a familiar feeling. One she could harness.

The cool metal of the gun lit up her hand. The courage to use it again rose inside her.

Ryan was scrambling to his feet, and she lifted the gun again. Her hands were still shaking, but she would make a better shot this time. The confidence settled over her, and she took one last breath.

Squeezing both hands on the gun, she squeezed the trigger.

It moved, but the loud shot didn't fill the room.

Jess pulled it again, but the gun only clicked.

It was Ryan's gun, and it was empty.

Ryan's grin only fueled her fire, but she only had a second to brace herself before he lunged for her.

The back of her head hit the floor, jarring all of her teeth as the old wound took another hit. She gasped for air, but Ryan's weight pinned her down.

He lifted onto his arms, and she tried to follow his movements. Stars flashed and danced on the edges of her vision.

He looked over his shoulder, then back at her. "Had to make sure he was watching," Ryan said. His dark hair hung over his forehead, casting a dim shadow over his dark eyes, and his grin spread wider. "He needs to know what it feels like to lose it all."

A numb warmth spread over the back of her head, but she held his gaze as she stared up at him. Teeth bared and ready to fight to the end. "He'll kill you for this."

Ryan chuckled, low and sinister like he'd won the day. "I'd like to see him try."

CHAPTER 43
LINC

L inc growled through the pain. It was the only sound he was capable of at the time.

Fitting for his attitude too.

His nostrils flared as he took deep breaths. His teeth gritted together, and he let out another groan.

Ryan was a dead man.

Linc raised his head and blinked through the fuzziness in his vision.

Ryan was on his hands and knees. Where was Jess?

"He'll kill you for this," she seethed.

"I'd like to see him try."

Oh, that could be arranged. There was no way on God's green earth Ryan was getting his way today.

Linc pulled one knee up until his foot rested flat

on the floor. Blood soaked everything around him, but he couldn't tell if it was his or Ryan's.

Probably Linc's, judging from the heaviness in his limbs. He had to work fast or he'd miss his opportunity. He could push past the pain only until his body decided to run out of blood.

Jess said she called for help. They'd better be breaking the speed limit to get here.

When he lifted his head again, Ryan was a little clearer.

And Jess was pinned beneath him. She jerked and bucked, giving it everything she had, but Ryan was stronger.

This wasn't happening. Not while Linc still lived and breathed.

The guy was going to be sorry when this was over. Sorry he'd ever laid eyes on Lincoln North again.

The edges of his vision reddened. Ryan wanted scorched earth? He'd get it.

Linc lunged at Ryan, pushing him off Jess and pressing him into the floor. With his forearm over Ryan's neck, Linc leaned all of his weight onto his old friend.

Ryan's eyes widened, and he sputtered.

"Didn't catch that. What did you say?" Linc taunted.

Ryan's mouth opened and closed while his hand clawed at Linc's arm.

"Who thought it was a good idea to touch my girl?" Linc asked.

Ryan's eyes darted left and right, back and forth. He squirmed from side to side, trying to pull one of his arms out from underneath Linc's leg.

His face swelled, turning a deep blue. Ryan jerked one more time, pulling his arm free and slashing it out to the side.

"Ahh!" Jess screamed.

Linc's attention jerked to where Jess lay on the floor beside them. Ryan's flailing had dragged the blade of his knife across Jess's side.

"Jess!"

She writhed to one side, clutching her abdomen.

Linc pushed off Ryan and scrambled for Jess. "Talk to me. Talk to me." He ran his hands over her arms and sides.

There was so much blood.

She gasped in short breaths. Her eyes were wide with a terror she couldn't hide.

"It's okay. It's okay," Linc repeated. Half to himself and half to her.

The small whisper of a siren lent him a surge of energy. "Hang in there, babe." He pressed a hand over hers, putting pressure on the wound. How deep was it? Were paramedics coming too?

Ryan coughed and sputtered, catching his breath from having half the life choked out of him. Too bad Linc hadn't been able to finish the job.

Jess grabbed Linc's arm so hard her fingernails dug into his skin. "My gun. I dropped it."

Linc scanned the room, but he only saw Ryan's. Where had she dropped it?

Ryan turned and spat blood onto the floor before lifting his glare to Linc.

With no sign of the gun, he'd have to make do with what he had. The knife in his pocket had come in handy more than once over the years.

Ryan's nose wrinkled, and he flung a few curses at Linc.

Words. The guy was wasting his energy on words, but it was to Linc's benefit. The longer the guy lingered, the closer the cops got.

In the blink of an eye, Ryan lunged forward, grabbing Linc's shirt and pulling. He had Ryan pinned again within seconds, but the last of his energy was waning.

The sirens were getting quieter and quieter. Were they leaving? They couldn't leave.

"Give up," Ryan snarled through gritted teeth.

Well, that wasn't an option. Not for him, and not for Jess either. She had to hang in there. He had to save her.

Ryan bucked his hips and turned in one motion, toppling Linc off onto the floor. The wood met his face in a rush. Almost too quickly.

Come on. Come on. Come on.

"Ryan!"

Linc and Ryan both turned to Jess. She stood in the middle of the room with a gun pointed at them.

She was still bleeding, but the fire in her eyes said she wasn't ready to give up yet.

A rush of pride welled in Linc's chest. *That's my girl.*

"Step back, or I'll shoot," she said calmly.

Linc raised a hand, but it fell back down. "Don't do it." The last word sounded funny. Almost like he was in a dream or underwater.

"You can't shoot me," Ryan panted. "You might miss and hit him." He jabbed a finger toward Linc.

It might not even matter soon. The room was fading, and Linc's shoulders were getting heavier.

Colorful lights flashed through the window, and Ryan turned. His eyes widened as the shadows fell over his face.

Had Ryan not heard the sirens? Why couldn't Linc hear them anymore?

Jess screamed, then a blast rumbled the floor. Linc braced his hands on the wood, letting the blood trickle a hot trail down his forearms. It dripped from his hair and fell into his eyes. He couldn't see anymore, and his arms collapsed just before his head hit the floor.

CHAPTER 44

JESS

Jess rubbed the pads of her thumbs over the back of Linc's hand. She'd been silently praying for hours at his bedside, but his condition hadn't changed.

The sterile smell hung in her nose as she sniffed. She hated the waiting. Hated sitting here helpless while Linc needed a miracle.

God, please.

The surgery went well last night, and the doctor had been able to repair most of the damage in Linc's shoulder. Even with the best medical intervention, no one could guarantee he'd make a full recovery.

Bandaging covered his whole shoulder, and another wrapped around his middle. The cut on his side had been tedious to repair too, but the doctor seemed to be more concerned with the shoulder.

There was a quiet knock on the door before

Hillary walked in. She'd been his nurse since early that morning. It took a special person to be a nurse, and Jess appreciated the attentiveness.

"Still the same?" Hillary asked.

"I guess so. He hasn't moved."

Hillary stepped up to the computer beside the bed. Her dark hair was pulled back into a tight ponytail, and she couldn't have been much older than Jess. "Just checking some things."

More checking when Jess wanted action. Impatience had been her enemy for the last twelve hours.

"Everything still looks okay. Call me if you need anything or if he wakes up."

"Thanks," Jess whispered as Hillary left as quickly as she'd come.

Jess let out a deep breath and rested her forehead on the back of his hand. The bending tugged at the stitches in her side, but she didn't care.

She'd prayed about everything she could possibly think to pray, but nothing was changing. Linc was still lying in the same position he had all day.

A knock on the door startled her, jerking her from a weird dream.

"Knock, knock," Brett said as he walked in, followed by Vera.

Jess sat up, blinking past the grogginess. How long had she been asleep?

Brett set a large bag filled with food containers

on the tray. "We brought food. Well, Vera brought food."

Vera patted Brett's shoulder. "You carried it, so you did your part."

"Thanks. I don't know if I could eat, and Linc hasn't woken up yet."

Brett's eyes squinted as he gave Linc a once-over. "Still no change?"

"No. The doctor and nurses said to be patient."

Brett chuckled. "How's that going for you?"

She glared up at her brother. "Not great."

"I do have good news. I talked to Camille this morning. She's pretty up-to-date on what's going on, and she said she'd represent you and Linc if any charges get brought up."

Jess straightened. "Why would that happen? Ryan attacked us."

Brett lifted his hands. "I don't know, but I thought it would be better to be prepared just in case. You shot someone, so I figure there will at least be an investigation."

Jess rested her forehead in her hand. The fever hadn't come back, but the exhaustion still hung over her like a thick blanket. "The police have already been by to talk to me. I can't believe I shot someone. Even if it was Ryan."

Vera rubbed a hand over Jess's back. "Don't beat yourself up. You did what you had to do."

"Yeah. At least Ryan will be leaving here in cuffs," Brett said.

"He hasn't been released?" She'd been so worried about Linc, she hadn't thought to get an update on Ryan.

"Nope," Brett said. "He had surgery too. You got him good."

The anger swelled in her chest again, but she didn't have the energy to maintain it. Ryan had barged into their happy life they'd been building and tried to destroy it brick by brick.

Jess rubbed her eyes. "Thanks for coming to help. I hadn't even thought about legal stuff."

"Don't mention it. I wish I could have gotten to you sooner."

Jess lifted her head and looked up at her brother. "I know what you went through with Thea now. I'm sorry I wasn't there for you more."

Brett squeezed her shoulder. "No worries, sis. We're gonna get you two through this. Speaking of Thea, she's loving running the barn right now, and she's doing an awesome job. Don't worry about work for a while."

"I hate she's been working so much overtime," Jess said.

Brett shrugged. "She said she likes being with the horses all day anyway. Don't worry about her."

"What would we do without her?" she asked.

"God knew we'd need her."

Jess eyed the bags of food. "Thanks for the food. Knowing it's going to be delicious might force me to eat it even without an appetite."

Vera chuckled. The woman didn't make a bad meal, but she still glowed with every compliment she received. "You're welcome. I'll bring more whenever you need it."

"I hope we get to leave soon," Jess said, knowing the possibility wasn't likely.

Linc's hand gave Jess's a small squeeze, and she gasped. Looking between his face and the hand holding hers, she waited for another sign.

"I think he's waking up."

Linc's eyes opened a small sliver before closing again. He blinked a few more times and stretched his back a little.

"Don't try to move," Jess said, standing by his bedside.

"Jess?"

"I'm here. I can't believe you're awake!"

Linc squinted at her. "Are you okay?" His words were low and raspy.

"I'm fine. Just got a few stitches in my side. You got some too."

He looked at his shoulder and frowned.

"The shoulder took a little more than stitches, but the doctor seemed content with how the surgery went."

"Surgery," Linc said, resting his head back

against the pillow.

"Yeah, not fun, but hopefully it'll heal and be just fine," Jess said. She poured all of the confidence she had into the words, hoping to assure herself and Linc.

"Hey, man. Glad you're awake," Brett said.

"Me too, I guess. Where's Ryan?"

"Still in recovery," Brett said. "He has a chaperone with him, since he's under investigation."

Linc sighed. "Man, I'd like to be rid of him."

"Wouldn't we all. Man, I know you don't have many friends, but if they're all like this guy, just don't tell us," Brett said.

"Sorry 'bout that." Linc glanced at Jess before hanging his head.

Vera rubbed her hands together. "Well, we'd better go. You probably need some rest. Just call us if you need anything."

"Thanks so much," Jess said.

"Oh, and we'll have your house cleaned up before you get home. At least, we'll try to. It's still a crime scene right now. Paul already got a new door, and we're just waiting on the go-ahead to fix it."

Jess's face grew cold remembering the mess in her living room. The front door was busted, and there had to be blood everywhere.

"Ms. Landry is having the time of her life," Jess explained. "Actually, she called the police before Brett got a chance. They were already on their way."

Linc huffed. "That woman is my new best friend."

Brett crossed his arms over his chest. "What? I called too! And I've been trying to get even a friend status for years. This is bogus."

"You can have friend status, but Jess still outranks you," Linc said groggily.

Brett nodded. "I guess that's fine, as long as you treat her right."

Linc squeezed Jess's hand, sending a surge of warmth up her arm. "You don't have to worry about that."

"Well, we'd better get going. See you two back at the ranch soon."

Soon? How long would that be? All of the chores that needed to be done before the tourist season started would be taking a back seat while Linc recovered. She didn't intend to leave him unless she had to.

Brett wrapped her in a gentle hug, careful not to touch her injured side.

"Thanks again," she whispered to her brother.

"Don't mention it. Love you, sis."

"Love you too." She had a new appreciation for love lately. Not only did she have a family she could count on, but she had a man with no obligation to her who would risk his life for her.

Linc.

After Brett and Vera left, Linc squeezed Jess's hand again. "Are you sure you're okay?"

"I'm fine. Really. I was discharged last night."

Linc rubbed his thumb over her hand. "I'm sorry."

"You didn't do anything wrong."

"But I did. I did everything Ryan said I did. Now, I put you through this because of the things I did–"

"In the past," Jess finished. "If you did those things, they've been forgiven."

"I need to tell you about the woman," Linc said, looking down at their linked hands.

Oh. That. She'd been hoping to avoid talking about it for a while. Was she ready to hear it?

"I burned buildings. It was stupid. I was angry, and I didn't care about anyone but myself. We mostly burned abandoned buildings. Old stores, run-down sheds, things like that. One night, Ryan set fire to an abandoned apartment building. We hadn't talked about it before, and when I got there, he handed me the lighter."

Jess's pulse pounded in her head. She didn't want to hear the story, knowing the outcome was so awful.

"I thought to ask if he'd checked the building. I always did that. He said he hadn't, so I panicked. I went in, but I couldn't see through the smoke. By the time I ran back out, the police and fire departments were already there, and I was arrested."

"And someone was in the building," Jess said, filling in the blank with the information she already hated.

"I don't know who it was. They couldn't identify her. The investigators said she was probably homeless, but that doesn't make it any better." He covered his face with his hands. "I did that. I killed her."

The gripping in Jess's chest ached, stealing the breath from her lungs. It was as bad as she'd feared. A woman was dead.

"Do you see why I tried to stay away? Why I warned you? I can't make up for that. I can't forget it. Ryan was right. I can't just live my life like it didn't happen."

All the things Ryan had said about Linc were true, but it didn't add up. They didn't describe the man she knew. Linc had done some bad things, but she believed him when he said he didn't mean to kill someone.

"We can't fix all of our mistakes, but God offers us forgiveness."

"Even for taking a person's life?" he asked.

Jess nodded. "I think that one is included."

He looked away from her and whispered, "I doubt it."

She grabbed his hand and held it between both of hers. "It's never too late to do the right thing. You know the Lord now, and you gave your life to Him.

He washed away your sins. You made a mistake, and you tried to fix it."

"I didn't. I couldn't."

"But He did. Linc, it's time to put it in the past," she said with finality. "You can't change it, but you're a new person now. You have to let it go."

He shook his head. "I'm sorry."

"I don't know what you're apologizing to me for. You already apologized once. I've forgiven you."

He looked up at her and chewed on the inside of his cheek. If he thought about it too much, he would cling to the guilt.

"The things Ryan said about me were true too," she said.

That lit a fire in Linc's eyes. "Don't even start."

"I would repeat them, but there were a lot of curses in there," she said.

"None of that was true."

"Mouthy was true," she said.

Linc chuckled once and immediately reached for his side. His brows pulled together in pain. "You're not mouthy. You're just opinionated."

"Same thing."

"I love you just the way you are."

She leaned in, resting her elbows on the side of his bed, despite the pain, and whispered, "Same."

He brushed a hand over her hair. "You're the best thing that's ever happened to me. Meeting you changed everything."

"Don't get sappy. Sometimes, we let the hateful things people say take up space in our heads. We have to decide to learn from those things and trust God to forgive us and help us move forward."

Linc rubbed his thumb over her cheek. "You're a good woman."

"And you're a good man."

Linc swallowed hard and whispered, "Let's make a promise."

"What kind of promise?" she asked.

"That we won't let what happened last night take anything else from us. I know you love your place, and I don't want to let what Ryan did ruin that for you."

Ugh. Her house. He'd destroyed the living room. "I don't want to see it right now, but I do love it."

"I know, and as bad as it might look, you won a big fight there, and that's something to be proud of. I'm proud of you."

She scoffed. "If I was brave, it was only because you and God were beside me."

Linc lifted her hand to his lips and kissed it. "If I'm a better man, it's only because you and God are beside me."

CHAPTER 45

JESS

The dining hall was packed, and the roar of all the talking and laughing buzzed over Jess's skin. Having the guests back at the ranch had been a perfect distraction. She could go a full ten hours a day without thinking about the mess Ryan created.

On the flip side, it also left little time to spend with Linc. Sure, they sought each other out every chance they got, but between workdays and Linc's follow-up appointments with doctors, their alone time was pretty sparse.

She scanned the crowd for him now. He should've already been back from his appointment.

Fingers touched her shoulder, and she turned, trying not to recoil. Touching still triggered her old fears sometimes, but she'd come a long way lately. Linc was patiently breaking those walls down.

It was Mrs. Shepherd, a dark-haired woman Jess

had met earlier that week. "Hey! How is Penny doing?"

"She's doing okay, but she's still a little timid."

Penny was a sweet girl with a love for horses, but her fear of heights was getting in the way. Knowing all she was going through to conquer her fears, Jess couldn't help but be proud.

Mrs. Shepherd wrung her hands. "I know. I was worried about that."

"Don't be. She'll get through this. I can tell she's determined. She's already come a long way."

A soft smile bloomed on Mrs. Shepherd's face. "You're right. I'm so glad she has a patient teacher. She can't stop talking about you. I think you're her new role model."

Jess swallowed hard. Her? A role model? It didn't seem possible, but she wanted to hang onto the words.

"Thanks for saying that. Don't worry about Penny. She's doing a great job."

Mrs. Shepherd's smile beamed as she jerked a thumb over her shoulder. "I'd better get back over there. She's talking some poor stranger's head off."

"See you later," Jess said as she continued her path through the large room.

Still no sign of Linc.

Pushing the unease down into her gut, she pulled out her phone to call him, but a text she hadn't noticed lit up the screen.

Linc: Come to the supply shed behind the archery range.

Jess pocketed her phone and wove her way through the crowd. He hadn't called her after the appointment or texted to let her know everything was okay. Hopefully, that didn't mean he'd hit any setbacks in his recovery.

She prayed for good news as she pushed out of the double doors and cantered down the steps toward her truck. The late spring had achieved pleasant status about a week ago, and the waning of the season made her itch with the promise of summer warmth.

She pulled up at the shed and shifted into park before coming to a complete stop.

Oops.

After a jerky entrance, she hopped out of the truck and jogged inside. The squeaky door announced her arrival, and Linc lifted his head, letting go of the bag he'd been packing.

Jess opened her arms. "What's the word?"

Linc turned to show her his arm, and she gasped. The brace was gone.

"You don't have to wear it anymore?" she asked, praying this wasn't a joke.

"I'm free," he said, meeting her in the middle of the room.

She slid her arms around his waist and tilted her chin up to him.

At what point was the giddiness supposed to fade? People were starting to worry about her. She'd been walking around with this ridiculous grin on her face for weeks.

She'd probably stop the madness if she had a choice. The muscles in her cheeks tingled relentlessly.

Linc framed her face with his hands and pressed his lips to hers, setting off a burst of explosions inside her.

He pulled away but thankfully kept his hold on her face. There was a slight chance she'd melt to the ground in a puddle if he let go.

"Sorry I didn't text sooner. Mrs. Grant called."

"Is she okay?" It bothered Jess a little that the older lady lived so far up the mountain alone. It was a good thing she had Linc's number on speed dial.

Linc brushed his fingers through her hair. "She's fine. Her hot water heater was on the fritz, and she said she wanted it fixed before her book club ladies came over tonight."

"Book club?" Jess asked.

"She said Ms. Landry was coming. I think book club is code for gossip and wine."

A forceful laugh burst out of Jess's throat, and she buried her head in Linc's chest. "Gossip and wine. That's probably close to the truth."

"If Ms. Landry is there, then yes." Jess looked up at him and tilted her head. "Those two became fast friends, didn't they? I can't believe Ms. Landry is actually getting out of the house."

"I don't mind," Linc said. "At least she isn't watching me come and go from your place every night."

"Speaking of my place, how much longer are you gonna be here?" Jess asked.

"Are you saying you don't have a lesson this evening?"

"I'm free as a bird," she confirmed.

Linc gave her a slight shove and rushed back to the bag he'd been packing. He pulled things from one shelf, then another, before securing the bag and setting it to the side.

He walked by her with purpose, grabbing her hand as he passed. "Let's get outta here."

"Are you serious? Do you actually have work to do?"

"Nothing that can't wait till tomorrow, babe. I miss you, and I need alone time."

Linc practically dragged her to her truck, opened the driver's side door, pressed a quick kiss to her lips, and jogged off to his own truck.

"Well, bye," she shouted after him.

"See you in a sec," he said before closing his door and starting the truck.

Jess bit her lips between her teeth as she drove home. She was looking forward to watching *Jeopardy* with him for the first time in weeks, and now she could actually cuddle up beside him without hurting his shoulder.

Cuddling. Who would have guessed she was a cuddler?

Better yet, who would have guessed Linc liked it even more than she did?

They parked in front of her house and met on the porch. Twilight shaded everything in a blue glow, and the only thing lighting the evening was Ms. Landry's porch light.

"I miss her when she's not home," Linc said. "She still disappears behind the curtains when I wave."

Jess pulled out her keys and unlocked the door. "Stop pestering that old woman. We probably scarred her for life after the Ryan incident."

She tossed her keys on the table by the door and sighed. Home at last.

Linc wrapped his arm around her waist and twirled her around, whipping her hair out in a wide fan.

"Hey—"

He cut her off with his mouth against hers. The kiss started off slow and guarded, then poured out in a rush. His breath was hot against her lips as he sipped and drank everything from her.

When she pulled away gasping for air, he trickled soft, tame kisses onto her cheeks.

"I have been dying to kiss you. All day. It's torture, really," he said against her jaw.

"We sound like one of the other sappy couples," she joked.

Linc lifted his head. "Ridge is the worst."

"I know! So surprising that the burly football player is a total sap."

"Your voice is my favorite song," Linc mocked in a deeper tone.

Jess covered her mouth to stifle the laugh. "Thea is just as bad. I think I heard her tell Brett she missed him even when he was right beside her the other day."

Linc's hearty laugh burst through the air. They might be joking, but she knew exactly what drove her friends to say and do such ridiculous things. Love had been having its way with her for weeks now, molding her into a different person. A better version of her old self.

Linc's rough hand slid up her neck and into the hair at the nape. His gentle pull coaxed her to tilt her head back as he trailed soft kisses up the sensitive skin of her neck.

His warm breath brushed against her ear, sending a tingling down her spine. "You know what I want?"

Oh, wow. That was one way to make her heart stop. "What?" she whispered back.

"I want...a grilled cheese sandwich."

All of the air in Jess's lungs left in one swift whoosh as she doubled over in laughter.

"With tomato soup," Linc added.

Jess wiped tears from the corners of her eyes as the laughter faded. "I love you. So much."

The open smile on Linc's face changed into a guarded grin. "Really?"

"Yeah, really. Haven't I said it enough? I'm crazy about you. Your horse and hay smell makes me happy. I even love you when you mumble while you work."

"I don't do that."

"You most certainly do." She propped her hands on her hips. "But anyway, that's about the sappiest love confession I can think of, but it's true."

Linc stuck his hand into his shirt pocket and pulled something tiny out.

It was two tiny somethings. Rings.

"What's that?" she spat before thinking.

Linc knelt in front of her and held up the two rings. "Jess–"

"Why are there two?" she asked, impolitely cutting him off, but she didn't care.

"Because one is a promise ring, and one is an engagement ring. I thought I'd let you choose because I don't want to scare you off, but I also want you to know I'm all in either way."

Jess's eyes widened. He bought two rings.

"You're crazy!" she shouted. Why was she shouting?

"Crazy in love," Linc said with a grin.

She covered her mouth with both hands and looked back and forth between the rings. He bought two rings. He bought two rings so she could choose how fast things moved between them.

Her breath hitched, and she wrung her hands in front of her chest. "Why would you want to marry me?"

When she finally got up the courage to look at him, the softness in his eyes begged her to trust him. She could see the fear pinching the edges of his eyes closed. She'd asked a question instead of answering the silent one he hadn't asked yet.

"For the first time, I know what it's like to love, and I don't care if someone makes fun of me for telling you exactly how I feel about you."

He lowered the rings, still holding one in each hand. "You deserve better than me, but I couldn't stand the thought of seeing you with someone else. So I became a better man. I'm still working on it, but one day, I hope to be the man you deserve."

Jess crouched and slipped her hands around his, lifting them both between them. "Which one is which?"

He lifted his left hand. "Promise." Then his right. "Engagement."

Jess wrapped both of her hands around his hand holding the engagement ring. "This one."

"Are you sure?" he asked, barely breathing as he pinned her with an intense stare.

"Absolutely sure."

Linc rose to his feet in one swift movement, wrapping his arms around her on the way up and taking her with him. "Wait!"

"What?" he asked.

She'd wrapped her legs around him on instinct, and now she clung to him with her lower half while leaning away at the top. "Your shoulder."

"Nothing could stop me from kissing you right now." He pressed his lips to hers, hard and sure before pulling right back. "I love you."

"I love you too. Even if you're sappy sometimes." She leaned in to whisper, "I won't tell anyone."

EPILOGUE
JESS

The sun glistened over Jess's diamond ring. Tilting her hand one way, then the other, she admired the beauty. She'd never been interested in jewelry before. Never even owned a necklace.

But the ring on her finger had changed that. The solitaire wasn't huge–just a small oval–but its weight drew her attention over and over. Clasping her right hand around it, she peeked around the side of the reception hall. A vine of greens with little white flowers mixed in wound its way around the wooden arbor. A few dozen chairs were lined up in rows with a person in each seat.

So many people. And they were here for her and Linc.

It was perfect.

Everly had squealed and cried when Jess mentioned getting married at the ranch. There were real tears, and the tingling behind Jess's eyes told her more tears were about to join.

So she'd spat out a quick, "Whenever you're not too busy. Just something simple," and made a hasty escape.

She'd expected a long engagement. The ranch booked up months in advance. Everly had said before that they had weddings on the calendar years out.

That didn't stop her from setting aside a few hours on a Sunday afternoon to give Jess the perfect, small wedding. The September midday sun was high in the sky, and a light sheen of sweat beaded on her brow.

Don't be nervous. Don't be nervous. Ten minutes.

Ten minutes was her focus that kept the roiling in her middle from growing into a storm. Everly promised her the whole thing would be over in ten minutes.

Then, she'd be married. To Linc.

Dizziness had her swaying, and the edges of her vision blurred. She was getting married.

Her. Getting married.

To Lincoln North!

"There you are," Everly said.

Jess blinked, clearing the fuzziness in her sight. "Yeah. I'm here."

"You were supposed to wait inside. What if someone saw you?"

"Aren't they about to see me?"

Everly rolled her eyes and smiled. "You know what I mean."

She actually didn't, but that was probably not what her friend wanted to hear.

"Is it time?" Jess asked.

"It's time." Everly wrapped her arms around Jess and pulled her in close.

Sinking into the warmth of the hug, Jess closed her eyes and rested her head on Everly's shoulder. "Thanks for this. I don't know what I'm doing."

"Sure you do. You're marrying your best friend. Trust me, you're gonna love it." Everly pulled back and grasped Jess's hands. "I'm happy for you."

"Thanks. I'm happy for you too." Jess winked and squeezed the hands she held.

Everly's eyes turned glassy. "We're excited, but the hormones are major. Especially when I get to make people happy all the time."

"At least they're happy tears," Jess said. "You're gonna be a great mom."

Everly pulled a tissue out of the pocket of her sundress. "I hope so."

"I know so," Jess said with another squeeze.

Everly looked down at their linked hands. "You're supposed to take that ring off. He has a wedding band to put on that finger."

Jess shook her head. "I don't care. I'm not taking it off."

Everly's shoulder slumped. "Come on. I know what I'm doing."

"And I do too. Not taking it off is what I'm doing."

Everly's smile grew wider. "Linc is one lucky guy."

Jess looked over her shoulder to where the guests were seated. Linc waited just around the corner. "I'm pretty lucky too."

"I'll be right back." Everly peeked around the corner, waved her hand, and came back to Jess's side. "Ready?"

"Ready." Boy, was she ever. There hadn't been a doubt in her mind since Linc asked her to marry him, and now, their life together was finally beginning.

Mr. Chambers stepped around the corner and tipped his cowboy hat to Jess. The wrinkles on the outsides of his eyes were deep, and his cheeks bulged with a grin.

She'd never put much thought into getting married before, and the tradition where the bride walked down the aisle with her father reared its ugly head early on in Everly's planning.

Then, Mr. Chambers called Jess and asked her to meet him on his back porch for a chat. He asked if he could walk her down the aisle, and she didn't think about her answer before it was out of her mouth. It felt right having the man who'd saved her from the same fate as her family by her side right now.

Jess bit her lip and blinked back the moisture in her eyes. Oh, no. She was going to be one of those mushy brides. How embarrassing.

Mr. Chambers gave her a once-over. "You clean up good, baby girl."

Well, the tears were gonna come anyway, so she wrapped her arms around Mr. Chambers's barrel belly and buried her face in the collar of his shirt. The smell of coffee clung to him, and she breathed it in, letting it settle her nerves.

"Thanks for doing this," she whispered.

"Wouldn't miss it for the world. He's a good one. He'll take good care of you."

A small tear leaked out of the corner of her eye, and she wiped it on his shoulder. "I know."

"And you take care of him too. He needs you in ways you don't understand yet."

She nodded, using the movement to dry her eyes again.

"Don't mess up her makeup," Everly said.

Jess lifted her head and swiped at her face again. "I don't know why I had to wear it anyway."

"You didn't have to, but it'll look good for pictures. You only get one wedding day," Everly said with a smile.

"I remember my wedding day. It was a lot like this," Mr. Chambers said.

"You married Lottie in the summer?" Everly asked.

"Nah. It was in the fall. On a Tuesday, actually."

Jess laughed. "Then how was it like this?"

"There was a lot of happiness. We knew we wanted to spend the rest of our lives together, so we didn't wait. I'm glad we didn't. I never took a second with that woman for granted."

Jess peeked around the side of the building and found Linc standing in front of the crowd. He wore dark jeans and a light button-up shirt. His dark cowboy hat left a shadow across his face. He stood with his hands clasped in front of him, and his weight shifted slightly from side to side.

She didn't want to wait. Not another second.

"Can we go?" Jess asked.

Everly nodded and handed over the small bouquet. "I'll let them know to start the music. You two can start walking after a couple of beats."

"Everly," Jess called after her friend.

"Yeah?"

"Thanks for being my friend. For everything."

Everly grinned and nodded. "Always."

Jess sniffed and brushed a hand down the white sundress she'd found at a boutique in Cody. The top had a thin layer of lace while the bottom flowed out in a skirt that hit just past her knees.

"You look great," Mr. Chambers said.

He offered her his arm, and she rested her hand

in the crook of his elbow. "Thanks."

The music started, and Mr. Chambers whispered, "Lift your chin up, baby girl."

She did as she was told and took the first step alongside him. Everyone was on their feet and looking at her. For once, she didn't mind being the center of attention.

But she had her eyes on the prize. Linc stood at the end of the aisle, piercing her with an intense stare.

Wow. That was her man. Forever. It didn't seem real.

Mr. Chambers gave her a little squeeze as he handed her off to Linc. When she was in her soon-to-be husband's hands, he pulled her in, brushing his lips gently over her ear.

"You're so beautiful. Inside and out," he whispered. "I love you."

"I love you too," she whispered back. Those words held so much weight, but it wasn't enough. She'd search the whole world over to find the words that accurately described how she felt about Linc.

She followed him to the center of the arbor and kept her focus on Linc as Brother Higgins led the ceremony. It was as short and sweet as Everly had promised, and Jess's hands shook in Linc's the entire time.

"I believe the couple has chosen to recite their own vows," Brother Higgins said.

Linc brushed his thumbs over the backs of her hands. He paused a second before beginning. "I always knew it was you. It'll always be you. I didn't come from much, and I'm not much to write home about."

He swallowed and looked down at their joined hands. "But you saw me. And you stayed." His gaze lifted to her, and the glistening in his eyes had her biting her lip and inhaling a deep breath.

"You stayed. No one has ever stayed," he whispered.

Everly would complain that the guests couldn't hear their vows, but Jess didn't care one bit. These words were for her ears only, and she wasn't too keen on sharing.

Linc cleared his throat. "I promise to love you forever. I promise to help you when you're hurting. I promise to put God first in our lives. I promise to protect you. And if I only do one thing well in this life, it'll be loving you."

Brother Higgins looked to Jess. "Jessica Patton, you have vows for your husband?"

She lifted her shoulders and chin as she looked up into Linc's eyes. "Hey."

He chuckled and whispered, "Hey."

"You came with a warning. I'm glad I didn't listen."

Linc looked down at their hands again. He did need her, and she'd always be right beside him with a reminder that he was a good man. He'd shown her over and over again.

"You saw me too. When no one else took the time to figure out what was going on in my head, you did. And you helped me understand myself. You helped me understand everything. You showed me how the Lord can lift us up off our knees and put us on our feet again. I promise to love you with my whole heart for my whole life. I promise to stay by your side when things get tough. And I promise I'll keep God first in our lives too."

Linc looked up at her and mouthed the words, "I love you."

"I love you too," she whispered back.

With rings on their fingers and sniffles in the warm afternoon air, Brother Higgins lifted the Bible in his hand. "I now pronounce you husband and wife. You may kiss the bride."

Linc took a step toward her and cradled her face in his hands. Slowly, he pressed an achingly soft kiss to her lips.

And the world shifted beneath her feet. She held onto his shirt at his sides and kissed him back as the guests cheered.

They were one now, made of hope and trust that wasn't tainted by the past. There would be ups and downs, but they were headed for happier days.

Forever sounded like an adventure with Lincoln North by her side.

BONUS EPILOGUE
AVA

Ava rested a hand on Ron's little knee in the carseat beside her. The bulky seat cradled him like a bowl, wrapping around his tiny body.

Jameson's gaze caught hers in the rearview mirror, and he gave her one of those heart-melting winks. Every emotion was running high, but her gratefulness was overwhelming today.

"Well, buddy. This is home," Jameson said.

Tall evergreens passed as he turned into the private drive leading to their house on the ranch. The cabin was nestled in a secluded meadow with a small creek running along the eastern side. A wall of tall windows covered the front, and a porch wrapped around one corner.

Some days, Ava woke up wondering how she'd gotten here. Other days, she couldn't remember her life before she moved to Wolf Creek Ranch.

She looked down at Ron and gently lifted his hand with two of her fingers. She'd waited weeks to hold the fragile hand. Now, she couldn't go a second without touching him.

They'd prayed for a baby, and those first prayers were calm and respectful. Then, as time drew on, the prayers became more urgent and fearful. The requests were so general.

Please, Lord. We just want a baby. Someone to love. Any baby will do. Girl or boy, we'll love the baby with all our hearts.

When the good news came, nothing could have dampened that happiness. Not even the morning sickness that ruled her life for countless weeks.

And when she'd laid eyes on Ron for the first time, it was almost like meeting an old friend. The Lord had made the perfect little boy for her and Jameson. Ron was exactly as he was supposed to be. She couldn't have imagined him any different.

Through the long nights of worry and uncertainty, she'd sat by his side, praying she could keep him.

In His time, the Lord had answered her prayers, and they were finally home. Though the weeks in the NICU would be a time in her life she'd never forget. Everything they'd gone through to get to this moment was worth it.

"We're home," she whispered to Ron, who slept softly in the bucket seat.

"Looks like Colt and Remi beat us here," Jameson said.

Ava looked up to see Colt's truck parked in the driveway. Ben and Abby waved their hands over their heads from the porch.

"They couldn't wait to meet you," Ava whispered.

Jameson parked the car, and the kids leapt from the porch.

Ben plastered his face and hands to the truck window and gasped. "He's tiny!"

"Let me see!" Abby shouted behind him.

"Kids! Keep your voices down!" Colt demanded from the porch.

Jameson opened the door to the backseat, and Ben and Abby shoved back and forth trying to get a better view.

"Why's he so little?" Ben asked.

Abby clutched her hands to her chest. "Can I play with him?"

"Let's get inside first," Jameson said, reaching around the kids to unlatch the baby carrier.

Ava stepped out of the truck and took the longest, deepest breath she'd had in months. They were finally home.

Colt and Remi waited on the porch with baby Landon. They'd only been released from the hospital two days ago, and Ava hadn't gotten the chance to meet the newest bundle of joy at the ranch.

Remi held the baby in one arm and opened the other for a hug. "I'm so glad you're home."

Ava sank into the embrace. "Me too. I'm glad you're home too." She smiled down at sleeping Landon. "Hello, little love."

Remi stretched her back. "We've already started calling him LJ. I guess we're destined to have shortened names in this family."

"LJ sounds cute for Landon Joshua," Ava said. "I like it."

Remi looked down at little LJ with a smile. "Maternity won't be so lonely now that we get to do it together."

Jameson stepped onto the porch with Ron in the carrier. Ben and Abby trailed right behind him. "I think the babies have a fan club."

Ava bit her lips between her teeth. These kids were loved more than they could imagine, and they'd get to grow up together. Being an only child hadn't been terrible, but she wouldn't trade this life for the world.

Jameson must have picked up on the emotion welling inside her because he ushered everyone toward the door. "Let's get inside, and everyone can take turns staring at the babies."

Colt, Remi, Ben, and Abby made their way inside, and Jameson hung back to wrap Ava in a hug. She nuzzled into his neck and squeezed his middle.

"Welcome home," he whispered into her hair.

Paul's truck headed up the drive, and Ava reached down to get Ron from his carrier. "We'll be right in."

Jameson gave Paul a wave as the truck parked in front of the house. "Take your time."

Ava bounced Ron against her chest as Paul met her on the porch. His dark eyes met hers, and his mouth turned up in a grin beneath his short beard. "You doin' okay?" he asked.

"Better than okay."

His rough hand cupped the back of her head as he pulled her close to place a light kiss on her hair. "You're a great mama."

Thane stopped beside her and rested his head on her foot. Even the tough wild dog was calmed by the baby.

Ava looked down at Ron and repositioned him so Paul could get a better look. "All I've done so far is sit by his bedside. I've been pretty helpless."

Paul turned his attention to the baby and let out a deep sigh. "That was all you needed to do. Just love him."

"Got that part down," she said.

"You forget I found out about you after you were already grown. I didn't have to do much either."

She'd grown up with a great dad, but Paul had been the blessing she hadn't expected. How many people got to have two amazing dads in their life? "You didn't have to do anything."

"I guess the first step is just loving your kid. Things probably fall into place after that."

Ava nodded, unsure if words would start the waterworks she'd been holding off for weeks.

Her baby was home now. They were happy tears.

"Thanks for everything," Ava finally said.

"I love you, Ava. And I'm glad I get to see Ron grow up."

"You didn't miss too much. I'm still growing too."

Paul's big hand brushed over baby Ron's head. "I know. But you don't need me anymore."

Her chin quivered, and her vision went blurry. "That's not true. I always need you."

He wrapped her and Ron in a warm embrace. "You'll always have me."

When her dad released her, she wiped at her face and bounced Ron in her arms. "Will you come over for dinner tonight? Vera said she'd stop by with food after the dinner rush."

"I wouldn't miss it. I think that means I better get back to work."

Paul turned and headed back toward his truck, and Ava cleared her throat before shouting, "Love you, Dad!"

Jameson and their friends were inside waiting, but she watched her dad drive away until his truck disappeared from view.

She'd come to the ranch years ago knowing she was probably severing ties with her mother, the only family she had left. Now, she had a Heavenly Father, dad, grandpa, husband, son, and countless friends. She even had a loving mother. They'd turned their relationship around, and they spent as much time together as possible.

Sometimes, life works out for the better when you least expect it.

Colt

Colt bounced LJ in front of him, but his baby eyes stayed closed. "How can he sleep through all the noise?"

Ben and Abby were fighting for the babies' attention. Ben was telling them about all the fun things to do at the ranch, and Abby was showing off her latest dance moves.

Remi shrugged, bouncing Ron in her arms while Jameson and Ava unpacked the hospital bags. "Probably the same way you sleep through the alarm clock in the morning."

She was right. He'd started snoozing the alarm lately. Ben and Abby sucked out all of his energy. Adding a newborn to the mix had him walking through the days like a zombie.

That wasn't even talking about the nighttime feedings. He'd heated a bottle last night and walked out onto the porch with it before he remembered what he was doing.

Colt sighed. "I can't stop looking at him. What is wrong with me?"

"I know. It's weird right?" Remi asked.

Colt leaned LJ over until he touched Ron's side. "This is your new friend, bud."

"They'll get to grow up together. I love it," Remi said.

Colt tilted his head to the side, studying the little boys. "They look the same."

"They do not," Remi said, pushing his shoulder with hers. "Ron actually has hair."

"LJ has a funny shaped head. Should we be concerned?"

Remi rolled her eyes and groaned. "It won't stay that way. Did you read the book I gave you?"

"I skimmed it. Nothing about head shapes."

Remi reached over and brushed the pad of her thumb over LJ's cheek. "He's perfect."

"I agree. Let's have another one," Colt said as the idea bubbled in his middle.

Remi leaned back, and her eyes widened. "I am not ready to relive what happened four days ago."

"Okay, but in a few months, can we–"

A knock at the door interrupted Colt's plea.

"I'll get that." He looked over his shoulder at Remi as he headed for the door. "This isn't over yet, princess."

Her grin told him she'd give in pretty soon. If he had his way, they'd have a handful of little Walkers running around.

And Remi? She'd be the best mom. She already was. Ben and Abby loved her, and no one could mistake how head-over-heels she was for little LJ. She'd barely slept in days, but she was rocking the new mom thing.

Colt was doing a good job as a trusty sidekick. He should have just read the book.

He opened Jameson and Ava's front door, welcoming Ridge and Cheyenne in. "Welcome to the babysitters' club."

Ridge

Cheyenne gasped when Colt turned the baby around for her to see. "He's so precious!"

"Wait till he fills up that diaper," Colt said. "That is *not* cute."

Ridge's mouth went dry. Coming over to see the babies was either going to be a good thing or a bad thing, and he was waiting on cues from Cheyenne to see which way things would fall.

Cheyenne cupped her cheeks. "Can I hold him?"

Colt jerked his head. "Come on inside and get all the baby cuddles."

Once they were through the doorway, Ridge took a deep breath. *Here goes nothing.*

Remi sat on the oversized couch, while Ben and Abby darted around the open living room.

"I found villagers," Colt announced. He turned back to Cheyenne and held out baby LJ. "I've heard it takes a village. Hopefully, a ranch will work too."

Cheyenne tentatively wrapped her arms around the baby, and Ridge noted the moment when she sucked in an extra inhale.

This wasn't going to go well. He could feel it in his bones.

Hoping to pass some kind of calming to her, Ridge pressed a hand against Cheyenne's back. "You okay?"

"Yeah. I think," she whispered, never taking her eyes off the baby.

Then she looked up at him. The tears welled in her eyes, and her chin quivered.

Mayday. Mayday. Abandon ship.

Ridge looked up at Colt. "We're gonna take this one for a walk."

"Just bring him back within the hour," Remi said, looking at her watch. "Well, within half an hour. How is it already feeding time? I just did that."

Herding Cheyenne out the front door with a gentle push against her back, they made it onto the porch before the waterworks started.

Cheyenne hugged LJ to her chest and rocked back and forth. "I'm sorry."

"It's okay. I knew this would be hard." Technically, it was hard for him too, but he couldn't show it. Not in front of Cheyenne when she was already breaking down.

She wiped her eyes. "I'm happy for them. So happy. I just..."

Ridge wrapped his arms around her and the baby, rubbing circles over her back. "I know. It's only been five months."

He knew that wasn't what she wanted to hear. Five months had felt like a lifetime when they were waiting for a baby. Impatiently waiting was different from casually waiting.

"You want me to pray?" he asked quietly.

Cheyenne nodded against his chest and sniffed.

"Lord, thank You for the new kids in our life. Thank You for standing beside us." He took a second to swallow past the knot of sadness in his throat. "Help us to put our hope in You. Your timing is perfect, and we just don't know what that looks like. If a family doesn't come for us when we want it, help us to be strong and trust in You."

Cheyenne nodded her head up and down, agreeing with the prayer that they'd both been through so many times.

"Cheyenne would make a great mom," Ridge whispered. "You know that. Show us how to be grateful for what You've already given us. Amen."

Cheyenne looked up at him, and a small smile

lifted her cheeks. "Thanks for that reminder. I needed that."

Ridge pressed a kiss to her forehead. "Anytime."

She looked down at LJ, who was starting to squirm. "I think he's ready for that meal Remi said was coming."

Ridge jerked his head toward the door. "Let's get him back to his folks."

"Then I can hold the other one?" Cheyenne asked hopefully.

"If you want, I'm sure Jameson and Ava will let us all pass him around."

Cheyenne stepped through the door first and wiped her face. "These babies are so loved."

"Ours will be too."

She stopped and turned to face him. "We could adopt," she said in a low, hesitant voice. "Or foster."

An immediate war raged inside him as the thought came to fruition. Those options were just as scary and unknown as waiting for a baby of their own. "Let's pray about it."

Cheyenne nodded, seeming happy with the answer. "You're right. I just want you to know that I'm not opposed to it."

Ridge brushed the pad of his thumb over her cheek. She still took his breath away every time he looked at her. When she was sweet and loving like right now, he wondered if his heart would burst in his chest. Loving Cheyenne caused the same physical reactions as NFL practices had all those years ago.

Ridge pressed a soft kiss to her forehead. "I'm up for anything, as long as we're together."

Thea

Brett's heel tapped a quick rhythm against the floorboard of the truck as they drove toward Jameson and Ava's house.

"Are you gonna be okay?" Thea asked.

"Aren't you excited?"

She chuckled. "I am, but I'm not going to jump out of the truck before we come to a complete stop."

Brett reached over and grabbed her hand. "We have two babies at the ranch. Two!"

Thea's heart squeezed in her chest. It didn't take much to excite Brett, but his joy today was extra special.

"Can we tell them?" he asked, gripping her hand like a lifeline.

Brett's nervous energy transferred to her. They had baby news of their own, and while the excitement was a living, breathing thing inside of her, apprehension held her back. "Um, maybe some other day."

Brett squeezed her hand again. "They're going to be happy for us."

"Yeah, until they realize the baby is due in the

height of tourist season. Jess will have her hands full without me."

"You forget we live close enough that I can hop over to the stables and help Jess anytime."

Thea let out a controlled exhale, pushing the worries out as Brett massaged her hand. "You're right. And the new workers might come back next year. Some of them."

Brett lifted her hand and pressed a kiss to her knuckles. "Don't worry about it."

"And Everly's baby is due at the beginning of the summer. Ron will be less than a year old. Jameson and Ava are going to–"

"They are going to be just fine," Brett said as he parked in front of Jameson and Ava's cabin. "Business is good, and they've always treated us like family. We work hard for the ranch, and we don't take advantage of the good thing we have going here."

"Family," Thea whispered. He was right. They were closer to Jameson and Ava than they were their own families, and the loyalty and friendship went both ways.

Brett shifted into park and turned his body to face her. There were still times when she couldn't understand how they'd ended up here.

Family.

Friends.

God.

So much love.

It was straight out of a fairy tale, but it was their *life*. She woke up every day pinching herself.

"Family," Brett repeated. "We can trust them, and they can trust us. Plus, I figure you won't stay away from the stables even on your maternity leave."

Thea chuckled. "You got me there. She'll be growing up around horses. Might as well introduce her early."

"She?" Brett asked with wide eyes.

"Oh, I don't know for sure it's a girl. They can't tell this early I don't think. I'm just...I don't know. I just said it."

Boy. Girl. Thea didn't have a preference.

"I kinda hope it's a girl." He gave her a playful grin. "Then, I can spoil two ladies."

"You would be in so much trouble. We already have two boys growing up on the ranch."

Brett's eyes widened. "They can be like big brothers, but that's all."

Thea laughed and reached for the door. "Good luck with that."

Brett jumped out of the truck and met her at the bottom of the porch steps. "Seriously, they can't have my little girl."

Thea pressed a hand to his chest. "Relax. She isn't even born yet. You have years before this is even an issue."

Brett's strong arm wrapped around her, pulling her in. She melted against him and met his kiss as the world stopped spinning around them.

He was going to be the best dad. He was already the best husband and friend.

Thea's head swirled in dizziness as Brett pulled away. She hummed through a smile. "I love you."

"I loved you first." He rubbed a big circle over her stomach. "And I love this little one too."

Jerking her head toward the door, Thea grabbed his hand, pulling him behind her. "Let's go meet the new babies."

Linc

Linc walked into the stables and scanned the arena for Jess. He'd gotten stuck doing inventory in the storage shed and pack room all day, which meant he was thoroughly bored.

And missing the woman who'd been on his mind all day.

Who was he kidding. She'd been on his mind for years, but the jolt of pure excitement in his veins when he remembered she was his wife hadn't faded.

A soft light shone out of her open office, and he directed his course toward it. Thankfully, the barn seemed empty, and he could greet her the way he wanted.

He stepped inside and made his way over to her. Jess looked up with tired eyes, but they lifted at the corners with her smile.

"Hey, handsome."

He rounded the desk full of papers and reached for her hands. Pulling her to her feet, he slid his hands around her waist and wrapped her up.

"Hey, gorgeous." He dipped his chin and pressed his mouth to hers.

It took her half a second to catch up, but when she did, everything clicked into place. Her body fit perfectly against his, and her kiss matched his need with every movement.

He'd never get enough of this–enough of her. He'd be seeking her out and pouring his love into her every chance he got.

What else was he supposed to do with the unquenchable emotions she stirred up in him? Sometimes, he wondered if she'd ever understand the magnitude of his love for her.

He peppered small kisses over her jaw and down her neck, breathing in her unique scent. It wasn't flowers or fruit. It was Jess.

It was *his*. Just like her.

"Did you have a good day?" she asked.

"It was fine," he breathed against her neck. "Better now."

He lifted his head and raked his gaze over her face. "How was your day?"

She smiled—a bright and genuine one that set his world on fire. "Perfect."

"Good." He scanned the desk. "How much longer do you have here? What can I do to help?"

"I'm finished. Just need to clean up."

"Hey, guys!"

Linc and Jess both jerked at the sudden words.

Jess rested a hand on her chest. "Brett, announce your presence first."

Brett propped against the doorway and folded his arms. Thea stepped up beside him and wrapped her hands around his arm. "I wasn't necessarily tiptoeing."

"Have you seen the babies?" Thea asked. The sparkle in her eyes was unmistakable.

Baby fever. Linc had always thought it was a figure of speech. Now, he was wondering if it was contagious and came with a raised body temperature.

"Not yet," Jess said beside him.

Thea did a little dance and giggled. "They're adorable!"

Jess straightened the papers on her desk. "I'm sure they are."

"She's right. Although, Ron lost his mind for a minute, and I thought he was going to break glass with that scream." Brett shuddered.

"We might head over there later. I still have a few things to finish up here."

Interesting. Jess suddenly had things to do when someone brought up the babies. They'd talked about kids a few times, but Jess was undecided on kids. Linc understood her hesitation. Neither of them had grown up in model households.

Plus, Jess didn't like to jump into things unless she knew what she was doing. He admired her confidence, but she avoided getting herself into situations where she was at a disadvantage.

"Sounds good," Brett said. "We're helping Ridge and Cheyenne move the horses back over here tomorrow. Did you mark the stalls you want them in?"

"I did." Jess picked up a page from her desk. "Here it is."

Thea took it and scanned the chart. "Looks good. We'll get it done."

"Linc, you helping?" Brett asked.

"I'll meet you there." Linc's attitude toward Brett had changed lately. Mostly because he understood why the guy was so happy. Having a good woman beside you changed a man for the good.

The happiness was ridiculous. Almost unbelievable.

Yet, Linc was living in it every day, and he'd never take a second for granted.

"Great. I'll bring breakfast," Thea said.

"See you in the morning," Brett said with a tip of his hat.

"Bye." Jess didn't look up from the papers she shuffled into folders.

Linc propped his hip against the side of the desk. "Everything okay?"

"Mhm," Jess hummed. "Yep. You ready to go?"

"You don't want to see the babies?" Linc asked, hopefully leaving room for her to casually decline if she didn't want to go.

She rubbed the back of her neck, careful to avoid his gaze. "I'm not sure."

"We don't have to. I'm sure they're tired of visitors anyway."

Jess sighed, and her bright-green eyes lifted to his. "I'm kinda scared."

"I don't think they bite, but maybe keep your fingers away from their mouths, just in case."

"Not of that. I don't know a lot about babies, and..."

"And why does that scare you? You don't have to hold them if you don't want to."

"I don't even know how to explain it. I don't know why I'm scared. They're just...a big deal."

"You're not being pressured, babe. We don't have to have kids, and we don't have to go visit the babies. You don't have to do anything you don't want to do."

She stepped closer to him and rested a hand against his chest. The small touch warmed everything inside him, and he wrapped his hand around hers.

"I know you've never pressured me. I think I'd like to have kids one day. I just feel completely unqualified."

Linc couldn't stop the grin that spread over his mouth. "That's fair. I don't think I'm qualified to be a dad either." He pressed his forehead against hers. "That's a decision we'll make together, and it doesn't have to be now. You can relax."

She took a deep breath and let it out. "Okay. You're right."

Linc lifted his head and brushed his fingers through both sides of her hair. "That might be the future for us, but it might not. The Lord has a plan, so we might as well not worry about it."

"Now I feel silly," she whispered.

"You're not. We've talked about it before, but we needed to talk about it again. We'll keep talking about it every time it comes up, and we'll always make these decisions together."

She rested her head against his chest. "Thank you. Have I told you how much I love you today?"

"Yes. You told me this morning," he reminded her.

"I need to tell you again. Just to make sure you know."

Linc rubbed a hand in circles over her back. "I don't forget." Though, he could see why reassurance was important to her. They'd spent so much of their lives without love, they sometimes needed an extra reminder. "I love you too. Don't ever question it."

"I don't," she said with a resoluteness that put the matter to rest. "You'd make a good dad," she whispered.

"Only if you're beside me."

She squeezed her arms around him and sighed. "Always."

Everly

Everly huffed and pushed her hands into her hair. Words were hard.

Which wasn't always a problem, but it was when it was her job.

This wouldn't be so difficult if Jess wasn't on her delayed honeymoon. She and Linc rode horses for a living, and they thought a trail ride in Montana was a good honeymoon destination.

A trail ride with no cell service. Convenient for those two introverts.

The hum of the garage door opening only heightened Everly's anxiety. She had to get this book finished, but she wanted to spend time with Blake.

A grin spread over her face, and she covered it with her hand. Alone time with her husband was going to be hard to come by soon. Her other hand rested on the swell of her belly. They'd be a family of three in a few months.

The door in the mud room opened, and Blake tossed his keys onto the counter. "Ev?"

"Living room!" She was wrapped up in two blankets, and fighting her way out of the burrito didn't sound like something she should attempt on her own. Not when she'd become so front-heavy lately.

She tried to look over her shoulder as Blake entered the room. "How was work?"

"Cold," Blake said as he rounded the couch. "Long."

He sat on the couch beside her—as close to her as possible—resting one arm on the back of the couch behind her and one hand on her belly. She moved the blankets so he could see better.

"She's been kicking. And squirming. And doing somersaults," Everly said, guiding Blake's hand to the harder spot on the right side of her bump.

They sat still and quiet for a few seconds before the baby started kicking against Blake's hand.

"I'll never get used to that. It's amazing." His voice held all the awe she felt whenever she thought about the baby growing inside of her.

"She missed you. I did too."

Blake brushed a hand over her cheek and pressed his lips to hers. She breathed him in, relaxing into the peace and love he radiated.

"I missed my girls too," he whispered before pressing another quick kiss to her lips.

Then he readjusted in his seat until he leaned over her belly. "Hey, sweet pea. It's daddy." His hand roved over Everly's side, chasing the tiny pulses. "Mommy said you've been practicing gymnastics today. I can't wait to see you do flips one day."

Everly grabbed his hand and pressed it to the spot he was searching for. Blake liked to talk to the baby every evening, and she always jumped and kicked even more when she heard his voice. It was the strangest thing Everly had ever seen, but there was definitely more movement when Blake was around.

Blake shook his head. "I can't wait to hold her, but I'm gonna miss this."

"You're telling me. I'm anticipating the separation crisis already."

He looked up at Everly, and his smile grew. He'd been growing his beard out lately, though he talked about shaving it every now and then.

Truthfully, Everly loved the bearded look on him. He looked more like a dad than the GQ model sports agent she'd met all those years ago. He'd traded in his suits and ties for flannel and boots, and she wouldn't change a thing.

She'd been stepping away from the event venue at the ranch over the last few months, spending most of her time training the new event coordinators. She loved the work, but she wanted to be a stay-at-home mom. Blake completely supported the move.

Blake's gaze shifted from her eyes to her mouth and back again. "I love that she's a part of you," he whispered.

Oh no. That was too sweet, and the waterworks were about to start flowing. "I love that she's a part of you too."

"The best parts of both of us." He brushed a hand through his tousled hat hair. "I might not sleep until she gets here. I'm so excited."

Everly chuckled and patted his cheek. "Better sleep now. We'll be wishing for it after she's born."

"You're right." He tipped his chin toward her laptop. "What are you working on?"

"The book is due to my editor next week. I'm having a hard time writing the ending."

"Is this Linc and Jess's book? The end is that they live happily ever after and ride off into the sunset. Literally, they're riding in Montana for the next few weeks."

Everly playfully shoved his shoulder. "I know how it ends. I'm having trouble with the actual words. What's a good way to say 'I love you forever' without using those words?"

Blake frowned. "Who is saying it? Jess or Linc?"

"Linc."

"He'd just buy Jess a new saddle or something. He's not big on the words."

Everly tapped her thumb against her lip. "You're probably right. He did get her a saddle for Christmas."

Blake reached for her hand, pulling her jittering thumb away from her mouth. "No stressing. You know your editor always loves your books. Then, the readers love them too. No stressing. Remember, this is something you love, and it's how you like to share the gospel. You're the boss, and the only one you have to report to is the Lord."

He was right. She prayed for these stories every day. Ever since her friends had agreed to let her write their stories, she'd made sure her work would glorify God above all else.

"Thanks. I needed to hear that."

Blake pressed a kiss to her lips before sitting up beside her. "So, you're sending this one off next week. Who's next?"

A surge of excitement had the baby kicking harder. "Asa and Lyric."

"Oh, that'll be a good one. The outlaw and the lawman."

Everly laughed. "That makes it sound like a historical western romance."

He snapped his fingers as the idea came to him. "The Cop and the Criminal."

Everly scrunched her nose. "I don't think Lyric

would be too happy to be labeled the criminal. She's changed."

"I know, but it sounds cool."

"Actually, I've been thinking about Gage and Hadley too. Hadley hinted that she wanted a story."

Blake nodded. "Yep. The Mechanic and the Informant."

Everly laughed again. "What kind of books do you think I write?"

"Well, the last one I read was Brett and Thea's story, and I'm still tense about it. That was a wild ride."

"Yeah, and Gage and Hadley were a part of that. Still, I think I need to make them sound like romantic suspense books instead of thrillers."

Blake swallowed hard, and his smile faded a little bit. "Have you thought about Paul and Vera?"

She shook her head. "I'm not ready to write that one." Paul and Vera's story was special, and those two were still clinging to each other after all that happened. "I'm not going to ask them yet."

"Probably a good call," Blake said. "Are you going to finish working, or are you ready for bed?"

She glanced at the laptop, and as strong as her responsibility was to get the story done in a reasonable time, she had a husband who meant more to her than a few extra lines in the manuscript. "I'm ready."

Blake stood and started pulling blankets off her.

When she was sufficiently unwrapped, he slid his arms behind her back and legs.

"I'm going to get too heavy for you soon," she whispered against his beard.

"Woman, do I look like I'm struggling? I got this." He lifted his chin and headed for the bedroom.

Everly wrapped her arms tighter around his neck. Soon, he'd be carrying their little girl, and she'd gladly start walking herself to bed.

For now, she'd let her husband adore her every second they were together and leave the manuscripts unfinished. There would always be another love story to tell in Blackwater.

OTHER BOOKS BY MANDI BLAKE

Love in Blackwater Series

Small Town Series

Love in the Storm

Blackwater Ranch Series

Complete Contemporary Western Romance Series

Remembering the Cowboy

Charmed by the Cowboy

Mistaking the Cowboy

Protected by the Cowboy

Keeping the Cowboy

Redeeming the Cowboy

Blackwater Ranch Series Box Set 1-3

Blackwater Ranch Series Box Set 4-6

Blackwater Ranch Complete Series Box Set

Wolf Creek Ranch Series

Complete Contemporary Western Romance Series

Truth is a Whisper

Almost Everything

The Only Exception

Better Together

The Other Side

Forever After All

Unfailing Love Series

Complete Small-Town Romance Series

A Thousand Words

Just as I Am

Never Say Goodbye

Living Hope

Beautiful Storm

All the Stars

What if I Loved You

Unfailing Love Series Box Set 1-3

Unfailing Love Series Box Set 4-6

Unfailing Love Complete Series Box Set

Heroes of Freedom Ridge Series

Multi-Author Christmas Series

Rescued by the Hero

Guarded by the Hero

Hope for the Hero

Christmas in Redemption Ridge Series

Multi-Author Christmas Series

Dreaming About Forever

Blushing Brides Series

Multi-Author Series

The Billionaire's Destined Bride

ABOUT THE AUTHOR

Mandi Blake was born and raised in Alabama where she lives with her husband and daughter, but her southern heart loves to travel. Reading has been her favorite hobby for as long as she can remember, but writing is her passion. She loves a good happily ever after in her sweet Christian romance books and loves to see her characters' relationships grow closer to God and each other.

Acknowledgments

My writing journey has been filled with support and encouragement. I love writing, and knowing that I don't have to do it alone is a blessing.

I have an amazing group of beta readers who give me honest feedback for every book. They keep me on track with the story and its message, and I appreciate their dedication! Thank you Kera Butler, Natasha Wall, Demi Abrahamson, Haley Powell, Vicci Lucas, Jenna Eleam, Elizabeth Maddrey, Tanya Smith, Laura Dela Torre, Stephanie Palmer Taylor, Jess Mastorakos, and Kendra Haneline.

My editor, Brandi Aquino, of Editing Done Write is amazing, and I'm so glad she has stuck by me through EVERY book. Same for Amanda Walker, who has designed so many beautiful book covers for me. I couldn't do this without either of them.

I also want to thank my writing circle for every encouragement. This book was one of my favorites to write, and I believed in this story because of their support.

Last, but not least, thank you for reading this story. I know you have countless entertainment options, but knowing you took the time to read my book makes me happier than I can explain. I love writing Christian romance books, and knowing you're along for this amazing ride with me is a blessing. I may not know you by name, but I love you immensely, and so does our Lord.

LOVE IN THE STORM

LOVE IN BLACKWATER BOOK 1

When a snowstorm sneaks up, she gets stranded with the handsome man who once arrested her. Will he be able to forgive her when the truth comes out?

Lyric Woods has been sober for years now, but nothing about picking herself up from rock bottom has been easy. She's behind on bills and on the verge of getting evicted, still paying for the mistakes of her past. When she is stranded with the deputy who doesn't remember her, she gets a second chance at a first impression.

Asa Scott isn't complaining about being stranded with the beautiful Lyric. The kind woman tending his wounds after a wreck in the storm is the first to make him think he could move on after his wife's death. But when he finds out about her record, he can't reconcile the woman from the past with the woman who cared for him at the cabin.

When Lyric needs his help after they're rescued, Asa treads carefully. Helping her is fine—letting her into his life and trusting her near his son is another story.

Despite his fears, Asa can't fight the way he feels about the resilient woman who helped him. But when it looks like Lyric has fallen back into her old ways, will Asa trust the evidence or believe the woman he's falling for and fight to clear her name?

If you loved the Blackwater Ranch series and the Wolf Creek Ranch series, get ready to fall in love all over again in Blackwater, Wyoming.

Made in the USA
Columbia, SC
20 November 2023

26579334R00293